TILL THE LAST BEAT
OF MY HEART

TILL THE LAST BEAT OF MY HEART

LOUANGIE BOU-MONTES

HARPER

An Imprint of HarperCollinsPublishers

To Christian:
I will never get over the irony of using your name for my love interest only to have you become my real-life love interest.

ONE

Christian Reyes is dead, and he's in my basement.

I had nothing to do with either of those things. I'm . . . still processing. Yesterday afternoon, Christian was trying to invite everyone in our math class to the party at the Davies twins' house that night while me and Regan pretended to be too sucked into our work to talk to him. Tonight, he's on the steel table in my basement while I'm sitting on the blue and bronze patterned Persian rug in the parlor right above him, staring at my chemistry textbook.

My mom runs a funeral home, so we're always among the first to know when someone's died in Jacob's Barrow. We also live here; Mami apprenticed under the last guy who owned it and he let her stay in the upstairs apartments when she and my dad were broke, new parents. When she took over the business, we kept the apartments, so I've had all sorts of dead people in my basement. From grandparents to teachers to neighbors. It's not unusual to know the person on my mom's worktable in a town as small as ours.

This is my first time having a classmate down there, though.

Mami can be kind of stoic, but I know she likes her job. She talks to me about it all the time; I know she prides herself on mixing skin pigments that suit bodies better than the three or four shades suppliers have available, and I know she finds purpose in providing comfort and closure to people in their darkest time. She doesn't hide any part of her job from me, ever.

So when she spent a solid ten minutes blocking me from the basement doorway, evading my questions about the body delivered to us today, looking at me with *tears* welling in her dark brown eyes, I knew something was wrong.

"Jaxon, baby," she'd said after I insisted that she tell me what was going on about a hundred times. Though she's always been soft-spoken, her voice wavered like it almost never did. "It's Christian. Conce's boy. He got into a big accident, and he . . . he didn't make it, mijo."

Since then, the inside of my head has felt like a crystal ball: foggy, swirling, full of pictures and ideas that don't make sense.

It's weird. I want to text Regan and tell her, but how do you tell someone that the kid we used to watch horror movies with in elementary school is dead? Christian's not even our friend anymore; now he's a guy from our neighborhood who hangs out with the crew team at school and wanders around on his own at night trying to get pictures of cryptids. I could go on a walk to try telling her face-to-face but I would have to pass Christian's house, and I don't know about all that.

The whole thing feels surreal.

Mami comes up from the basement, her heels clicking on the wooden steps before she comes through the door. She always looks regal, with her hair shaved almost as close as mine, her neck and shoulders upright, adding as much height as she can get on her short frame. Today, her face looks drawn, the deep brown of her cheeks gone ashen. She looks at me, sitting in the middle of the parlor, shaking her head.

"I'm not sending you to school on Monday," she says, coming over to sit on the floor beside me. "*I* can't even get work done right now. He's a little more cleaned up, but . . . I don't know. I might call Monica in and oversee instead."

Monica is my mom's apprentice; she does good work. She took care of my dad when my mom was too messed up to go anywhere near him but wanted him done here with us.

"That's probably a good idea," I say, closing my chem book. "Are you gonna be okay? I've never seen you this upset even when you worked on people you knew."

She smiles, a soft, sad smile that doesn't reach her eyes, and pulls me in by the shoulder, leaning down to press her lips against the top of my head.

"Me and Conce were pregnant at the same time." She brushes her fingers over my tight fade, probably trying to rub the lipstick off my hair. "It was my first time ever, and she was having her first boy . . . I don't know. Maybe I should have said no. I think it means a lot to Conce that he's here. Like he's with family."

I don't know what to say to that. Christian's never felt like family to me, even when we were friends. First of all, I had a huge crush on him . . . not that my mom knew. Second, he was always loud and kind of annoying, which never really changed as far as I could see. It just got less cute to me after middle school, I guess. If anything, he's more of a nuisance.

Was more of a nuisance.

A wave of dizziness hits me out of nowhere and I press the heel of my hand against my forehead. Mami rubs circles between my shoulder blades, sighing.

"Oh, baby," she whispers, pressing her cheek against my shoulder. "It's gonna be okay."

"No, I'm fine." And I am, I think. There's no reason for me to be this upset, really. "I think I'm still . . . shocked."

Mami tries to look into my face, her eyes searching, thin eyebrows drawn together in concern. She pulls away after a moment, squeezing the nape of my neck.

"I need to take a drive. You wanna come with me? We can get something to eat."

I shake my head. Mami takes comfort in food when she's upset, but I can't think about eating. My stomach feels like a dank old cave, cold and empty. I'm pretty sure it's gonna feel that way until Christian's out of our basement and in the ground.

"Nah . . . I'll stay."

Mami looks at me like she's gonna try to change my mind, but instead she pulls me in to kiss the top of my head again. She stands up, brushes her hands over her dark, high waisted pants, and looks at me.

"You'll be okay? I can order in instead."

I nod. "I'll be fine. Bring me back some fries?"

"Sure thing, mijo." She pats her pockets for her keys, then looks at me as she grips the keys in her palm. "*Don't* go down there. Alright, Jaxon? Kids shouldn't have to see their friends like that."

"I know, Mami." I resist the urge to roll my eyes. I'm turning seventeen next weekend, I'm not some impressionable little kid. Anyway, I've been around dead bodies since before I can remember. They haven't messed me up yet; one more's not gonna do it.

She pauses for another moment, looking like she wants to say more, but she gives me a sad smile before heading out through the foyer.

We both know I'm going down there. How can I not? And it's not morbid curiosity, really. It's a need to make this . . . real. Christian Reyes, the occult-loving nerd from elementary school who got too handsome to stay uncool, dead?

I know death can feel unreal. After years of helping my mom choose options for tiny baby coffins to attending my father's funeral, I know how hollow and fucked up death can be. Processing that someone who shouldn't be gone has gone anyway is like watching an asteroid approaching earth. There's nothing you can do. You know it's happening. All you can do is sit there bracing for impact.

Seeing the body speeds up the process. So that's what I'm gonna do.

Grimalkin, our cat, comes down to the parlor when she hears Mami's heels clicking against the stone path leading to our driveway. She meows at the door, then turns her big orange eyes on me and stalks over to bump her head against my arm. She sits down primly on my chem book, looking like a smug, slate-gray gargoyle. I pet her head while I wait to hear the car engine start and the crunch of the tires rolling over the asphalt.

It's time. I walk through the parlor, past the small showing room into the kitchen. The downstairs kitchen, like the rest of the first level of our house, isn't for daily use. At most, Mami makes tea to comfort the bereaved as they make funeral decisions, and at some wakes, they have small food platters that we keep in here. More than anything, the downstairs kitchen holds the gateway to the basement.

Grimalkin follows my heels only to meow in annoyance when she sees where I'm headed. The cat, obviously, isn't allowed in the mortuary. She hates not being allowed anywhere.

"Sorry, Grim," I say, shooing her away from the basement door as I go through it. She tries to squeeze through with me, but I manage to get in, shutting the door before she can poke her head through. She wails at me from the kitchen, accompanied by the gentle thumps of her head and the scritch of her paws trying to open the door. "I'll be back; be patient."

The light in the staircase is a single, dim bulb, but the lights are on downstairs. In Mami's mortuary, she's got bright overhead lights that gleam off the white and steel surfaces of the room. It's a harsh, unforgiving brightness, and as soon as I get far enough down the stairs to see the steel table in the center of the room, the glare feels like an icy stab to the chest when it reveals Christian's body lying prone on the table.

It doesn't look like him. Under the cold light, his skin looks gray, traces of dried, brown blood matting the curls on top of his head. It takes me a while to come any closer than the foot of the stairs. From here, that body could be another boy that looks like my classmate—another lightskin boy with big feet and curly hair.

But I know it's him. The weirdest thing is that it's not because Mami told me, or because I can kind of see his face under the glare of the light. It's like the air itself down here is thick with Christian's absence. It's the feeling of knowing down to your bones that some-one is in the next room, so you start talking to them before you even get in only to find that they're not there after all. Christian's as much on the table as he is nowhere at all.

When I finally come up to him, it's weird how much it does and doesn't look like Christian. The sharp, handsome lines of his jaw and the manicured shape of his eyebrows are distinct, but the grimace left across his face by the rigor makes it hard to recognize him.

He'll be easy enough to make look good for the funeral, at least. The brunt of the damage is on his chest: a dark, massive bruise that spans from the edge of his collarbones to the top of his stomach and a caved-in sternum. Most of the lacerations on his face are thin, weblike scratches I can barely see now that he's been cleaned up and livor mortis has pulled his blood to the back of his body. The only injury that will take my mom a little more wax to cover up for the viewing is the gash stretching from above the arch of his left eyebrow to the highest edge of his cheekbone. His neck's broken, but Mami's fixed up about a thousand broken necks.

"You know something," I start, my voice too loud in the sterile silence of the room, "I never thought you were such a dumbass. Mami told me the hospital said you were texting and driving."

Mami broke most of the rigor setting into Christian's limbs. I pick up one of his hands, cool to the touch, turning it over to look at the crescent-shaped indents on his palms left by his fingernails. I imagine Christian, slumped dead over his steering wheel, then alone in a hospital morgue before they called his mom.

Christian and I . . . our friendship ended kind of abruptly. After the stuff with my dad's passing, we never really recovered. He got involved with sports, I didn't, and we drifted apart. My painfully huge crush on him didn't help either; that's not Christian's fault, obviously, since he didn't even know. All the same, it made it twice as hard to find my footing in our relationship again.

My chest aches for him, naked and mangled on a table in the basement of the guy he fell out with. Who would want that? A smart kid like him—even a weird and kind of annoying one—dying for such a stupid mistake feels so wrong.

I place Christian's hand back in the position I found it in, his cold, stiff fingers curving gently over the reflective surface of the table.

"Christian . . . it felt so impossible before to approach you and try to be . . . friends again. Forget actually telling you how I *felt* about you. It really is impossible now, and I wish I'd known we were gonna run out of time." I keep my eyes on his pale gray nail-beds as I whisper. It's painful, and embarrassing, to stand here knowing I'll never know what could have been if I'd swallowed a little pride instead of holding grudges. "If I could breathe you back to life right now, I would. Not just for me. You deserve better than this."

My head swims for a second, and I grip the edge of the table to hold myself steady. In the next moment, something drips out of my nose, but before I can plug it with my wrist, two red drops of blood land on Christian's arm.

I curse under my breath and use the edge of my sleeve to wipe the blood off his skin, glancing up at him apologetically as if he felt it.

Christian's face moves then, which isn't as weird as it sounds. People think dead bodies fall prone and never move again after death, but it's not true. Mami must not have gotten through massaging out all of Christian's rigor mortis, so his body's in an awkward state of half-stiff and half-slack; it's not unheard of for muscles to shift after death, especially in this state. A soft huff comes through his nostrils, and his expression changes, his eyelids going smooth as if he's only sleeping.

With his pale face strangely tranquil, I feel like I'm trespassing on him as he tries to rest from his injuries.

"I should go," I tell him, backing up toward the foot of the stairs again. "Promise we'll give you a good funeral. It's the least I can do."

I walk backward until the backs of my heels touch the lowest step. I look up to see Christian one last time before he's dolled up to look a little less dead.

And he's looking at me.

Clumsy as ever, I stagger back in alarm and trip over the stairs, falling so hard on my butt my tailbone rumbles against the wood. My hands scrabble over the thin carpet lining the steps as I try to climb backward, getting a full three steps up before I realize he's *not* looking at me. His eyelids have flipped open, and his head is tipped sideways, which . . . well, that happens sometimes too.

It's never happened to *me* . . . and my mom's never told me about something like that happening to *her*, but . . . Mami says bodies do crazy things. Even from here, I can see the dull haze beginning to creep over Christian's unfocused eyes.

It's probably nothing. All the same, a cold wave of dread raises goose bumps all over me. Staying down here doesn't feel right. It feels stupid to say goodbye, but it also feels wrong to say nothing at all.

"I'm . . ." I straighten up, climbing the stairs step by step, backward. "I'm gonna go."

It takes twice as long to go backward up the stairs, but the thought of turning my back on Christian's restless body makes the hair on my arms staticky with anxiety. I'm used to dead bodies, but I can't shake the image of Christian crawling up the stairs after me like something from *The Exorcist*. It's only when I'm back at the top of the stairs, listening to Grimalkin still trying to force the door open, that I turn around. I nudge Grim away with my foot and shut the door behind me, keeping it pressed closed with my hand flat against it until I turn the lock on the knob in place.

"Let's get out of here, huh?" I say to Grimalkin, who stares up at me for a beat before meowing in response. I stoop down to gather her in my arms, and she nestles against the thick black sleeves of my hoodie. We duck back into the parlor to grab my phone, then make our way upstairs.

The second floor is where most of our living spaces are: the small landing with a fireplace we use as our living room, the secondary kitchenette installed back when my parents first moved in, and one large bedroom Mami and Dad transformed into a personal library, shelves stuffed with books he'd written. When my dad was alive, and home, he usually did his writing in there. Guests, even grieving ones, are nosy, however, so our bedrooms are all the way on the third floor.

By the time I make it to the third-floor landing, Grimalkin is squirming in my arms. I put her down, letting her lead the way, slinking along the runner lining the hardwood floor.

Grimalkin stops in front of my door, marked by the vintage *Night of the Living Dead* poster taped over it. I turn the doorknob as Grimalkin, impatient as ever, presses her face against the crack in the door until it's wide enough for her to dart through.

I follow her, shutting the door behind me. In my room, more

vintage horror posters line the walls in shades of black, yellow, red, and green. I have everything from *Creature from the Black Lagoon* to *Them!* to *Mothra*. Every year, Mami finds me more. The hardwood floor is bare, but it's early enough in October that the chill doesn't reach the third floor yet. Grimalkin walks up to my tall oak bureau and rubs her face against the edge of it, sitting back on her haunches, considering the height she'll need to clear to jump to the top.

"Grim," I groan, coming over to shoo her away, "not up here, okay? This stuff can break."

Most of the things in my room are pretty benign or at least cat-proof. I've got a collection of weird rocks from the woods scattered around different corners of the room, a bookshelf packed with books and movies, a couple spiritualist knickknacks that don't work—Ouija boards, pendulums . . . shit like that. On the bureau, though, I've got a few cool bones I picked up in the woods. The owl skull I found the morning before my father died, the fox skull a few weeks after that. I cleaned them up and set them on my bureau to flank the only thing my father left me: an old, broken pocket watch that I don't know how to fix.

Dad was . . . distant. Literally, he was physically distant, often gone for weeks on end. When he was home, he was quiet and with-drawn, holed up in the library writing most of the time. Sometimes he joined us for meals or go out on a drive with me or something, but as I got older, we saw him less and less until we barely ever saw him at all. And then he died.

He was like a ghost to begin with. A faint presence, more felt and talked about than seen.

I tear my eyes away from Dad's watch, shaking off the memory as I head to my bed tucked into the far corner of the room. I drop down onto it on my back, shuffling on the mattress until I can pull my purple comforter with black bats over my head. A moment later, Grimalkin hops up onto the bed, climbing on top of my stomach and kneading her paws over the comforter.

I should tell Regan.

There are no messages on my phone, which is typical but also tells me that word hasn't spread about Christian yet. I open Regan's texts, though I can't think of anything to say. The last thing Regan texted me was a long rant about how she ate shit on her longboard and almost lost a tooth. The last thing I said to her was: *one day you're gonna kill yourself on that thing.*

It's too weird. I call her instead.

She picks up after one ring.

"Hello?" she answers, her voice lilting up with surprise. "Jax?"

"Um . . . yeah. Hey."

"Hey! You never call!" She pauses. "*No one* ever calls. What's up?"

"Um . . ." I push the covers off my head and sit up, which earns me a soft, irritated growl from Grimalkin, who refuses to move. "Something happened. Something bad happened."

"What?" Regan's voice goes sharp and clear. I can't see her, but I can tell she's frozen wherever she is. "Are you okay? Is Tessa okay?"

"Yeah, I'm fine, Mami's fine."

"Is Grim, okay??"

"Yeah, Regan, Grim's good." I reach down to scratch the top of her head, but Grim swats my hand away. "It's . . . there's a body here. It's—"

"A body? Who died?"

"It's Christian."

"*Christian*?" she echoes immediately, like she thinks she's misheard. "What?"

"It's Christian Reyes from school. He's here. He's . . . he's dead. In the basement."

Regan stammers for a second, no words forming. Then she falls silent. She takes so long to respond that I pull my phone away for a moment to check that the call hasn't dropped.

"Are you okay?"

"Yeah," Regan says, breathless like she's been punched in the stomach. "Jesus Christ, Jaxon. Are you sure?"

"Positive."

"What *happened* to him?"

I close my eyes, squeezing hard, trying to block out the mental image of Christian's chest sunken in and marbled with bruising.

"Crashed his sedan into a truck. No seatbelt. Airbags didn't deploy."

Regan hisses on the other line. "Oh, Christian . . . oh, God. God. I can't even believe that!"

"I know. I'm really sorry to tell you."

"God, Jax . . . man. We never really made up with him."

I rub my fingers against my temple, leaning back against the wall. "Nah. *I* never really made up with him. You were nice to him sometimes."

"Sometimes," she agrees, not sounding convinced.

I let my head drop back against the wall with a dull thud. "We didn't know something like this was gonna happen, Regan."

"Yeah . . ." She exhales hard. "I gotta tell my family."

"Okay. I'll let you go. You can call me later if you want. Or text, whatever."

"Thanks. And thanks for telling me."

"Yeah," I mutter for lack of anything better to say. There's no one else I *would* tell. "Bye."

"Later."

I spend the rest of the afternoon in my room, trying to fight off the sharp spines of anxiety digging into my chest. Lying in bed keeps me from getting lightheaded, and Grimalkin's warm weight and purring is comforting against my stomach. Through the window next to my bed, I watch the light filter through the bright yellow leaves of the giant elm tree in our yard, the blue of the sky between the gaps deepening into pink as evening comes closer.

I don't know when I fall asleep, but when I wake up again, it's almost pitch black in my room except for the pseudonight-light on my bedside table, a mason jar of sheep eyes preserved in formaldehyde sitting on top of a small grid of purple LED lights. Grimalkin paws at my closed door across the room and I sit up, turning on the actual lamp at my bedside. I can't tell what woke me—the dull ache in my head and limbs or the butter, garlic, and onion smell coming through the floorboards.

Of the two, the smell interests me more. Mami must be home.

I roll out of bed, let Grim out through the door, and the smell hits me harder in the hall. The garlic and onion joined by the sweet smell of chicken and the achiote-cumin scent of habichuelas guisadas is enough to make me rush down to the second-floor kitchen.

Mami's standing at the stove, barefoot, switching between checking the chicken in the oil and stirring the thick, red sauce the beans cook in. At the square table on the other side of the kitchen, she's already laid out a plate of fried tostones, steaming and glistening, fresh out of the frying pan. Beside it, there's a small bowl of mayoketchup.

I know I told her I wasn't hungry, but I can't help smiling.

"Mami . . ."

She looks over her shoulder and nods me over, a small smile gracing her lips.

"Hey, baby. I was going to wake you when it was done."

"I thought you were gonna get fast food? You're throwing down in here." I come over and pick up the fork for the chicken, standing in front of the sizzling pan to take over for her.

"I thought it'd inspire a little appetite in you." She wraps her arm around my shoulders and kisses my cheek, shaking me gently. "¿Qué te parece? Family dinner? You can even call Regan over, si quieres."

Mami, despite being Dominican and knowing a wide breadth of Dominican and, thanks to my dad, Puerto Rican dishes, speaks very little Spanish. I speak even less. I only ever try with her.

I lean my head down against hers. "Nah. Mejor solo nosotros."

Mami turns off the burner, bringing plates over to scoop white rice onto, then beans. She glances at me, raising an eyebrow. "¿Encima o al lado?"

I roll my eyes. I haven't asked for beans on the side since I was like ten, but she still asks. "Encima is fine."

I grab a plate, cover it with paper towels, then fish the fried chicken out of the oil, setting the pieces down on the table to finish popping and sizzling as they cool. Mami sets our plates down as I fill cups with water. It's comforting, falling back into a routine after a day so out of the ordinary.

"Pues, go ahead," she says.

I grin, dropping a drumstick on my plate quick before it burns my fingers. I didn't realize how hungry I was until this moment. Eating a forkful of rice and beans, salty from the tocino but sweet from the tomato sauce, my mouth waters, and my stomach growls with sudden awareness of how long it's been since I put anything in it.

Mami points her fork at me, smirking triumphantly.

I point my fork back at her, dabbing my eyes with my sleeve as if crying in defeat.

"It's *really* good."

Even if it wasn't, I'd tell her it was just for the way her chin lifts, eyes gleaming with pride. She eats in delicate forkfuls, the triumphant look staying fixed on her face, pushing more food onto my plate whenever it starts clearing up. It feels weird to smile and laugh over dinner while Christian is two floors below us—I can't push him out of my mind; he's like a constant fog over my brain— but I'm warmer and lighter knowing that my mom's happier.

It isn't until we've scraped our plates clean that her face fades from pleased to gray with exhaustion. She leans her head on her hand and rubs the space between her eyebrows, sighing through her nose.

"You should get some rest, honey. And try to be out of the house tomorrow. I don't want you here while me and Monica are . . . working. Okay?"

I stand up, gathering our plates. "Yeah. I'll clean up if you wanna take the first shower?"

Mami squeezes my elbow as I pass by, then scrapes her chair back, getting up.

"Alright—but don't you dare go back down there again, you hear me?" She holds her finger up at me as I open my mouth to lie. "I know you went. You moved the body around."

"I didn't move it around," I say, placing the dishes in the sink as she narrows her eyes at me. "It just moved . . . while I was down there. I'm sorry."

She shakes her head and waves a hand in my direction, heading for the doorway. "Don't do it again."

"It was like a weird rigor thing, I swear."

"Ya te dije. Seriously, Jaxon."

I turn on the tap and start washing. "Yeah, okay."

I can't lie; I feel a pull to go back to the basement. I know Mami's probably wrapped Christian up so it would be way more trouble than it's worth to look at him, but it's like there's a wire pulling me from the pit of my stomach down through the floorboards into the morgue.

I ignore it, scrubbing the plates and pans, leaving the kitchen as orderly as I can before heading upstairs. The pull in my stomach stays; like a dog on a leash, tugging against it makes my insides constrict.

Mami really will kill me, though, if I do. It's not an option.

At my door, I click my tongue a few times, calling for Grim. Now that I think of it, I haven't seen her since dinner, which is strange. She usually likes to eat her meal along with us, but I don't see her for the rest of the night, even after my turn in the bathroom.

I leave my bedroom door open in case she shows up.

TWO

Consciousness hits me like a meteor to the chest in the middle of the night. The first sound I hear before my eyes open is my voice leaving my throat in a strangled cry. I roll onto my side, nauseous, breathing so hard I cough and choke on the air. The first coherent thought that manages to filter through my brain is: *Christian*.

He's dead. I didn't dream that . . . right? No, he's dead. But he floods my every thought even as I try to regain my bearings. The image of him on the table, the darkness of the morgue, the frigid stiffness of his fingers, the mottled coloring of his bruised, sunken chest.

Trying to shake the images out of my head, I reach for my phone. The screen is blinding in the darkness of my room. I can't focus on the numbers or the tiny letters on the push notifications filling the lock screen, so I drop my phone on my comforter, reaching to turn on the light instead.

Was I having a panic attack in my sleep? Is that possible?

I stumble out of my room, legs shaking hard enough to make my knees buckle as I crash my way into the bathroom. I flip the lights on and drop down onto the cool tile floor, pressing my hands against it, blinking hard to try to stop the spinning in my head.

I barely register that I woke Mami until she's in the bathroom with me, kneeling on the tile in her white nightgown. She presses her soft, warm hands to my cheeks, my neck, and the top of my spine as she pulls me into her. She smells like lavender vanilla lotion; it's familiar enough to quell some of the lurching in my stomach.

"Breathe, Jaxon," she murmurs, rubbing wide circles over my back and holding my head against her shoulder. "I told you *not* to go down there, you see?"

"I feel—" I say, sitting up straighter, trying to shake my head clear.

I stop then because Mami clamps her hand over my mouth, her entire body suddenly as straight and rigid as a gravestone. Her expression is tight, her eyes wide, nostrils flared. I freeze with her, straining to hear something beyond the autumn wind outside and faint creaks of the house settling in the cold.

Then, I hear it.

It's a faint but distinct crash. A clanging clatter from somewhere downstairs. My stomach strains, like it's trying to find its way outside of me. Grimalkin meowls from downstairs.

"Someone's in the house," Mami whispers, cupping a hand around the back of my head. "Come to my room. I'm calling the police."

I feel sick. Grimalkin yowls again.

"It's coming from the morgue," I say. I don't know why I'm certain about it. It's like the wire I felt pulling me down there earlier has become electrified. "It's Christian."

I expect Mami to clamp her hand over my mouth again, but instead she stares at me, her eyes flitting back and forth between mine. She looks down like she's trying to see the morgue through the bathroom floor, her arms tight around me to keep me from moving.

"What did you do?" she asks.

I stammer at her for a moment. She thinks I caused this? *How*?

"I . . . I . . . I don't know! I feel it . . . it's him, he's—"

I stop because I don't know *what* he is. He's down there, he's dead, and he's calling me.

"Get your father's watch."

"What?"

She wraps her hands around my upper arms and stands, looking into my eyes as she hauls me up with her.

"Your father's pocket watch. Did you lose it?"

"*No*, but—"

"Grab the watch and come downstairs."

"Mami, what's going on?"

She shakes her head, lips pulled thin in impatience as she turns me around and pushes me through the door.

"Don't go down there without me," I tell her over my shoulder, staggering toward my room.

"Jaxon, baby, *get* the watch," she orders sharply, already running downstairs.

I almost trip over my own feet running back into my room. Crashing into my bureau, I brace myself against the drawers as the fox skull goes clattering onto the floor. I grab the pocket watch, cold in my tight fist, and run, taking the stairs two at a time until I make it to the kitchen.

I hear him. I know Mami does, too; her hands shake as she unlocks the basement. The sound coming from downstairs is disturbingly human, wheezing cries, scraping coughs, and choking sounds. When Mami finally pulls the door open and flips the light switches on, the voice downstairs yelps in surprise, then lets out a scream that rattles my teeth in my skull.

We scramble down the stairs, but I trip over the last few steps as soon as I see Christian. My legs give way beneath me. I land hard on the concrete floor, my father's pocket watch skittering away from me, but all I see is *him*.

Christian's sprawled on his stomach on the ground, the steel worktable spilled over on its side behind him. He's pale, his lips and fingers and eyelids tinged with blue, his entire back still deep purple from the livor mortis, skin drenched with sweat. He looks at me, and his eyes—dull and filmed over earlier this afternoon—are bright with tears and bloodshot, wide with desperate fear.

"*Jaxon?*" he cries, lungs wheezing audibly.

I don't have to look to know the state his lungs are in.

"It—it's okay, Christian," I stammer, voice shaking as I look to my mom. Her face looks blurry. I squeeze my eyes shut for a second to try to bring the world back into focus.

Mami rushes over to kneel by Christian's side, placing her hands over his hair and on his back, shushing him. He clutches at the skirt of her nightgown, trying to breathe through his gasping and choking.

"Get the pocket watch," she says to me, pointing her chin to where it landed on the ground. "Grab the watch, baby. Avanza."

I crawl across the floor as my mom tries to soothe Christian with soft reassurances, brushing her fingers through his curls. Even on my hands and knees, my limbs tremble like they can't bear to support my weight, but I make it far enough to grab the pocket watch again and sit on my knees.

"Mami . . . what do I do?"

"Open it," she instructs, pulling Christian up into her lap by his shoulders carefully and running her hands over his back to calm his shaking. "Then touch him and turn the hands back."

My first thought is *that sounds ridiculous*. But I go with it, stumbling over to them and taking Christian's frozen hand. His fingers clench around mine so tightly my knuckles grind together. The look in his eyes—wild, alert, alive—makes the bile rise in the back of my throat.

I flip the watch face open, the inside of the cover flashing *Jadiel*, my father's name, carved into the metal under my grandfather's name. My fingers still shake, but Christian's vise grip and shuddering, reedy breaths keep me focused on the task at hand.

Dad taught me how to do this once, weeks before he died. I imitate the motions now, tracing my thumb along the edge of the dial, swinging the lever away from it with my nail, and twisting the crown at the top with my thumb and forefinger. I open my mouth to ask my mom what I'm supposed to set the watch to, but before I can get a word out my body shudders hard and I cry out, tightening my grip on Christian's hand.

Blood pounds in my ears, my arms are vibrating, and my heart is banging against my sternum. My breath stutters out of me, lungs struggling to inflate as my vision flashes with black.

It *burns*. Everywhere, every inch of my body inside and out, feels sharp and hot and alive.

I can't hear anything. The rushing sound in my ears blocks almost everything out. Only Christian's screams, sharp and piercing, cut through the static. I grit my teeth, molars grinding hard against each other, squeezing my eyes shut as I keep turning the crown of my father's watch, faster now, trying to stay focused. The pain ebbs, gradually dulling into a sharp ache in my chest and the side of my head. A sharp *crack* and a yelp from Christian prompts me to open my eyes.

He's changed. His brown skin is still pale, but now it's even and unmottled, the white lights gleaming off the sheen of sweat covering his body. He takes a deep, rattling breath and coughs. Blood splatters from his mouth, bright red, spraying my mom's nightgown and dripping from the end of his chin, but his next breath sounds normal. When he groans, it's clear, no reedy wheeze.

"Set it there, Jaxon," Mami says to me, turning Christian's face delicately with her fingers. The gash across his eye is bleeding anew, deep red.

I push the lever back in place, then shut the watch. When I let go of Christian's hand, I sway, head swimming, but Mami reaches out to steady me. Her hand feels cool and soft against the back of my neck.

"You're right here with me," she murmurs. "Breathe."

I do, my breath shaking with the trembling rocking my whole body. My face feels wet, and touching over my lips, I find my nose has started bleeding again, profusely this time. Christian's out cold, draped over my mom's lap, his back rising and falling with new, steady breaths. She keeps running her other hand through his hair and across his shoulders as if he might still be in pain, but her face is sober and thoughtful.

"What's happening?" I ask her, my voice coming out higher and thinner than I expected.

"Let's talk about it in the morning, Jaxon," she says, turning her face to me and squeezing the back of my neck. "You should clean up and get some rest."

"Rest?" My voice cracks, I sway back like I might fall over even on my knees. "I can't go to sleep! Did you see what I did? We have to call Christian's mom! We have to call her right now!"

"No, we . . ." She stops, letting go of me to pat Christian's face, testing how passed out he is. "Let me think. Let me think what to tell her."

"What are you talking about? You can tell her whatever, nothing makes sense! Tell her it's a miracle; they're Catholics!"

In the end, Mami calls Christian's mom while I turn on every light in the house on my way upstairs to grab clothes to put Christian into. I can't stand the dark right now; I keep seeing Christian's sweat-drenched face and horror-stricken eyes in it. By the time I get back downstairs, Mami's already put on a pot of coffee and laid Christian out on the couch in the receiving room.

I don't know how she carried him up here alone; he's huge. I go over and wrestle him into a pair of gray sweatpants and a blue hoodie, feeling like I'm in a weird dream all the while. My brain feels like it's been pierced by a thousand tiny needles; my hands are numb. Christian is like a rag doll in my arms, groaning, his eyes moving behind his eyelids as I dress him.

The sweatpants leave a solid three inches of ankle showing but that's the best I can do. I notice belatedly that the hoodie I put him in says *The Evil Dead* in bright red lettering with a hand bursting up behind it as if coming out of the ground. I consider swapping hoodies with him, but before I can make a decision, there's frantic knocking at our main door.

"That's Conce," says my mom, as if it could be anyone else

at this hour. "Get the door, honey."

I get up, watching Christian as I move to the door, mentally begging him to wake up. He's warm, he's got a pulse. Even though I can see and feel he's alive, I can't help worrying his mom's gonna come in and he'll be dead, and she'll think we're crazy. Or cruel. Or both.

I open the door.

Christian's parents are on the other side, along with his older sisters. His mom, Concepción, or Conce for short, is a small lady with bronze skin and long, pin straight black hair with premature gray streaks in the front. She takes my hands as soon as I open the door, eyes red and swollen.

"He's here? He's alive?"

My mouth opens and closes. I nod, stammering. "Uh, he . . . he's . . . yeah, he's asleep."

Christian's dad, a man who looks like a surlier version of his son with a serious mustache and deep brown skin, pushes his hands back into his close-cropped hair and blows out a sigh. Christian's sisters, both of them tall and curly haired like Christian but darker like their father, look at each other in bald-faced shock. I can't blame them.

Conce kisses my hands and pulls me down to squeeze her arms around me, kissing my cheek too. "¡Gloria a Dios!" she cries, letting go of me to wipe her eyes and making the sign of the cross before heading inside. "Where is he?"

The rest of the family rushes in past me into the main receiving room. When they go through the doorway, Conce cries out and dissolves into sobs, rushing over to drop on her knees beside Christian on the couch. One of the sisters kneels beside her and the other leans over the back of the couch, the three of them pressing their hands to Christian's face, neck, and hands. Mr. Reyes stands behind Conce, his hands on her shoulders as if anticipating having to comfort her when it turns out Christian's dead after all.

"He's warm!" gasps one of the sisters.

"Ay, mi niño," Conce moans in her song-like Central Mexican accent, circling her hands around Christian's face and stroking her thumbs across his cheeks. "Despiértate, mi nene precioso, por favor."

My mom comes into the room with a tray of coffee cups and a plate of sliced pound cake. She sets the tray on the low table, coming to stand beside me, slightly off to the side.

"He was awake earlier," says my mom, wrapping an arm around me. "When Jax found him, he was awake but confused. I think the shock of everything wiped him out."

"How does something like this happen?" asks Mr. Reyes, still staring down at his son.

"Yeah," the sister behind the couch chimes in. She looks up at us, her eyebrows knitted together. "Amá said . . . she said his chest was caved in! He couldn't have lived!"

"Bodies are pretty incredible," my mom explains, squeezing me a little closer to her. "Sometimes they handle trauma that seems impossible. This isn't the first time something like this has happened to a mortician, actually."

Conce runs her hand over the lettering on Christian's chest. My mom's fingers tighten around my arm when she notices what it says, but Conce doesn't say anything about it. She gazes at Christian, willing him to wake up.

I stand up, jittery with the anxiety that he'll drop dead if I don't do something, and edge up beside Conce, leaning over to pat Christian's cheek lightly. Dried blood still clings to my fingers in streaks from my nosebleed, some packed under my nails. I hope his family doesn't notice. "Come on, man . . . wake up, please."

Almost the same moment as I say it, Christian's eyes open. He looks up at his mom, dazed and lost for a moment before recognition sets into his eyes.

"¿Amá?" he mumbles drowsily, reaching up a pale, shaking hand and touching it to her cheek. He looks around to the other faces around him. "Apá . . . Alondra, Rosa . . . ¿dónde . . .?"

All of Christian's relatives make a clamor of voices at once, Conce wailing louder than all of them and pressing her head against Christian's, her long black hair making a curtain around his face.

They stay a while after that, Christian surrounded by his family on all sides as they nurse coffees and talk with my mom about the miracle of Christian's survival, what they'll have to say to the priest after they'd called on him to deliver Christian's last rites, and what they need to do when they report back to the hospital and the authorities about the mistake they made. She offers to go along with them, and Conce trips over herself thanking her and calling me a sweet, beautiful boy for being the one to find Christian still breathing.

Christian keeps looking at me when he thinks I'm not looking, which has my stomach in knots. I wonder if he remembers how he came back, but I don't get a chance to ask him. By the time they leave, the sun is coming up over the rooftops and trees on our street.

I've never felt so awake.

THREE

Grimalkin shows up late in the morning. I don't know where she's been lurking, but she's twitchy and wary, her orange eyes flitting from corner to corner as she creeps into my room and hops up on the bed beside me. I haven't slept. My brain feels like thick sludge pushing against my eardrums and the back of my eyes. Grimalkin curls up next to my face and I push my nose into her fur, patting her head.

"I'm freaked out, too," I tell her.

Even with Grim here, I can't sleep. When I close my eyes, I remember the deep pull of panic and dread that shook me into consciousness in the middle of the night. I picture Christian mangled, in pain, staring up at me for help. I'm wired, skin prickling from all the excitement.

Without my mom here, I don't have anyone to answer the million questions I have about all this. I'd call Titi Clío, my dad's sister, but how would I begin explaining the situation to her? The only thing I can say for sure is that my dad must be involved since it was his pocket watch Mami told me to use on Christian. I feel like Titi Clío must know *something* if he's tied up in all of this. They were close in age, they seemed to be able to communicate through eye contact sometimes. If my dad had secrets, Titi Clío is definitely the person most likely to know them, along with my mom.

But if I'm wrong and she doesn't know, then I don't want to be the one to get her involved either.

I lift my head, looking at Grimalkin. I gotta do something else until Mami comes back, at least.

"Wanna go see Regan?"

She runs her sandy tongue over my short hair, which I take as a yes.

"Come on, then," I say as I pick Grimalkin up to pack her in my bag. She's a good sport about it as usual. I think she enjoys getting a chance to take in the sights and smells on the walk to Regan's place.

Regan lives in a rectangular white house with a black roof and a wooden porch. She's a few streets away from me, but the houses in her neighborhood are more isolated than mine, with short stretches of trees between each. When we were little, we used to peel strips of bark off the birch trees in her yard and pretend they were magic scrolls while her dad watched us from the porch. Her dad's there now, sitting in one of the plastic chairs having coffee and bread.

Grimalkin pokes her head out of my backpack, meowing as if in greeting. I raise a hand, as he nods at me.

"Hey, Carlos," I call to him.

"Hey, Jaxon." He smiles. He has Regan's dimples and sunny brown skin, but his hair's gone salt and pepper, lines forming around his eyes when he smiles. "Go on in. Regan's still in her pajamas, but she'll want to see you. You holding up okay?"

"Uh, yeah," I say, grimacing. "Actually . . . Christian's still alive. He woke up in our morgue."

Carlos's eyes widen and he raises his thick eyebrows at me. "What?! They sent you that kid alive?"

"I know, right?"

Carlos lets out a low whistle, shaking his head. "Anything like that ever happened to one of my girls . . ."

I laugh nervously, heading for the door. "As long as you took it out on the hospital, not us."

I leave Carlos on the porch, shaking his head at the shame of someone pronouncing a kid dead before checking well enough, and I try not to look suspicious. Inside, Regan's mom, Simone, is in her scrubs with her bag slung over her shoulder, running around to kiss her daughters goodbye.

Regan is lying on the couch in her gingham pajama pants and an oversized shirt with her legs over the armrest. She's sucked into whatever's happening on her phone, so Simone and Regan's kid sister Robin notice me first. Robin's fluffy brown curls have been wrestled into twin braids tied off at the ends with bobble hair ties that clack when she leaps out of Simone's arms and runs to me.

She's eight now—way too big for this—but I still catch her when she takes a running leap into my arms.

"It's Jaxon!" she announces.

Simone's already at my side, all frantic energy. I'm sure she's running late to get to the nursing home; that's usually the case.

"Hi, hon," she greets, placing her hand on my shoulder as she kisses my cheek. "I gotta go, but if you're hungry there's still arroz con gandules and chuletas from yesterday. You know you can have whatever's in the kitchen."

She kisses the top of Robin's head again for good measure and looks back at Regan, who's sitting up now, her sleep-rumpled ponytail sticking up on one side, her edges starting to curl out of their formerly flat-ironed state.

"It's almost noon," she says to Regan, giving her a pointed look as she pushes the door open. "You better not be wearing those same pajamas when I get home tonight."

"Okay, Mamá. Bendición." She sighs, raising a hand to me in greeting.

Simone huffs a fond sigh, hurrying outside as she tosses a "Dios te bendiga," over her shoulder. I hoist Robin higher up as she begins to slide out of my grip, walking over to Regan.

"How are you guys?" I drop Robin carefully on the couch beside Regan and sit on the other side of her. "Me and Grim came to give you guys some updates."

"Lemme see Grim!" says Robin, already unzipping my bag. She laughs as Grim hops out and brushes her big fluffy tail against her face before jumping off the couch.

"Updates on Christian?"

Even as Robin's making to follow Grim around the house, she looks back at me when Regan says that.

"Is there gonna be a funeral at your house?"

"Uh . . . no."

Robin takes that answer with a shrug, stalking after Grim, who keeps moving out of her reach. Regan, however, frowns and shakes her head like she didn't hear me right.

"No funeral? Can the Reyeses not afford it? We can start a fundraiser if we need to."

It's just like her to jump into problem-solving mode. Regan's always been bad at sitting idle and amazing at tackling issues relentlessly. Even now she's already whipped out her phone and started googling "funeral financing options." If it were something like that, I'm sure Regan would have a full-service funeral funded by Monday afternoon.

"No, that's not it." My stomach churns. In my head, I can hear my mom telling me to tell people as little as possible about Christian being alive but it's Regan.

I glance over at Robin, following Grim into the dining room, then I wince at Regan. "He woke up in the morgue, Reg."

Regan's dark eyes go wide. She lifts her gaze from her phone to blink at me in shock.

"He *what*?"

"He woke up." I lean in to lower my voice. "It was freaky. I wanna tell you how it all went down, but . . ."

Regan is still staring at me like I'm speaking a language she doesn't understand. Her eyes flicker over to Robin sitting on the dining room floor, letting Grim rub herself against her hand. Regan starts getting up, tucking her cellphone into the waistband of her pajama pants, and nods for me to follow.

"Robin, watch the kitty. Jaxon's gonna help me with something."

"Okay!" she calls, wrapping her arms around Grimalkin despite the low growl Grim lets out.

"Be good, Grim," I call over my shoulder as I follow Regan down the hall to her room.

When we enter her room, Regan snaps the door shut behind us, pulling out her phone to connect to her speaker, playing some lo-fi beats to drown out our conversation in case Robin gets it in her head to eavesdrop. Regan backs into her bed, dropping onto the tangled pile of her lavender comforter and sunset-pink sheets. I sit in her computer chair, stark black against the twilight pinks and purples she liked as a kid, rubbing a hand over the top of my head as I figure out what to say.

"So he's alive," she prompts.

"Yep." I take a deep breath. I know I can trust Regan. "But he was dead when he came to us. He *woke up*, Regan."

Several different expressions pass over Regan's face in the span of a second. Her eyes widen in shock, her eyebrows furrow in disbelief, her head tips in confusion. Finally, she stares at me while shaking her head.

"Okay, slow down, Jaxon. What are you saying? Like . . . you guys resuscitated him?"

"No," I say, feeling a little crazy. "More like . . . *resurrected* him."

She blinks at me. The set of her mouth and the small wrinkle between her eyebrows tell me she doesn't believe me.

"Maybe they got something mixed up at the hospital. I've heard that can happen—people waking up on autopsy tables and stuff like that."

"*No,*" I insist, looking down at my knees to avoid looking at her face. The doubt in Regan's eyes is hard to look at; I already feel insane. "I know a dead body when I see it, okay? His chest was all . . . it was like punched in by the steering wheel. No one could've survived what his body went through. Seriously, Regan."

"But he's alive now?"

"I know how this sounds, but I swear I resurrected him or—or something. I touched him, and he woke up."

"Well, where did you touch him?"

I look up at her, puzzled. "His hand. Why?"

"Well, I don't know!" She shrugs helplessly, rubbing the heel of her hand over her forehead. "Maybe you touched a pressure point or something that, like, jolted him out of, like, a coma." ·

"I don't think that's how that works."

Regan sucks her teeth, rolling her eyes at me. "Okay, well, *resurrection* is a lot to swallow, too."

Logically, Regan's trying to rationalize something totally fucking nuts. But I really want her to make me feel like *I'm* not the one who's nuts.

"Look, I wouldn't bullshit you, okay?" I snap, getting up out of her chair and moving to the door. "And I'm not *crazy* either."

Regan hops off her mattress, bounding over the laundry on the floor to reach the door before me with her long legs. She stands in front of it, holding her hands up peaceably.

"I know. I'm sorry . . . I'm just trying to make this make sense."

"So am I!"

"Okay . . . okay." She puts her hands on my shoulders, walking me back to sit on the computer chair. She sits on her bed again, crossing her legs under her. "So how did it happen?"

I explain it to her from the beginning. I tell her how I went into the basement when I shouldn't have and how Christian turned to stare at me with his dead, unseeing eyes. I tell her how I woke in a panic in the middle of the night and how, when I went down there again and found him writhing on the floor, his eyes were clear.

"How did you know?" she asked.

"Know what?"

"To turn the watch back?"

"My . . . my mom told me to."

Regan rubs the space between her eyebrows, frowning at her

lap in thought. "Tessa hasn't said anything else? Since it happened?"

She hasn't had a chance to, but this is also the first time I'm clear-headed enough to think about it. From the moment I told her I could feel it was Christian crashing around in the morgue, she'd known exactly what to do.

"Not yet. We had to get Christian dressed and call his parents and all that stuff. She's with the Reyeses right now, sorting Christian's shit out at the hospital."

I press the heels of my hands against my eyes, exhaling through my nose slowly. Panic twists my stomach into a hard knot, sour bile climbing up the back of my throat, and I don't want to go there. Not right now.

"I'm so tired," I sigh, rubbing the sleepy itch out of my eyes. "I haven't slept in like . . . I don't even know, a day, I guess?"

Regan isn't ready to drop this subject. She leaves a long, tense pause before she speaks again. Her eyes are torn, squinting at me like it's taking physical effort to hold back more questions, but she decides against pushing it.

"You wanna lie down? Your house is so big and scary, it might be easier to take a nap here."

I nod, finally pulling my hands away from my eyes. There are spots in my vision from how hard I pressed against them.

"Is that cool?"

"Yeah, Jaxon, of course," she says, standing up to shake out her sheets and comforter so they're usable rather than in a big tangle. "Lie down. I gotta do some chores anyway."

I get up and climb into Regan's bed, immediately sinking into the warm spot she'd been sitting in while burying myself in her comforter. It smells like Regan in here, a combination of soft scented lotion and the sweet, candyish scent of her heat protectant. Outside the room, Robin coos over Grimalkin.

I think I can sleep here.

"Thanks," I murmur, half-muffled in the blankets.

It's easy to sink into the warm comfort of sleep at Regan's house, surrounded by sounds of life. When I wake again, the light shining through Regan's gossamer curtains is that persimmon color the sky turns into during early autumn evenings. My eyes feel sticky with sleep, but the static in my head is clearer. I feel almost fully human again.

I get up, a little unsteady on my feet for a second, and pull my hood up over my head. It's cold outside of the enveloping warmth of Regan's comforter, the smell of chocolate is coming from the kitchen, and I can hear my mom's voice along with Regan, Robin, and their dad.

Grimalkin's the first to greet me as I trudge down the hallway. She hurries over to me and winds around my legs as I walk, half curling her smoky gray bottle brush tail around my ankles.

"Grim," I chide, slowing down so I don't trip over her. "Girl, what're you doing? I don't wanna step on you."

The voices in the living room pause when they hear me, the couch springs creaking. In a second, my mom is at my side looking twice as exhausted as I felt earlier today. The shadows under her eyes are dark and deep, but even dressed down in sweatpants, she still carries herself with her usual poise. She presses her cool hands against my cheeks, looking me over as if I might be sick.

"How are you holding up, Jaxon?"

"I'm fine. You should be at home, Mami. You've been up for way too long."

She smiles, placing her hand between my shoulders to usher me toward the living room.

"I was filling Regan and her dad in on how Christian's doing at the hospital," she said, giving me a meaningful look I'm not sure how to read. "Besides, I'm not going home without you."

That's fair. I don't want to be home without her either.

In the living room, Regan looks up at me, raising her eyebrows a fraction before smiling normally. She tells me plenty with that micro expression: my mom's explanation doesn't match up with mine. No surprise there. If nothing else, two very different reports should confirm for her that something weird happened last night.

"You want some hot chocolate before you go?" Regan asks, raising her mug.

The chocolate in her mug is thick and milky, dotted with specks of brown from the melted bar her dad used to make it. Carlos makes the best hot chocolate in the world.

I look at my mom. "Do you wanna head home now?"

"I can wait a little bit. Go ahead." She cups her hand around the back of my head, stretching up to kiss my temple.

Carlos is already coming in from the kitchen with a mug for me, pushing a sleeve of saltine crackers into my hand. "You should eat something. You've been sleeping for a while."

"Yeah," I say, taking the mug in one hand and the sleeve in the other. The hot ceramic burns the pads of my fingers, so I sit on the couch between Regan and Robin, setting it down on the coffee table. "Sorry about that. I've been too freaked out to sleep."

Carlos shakes his head, waving off my apology. "You can sleep here any time. Just make sure you get rest tonight, too."

Mami sits on one of the armchairs, waiting until I've pulled the sleeve of crackers open to take one.

"Don't worry, Carlos," she says, smiling demurely at him. "He'll be fine."

Though it's nice sitting in the warmth and good humor of Regan's living room, we don't stay much longer. My mom reiterates a few times that she doesn't understand how Christian woke up and how it's never happened to us at our funeral home before. Each time she does, Regan bumps her leg into mine without looking at me.

I know Regan wants to talk more, but my brain feels as ragged and shriveled as a popped balloon. As soon as we leave her house, I turn my phone off.

"I know you have a lot of questions," my mom starts before I can say anything, toeing her shoes off in the doorway when we get home as she presses a hand against the wall to keep her balance. "I promise we can talk about what I know. But can I lie down for a little while first?"

If she's going to talk to me about *what she knows*, that means I was right, there's more she hasn't told me. It's weird to think there's any amount of information she's been deliberately hiding from me for a while.

I'd feel like a dick insisting on talking *now*, though. She's exhausted.

"Go to bed, Mami." I squeeze my arm around her shoulders, leaning in to kiss the top of her head. "We can talk tomorrow. Christian's doing okay?"

"Yeah." She looks more tired when she says that, taking a deep breath and letting it out slowly. "I don't know where your head's at on this, honey, but you saved him, you know."

I'm not sure what to say to that. I don't know how to even start thinking about what I've done to Christian. It doesn't feel *good*.

"Yeah." I shrug. "We can talk about it when you wake up later."

FOUR

I'm not proud to admit it, but I wake up in my mom's room late on Sunday morning. After napping the day away in Regan's house, it was too hard to sleep and being alone in the dark felt bad, so I went to go sleep with my mom like a little kid. She was so tired she didn't even notice me come in.

She's not here when I wake up. One of my dad's old paperbacks sits on her bedside table, page marked with one of her engraved metal bookmarks even though she must have read all his books at least a dozen times over by now.

I'm still tired, but her side of the covers are neatly tucked in. She must have been up for a while. I don't get *how* when I got more sleep than she did.

I sit up, yawning so wide my jaw makes a soft popping sound, and rub the crusty stuff out of my eyes as I swing my legs over the side of the bed. I can tell, already, that today is going to be one of those freakishly hot October days because the floorboards feel warm under my feet and the sun outside the tall windows beats down on the orange maple trees, lighting them up.

It's hard to appreciate it. Today was the day Mami was gonna call her assistant over to finish prepping Christian's body.

I shake off the thought as I straighten out the blankets on my side of her bed, tucking the corners of the gray comforter in tightly like she always does. It's weird having Christian taking up so much space in my mind over the past day. Before this, I only thought about him this much back when I was in danger of catching feelings for him again. I know, with time, the shock of everything that's happened will wear off. But I don't know how I'll go back to blowing Christian off.

Downstairs, Mami's throwing down in the kitchen again. As soon as I walk in, the smell of fried salami and red onions cooking in sweet vinegar hits me. My stomach growls as I pad into the kitchen; it's been a minute since the last time I ate something.

Mami's standing at the stove, sautéing the onions and frying cheese and salami in her robe. On the table, there are two plates of soft, creamy mangú. It's been forever since the last time she had the time and drive to make it.

"Morning, Mami," I say, coming over to squeeze an arm around her shoulders. "You sleep okay?"

"Yeah, baby. Did you?"

"Yeah. Thanks for making breakfast. Smells wicked good."

Mami comes over with the onion pan, dishing some on top of my mangú, then some onto her own. I grab us utensils as she gives us each our share of salami and cheese, then she gestures for me to start eating. When she sits across from me, it almost feels like a holiday or a birthday morning—up late, special breakfast. Instead, we're recovering from the shock-hangover from everything yesterday.

"Couldn't sleep in your room last night?"

"Sorry," I say, instantly regretting eating a slice of salami it when it burns my tongue. I inhale awkwardly to cool it off as Mami wrinkles her nose at me when I talk with my mouth half-full. "Just can't stop seeing what happened. It's starting to feel like . . . I don't know. Like a really weird nightmare."

She mulls that over in silence, frowning down at her plate as she pokes absently at her mangú. Finally, she sets her fork down before lifting her dark eyes to meet mine.

"It wasn't, though. A nightmare."

"I know."

There's another pregnant pause. She looks at me like she's waiting for something, and I know I should be asking her questions, but I don't know what to ask.

"Are you angry with me?" she asks after we've gone more than a few seconds in silence.

"No!" I say, widening my eyes. "Why? Should I be?"

She blinks at me as if that should be obvious.

"Because I've never told you something like this was possible? I've never told you the truth about the pocket watch your father gave you."

"So like because you were hiding things from me, you mean?"

"I wouldn't . . ." Mami winces, lifting a finger in protest. "I don't know that I'd say *hiding* exactly."

I raise my eyebrows at her; what else would she call it?

"I'm not mad," I insist. "I'm . . . confused. I'm guessing you never thought something like that was gonna happen? Or something."

Her eyes scan my whole face, like she's trying to figure out if I'm lying. I stare back at her, trying not to show it bothers me. When do I ever lie to her?

"Mami," I say, frowning at her, "I'm not mad. Why wouldn't I tell you if I was mad?"

She looks ashamed when I ask that, turning her eyes down and pressing her lips together. She turns back to her plate again, picking up her fork. "Sorry. I know you wouldn't lie to me; I'm just freaked out."

I shrug, smiling at her weakly. "Me too."

"I know. Listen, baby, today I want us to spend some time talking about this when we finish breakfast. After that, I want us to go back to normal."

I'm nervous and relieved at the same time. I don't know what to expect, but maybe she'll say something that'll make my head spin a little less.

It must be about Dad. If my mom was going to have a reason to hide things from me, it would be for him.

We eat quietly for a bit, Mami getting up when the coffee maker beeps and pouring out cups for both of us. As she pulls the creamer out of the fridge, our mechanical doorbell dings three times. Mami looks up at the clock, rubbing the space between her eyebrows as she heaves a sigh.

"Did I forget to tell Monica we don't have a client today?"

"I got it," I say, rising out of my chair and flapping a hand at her. "Don't worry, Mami."

She wraps her robe tighter around herself and picks up her coffee cup, nodding at me gratefully. "Thanks, baby."

Grimalkin sits on the banister of the main staircase, meowling at me as if to inform me of the visitor at the door. I pet her head, scratching between her ears, then climb down as she follows me along the banister. Down at the front door, the doorbell dings again, three dings in quick succession.

"Coming!" I call down to the person at the door. Taking the stairs two at a time, I head into the foyer with Grimalkin at my ankles. I unlock the latches and bolts on the door, swinging it open.

Titi Clío's on the other side, eyes lighting up as soon as she sees me, smiling like she's been let in on a big secret. She throws her arms around me before I get a single word out, and I laugh in surprise, squeezing her rail thin body. Her locs smell like rosewater and peppermint. A surge of nostalgia hits me hard.

"¡Titi! ¡Bendición!"

Titi Clío smacks a big kiss on my cheek, then pulls back to look at me. Even in her flat brown sandals, she's as tall as I am, long and willowy like my dad was. It's still morning, but since it's so unseasonably warm, she's wearing denim shorts and a stone-washed t-shirt with a fading logo under her long crochet lace cardigan.

"Surprise! Dios te bendiga, mijo." She laughs, hefting her hemp bag higher up on her shoulder and grinning at me. "You look even bigger than the last time I saw you."

"What are you doing here?" I ask, taking her bag and letting her into the foyer. "Mami didn't say you were coming."

"I was spending some time up in the mountains," she says, looking around as she heads to the stairs. "I decided to take a little detour at your house before heading back home."

That feels . . . convenient. When Titi comes out to Western Mass, she usually calls or texts us. I don't think she's ever gone to the mountains and forgotten to let us know she was nearby.

I'd better not push that for now, I guess, especially until I find out what Mami was planning to tell me. Besides, what would I say anyway? *I think you're here because I brought my friend back to life.*

Grim bumps her head against the back of my calf as I shut the door behind us, then runs on ahead of me, hopping up on the banister and climbing up. I follow her and Titi Clío, slinging the bag over my shoulder.

"Um . . ." I pause, not sure how to put it. "Titi, I don't know if now's like a great time to visit. Mami's pretty stressed out. She didn't get a lot of sleep, you know?"

"Oh no," she says, glancing at me over her shoulder to offer a sympathetic pout. "Well, that's fine. I'll help out, and we can let your mom get some good rest."

"Uh . . . right, yeah."

She hangs back for a moment at the landing, reaching out to run her hand over my hair and straighten out my eyebrows with her thumb. She smiles at me, pride shining in her eyes, which are so light brown they're almost golden.

"You look more like Jadiel every day. Handsomer, though."

I laugh awkwardly. It's true that I look like my dad, kind of. I know I have his sharp, narrow brows, and his big front teeth. I'm darker, broader, and shorter than he was, and I really can't speak to *handsome,* but Titi's been saying that since before my dad passed away.

"Thanks," I say, because it would be rude not to.

"You got a noviecito somewhere around here?"

My cheeks turn hot immediately as I roll my eyes, clicking my tongue against my teeth. Like I'd ever find a boyfriend at Jacob's Barrow Regional of all places. Christian's face pops into my mind, which I immediately push away. That's a level of delusional above wishful thinking. If I were in his place, I don't think I'd ever want to look me in the face again.

"No, Titi, not even close," I mutter, shaking my head. "The boys at my school are all straight or stupid. Or both."

She smiles like she thinks I'm lying, going into the kitchen ahead of me.

Mami is already up, searching through the cupboards for a plate for Titi Clío. The circles under her eyes betray how tired she is. She smiles at Titi, gesturing for her to join us for breakfast.

"We'd sat down to eat," she says, and I wonder if my aunt can hear the tinge of irritation barely staining her words. "You still eat plantains and everything, right? Just no animal things?"

Titi Clío pulls out one of the chairs and sits, sighing as if she's weary from her travels. I follow, setting her bags down between her chair and mine, then sit down again.

"Don't worry about me, Tessa. Siéntate y come. I don't wanna put you guys out."

"It's really no problem," my mom insists. "Ah, but I used butter in the mangú. You can't eat that, can you?"

Titi Clío's vegan diet bothers everyone in the family, right up to my grandma when she was alive. Titi is always cool about it, smiling through the criticisms both veiled and unveiled, while sticking staunchly to it.

"I'm good," she chirps cheerily, beckoning my mom back to the table. "I had a ton of granola and cashewgurt this morning."

"*Cashewgurt*?" I ask her, waiting until my mom sits back down before I pick up my fork again.

"Cashew yogurt. ¡No me des esa cara, it tastes good!"

"Sounds nasty," I say, pulling a face as I remember the time she convinced me to try vegan cheese.

"So," my mom cuts in abruptly, though her tone is warm. "What brings you here, Clío?"

"Came to see my favorite nephew," she says, widening her eyes like that should be obvious and reaching over to scrub her hand over the top of my head. "It's been some time, you know?"

"You could've called." My mom's trying to sound gentle, but it still sounds like a scolding. Or maybe it sounds that way to me because I'm used to hearing that little shift in her tone.

I focus on eating. The mangú is perfectly mashed, soft, creamy, and buttery. I know Mami takes out her stress sometimes by cooking, but I can't help feeling grateful for it.

The silence between them stretches for a few seconds while Titi Clío tries to bite back whatever retort she had in her head.

"I know, sorry," she admits finally. "I should have. I also heard you guys . . . tuvieron una *situación* aquí."

My mom's eyebrows knit together, her lips going thinner in disapproval. "You heard about the mix-up with the body?"

Titi Clío leans back in her chair, tipping her head, with a disbelieving smile spreading across her face. Her eyes dart to me for a fraction of a second, then she raises her brows a fraction at my mom, nodding once.

"Yeah," she drawls, tone laced with sarcasm. "The *mix-up*."

My mom's quiet for a long moment, like she's trying to figure out how to keep talking without saying something wrong.

"How'd you hear about it, Titi?" I ask, breaking the tense silence.

She shrugs. "It was on the radio this morning while I was driving. Dead kid ended up not-so-dead at a funeral home in Jacob's

Barrow. The *only* funeral home in Jacob's Barrow is the Santiago-Noble Funeral Home, so . . ."

Mami pinches the bridge of her nose, leaning her elbow on the table. "The *radio*? Already?"

"It's kind of a big deal, Tessa." says Titi Clío plainly. "So, I came because I figured maybe it was *time* to . . ."

She trails off, tipping her head toward me pointedly.

Why didn't it hit me until now? She *knows* what happened, and she knows it was me that did it. She didn't just hear about Christian waking up in our morgue; she has all the information to connect the dots and came to the right conclusion because she and Mami have been keeping this secret *together*.

That's why my mom was apologizing. Because everyone knows except me.

"You could have waited until I called you," says my mom, lowering her volume as if she's subconsciously trying to prevent me from hearing.

"Well, I wasn't sure you would! Jadiel siempre con sus secretos, y—"

"Can I be excused?" I ask, pushing my chair backward and standing up.

"Jaxon," Mami looks up at me with wide eyes as I gather my plates, "you barely ate anything."

"I wanna lie down for a minute. Sorry."

My aunt reaches for the back of my chair, gesturing for me to sit back down. "Jaxon, mijo, finish your breakfast. I'm sorry. We can put this off till later."

"Nah, I need to lie down."

I don't let them say anything else. I turn around, heading

straight up to my room, burying myself in my comforter. They don't follow me, though Mami calls after me half-heartedly one more time.

I shouldn't be surprised that they were *both* keeping secrets for my dad when I already suspected. But it still sucks.

I spend my time catching up on what I've missed on my phone. I get the barrage of texts I expected from Regan, but I also get a bunch of texts from kids at school I never talk to. Some of them don't even have names attached to their numbers. They all follow the same pattern.

Is it true about Reyes??

What happened to Reyes?? Did you see when they brought him in?

What happened when Christian Reyes woke up?? Did he wake up in a body bag? In a coffin??

It's the same on my Instagram, a bunch of messages from people I never talk to about Christian. I resist the urge to block everyone, texting Regan back instead. Her chatbox is full of link after link to obscure webpages about necromancy and black magic, but I ignore them.

Not looking at all that shit, I type. My family knows way more than they wanna tell me.

The thought bubble that means she's typing comes up immediately. A second later, she says,

Regan: Oh shit! Jax, you gotta get answers!

Me: I'm trying. Lemme call you later?

Regan sends me a thumbs-up emoji followed by a bunch of black hearts and skulls. I roll my eyes, but it does make me smile a little bit. I put my earbuds in, play some music, and put my phone on Do Not Disturb so I can turn my brain off and play a mindless game for a while.

It's normal for me to space out while I'm playing phone games. It quiets the anxious buzz of thoughts that won't shut up in my head down to a dull hum. Music helps with that, too. The music drowns out the unwelcome thoughts that drift up to the surface every now and then.

This time, I keep getting spikes of thoughts cutting through all the distraction. But the weirdest part is they don't feel like they're actually *mine*.

I keep thinking things like *I can't sleep. I don't want to sleep.* which I don't get because I'm not *trying* to sleep. My eyes aren't tired, I'm not groggy, but thoughts of sleep plague me anyway. Every time I think about it, my heart starts beating hard and fast, like a scared hummingbird trapped inside a fist.

I tug my earbuds out of my ears and put my phone down when another small wave of panic hits me. The voice in my ear carries on warning me away from sleeping. I figure it probably isn't coming from Spotify, but I don't know how to explain it to myself.

"Hey," I say out loud. My voice sounds ragged, as if I've been sleeping. "It's okay."

I don't know who I'm talking to or if I'm talking to anyone other than myself at all. There's a moment where my heart sinks into cold fear, then, with a full-body jolt like a bolt of electricity up my spine, the voice in my head is gone, my heart goes back to normal, and the threat of sleep leaves like a thin veil pulled away from my face.

I could step out of my room and ask my mom and my aunt what

happened to me. Odds are they'd have an answer. But they left me with nothing for this long.

I pick up my phone and text Regan.

Actually, can we meet up? Like in a couple minutes? I have an idea.

FIVE

The nice thing about living in a big Victorian house is how many ways there are to get out. I know my mom won't stop me if I tell her I'm going somewhere, but I don't feel like telling her, and I'm sure Titi Clío will try to intercept me. She's not used to me being upset with her; she's usually the one I complain to when I'm annoyed with my mom.

I take the back stairs that lead all the way down into the pantry on the first floor. They're narrow and dank but familiar and nostalgic. I used to sneak around the house when I was little, spying on my parents or pretending to live in a castle with secret passageways. From the pantry—it's more like a small room lined with shelves and cabinets than a standard pantry—I sneak into the kitchen, heading for the back door.

Grimalkin cuts me off, meowing dolefully up at me. I glare at her, holding my finger to my lips to shush her, then shoo her away from the door before slipping out silently.

The sun is hot on the back of my neck. Although I feel weird without a hoodie on, I have to take it off and tie it around my waist. By the time I make it to the hospital, the back of my shirt is sticking to my shoulders. I fan my stomach by flapping the front of my shirt by the hem and wave at Regan, who's sitting with her board on the sidewalk leading up to the main entrance.

Regan waves back, standing up and stowing her board in her backpack, more than half of it still sticking out. She's dressed for the heat; all of her hair is pulled up into a tight bun at the top of her head, her baby hairs slicked into neat little swoops. Her shorts are so short the pockets hang down past the denim, and she's got a crop top on under her lime-green hoodie.

"Feels like summer out here," I say, nodding at her. "What's up?"

"What's up?" she answers, shoving her hands in her pockets. "Did you call to see if he's here?"

"No, but I'm sure he is. They're probably freaking out, running tests and shit, right?"

"Probably? I mean . . ." She lowers her voice as we approach the doors, glancing around surreptitiously. "How sure were they that he was dead when they called it?"

"Uh . . . very. Blunt trauma to the chest and head. Broken neck. Caved in chest."

Her face pulls into a grimace, her nostrils going wide and round in disgust. I shrug at her.

"It's never pretty. Remember that one guy that got his leg ripped off when his car—"

"Yeah!" she yelps, cutting me off and covering her ears. "I remember, I remember! That was so fucked up . . . don't remind me."

"It was way harder looking at Christian, though," I admit, heading into the lobby. "It was . . . so weird. I don't know."

"You think he'll remember anything?"

"I don't know. He might. He was really staring me down when he woke up, but he didn't say anything."

Regan rubs her hand over her chin, squinting thoughtfully. "He *could* remember something . . . how it felt or *something* . . ."

"We'll at least know more than we know now. And, to be honest, even if my mom and Titi tell me anything, Christian's less likely to hide things or try to twist his story."

Regan furrows her brow like she wants to say something—probably to defend my mom. We've grown up so close my mom's practically her tía, and Regan's parents are like tíos to me as well. I get it: before this, I never knew my mom to lie to me. I can't defend her there now.

I cut Regan off before she can say anything, nodding toward the front desk.

"Can you . . ."

I don't need to say anything more; Regan understands my anxiety struggle with asking random strangers stuff. She nods, walking ahead of me.

"Hey," she greets the lady behind the desk. The lady looks up at her, smiling politely. "I think our cousin's here? Christian Reyes?"

There's instant recognition in her eyes. That's not surprising; it's not every day they send a patient off to the funeral home only to get him back.

"Oh! Yes, he's . . ." She pauses, typing on her keyboard and looking at the computer screen. "Still in the ICU. Head down that hall and take a right. The nurse at the booth will let you in."

"Thank you."

Regan looks at me wide-eyed as we turn to follow the lady's directions. She's pale, like the reality of the situation is sinking in for her. Maybe it makes this feel more real to hear someone else acknowledge Christian's situation. For me, it's felt real and unreal at the same time from the moment I saw Christian on Mami's prep table.

If anything, it helps get us into the ICU that much faster when Regan lies about us being Christian's cousins again at the booth. The nurse gives us a sympathetic look, Regan with her round eyes and me leaning close with a comforting hand around her shoulder, then unlocks the door as soon as we give her Christian's name.

Most of the rooms we pass on the way down the corridor have the curtains drawn so we can't see inside. The few that don't show mostly elderly people hooked up to tubes and machines. Regan blanches even more when she glances at them.

"Are you freaked out by hospitals?" I ask, keeping my voice in a low murmur.

"Not really," she whispers, shaking off a shudder. "Maybe just the ICU. These people look . . ."

I lift the corner of my mouth at her in a half smile. "I've seen worse."

Her eyes narrow. "You know that's not even funny."

"Sorry." I brace her arm gently as we turn to Christian's door and knock.

Multiple voices call, "Come in!" in English and Spanish at once. I push the door open to peer in, Regan scooting in right beside me to get a look as well. My shoulders loosen as soon as I spot Christian, and Regan's tension dissipates beside me as well.

Christian looks fine. He looks better than fine; he looks great. All the color is back in his warm brown skin, eyes lighting up behind the round frames of his glasses when he sees us. I try not to stare too long, my relief combined with how unfairly hot he looks even laid up in a hospital bed making it hard to tear my eyes away.

He waves at us from his bed, with his parents sitting in the chairs at his bedside and a priest standing nearby, gathering up his effects.

"Hey, Jaxon! Regan!" Despite his apparent perkiness, he's hooked up to all kinds of wires connected to the monitors beside him. He waves awkwardly, trying not to jostle them too much.

Christian's mom, Conce, is up out of her chair before either of us respond to him. She practically flies across the room and throws her arms around me, pulling me down into a hug.

"Thank you," she exclaims, kissing my cheek three times in quick succession. "Thank you for being here, and for helping my nenito and for everything, thank you! Padre, ¡este es el que lo encontró!"

I give her a quick, awkward squeeze and pull away, trying to smile at her and the priest like I don't feel super inappropriate being here.

"I didn't really do anything . . ." I mumble.

The priest smiles in that weird, paternal way priests do, patting my shoulder. "You appeared where and when God needed you."

Conce nods emphatically. "If you hadn't heard Christian, he wouldn't be here right now. I know it."

"*Amá*," whines Christian. "Can I say hi to them?"

"Ay, mijo," chides Conce, turning to look at him as she sets her hands on her hips. "Why can't I say hi, too?"

"I didn't say you couldn't!"

Christian's dad stands up with a sigh, reaching out to ruffle Christian's hair before coming over to us, placing a hand over Conce's shoulder. He gives me a tired smile, the shadows deep and dark under his eyes. He looks even more like Christian when he smiles. Even weighed down with exhaustion, he speaks with

Christian's same energetic, assertive affect.

"We were about to go to the cafeteria. Let me get you something. Soda? Candy? Lunch?"

Regan shakes her head. "No, no, thank you, don't worry about us."

"Chale, déjenme comprarles algo."

We shake our heads again and he sighs in defeat. Conce looks irritated to be steered away from the room, but Christian lets out a soft breath, leaning back against the head of his bed as his parents leave. He smiles as we come closer to him, gesturing toward the chairs his parents vacated.

"Sit down, it's fine! I had a couple visitors earlier, and my dad did the same thing. They'll be down there for a little while."

Regan sits in the chair closest to the head of the bed. I take the one further away. She puts her backpack down between her legs and reaches into it, pulling out a card in a pastel yellow envelope.

"My family signed this card for you," she says, passing it over to him. "They're all worried about you. How are you doing?"

"¡Qué chido!" He grins, tearing the flap open to pull out the card. It's got a photograph of a puppy in a cone on the front, which he laughs at even though it's not that funny. His chest makes a thin wheezing sound. "Tell 'em I'm doing fine! I don't even know why they still have me here, to be honest. All they told me so far is I have a concussion and a couple busted ribs."

I wish Regan had told me she had a card for Christian. I would have at least faked one out of the more ambiguous sympathy cards we have back at home. It's weird; I don't have anything for him but questions.

He reads Regan's card and thanks her profusely. Though he

does look well, up close his eyes are red, the shadows under them even darker and deeper than his dad's. His attitude is bright and sunny, but his exhaustion is palpable, from the way his eyelids hang over his eyes to the tremble of his fingers as he holds Regan's card.

He looks at me when I go a little too long without saying anything, raising his eyebrows and smiling hopefully. Infectiously sweet since elementary school, Christian's always had a way of making me feel like the most important person in the room when his eyes land on me. Now that he's grown handsome on top of sweet, it's hard not to blush like an idiot under his gaze.

"I didn't think you'd wanna come see me, Jaxon."

"Well . . ." I pause, reaching for an answer to that. Regan turns to look at me too, which isn't helpful. I look down at my knees, the dark brown of my skin showing through the frayed denim of my jeans. "I don't know, I guess . . . last time I saw you, you looked like you'd been in a car wreck, so . . ."

Christian laughs at that but not hard enough to make his chest wheeze again.

"So," I continue, looking up at his face, "I wanted to make sure you were really doing better."

Regan pats between my shoulders and smiles at Christian, nodding earnestly.

"Jaxon's been legit worried about you," she says, scrubbing her hand over my hair before I push her away gently. "You were our friend, you know?"

Something flickers over Christian's face when she says that. For a split second, he looks like he wants to argue. He stops himself, still smiling wearily.

"Yeah. Well, thanks."

An awkward silence settles between us, and I rub the space between my eyebrows. We didn't come here to hash out ancient middle school drama. I came here for answers.

"Christian," I say, leaning forward to rest my elbows over my knees. "Can I ask you some stuff? About the night you woke up in the funeral home?"

"I don't remember a lot." He grimaces apologetically. "But yeah, sure, you can ask. Are *you* gonna tell me too?"

That's entirely dependent on what and how much he recalls about everything. But I can't say that, obviously.

"I want to see if our memories line up," I tell him slowly, raising my eyebrows pointedly. I don't want to give myself away if he doesn't know what happened. If he *does* know, I don't want him to hold back. "So can you tell me what you *do* remember?"

Christian looks at me doubtfully, sharp enough to notice the careful evasion of a direct answer. Despite that, he closes his eyes, pressing his head back against the pillows as he thinks. "I remember getting in my car. Then the rest feels like a dream until I got to the hospital. I'm not sure which parts are real and which parts aren't."

"You don't remember waking up?"

"I don't know," he says, opening his eyes and looking up at the ceiling tiles. "I remember random things. Like I remember it being really dark, and I remember seeing you. I remember weird stuff. I don't know, I can't describe it."

"What kind of weird stuff?"

Christian reaches up to rub his eyes under his glasses, his light brown skin flushing pink across his cheeks. "I don't know . . .

really weird. Like I think I had some weird dream while I was in the morgue? Like one of those falling dreams, only the falling didn't wake me up. I could hear *you*. You were calling me."

"In your dream?"

"Yeah. I don't remember what you said. Half the time it sounded like you were talking to me underwater."

"How'd you know it was me?"

He's quiet for a moment, like he's trying to think of a good answer. I think I get it regardless; it's the same way I got that weird feeling pulling me down to the basement. The same way I knew something was up with him.

"It felt like you." He turns to me, shrugging weakly. "It felt like . . . I don't know. When I heard you, it felt like it always feels when you talk to me. Or when you used to. You know?"

Regan blinks at him, her brow furrowed in confusion. She raises an eyebrow, waiting to see what my answer is.

Weirdly, I do kind of get it. There's an almost tangible familiarity when you're near someone you've known for a long time. Even though Christian and I haven't talked much in the last few years, I think I'd recognize him even walking into a pitch-black room. Christian is hard to miss in general. He's always had a magnetism about him.

For me, anyway.

I nod, ignoring the heat rushing to my ears. "Yeah. I know what you mean."

"What do *you* remember?" He asks, looking at me pointedly as if to say *I showed you mine*.

I should have been prepared for this, but it throws me. I can't stop myself from floundering, looking to Regan for help. I still can't tell what he actually remembers or believes; his thoughts are all jumbled up, which makes sense. Is it even helpful to throw my version of events at him while he's wheezing and exhausted like this?

Regan stares back at me, her expression telling me she knows what I'm thinking. She opens her mouth, tearing her eyes away from mine to look at Christian. "You—you have a concussion, right? You're supposed to be on brain rest. Maybe in a couple days we can all get together and talk about it."

Christian's eyes flicker from Regan's to mine a few times, pressing his lips together irritably. I reach out, putting my hand on his calf over the blanket. Even through the fabric, I get a shock from him that makes us both jump in surprise, so I pull my hand back immediately.

"I promise we can talk about it when you're out of here. I don't wanna freak you out."

"¡Vete a la verga! I'm already freaked out!" He pushes his glasses higher up on the bridge of his nose, sitting up and trying not to get tangled in his wires. "I can't even sleep. I feel like I'm gonna drop dead if I do!"

"I'm sorry," I say, exchanging anxious glances with Regan. "I don't wanna freak you out *more*."

One of the monitors Christian's hooked up to starts beeping faster and his ears start turning red all the way down to his neck. He balls his hands into fists over his blankets, and a heat settles into my chest, dark and smoldering like an ember.

"Jaxon! Why are you always like this?! You can't come here asking me shit and then refuse to answer *my* questions!"

"I am *not* always like this!" I fire back.

"Yeah, bullshit! Even at school it's like *you* can say hi to me or ask for a pencil or whatever, but when *I* do it, you look at me like I spit in your face!"

My face burns with embarrassment. Is that true? That's not true. Right? "Okay, well, remind me not to say hi or ask for a pencil again . . ."

Christian groans in frustration, throwing his hands up and making the tubes tied to him jostle enough to make him flinch. "That's *not* what I'm saying!"

"Stop doing that, stupid, you're gonna tear your IV out!"

"Guys—stop. We're not refusing to answer questions!" Regan holds her hands up peaceably, looking between me and Christian like she can't believe we're arguing over something so stupid. "Just . . . later! You're still recovering!"

"*Recovering*? ¡No mames! If you know something about what happened to me, you need to tell me!"

The hot anger blooming in my chest gets hotter, but it feels foreign, like someone forced it down my throat, and my body wants to reject it. Christian keeps gesticulating angrily, the scrapes over his knuckles from his windshield shattering over him in the accident starting to heal over. I reach out on instinct, placing my hand over one of his and coaxing it back down firmly, trying not to disturb the IV drip.

"You need sleep," I hear myself tell him. "Go to sleep and heal."

When my nose starts bleeding this time, I almost expect it. A couple drops land on my knuckles and Christian's wrist before I clamp my hands over it, the hot blood smearing against my palms.

Christian widens his eyes at me for a split second before sleep drops over him like a veil, his whole body relaxing, eyelashes drifting shut. His hands unclench, and I pull away, holding onto the side of my chair as the room tilts around me.

Regan half rises out of her chair, eyes blown wide, mouth hanging open. She holds her hand to his nose to feel for his breath and looks up at the monitors, their readings almost exactly the same as they were a moment ago. She turns to gape at me, shaking her head. "Wh . . . what did you . . . ?"

I shake my head back at her, but it makes the room spin more so I stop.

"I—I don't know," I whisper. "Is he okay?"

"He's sleeping! He just . . . *fell* asleep! How did you do that?! Are you bleeding?"

"Don't wake him up!"

Regan stands up straight, shifting her weight between her feet anxiously and biting her lip. I watch Christian's face, still and calm in deep sleep, his chest wheezing softly with each rise and fall.

"We should go. This is weird."

Regan doubletakes at me in disbelief. "What? No! Wake him back up!"

"*Why?*"

"Because! What if he can't wake up without you?"

That's a scary thought. I hate it, but I don't know what to say to that. She might be right for all I know; I haven't really learned anything yet. Christian's sleep looks normal, though—quiet and tranquil. He looks much more alive than he did on Mami's table.

To Regan's disgust, I wipe the blood on my palms off on my jeans before I reach out to place my hand over his again. His fingers shift under mine unconsciously.

"Look, just . . . wake up whenever you want, okay?"

Christian makes no sign that anything in him has acknowledged me.

Regan's lips go thin, nostrils flaring as she shoots me an impatient glare, then she leans over and jiggles Christian's shoulder. "Christian? You okay?"

Christian's lips part in a sigh, his eyes moving behind his eyelids. He makes a soft sound of acknowledgement, then shifts away from her hand, frowning slightly at the disturbance before drifting right back into peaceful sleep.

"He seems okay?" I offer, pulling up the bottom of my shirt to wipe the blood off my face. "Let's get out of here. There's literally no safer place for him to be!"

Regan straightens up, rubbing the heel of her hand against her forehead, as she looks down at Christian.

"Okay. Okay, fine. Let's tell his parents he fell asleep, though."

"Okay, yeah."

I cast a backward glance at the hospital bed as we make our way to the hall. Christian is definitely breathing; I can see the rise and fall of his chest even from the doorway. Still, the uncertainty of what I can do haunts me. The possibility that Regan is right, that he needs me to wake up, makes the pit of my stomach feel hard and frozen with fear.

That can't be right.

SIX

The only reason I don't bring Regan home with me to be a buffer between me and my family is because I know if they really do plan on telling me anything, they won't if Regan's around. Mami pulls the front door open before I can even get all the way up the porch steps, Titi Clío right behind her.

"Hey," I say, waving a hand weakly.

Mami's lips go thin as she huffs through her nostrils. She's little, but at the top of the porch stairs, with her finger pointing down at my face, she might as well be fifty feet tall.

"*Jaxon Santiago-Noble.* You think you're grown, huh? You think you don't have to tell me when you're gonna go take a walk to see your little friends?"

"No, Mami," I sigh, consciously trying to keep my eyes from rolling. "I'm sorry."

"I *know* you're mad," she continues like I didn't say anything. "But you don't get to walk off without telling me, especially because you don't *know* what you can *do*!"

Titi scoots past my mom, coming to usher me up to the door by my shoulder. "Let's bring this inside, okay? He said he's sorry, Tessa. Tómalo suave, chica."

"Clío, *don't* tell me to calm down or how to talk to my son," my mom snaps. She turns on her heel and storms through the front door.

Titi squeezes my shoulder as we follow behind her. "She's just anxious."

"I know," I say. Grimalkin rubs up against my legs as soon as I cross through the threshold. "So am I."

Titi rubs my back as we follow Mami up the grand staircase. Mami's chanclas thwack against the soles of her feet as she storms across the carpet, which gives me the hysterical urge to laugh. It's not actually funny, but she gets angry with me so rarely that I don't know what else to do when she gets like this.

I cough to cover up any nervous laughter, staring down at the vine patterns on the carpet running up our stairs.

We come to the small sitting room on the second floor. Mami sits on the high-backed armchair closest to the fireplace, placing her arms over the armrests like a queen in her house slippers. With the dark look in her eyes, she looks cartoonishly severe.

I sit on our overstuffed couch, on the cushion closest to her chair. Titi sits on the floor, making a triangle between the three of us.

I wait a beat.

"Mami, I should've told you I was gonna go out. Sorry. I was heated."

"Did you go see Christian?"

Titi stares at me, waiting. The room feels as tense as a violin string at the point of snapping and I frown, squinting uncertainly.

"Uh . . . yeah. I did."

"Baby." Mami leans forward in her chair, shaking her head

and sighing as she pinches the bridge of her nose. "You shouldn't have done that. You don't know what you could've done to that boy."

"It's not *my* fault I don't know," I snap, crossing my arms over my chest. "I thought maybe he'd be able to tell me something. You know, since no one else wanted to."

"You're gonna cut the sarcasm right now." She states it matter-of-factly; it's not a request.

Titi pipes in, "We want to talk to you about it! Honey, I've been waiting your whole life to talk to you about this; your father always forbade it!"

"Why would you listen to him? He never talked to me about *anything*!"

My mom shakes her head. "That's not fair, Jaxon. That's not true."

It *is* true, even if she doesn't want to admit it.

"Look, what did you think I was gonna do to Christian? Kill him again?"

Mami and Titi trade glances with each other, wincing. Titi looks at me, wrinkling her brows together sympathetically.

"Well, not on purpose, honey, but we don't know what you're capable of. I'm in my thirties and I still have a really hard time controlling my abilities sometimes." She smiles uneasily. "Did . . . *did* anything happen when you saw Christian? No le dijiste lo que en realidad pasó, ¿verdad?"

That bothers me so much I grit my teeth for a second. It annoys me because I already lied to Christian, and also because that's what they want—more lying.

"I didn't tell him anything. I asked him what he remembered."

Mami crosses her legs, one foot jiggling restlessly in the air. "What did he remember?"

"Uh." I clear my throat, thinking back to what Christian said. It feels weird to say it out loud—like I'm betraying some secret. "He says he dreamt about me. He doesn't know he was dead, so I think he thought he was in a coma or something, dreaming about me."

Mami rubs her fingers over her brow, mulling that over. Her posture loosens with relief, as she leans back, frowning into the middle distance as she thinks. "That's good. That's fine. You're the one that found him, so that can be explained away."

Titi Clío leans her elbows on her knees, looking up at me. "And he's fine still? You didn't affect him? Like seeing through his eyes?"

"Like how? Literally? What do you mean?"

"Can you see what he sees if you try? Or feel any control over his will—think like *Brides of Dracula*, sort of?"

"I think I would've been a little more upset if I accidentally turned him into my weird, sexy thrall." But the question shakes me. Even if Christian didn't turn ruthless or mindless, I did have some control. "I made him fall asleep."

Titi Clío tips her head, squinting as if to better parse out my meaning. "How did you do that?"

My stomach squirms unpleasantly. I know he's not dead; he was still breathing. He moved and reacted to us even in his sleep. The monitors all showed he was normal. But I can't swallow back the fear that my mom and aunt are going to tell me he's never waking up.

"I touched his hand and told him to sleep and heal. Then he fell asleep like a second later."

Titi and Mami exchange glances again before looking at me wearing matching expressions of apprehension.

"That can't be good." Titi scrunches her eyebrows, running a hand through her locs. "I'm not sure what to think. Jadiel and I . . . bueno, salimos bien diferentes. He had real talent for bringing just about anything back to life. Me—best I got is reanimation."

Mami raises her eyebrows at her meaningfully. "That's not *all* you got."

"No," Titi Clío admits, laughing awkwardly. "I'm also constantly trying not to suck the life out of things. Ojalá no hayas salido a mí."

My head feels as hollow and collapsible as a balloon. I blink, staring between them, struggling to understand. They're talking about this like it's in my genes or coded into my DNA.

"What do you mean? What . . . what does that even mean? Can you explain this to me from the beginning? What the fuck is happening to me?"

"Nothing is happening to you, baby," assures my mom, switching back into her soothing voice as she leans over to place a hand on my knee. "Your dad went through the same thing; it's natural. It runs in the family."

"*What* does?" I ask, hearing my voice climb into a more hysterical register. "*Necromancy*?"

Mami squeezes my knee, looking up sympathetically through her lashes. "I know that's hard to believe, but—"

I shake my head, squeezing my eyes shut and trying to make sense of what I'm hearing. On the one hand, I've put that much together already. On the other hand, I wanted a logical explanation, not a confirmation of crazy shit.

"So my dad . . ."

"And me, your grandmother, your great-grandfather . . ." adds Titi gently, ticking off on her fingers.

I rub the pads of my fingers hard over my eyes. I'm not sure how much of that I can process right now. What I do understand, though, is that Titi is worried about the state of Christian and what I've done to him.

"So, I did, like, a bad job with Christian?"

"No, mijo, no, no," she says, scooting across the floor to get closer to me. "It's not your fault. Jadiel should have been talking to you about this. I'm sorry we kept you in the dark."

"What's gonna happen to Christian?"

"You need to stay away from him," says my mom, spreading her hands firmly. "His life is tied to you right now; it's better you don't give yourself the chance to control him."

"Well, what happens if I leave him alone? Can he *do* things without me?" He's obviously not a literal thrall or ghoul or whatever; he's been surrounded by his family since he came back to life, and they definitely would've noticed by now.

"Yeah . . ." Titi Clío starts slowly like there's a *but* coming. A long silence follows, and neither she nor my mom seems willing to break it, eyes cast down at their laps. Eventually, Titi clears her throat and looks up at me, speaking with the melancholy sweetness of an adult explaining death to a toddler for the first time. "He . . . his time will run out, honey. He'll die. But it's not your fault; it takes a lot to resurrect a human being completely. You had no way of knowing!"

My head swims. I swallow thickly, trying not to show how much it feels like I've been dunked into a pool of ice water. I curl my hands into tight fists, my nails biting into my palms, hearing only dimly when my mom tries to give me a few words of comfort.

"I . . . I gotta lie down," I say.

Titi gets up off the floor, bracing her hand over my shoulders and peering into my face. She squeezes me, speaking firmly in a reassuring tone. "You know now. That's good. Now I can teach you."

"Titi, I . . . I'm killing someone."

"He was already dead. *You* bought him more time."

"*Okay*," my mom interjects loudly, coming in between me and Titi to press her cool hands against my face. "Let him take a breath, Clío. You know his anxiety's real bad."

Titi backs off at my mom's behest, gazing at me sympathetically. My mom runs her hand over the top of my head, leaning down to kiss my forehead.

"None of this is your fault. Take some time to breathe and we'll talk more about this later, okay?"

I do go lie down after that, unsure what to do with myself. I never thought of my mom as a heartless person, more levelheaded and matter-of-fact. Titi . . . she's always been a wildcard, but it still surprises me that she *and* my mom told me, without hesitation, that I should let Christian die.

How much time does he even have? I don't know if I have the mental strength to look for an answer to that. I fall asleep eventually and spend hours plagued with weird, fitful dreams where I'm tangled up in a silver spiderweb and can't get out.

SEVEN

It's dark outside by the time I commit to being awake. The only light in the room comes from the moon gleaming through the window, so I reach over to click on the LED lights under my eyeball jar. My room glows dim purple, the countless horror movie posters on my walls barely legible. Grimalkin wandered off somewhere at some point, leaving me alone.

I pull my hoodie off, stuffy and damp from falling asleep during a warm day. As I do, my phone vibrates from somewhere, the screen lighting up against the floor.

I lean over the bed to pick it up. The slew of messages from Regan don't surprise me. The texts from a local, unsaved number *do*.

I blink hard and unlock my phone, trying to make sense of what I'm looking at. It's normal to feel disoriented after waking up, but it takes me a couple attempts to look at the unknown texts before I slow down enough to read from the beginning.

Don't text this number back

Lost my phone in the accident

I'm gonna delete this before my sister sees

She doesn't know I know her passcode lol

Anyway

This is xtn

I know you put me to sleep and I KNOW you know stuff I need to know

I'm boutta get discharged so let's talk ok?

10 PM behind the snack pit

Please please show up jaxon

I'm really freaked out

I can't decide not to show up without leaving him hanging out there for however long he's stubborn enough to wait. I can't help wondering, though . . . is it worth it? What if I do something or say something that hurts or kills him? And how much can I even tell him?

The last time I hung out with Christian on purpose was in sixth grade. Since then, he's sprouted a bunch of cool, idiot friends and we've started existing on what might as well be two completely different planets. As much as Christian swears he hasn't changed, it feels unfair that trying to stay away from him now makes me feel guilty.

According to my phone, I've got a solid half hour to make it out there and meet him on time, though I don't know how Mami will feel about it. It's late. I climb out of bed, still unsteady and overheated, and strip out of my shirt to change into a less sweaty t-shirt. The night still feels balmy, but I grab a zip up hoodie to take with me anyway.

I poke my head into the second floor sitting room on my way out. Titi Clío and Mami are sitting exactly where they were before, Titi painting her toenails green while Mami eats a bowl of spaghetti. There's a bowl next to Titi too, which tells me Mami and Titi must have sorted out their feelings about all of this in the kitchen. They notice me after a moment, both turning away from the telenovela on the TV at the same time.

"Hey, baby," says Mami, smiling gently. "There's mushroom spaghetti on the stove. How are you feeling?"

"I'm okay." My voice is hoarse from sleeping so long. I reach up and rub the sleep from my eyes, trying not to betray that I'm about to lie. It feels bad, but I know Mami won't let me out to see Christian after everything we talked about. I can't leave him hanging, though; it's my fault he's in this situation in the first place. "Is it cool if I go out? My head feels cloudy."

Mami gives me a long glance, considering me as she breathes in slowly before opening her mouth to speak. "It's pretty late, Jaxon . . ."

"Please? Just to walk down to the river?"

She sighs through her nose, pressing her lips together but ultimately nodding. "Be careful. And eat something when you get back, alright? Don't be out long and don't go any farther than the river, I get nervous when it's dark out like this."

"I know, Mami."

"Text me when you're walking home."

Titi points at me with her nail polish brush. "I promise, you and me are gonna sort out all the answers you need tomorrow and going forward. Cool?"

"Cool." I toss my hoodie over my shoulder. "I won't be gone long, so maybe we can watch a movie or something later?"

"Your aunt's been wanting to watch *Pet Sematary* all night," says my mom, smiling even as she rolls her eyes.

"She can't appreciate it like you can, Jax."

That's a nostalgia pick for sure. It was the first horror movie I ever watched; I was in kindergarten at the time. It left me with nightmares but also a fascination with horror movies. Seems like a weird choice, given the circumstances. In all fairness, most of my favorite movies involve the undead.

"Sure," I say. "Be back in a bit."

The walk to the Snack Pit is short from my house. Cutting through the woods, it takes fifteen minutes to come up behind it. It's literally a shack—more specifically, a one-story shotgun house with a plastic sign out front reading SNACK PIT in purple Comic Sans. They're closed at this hour, but the frying oil smell hangs in the air.

The scent of fall leaves on earth is stronger than usual, especially when the breeze comes in from across the river. I like it—the earthy smell and the quiet, interrupted only by the rustling branches and the distant screech of an owl.

When I reach the clearing behind the Snack Pit, the silty riverbank gleams white under the moon. One of the only reasons people hang out here is because the backyard of the Pit opens up into one of the best swimming holes in town. The bottom of the river is soft and sandy here, and there's a tire swing over the water.

That's where I find Christian.

Christian sits on the tire swing, swaying slowly over the water. His toes skim the illuminated surface, and a shudder wracks my body, remembering the disquieting curl of his toes in rigor mortis. The memory of Christian's prone, broken body feels so wrong while I'm looking at him moving, breathing, virtually unscathed.

It's like the earth tilts under my feet as I walk over, struggling not to stagger.

"Christian," I call.

Christian turns his head. I can't see his expression from where I'm standing, but I don't think he's surprised.

"Hey, Jaxon!" he chirps, gripping the rope as he hops up to stand with his feet in the tire instead. Holding the rope with one hand, he swings a few times to build momentum before taking a haphazard leap backward onto the riverbank. He lands in a tangle of gangly limbs in the moss and silt, laughing at himself. "Ahh, valgo verga."

"You were just in the hospital," I scold in disbelief, coming over to offer him a hand up. "Don't you think you should be more careful?"

"I was just in a morgue, too," he reminds me with a wild-eyed grin, grabbing my hand to hoist himself up. He brushes the dirt off his butt, adjusting his glasses again. "Don't you think I should live a little?"

I swallow back the wave of nausea that statement gives me. How can I tell him? Living a *little* is literally all he's got left.

I clear my throat.

"Uh . . . sorry about . . . back at the hospital," I say uneasily, not quite meeting his eyes.

Christian tips his head until he catches my gaze, then smiles. "Me too. I'm not very good at staying mad, though."

"I remember," I say, rolling my eyes. "I'm still pretty good at it."

That makes him laugh, though it's a bit dry. "Yeah. I know. If anything, you've gotten better at staying mad. The last time you gave me the cold shoulder lasted, like, two months."

"Yeah, well, you shouldn't have regifted me the book I got you. That copy of *The Egyptian Book of the Dead* was like twenty bucks. Do you know how long it takes a ten-year-old to save up twenty bucks?"

Christian laughs for real this time, shrugging helplessly. "I know, I know! I said I was sorry! Six *years* ago!"

"I don't know how you could have possibly forgotten I was the one that gave that to you."

He grins playfully, though I'm trying my best to remain deadpan. He doesn't buy it, as that *was* one conflict we managed to get through unscathed. "I had the memory of a goldfish back then! I just thought 'oh, Jaxon would love this!' And, you know, *some* of us didn't have allowances at all, okay?"

I roll my eyes, smiling a little reluctantly. "Yeah, yeah."

"Any time I tried to pick a gift out for you myself, my amá would say, '¡ay, Jesús, mijo, eso es del diablo!' and refuse to get it."

We laugh together at his impression of his mom, which is spot on. Everything Christian and I liked, from *Child's Play* to *Coraline,* was of the devil in her estimation. The only remotely occult thing we could watch or talk about around her without her crossing herself and asking Jesus to forgive us was *Casper the Friendly Ghost.*

It's been a long time since then. The laughter between us dies after a moment, leaving the awkwardness of two people that once knew each other well and now have a gulf of a couple years between them.

I wrap my arms around myself, steering us back to why we met up here.

"So, you think I put you to sleep."

"I *know* you did!" Christian jerks his head toward one of the picnic tables up the way, heading up to sit at it. "You told me to go to sleep, then I passed out. Did you think I'd forget?"

I sit across from Christian, watching as he pulls out his canvas backpack from under the table. I don't know what the right thing to say here is, but I know gaslighting him is wrong. He saw what he saw; I panicked and fucked up.

"I guess I was hoping you would."

"Like you were hoping I'd forget how I woke up at the morgue?"

I eye him warily but he's too busy rummaging through the mess of papers in his backpack to look up.

"Yeah . . ." I say slowly.

Christian pulls a leather-bound journal out of his bag, stuffed so full with extra pages and clippings that the elastic around it strains to keep it all shut. I've seen it many times before—even back in middle school, Christian carried it around everywhere, sketching and noting down anything he found interesting. Now, he opens it to pull out a folded-up packet of papers, smoothing it out between us on the table.

"Got a flashlight?" he asks.

I pull my phone out of my pocket and turn the light on, shining it over the pages as I lean in to read the first few lines.

"Are these your discharge papers?"

"Yeah," he says, flipping back a few pages. "Also, the paper detailing the first time I got admitted, dead on arrival."

I breathe out slowly, curling my fingers around the edge of the picnic table bench as I lean in to read the words under the beam of my phone's light.

In plain, certain black letters, the document reads:

PATIENT DOA.

Patient arrived non-salvageable. Injuries sustained: massive collapse of chest cavity, bifurcated heart.

   Cause of death: blunt force trauma to chest due to vehicular collision.

I stare at the word *bifurcated* for a long moment, my mind's eye drawing up the unwavering image of Christian on the prep table with his sunken chest and open eyes. The splinters at the edge of the picnic table bite into my fingers, and I look up, finding Christian studying my face.

"That's how I went in, allegedly. Then they sent me to your house, I woke up, and—" He flips forward a few pages, stopping on his discharge summary. "Here's how I left today."

I look, uneasiness gnawing at the pit of my stomach.

DISCHARGE SUMMARY

Patient exhibits multiple pulmonary and bone contusions in the chest area and lacerations localized in the orbital, supraorbital, and temporal regions of the left side of the head. No extensive damage to vital organs. Injuries noted upon prior admittance not present and unexplained.

"Wow," I whisper.

"Exactly. They were pretty much only keeping me to be positive that I wasn't bleeding into my lungs and because every doctor in the building wanted to look at my charts. So, you see why I gotta get some answers, right? Imagine you were in my place right now.

You'd wanna know more, wouldn't you?"

I'm not in the same place as Christian—not even close. But I know what it is to have a part of you be a mystery, so I nod. We're both right to be looking for answers.

"Yeah. I would."

"Then you gotta tell me what you know," he declares, spreading his hands over the table and looking at me over his glasses. "Please, Jaxon. I know you wanna understand more about what happened, too. Maybe if you tell me, I'll remember more. We can help each other."

I can't deny he's being reasonable. If it were me, I would ask the same and hope the person I was trying to bargain with would get it. I want to help, but how do I say what I know?

Does anyone really want to know that they're undead and soon to be permanently dead?

"You might not actually wanna hear what I know, Christian. I don't have anything *helpful*. Maybe it's better if we pretend shit's normal again and leave each other alone."

"No way," Christian insists without a moment's pause. "You know what waking up in a morgue teaches you? That there's way too much shit that isn't worth it."

"Like what?"

"Like you and me," he says, gesturing between us emphatically. "Trying not to be friends! It's stupid, and I'm tired of it!"

That makes my insides flare like sparking metal. Christian can say that fine, but I'm the one who ended up a reject while he's graduated to hot, unattainable jock.

"So, what's that mean? I have to get over you acting like a tool because *you* think it's stupid that I'm mad?"

"Yeah," he says with complete sincerity. "And I'll get over *you* acting like you're too misunderstood by everyone to be friends with a tool like me."

I stare at Christian for a long moment in disbelief. Does he really think it's that simple?

"I can't be friends with you, Christian, because when my dad died, you didn't tell your idiot friends to stop spreading rumors about him being a drug addict who overdosed."

A heavy silence falls between us. Christian adjusts his glasses as the river flows quietly behind us, the branches of the nearby oak trees creaking in the tepid breeze. His regret is clear enough. The way his eyes move behind his lenses like he's scanning his brain for the perfect response tells me he knows better than to keep barreling through this conversation. A sharp, jagged sort of ache grows in my chest as my face grows hot. It's not fair that he's pushed me into this moment. I never wanted to have this conversation with Christian. I never prepared for it.

"I know. And I *am* sorry," says Christian, lacing his hands together as he shifts on his seat. "But you didn't even give me a chance to make up for it, Jax. You cut me off completely."

"Because it makes me sick that you of all people let them say shit like that! Now I get to be the dead junkie's kid! I was already the weird, clumsy kid *before* that!"

"I'm sorry, Jaxon! I didn't know what to say. You wouldn't even tell me what happened to your dad!"

He's right about that. It's because I don't even know what happened; no one does. As far as I can tell, he was a normal, healthy man barely in his forties. Then, one day, he woke up dead.

A thought hits me. My stomach churns unpleasantly. I look

down at the papers on the table, not really seeing them.

My mom and my aunt . . . do *they* know what killed him?

Christian tips his head, looking into my face and frowning. "Jax?"

I glare at him. "You don't get it, alright? I barely got to know my dad, and you knew that, so how do you think it felt hearing your stupid friends talk about him like *they* knew him?"

"Horrible," he says quickly. "I know. I'm so, *so* sorry, seriously."

He really can't understand. He and his dad have always been super close. When we were kids, Christian's and Regan's dads were the ones who did typical dad-things with me, like fishing and going to my first baseball game and whatever. If someone said something stupid about Christian's dad, I'd fight them myself.

But Christian didn't stand up for mine. Because my dad was like a ghost.

"You probably thought they were right," I mutter.

"No, Jaxon,*"* says Christian, shaking his head. "You've got it all wrong, seriously. If you give me a chance to make up for it, I will. Please? Life is short, man."

My brain skids to a stop. Life is *very* short for Christian. He's right about that.

I can't tell him.

I *have* to tell him.

But how?

"We're not friends," I grumble, crossing my arms over my chest. "But I'll stop blowing you off so much."

Christian leans over the table, grinning as he offers me a hand to shake.

"¡A huevo! I'll take it!"

I roll my eyes and take his hand, shaking it once firmly. A dull, static spark where our palms meet startles us, making us release each other immediately. Christian looks at his palm, touching his fingers on his free hand to the arm of his glasses.

He turns his eyes up to me, the white moonlight gleaming off his lenses as he pulls a pen out of his pocket. Flipping his notebook open and clicking the pen, he leafs through to find a blank page, then looks up at me expectantly.

"So," he says. "Tell me what you got. Please. Do you remember how I woke up?"

I take a deep breath, letting it out slowly through my nose as I look across the table at Christian's open, imploring face. I gotta do it. I can't be like my family on this one.

"Kind of. I don't really understand how it all happened, but I need to tell you something, and you need to not think I'm crazy if everything else I have to tell you is gonna mean anything to you."

Christian nods, scooting forward on his bench. "Okay. Go for it."

I charge ahead. Too late for takebacks.

"You did die, Christian. When I saw you yesterday morning, you were dead on the prep table in the basement."

An owl screeches in the distance again. Christian looks at my face, then turns his eyes up to look at the stars above us, tapping his pen over the table. He squints at the sky, pursing his lips like he's trying to put his words together. Finally, he clears his throat as he jots down something in his notebook, scrunching his face to push his glasses up higher on the bridge of his nose.

"Okay," he exhales, the boyish raspiness gone from his tone. "I thought so, to be honest. Then I thought maybe I was being . . ."

He waves a hand vaguely, but I get what he means. I saw everything happen—I *made* things happen—and it still feels a bit like I dreamt it all.

I shake my head, lifting the corner of my mouth in a wry half smile. "You're not crazy."

"That's the first time I've heard *that* from you."

"You're not crazy because of this, anyway." I swallow, flicking a loose splinter on the edge of the picnic table to give myself something to focus on other than the strangeness of everything. Christian looks spooked, even in the dark with his measured expression. "Do you, uh . . . wanna talk about this? I can't even imagine how you're . . ."

He shakes his head adamantly as I trail off. "No. Tell me what you know. I can handle it."

I can't help thinking that's not true. I can barely handle it, and I'm not the dead one. But Christian looks at me with a hard expression, his mouth a firm line, eyes shadowed by the set of his brow.

"Okay . . . well. The other crazy thing is I think I'm the one that brought you back."

"You *think*? Or you know?"

I look down at the surface of the table, shaking my head. "Uh . . . I *know* it was me."

Christian starts scribbling in his notebook again and I lean over, trying to make out his chicken scratch in the dark.

"Don't write that down!"

Christian clicks his tongue. "I'm not writing down identifying details, Jax, obviously. Anyway, this whole notebook's in code."

Sure enough, Christian is writing nonsense in his notebook. I can't see much on account of it being upside down and in the dark, but I make out the words "ORPHEUS," bold and heavily under-lined, and "dreamless rift."

"You call this a code?"

"Look, I've tried numbers and runes and shit. Don't you re-member? You always cracked my codes before I could even teach them to you. Better if it looks like a bunch of nonsense."

"Yeah, well." I try not to smile despite myself. He was always so proud of himself when he came up with a new alphabet, and then so mad when I'd crack it. "I bet I could still figure out your journal if I tried."

Christian does smile, rolling his eyes. "Okay, well, don't."

I don't see how having a notebook full of numbers and made-up symbols looks less crazy than word salad spilled all over the pages, but I keep my mouth shut. I'm here to be helpful, not to criticize Christian's eccentricities. As long as he's not writing down "Jaxon Santiago-Noble is a fucking necromancer," we're good.

Christian makes me go over the details of what happened as he takes notes. I try not to leave out anything, including the embar-rassing parts where I held his hand and talked to his dead body and the part where I woke up to a panic attack in the middle of the night. He listens to me all the way until I get to the pocket watch. Then he stops me.

"Pérate, pérate. There's, like, an artifact? A necromantic artifact?"

"I don't know if it's an *artifact*. My dad left it to me. I don't know anything about it other than that, but when I turned the hands back on it, your body kinda unbroke."

Christian raises his eyebrows as he scribbles fervently in his notebook.

"Um, so that's definitely a necromantic artifact? Obvi." Christian leans an elbow on the table, raking his fingers through his curls as he taps his pen against his lips. "Were you, like, moving back in time?"

"I don't think I was. I think *you* did."

I watch him draw a curved return arrow on his page of nonsense. Is he really going to remember what all his notes mean later? He traces over the line of the arrow a few times, making it bolder, eyes focused somewhere past his notebook. Finally, he looks up at me, rubbing his hand over his chest.

"Am I moving forward again?" His voice wavers. His eyes hold mine, waiting for me to confirm somehow. "Or am I moving in a new direction?"

I don't know how to answer him. My mouth is dry, guts shriveled with guilt. Everything I've learned so far supports what I can hear in his voice is his greatest fear: he's hurtling toward his death. If going backward brought Christian back, moving forward will kill him again. It makes sense when he puts it like that. But putting him on a new path in a different direction doesn't sound crazy, all recent events considered. Any other day, it would sound like Christian going hard on his sci-fi theories, but today . . .

"I . . . I don't know how to put you in a new direction. I just found out I can *do* stuff like this. But there has to be a way, right?"

Christian looks over his notes, scratching the side of his head with his pen. Even in the darkness, his eyes look round and fearful. I don't blame him. My lungs feel like they're full of worms—writhing, knotted. It's hard to breathe. I can't fail him.

I'm the one that brought him back. If he dies again, it's on me.

"I'm gonna figure it out. My tía's here; she's gonna help me learn more stuff about all this."

"How long do I have?"

"I . . ." My voice cracks and I cough into my hand. "I don't know. How do you feel?"

"Uh, scared?"

"Well, *yeah*. I'm talking about physically."

Christian looks down at himself, patting his hands over his chest and sides. He spreads his palms out in front of him, looking at them as he stretches and curls his fingers.

"I feel good. There's bruising and stuff, but not bad."

I inspect his face for a moment; his expression is open and earnest. No shifty eyes or pinched mouth to make me suspect he's lying. I rub a hand over my face, then back over the top of my head, breathing out slowly.

That's good. That means there might still be time.

"You have to tell me if that changes, okay? Like . . . immediately."

Christian nods. "Okay. *You* have to tell me anything you find out. Also immediately."

I cross my finger over my chest in an X, trying to look reassuring but I barely manage a grimace. "For sure. We're gonna figure this out."

Christian gives me a tight, nervous smile. "Yeah. For sure."

EIGHT

I spend most of the morning combing through the links Regan sent me and ignoring the still growing number of texts I'm getting from kids at school asking about Christian. I hate that they're still pestering me about it even though I keep leaving them on read. Dealing with them at school is going to be a nightmare.

Most of the links Regan sent are articles, some even from reliable sources, about historical and cultural aspects of necromancy. There's not much to them—some runes, a lot about spirits, divination, mentions of bells. I paste the parts that stand out most into a note on my phone to share with Christian and Regan later.

Last night, I stressed to Christian that it's important he doesn't show up at my house, but with his phone still busted and his parents refusing to let him out of their sight, I haven't figured out how we're going to make time to figure this out. Regan is game to be our point of connection, which is kind of a solution. However, my aunt's focus is completely revolving around me right now. I'm not sure how to move forward with her watching so closely.

Titi Clío has never been a morning person, but today she comes into my room before 11 a.m. with a look of determination on her face. She's got her locs pulled up high in a bun, wearing harem pants patterned with the vibrant greens and blues of a peacock's tail feathers and a knitted top. In one hand, she's got a big plastic cup with Mickey Mouse's fading face on the outside. Her other arm helps her balance a polished wooden box on her hip.

"Hey, Jaxon. Your mom's got a body today, so it's just us for a while." She crosses into my room and presses the cup into my hands. "It's a good time to get you acquainted with some of our family legacy."

In the cup there's a dark, thick liquid inside, the color of moss after a heavy rain. "What is this?"

"Green smoothie!" Titi Clío grins at me, nodding at the laundry on my floor. "Get dressed and come down. We'll go out in the woods today. Trae el reloj de tu papá."

"Okay," I say. "I'll be right down."

I take an experimental sip of the green smoothie. It's as thick as pudding and tastes like bitter, chalky peanut butter. Titi's already shutting the door behind her, but I hold back my choking cough until her footsteps go down the stairs.

Titi travels a lot. She doesn't so much cook as craft things that will keep her alive. But it was nice of her to make me something while my mom's busy, so I choke down as much of the sludge as I can before I hop up to pull on some jeans and a zip up hoodie over my t-shirt. As I head down the stairs, I shoot Regan a message.

Titi's gonna teach me some stuff today. Figure out with xtian when we should rendezvous?

Regan replies to me almost instantly, a brown thumbs-up and a simple *you got it!*

Downstairs, Titi sits at the bottom of the main staircase as Grimalkin rubs herself against the polished wooden box. I take the stairs two at a time to get down faster and stoop down to scoop Grim into my arms, smooching her furry face. She bats hard at my nose without extending her claws. Titi laughs at me as I let her go, hefting her box up again.

"Can I carry that for you?" I ask, reaching for it.

Titi shakes her head, heading for the foyer as she tosses a smile at me. "I'm stronger than I look."

I stick my hands in my pockets, tapping my fingers against the cool cover of the pocket watch, and follow her out the door, stomach twisting. Even if I'm not sure what she's going to tell me or teach me, I can't help feeling nervous. I don't know if I'm more nervous that she'll want to take it slow and won't teach me anything related to what happened to Christian, or that she *will*.

Either way, for better or worse, it's time to face this stuff head on.

We walk for a long time. Titi doesn't say much other than to comment on it being a nice day. It's cooler than yesterday, but there's still warmth coming up from the earth as we walk deeper into the woods behind my house. The sun must have soaked deep into the ground yesterday. The leaves underfoot smell rich and sweet; the ones still on the trees range in color from green marbled with yellow to brilliant reds and oranges. The deeper into the woods we go, the richer the smell gets.

"This is my favorite time of year," I say, looking up at the blue sky peeking through the canopy of vibrant leaves.

Titi Clío laughs kindly. "Well, your birthday *is* coming up."

"Yeah," I agree, though with everything that happened in the last few days, I haven't thought about it much. "But it'd be my favorite anyway, I think. It's the time of year when everything turns colorful and ripe and stuff, you know?"

She hums, nodding. "And then dies."

My stomach turns. That shouldn't feel weird; talking about dead stuff with Titi Clío is par for the course like it is with my mom. Unfortunately, everything about death feels weird now.

It sucks, because death has never been a source of anxiety for me. New people, speaking in public, stress about school, sure. All of that. The inevitability of dying was always reassuring to me. Losing someone is hard, but you have the comfort of knowing it happens to all of us in the end.

Death going from a solid, immovable fact of life to . . . whatever it is now. How am I supposed to make sense of it?

"Yeah . . . then dies."

Titi glances back at me when I hesitate, pausing so we're walking in step with each other. She wraps her free arm around my shoulders, squeezing me into her side.

"It's just nature, honey."

"I know."

Finally, we come to a clearing where Titi sets down her box. There's a splash of color at the edge of the clearing; one of the trees is charred and split down the middle, barren of leaves, with a reddish lump at the base. I jog across the clearing to take a closer look, slowing as I recognize the shape. It's a fox, dead at least a few days, curled up like it came here to pass in its sleep. Its pelt is striking: deep orange with a coal-black tail, belly and face. The only giveaway of its death are the maggots in its ears, mouth, and where its eyes once were.

"Titi Clío, look—a fox!"

She comes over to look, standing beside me. Her brown eyes

light up at the sight, squatting down to brush the maggots out of its eyes. I cringe internally, trying not to show it. Mami's dealt with maggots plenty of times—and worse.

"Qué bello," she says, looking into its empty eye sockets. "Bendito. Think it got struck by lightning when the tree did?"

I shake my head. "No singeing or anything on the fox that I can see."

She grins as she straightens up, guiding me over to where she set down the box she'd brought. "Ven, siéntate."

We sit in the soft grass, Titi's lacquered wood box gleaming in the daylight.

"So, what's up?" I ask.

Titi smiles at me, running her hand across the top of the box before lifting the lid. The inside of the box is lined with what looks like velvet.

"I've been waiting your whole life to tell you about this," she says, glancing up at me as she sets the lid aside and reaches in. "I'm really sorry I kept you in the dark, but I hope this makes up for it a little."

When she pulls a fucking sickle out of the box, I have to laugh. Titi laughs with me, setting the sickle down on the grass as carefully as if she were setting down a baby. The lacquer on the rounded wooden handle shines brighter than the curved metal blade, but the whole thing looks old. The blade is sharp at the edge, while the rest of the metal looks worn, especially the runes embossed along the curve. The handle warps in a weird way, like lifetimes of being held coaxed the wood into the shape of a grip.

"Let me guess . . . my great-great-great-grandfather's sickle."

"Don't be fresh," she says, lifting her light brown eyes to my face and smirking. "It's yours."

"Are you sure it's not the Grim Reaper's?"

"He carries a scythe, bobo. Not a sickle."

"Well, where'd you get this from, then?"

She shakes her head and holds a finger up to quiet me, then reaches back into the box to pull out a bundle wrapped in an iridescent purple scarf that shines blue when the fabric moves. She sets it down beside the sickle and unfolds the scarf, revealing a hand mirror. The actual mirror glass is black; it looks as deep, clear, and unscathed as a pond in the still of night. The frame of the mirror is white—maybe ivory. At the top, perched proudly over the glass, is the heart-shaped face of a barn owl, smooth black stones inlaid for its eyes. The owl's wings curl around the sides of the mirror, as if guarding it, and the handle is its legs drawn together, talons spread as if about to catch a field mouse.

"Whoa," I whisper.

"You like that one?" Titi grins, gesturing toward the sickle and the mirror. "They're yours; you can touch them."

I pick up the mirror, looking into it. It's heavier than expected, the ivory handle smooth in my hand. My reflection stares back at me, clear but dark, like the me in the mirror is in shadow.

"That's obsidian," says Titi Clío, "so you have to be careful with it. That one actually is a family heirloom."

"What about the sickle?"

Titi laughs a little and shrugs. "I stole that one a while ago. It worked better for me than the mirror, but who knows what'll work for you?"

I raise my eyebrows, looking down at the sickle. "You're passing down stolen goods?"

"I have a better one." She shrugs, smiling unapologetically. "Don't get all judgy. The guy I stole it from is dead."

"Alright," I say, setting the mirror down on my lap and shaking my head. "Can we start with the dead stuff? At this point, I understand that this isn't a dream or a weird prank but . . ."

"Okay." Titi covers the box again, resting her hands over her knees. "Our family has always had a special relationship with dead people. Or, at least, your abuela did, and she always told me and your dad stories about her mom and her abuelo."

"Stories about them raising the dead? Zombies?"

"*No*, not zombies. Ghosts. Spirits, you know?"

The owl's obsidian eyes stare at me. "And this belonged to . . . ?"

"Your abuela. Papi made it for her when they moved up here, based on a dream she had."

"He made it? Could he do necromancy too?"

"No. As far as I know, it's only ever been people born on Mami's side of the family as far back as we can remember. Jadiel was really into trying to trace it; he tried to put a family tree together at one point." Titi sits back on her hands, watching me examine the craftsmanship of the wings and the face. On closer inspection, I see the irregularities along the design of the owl, but it looks as close to professional as I've ever seen. "Mami used to look into that mirror, and the spirits would show her things."

"For real? What kind of things?"

"Secrets. Past, present, and future."

I squint at her, tipping my head. "How would spirits tell her things about the future? Why would dead people know anything about that?"

Titi considers the mirror for a moment while I wait, expecting her to say something about time being relative or a construct. Instead, she smiles, shrugging at me. "I don't know. I wasn't ever any good at getting ghosts to talk to me. But you might be! So, you get the obsidian mirror."

"What are *you* good at? Reanimation, you said, right?"

"That's right. Let me show you!" She nods toward the dead fox at the base of the charred tree. "We have a subject right here."

Titi sits up straight, dusting her hands off, and takes the handle of the sickle. She gives me a meaningful look before taking the point of the sickle to her palm, dragging it across it to draw a trickle of blood. I hiss, reeling backward in alarm, but she winks at me.

"Just watch," she says.

I bite my lip in sympathy, rubbing the center of my palm as I watch her cross the clearing. She twirls the sickle between her thumb and fingers by the handle as she approaches the charred, split tree, touching the point to the apex of the two halves. She stands there, holding her injured hand up, blood dripping onto the fox at the base of the tree.

A wind blows from behind me, hard enough to sway me forward, and the tree goes from partially charred to a husk of paper-thin gray-white ashes, half the branches blown away in the wake of the wind, sweeping through the air like snow.

Titi drops her fist by her side. She glances back to make sure I'm watching, then slashes the sickle through the husk of the tree. It crumbles like a sandcastle, ashes fluttering around her feet.

As the ashes settle, the dead fox rises shakily at her feet. Even from this distance, the maggots dripping from its mouth, ears, and eyes are visible. I shoot up, about to run over and check it out for myself, but she pats her leg like she's beckoning a dog to follow her. Titi Clío returns to me, the fox following her stiffly.

When Titi sits, the fox sits too. In a weird way, it's kind of comforting to look at. Even when he'd woken up in the morgue, Christian screamed his head off. He never sat there blank and calm like the fox.

"Tools like this . . . they could be anything. But the point is they should make sense to you, and they can help you focus what you're doing. Keep the power from going out of control. Like the watch Jadiel left you."

That's probably why Chrisitan went haywire when I brought him back. I didn't even know I was doing it, so there was no control and no focus at all. If I'd known—if I'd had something to help me focus—I wouldn't have brought him back half-alive in a broken body.

Titi Clío nods at me, prompting me to pull the watch out of my pocket. A watch turning back decay makes some kind of sense, I guess. A sickle reaps. A black mirror looks back at you in the dark. I open the watch, looking at Titi uncertainly.

She grins enthusiastically. "Go ahead. You know what to do with that, right?"

"Yeah. I mean, I think." I reach for the fox, scooting a little closer. "C'mere, fox."

Titi Clío pets its dark orange fur, nodding toward me. "Dale, zorrito."

The fox moves at her word, coming up close to me. Some of

the rot stench sticks to it, putrid due to its time in the sun. It's not the worst dead body I've smelled by any stretch of the imagination, though. I touch it with one hand, avoiding the maggots still clinging to it as best I can, and it comes closer still, black paws on my lap, empty sockets turned up toward my face.

With my other hand I turn the hands back on the pocket watch, the way I did that night with Christian. It goes about the same; a headache bursts behind my eyes, vision going white, hot blood spurting out of my nose, choking me. I continue despite the pain, squeezing my eyes shut, the fox making distressed chattering noises until I stop and set the watch.

When my vision clears, the fox standing before me flicks maggots out of its ears, looking up at me with bright, honey-gold eyes where there were only black sockets before, flecks of blood from my sudden nosebleed speckling its snout. In spite of everything— the headache drumming at my temples, the uncanniness of a silent, obedient wild animal at my lap—my heart pounds with excitement as I shove the pocket watch back into my jeans, rubbing my blood off the fox's fur.

"Hey, buddy," I say, stroking it like a cat. "There you are!"

It barks and I jump, snatching my hands back in surprise. But it only bounds away from me, leaping in circles around me and Titi, before returning to Titi's side, wagging its tail up at her obediently.

"Look what you've done," says Titi, grinning brightly. "You see?"

Getting to flex this kind of thing in a low-stakes way is exciting, I can't lie. And Titi Clío looking so proud of me is an addictive feeling. I look down at the other tools; the sickle Titi used to make an exchange for the fox. Even though my abilities are a little different, could I use it to give more life to Christian?

"So is the fox going to die again later?"

"Hm?"

"I mean . . ." I look down at the blade, staring at the point Titi used to cut herself. "Christian's supposed to die again, right? Whatever I did is gonna run out, you guys said. So is the exchange you made gonna run out?"

Titi's face softens as she squeezes a hand over my shoulder, sighing. "Well eventually, yes. But an actual trade was made, you know? So, the fox'll run out when she's spent whatever the tree had left to give. We're still not sure what kind of trade *you* made."

I pick up the sickle, running my fingers experimentally along the blade. "Could I make something pay the price with this? Like a tree or something like that?"

Titi's sympathetic half smile gives me my answer before she even opens her mouth. Beside her, her new fox friend sniffs the air, letting out a few short, yippy barks.

"I'm sorry, no. It's too dangerous, and the price is high, especially if you're not careful."

"But . . ." I shake my head, raising my eyebrows. "He's already *alive*. How hard can it be to make it permanent?"

"Jax, he's alive, but his soul isn't tied to this plane anymore. You fixed up his body with the watch, so now he's in a working body at least. He has a chance for a more peaceful death. Trust me; this is stuff you don't wanna mess with until you've learned more about how to do the easier parts. When he dies this time, it'll be quick and painless like falling asleep. That's a gift."

I don't understand how she can think that. She can't understand what it's like to have him now after he was ripped out of my life so suddenly and violently. She didn't see his family's faces when they came to our house or the way they looked at Christian when he opened his eyes. Christian's mom looks at me like I'm some kind of angel now. How could anyone see letting him die a second time as a gift?

"It's not a gift! I gave everyone false hope!" Heat floods my face across my nose and cheeks. I take a deep, steadying breath. "How long does he have left?"

"I can't tell you for sure—we don't do things exactly the same way, Jax. When I reanimate things, they're literally just . . . animate. Not alive. They're like puppets. I can see through them, I can tell them what to do. You pulled Christian's soul back into his body, that's nothing like what I do. For me, it's not long. Usually a couple days, give or take? Not enough time for you to learn how to help him, honey. I'm really sorry." Titi cups her palm around my cheek, stroking her thumb over my cheekbone.

A *couple days*? That's not a generous guess. I wonder if we even have that long. My head spins, my stomach turning. I squeeze my eyes shut against the sickness, breathing out slowly.

A handful of days to figure this out. And we've already lost so much time.

I rub my fingers over the space between my eyebrows, tension blossoming into a headache stretching from my temples down to my teeth as understanding sets in. I *have* to do something. I need to help Christian, and I'm going to have to figure it out on my own.

Titi pulls my hand away from my face gently, squeezing my fingers.

"Maybe that's enough for now. Why don't we go into town for some iced coffee?"

"No!" I shake my head fervently, squeezing her hand. "No, I wanna learn more, Titi."

She wrinkles her brow, pursing her lips. "Jaxon, I'm telling you, it's better if you stay away from that boy. Stop thinking about him. He was meant to die already. He died all on his own."

"I can't stop thinking about him," I say, widening my eyes at her. Even if I wasn't literally responsible for his life and death, I'd only just barely started to think a little less about him before he died. It was impossible to forget him before, and it's even harder now. "But even if it doesn't help him, I need to learn more stuff. I never wanna make a mistake like this again."

That eases the expression on her face slightly. She leans forward on her knees and presses her lips against the top of my head.

"Alright. A little longer. Then we'll think about lunch."

I nod, flexing my fingers around the wooden grip.

Just a handful of days.

NINE

I have my misgivings about letting Christian and Regan get close to the pieces my aunt gave me. Trusting them with information is one thing. Trusting them with impulse control is another.

My mom let me skip school today, and Christian's mom let him, too, so this is the first time the three of us are getting back together since we visited Christian at the hospital. I've got the mirror wrapped up in a scarf like Titi did, tucked into my backpack. The sickle doesn't really fit, but it's shoved in there too, blade all wrapped up in one of my shirts from middle school. The watch I've got safely tucked into the side pocket.

I sling my backpack over my shoulder, creeping down the hall that leads to the back stairs. Titi is downstairs, I think; there's salsa music playing from somewhere on the second floor, trumpets blaring up through the floorboards. Mami should still be down in the morgue with her assistant. I didn't see the body when it came in, but last I heard, the reconstruction of the face should take the bulk of the day. Wherever they are, I don't want to be seen with my bag, so I run down the stairs as quietly as possible and stow it away in one of the many empty cabinets in the butler's pantry.

I pull my phone out of my back pocket, but there's nothing from Regan yet. Squatting down near the cabinets, I send her a quick message to let her know I'm about to get on my way. As I finish typing that message, my phone buzzes with a notification from my mom even though she's only downstairs.

Your titi is making dinner. I didn't know how to tell her no. If you want to borrow the hearse and grab McDonald's with Regan, it's on me. Just bring some back for me.

I bite back a laugh, straightening up to peek out of the pantry before stepping out. Whatever Titi's got going on upstairs, she's feeling it. The floorboards above me creak as she dances around the second-floor kitchen.

What's she making?? I ask.

I'm not sure, says my mom. But she went out to the Whole Foods in Hadley this morning to buy seitan for tonight.

I climb up the stairs, schooling my face so I don't give away that I already know Titi has dinner plans for the evening. I don't know what seitan is, but I'm sure I'd eat it even if Titi's the one making it. I'm not picky.

What is that? I ask.

I don't know, but I don't want it. Get McDonald's and bring it down to the morgue for me. A chicken sandwich.

I send my mom a thumbs up then peek into the kitchen, finding my aunt standing over a pot, dancing in place as she stirs. It smells nice, actually; cumin and chili powder are thick in the air, wafting up from the clouds of steam rising from the pot. Whatever seitan is, I can tell Titi Clío wants my mom to like it.

"Smells wicked good in here," I say, leaning in the doorway. "I didn't know you were gonna cook tonight, Titi."

Titi flashes a big smile at me. Setting the spoon on the spoon rest on the stove, she heads to the counter, gesturing for me to come with her. She produces a handful of cilantro and a knife, setting them on the wooden cutting board on the counter.

"Well, your mom's been working all day. I thought it would be nice. Can you chop this up for me, honey?"

"Sure." I take the knife, holding down the stems as I chop up the leaves. "What are you making?"

"Seitan chili. There's real cheese for you and your mom, not vegan cheese."

There's no judgment in her words. If anything, she sounds proud of herself. It pulls at my chest a little, knowing my mom is dreading trying my aunt's food. If I had the time, I'd stay home just to eat in front of her. Even if it doesn't taste good after all, I can fake enjoyment pretty well.

"Can you set some aside for me, Titi? I didn't know you were making anything, so I made plans to go to the movies with Regan."

"Oh," Titi pouts, not bothering to mask her disappointment. She gives her chili a stir, shoulders drooping. "Well, of course, I can save you some. What are you going to go see?"

I didn't think that far. What's even playing right now? I hesitate, pretending to concentrate on chopping finely.

"Uh, I don't know. Some action movie Regan wants to see."

"Hm." When I glance sideways at her, she's looking into her chili pot like she's seeing through it.

I shouldn't have lied. I should have said I was going to McDonald's. Why did I lie more than I was already lying?

The cilantro crunches in my fist. There's a pile of pitch-black charred pieces where the cilantro should be. In my surprise, I drop the knife, sending it clattering to the ground as my heart jumps up into my throat. I lift my hand and the black ash flutters onto the cutting board.

"Titi?" I say, voice strangled by the lump in my throat.

"Yeah, honey?" It takes her a moment to look up, but when she does, she flies over to my side, grabbing my wrist and pulling me back from the cutting board. She looks at the black smudges on my palm, the charred flakes on the board, then at me, light eyes blown wide. "Jax what the—¿eso fuiste tú o fui yo?"

"I . . . I don't know if it was you or me . . ." I stammer. My face feels numb, a cold sweat breaking out over my temples. "I was cutting it, and it . . . I don't know, it did that!"

Titi Clío brushes the soot off my hand delicately, leading me over to the table to help me into a chair. I don't even notice the nosebleed until Titi grabs a paper towel to clean up my face. She runs the back of her hand over my forehead then searches my face, lines forming between her sharp brows.

"That . . . I guess it might have been me?" Even as she says it, she grimaces knowing we both know she's saying that to make me feel better. I'm the one with the nosebleed. "I . . . I don't think you should go out tonight, Jaxon. Me tienes ansiosa."

My stomach turns. I grip my knees, trying to get my heart to stop pumping so fast. She's not the only one who's anxious. "It's . . . it's just a movie."

Titi studies me as I stare back at her, trying to look honest. Her expression is grim, eyes hard, lips pressed tightly together. Whatever she's thinking, I can't stay home. Even if I want to go sit in my room and try to understand what I just did, I don't have the time.

I have a handful of days.

She sighs, knitting her eyebrows before taking my face between her hands.

"Don't touch anyone. Okay? We know you take after your papi, pero maybe también saliste un poquito a mí, so . . ." She trails off, stroking her thumbs across my cheeks. "So be careful. Don't touch anyone, ¿me oyes? And try to think happy thoughts."

I nod, anxiety knotting up my insides even more.

"Did it take you a long time to figure out, too?"

She sighs through her nose before letting go of me, turning to pick up the cutting board and knife from the floor, then scraping the ashes into the trash. "I didn't have the same situation. But no matter what, people like us need to have control. It's very important, Jax."

I turn my palms up on my knees, staring down at them. They're flushed pink like my heart's directing most of my blood flow into them. I flex my fingers, then curl them into fists. No touching anything, alive or dead. I can do that for now.

"Okay."

It takes me a bit to get it together. I sit in the hearse with my head against the top of the steering wheel, breathing slowly. If Titi Clío tells Mami what happened, Mami will tell me to come back home. I think Titi knows that, though, and she's never snitched on me before. Either way, I wait in the driveway for my lightheadedness to pass. When it does, I double check that my backpack is safely in the back seat before I go.

The hearse isn't the kind of hearse in movies and TV shows. It's just a big van my mom uses to transport dead bodies in. We had a classic hearse back when I was little that belonged to the funeral director my mom inherited the home from. It broke down when I was still in elementary school. Now the only thing that gives the hearse away are the letters across the white-tinted outside window reading Santiago-Noble Funeral Home with our number underneath.

Regan's still psyched to see it pull up when I get to the old Gibson house ruins she told me to meet them at. It's an abandoned lot a stone's throw from the cemetery where a house burned down a long time ago. The three of us used to hang out here when we were little, hoping to catch a ghost to no avail, but my parents forbade me from it when I slipped into the exposed basement and broke my wrist in middle school.

Regan hops up from the crumbling block of stone foundation she and Christian are sitting on, clasping her hands as she hurries over while I pull over at the side of the street.

"You brought the whip!" She wheezes with laughter, patting the side of the hearse like it's a horse. "I thought we'd be on foot!"

I roll my eyes, grabbing my backpack and stepping out onto the gravel street.

"My mom wants me to go on a McDonald's run. I can buy for you guys, too, if you want."

"Yes!" she cries, bouncing on her heels as she grins back at Christian. "You too, right, Christian?"

Christian doesn't react at first, glasses reflecting the blinding red glare of the sun through the orange leaves. He's staring at the hearse with an unreadable expression, but I feel his wariness in the pit of my chest and suddenly regret having brought it.

"Christian?" I try, gently.

He startles, turning to me hastily with a big grin. "Yeah! Yes, I want McDonald's, duh."

"Okay," I say, pretending to miss Regan's attempt to hug me as I set the backpack down on the rubble. Studying Christian's face closely, I wonder if the shadows under his eyes or the pinkness of his lips might tell me something about how long he's got left, but he looks as good as ever, if a little rougher around the edges. The shallow cuts around his left eye have started to scab over. "How are you feeling?"

"The same." He shrugs. "A little better, actually. My ribs don't hurt as much today."

"Cool . . . alright. You're sure, right?"

"Sure, he's sure," says Regan, sitting on the stone foundation again and slinging an arm around Christian's shoulders. "We're excited to get a look at that watch!"

"I've got it," I tell them as I unzip my bag. "And I've got some other things, too."

"Okay—wait, is that a fucking scythe?"

Christian answers her before I can open my mouth.

"*No*," he says, eyes wide, pushing his glasses up the bridge of his nose. "That's a sickle! A really *old* sickle!"

Christian's already pulling out his notebook, flipping it open and tapping his pen against the page as he studies the curved blade in my hand. Regan's right beside him, looking at the runes decorating the blade as she laughs in surprise. I smile a little in spite of myself; I had a feeling it would fascinate them.

"My aunt said she got it from some dead guy."

Christian, stupid like always, reaches out to touch the blade. I yank it out of his reach in barely enough time.

"Hey," he whines, frowning at me.

"*Hey*, this is for necromancy, stupid," I tell him, shaking my head. "You're undead, remember? What if it sucked the life right out of you?"

"Is that what it does?" he asks, bringing the tip of his pen to the paper.

"The point is you don't *know*, Christian!"

"Yeah, Christian, stop being stupid." Regan reaches for it, opening and closing her hand like she expects me to hand it over. After the episode earlier tonight, though, I don't think it's a great idea to pass around something that reduced a whole tree to ashes and reanimated a fox in one swipe.

"Look, nobody touch it. Maybe I can show you what it does."

It's a big maybe; I have no idea if it'll work for me the way it did with my aunt, but *something* will probably happen if I interact with a dead creature or plant, right? I straighten up, gripping the handle of the sickle and stepping back a few paces. Regan and Christian watch me expectantly, Christian with his pen ready to write, Regan with elbows resting on her knees.

Looking around the ground around the crumbling stone foundation, most of the dead things around me are brown leaves, but sprouting up through the decay there's a thin sapling, a couple red oak leaves clinging to it. I could bleed on the leaves and reap the sapling. It might work.

I wrap my hand around the sharp edge of the blade until it bites into my palm, which makes Regan and Christian leap up from the block of foundation.

"Dude, Jaxon!" Regan's voice is shrill.

"Tetanus!" cries Christian, knocking the sickle out of my hand before I can react and grabbing my hand.

"Don't!" I try to tear my hand away, but it's locked to his. My arm vibrates like Christian's hand is a live wire, a high-pitched buzzing ringing in my head. Christian's shaking too, eyes round and bright.

Our hands break apart with a static crackle. Christian stares down at his palm, smeared with my blood. My heart beats so hard I'm sure they can see it through my hoodie.

What was *that*? That had to be something more than a spark of chemistry, right?

"You can't get tetanus from a clean blade, you fucking dumbass!"

Christian gapes at me, holding his hand to his chest. "What . . . what just—"

"I know what I'm doing!" My hands are still shaking, now from nerves, as I stoop over to pick the sickle back up. I grab it with my uninjured hand as the cut disappears from my other hand. The blood is still there, still warm, but the palm of my hand looks untouched otherwise.

The warmth drains from my face as I look at Christian again, trying to see if anything's different about him. Did I take life from him?

"Regan, does he look okay?" I ask, backing up further to get a better look at him out of his reach. "Does he look normal?"

Regan raises her eyebrows in question, looking Christian over with her head tipped. "Um . . . I think? As normal as he gets."

"Are you okay, Christian?"

Christian also looks quizzical as he pats himself down, streaking blood on his white t-shirt. "I feel okay. Do *you* feel okay?"

I wipe my blood on my pants, holding my hand up to show them my healed palm. Regan bounces on her heels, covering her mouth with her hands as Christian steps closer, like he wants a better look.

"Stop!" I tell him, pulling my hand into my chest. "Don't touch me! Did you miss what just happened?"

"You've touched me like multiple times since I came back!" he counters.

"And? What if it's hurting you?"

Christian squints like the idea is farfetched, holding his hands up in surrender, then crossing his arms as double assurance that he won't touch me.

"I really don't think it is. What just happened *did* kind of hurt but it looked like it hurt you too."

I pinch the bridge of my nose, sighing. Isn't he supposed to listen to me? Wasn't that part of the problem with his resurrection in the first place? He's got a point, though. It did hurt me too. Maybe I didn't *take* from him . . . maybe I'm giving.

That's a big "maybe." Too big to rely on. I'm not even sure if that's better or worse.

"Okay, forget it. Just *don't* do anything like that again, Christian, you don't have any more spare lives. Don't you understand that? The sickle's supposed to drain life out of shit and move it into something else. I was gonna show you before you 'saved' me from tetanus."

"In his defense," says Regan, lifting a finger, "that blade doesn't really *look* clean. And you don't exactly have a great track record with holding sharp things safely."

Christian laughs like the little jerk he is, eyes lighting up as he remembers. "Oh no, the birdhouses in seventh grade!"

Regan nods, laughing along with him. "Jax's covered in blood like a little mini haunted house."

"The Amityville Birdhouse," Christian teases.

"No, please, I love reliving one of my top ten most embarrassing moments." I roll my eyes irritably. "And I only stabbed myself that *one* time in shop class, alright? That's not really a track record. Anyway, look—the *point* is, I don't know if I can make it work. But if I can, that would obviously be real useful."

Regan rubs her hands together, eyeing the sickle. "So how are we gonna figure it out?"

I shake my head. "*We* aren't. This is obviously too dangerous for you guys, so I'll figure this one out myself."

They whine while I wrap the sickle back up in my shirt, but there's no way I'm letting them sit in the temptation to touch it any longer. I keep imagining Christian turning into a pile of white ashes like the tree Titi drained or even Regan withering way. The mirror is a safer idea. It's not meant for anything more than looking into.

I pull it out of my bag, unwinding the scarf around it and holding it by the leg-shaped handle. The heart-shaped barn owl face stares up at me, as well as my dark reflection over the unblemished surface of the obsidian glass. Even in the red sunlight, the black mirror looks like a vortex covered by a thin, crystal sheen.

Christian sits on his hands to keep from reaching out, but the excitement colors the tops of his cheeks pink.

"That's a scrying mirror!" he says, grinning.

Regan looks at it, politely impressed. I get it; it's not as exciting as a blade.

"How do you know that?"

Christian gives me a flat look, holding up his overstuffed notebook pointedly. "Because I believed in this shit way before you turned me into a zombie!"

"What's 'scrying'?" asks Regan, looking back and forth between me and Christian. "Is it magic?"

I run the pad of my thumb against the owl's talons. I wish Titi could explain this with me. All I can do is repeat what she told me this morning, and not as well. If Titi Clío were here, she could explain how these things can help us. She could probably make Christian and Regan keep their hands to themselves, too.

"I guess it's like divination? You look into it to ask the spirits for secrets and stuff."

Regan leans back on her hands, squinting thoughtfully. "How does it work?"

"I'm not sure yet. Titi said she's not good at this, but since I might be, I get the mirror."

Christian cuts in, flipping his notebook open. "You need to go into a trance state, that's what they say. The more you practice, the easier it gets. When you're in the trance, that's when you'll start seeing answers."

"How do you get into a trance? Like hypnosis?" asks Regan.

Christian shakes his head. "Jaxon needs to be focused. Relaxed."

I look at the random doodles and phrases across Christian's notebook, raising my eyebrows at him. "According to what?"

Christian widens his eyes like I've insulted his grandmother.

Then he says, "According to my abuela! It's legit!"

Regan laughs at my expense, asking between giggles, "Was your abuela a necromancer?"

"No, she was like a curandera!"

Me and Regan exchange looks, raising our eyebrows at each other, Regan still laughing. Christian glares at us, his eyebrows are set heavy over his eyes.

"Look, I didn't get to visit her that much, but she knew a lot! My mom doesn't believe in this stuff, or *like* it, so I can't really ask her about it. She was a curandera, though, seriously!"

"Sorry, man, I believe you," I reassure him, waving my hands in a pump the brakes motion. "I don't even know anything about curanderas. That's like brujería right?"

"Yes! It's brujería. I know it's not the same, but . . ."

"No, it's worth a try," interjects Regan, shaking Christian's shoulder bracingly. "More than Jaxon's titi gave him to go on."

She's right about that. Titi Clío didn't say anything about how to use the mirror. Maybe she doesn't like the idea of trancing out with spirits. I'm not sure I do either.

"How long does it take to get good at trancing or whatever?"

Christian scratches his curls with the back of his pen, looking at me uncertainly. "I don't know. I guess it depends on how much you practice? And how quiet your brain is?"

That makes me laugh in despair. Quiet? *My* brain? I've had anxiety as long as I remember. My brain's *never* had a moment of quiet.

"I'll work on it . . ."

Christian gives me a sweet, encouraging smile. "You got this!"

My dark reflection in the mirror stares back at me, and it's looking doubtful. I'll have to work on it as much as I can *tonight*. Unfortunately, my long weekend is over. Mami let me take Monday off, but it's back to school tomorrow.

"Did anyone say anything at school, Regan?" I ask.

She laughs, thumping her hand over Christian's back. "They couldn't stop talking about it! Everyone was asking me where you were 'cause they all want a firsthand account of what it was like finding the living dead boy."

Christian looks as queasy as I feel, hearing that. He looks down at his notebook for lack of anything to say and starts trying to replicate the mirror in my hands, glancing up at it, craning his neck to get a better look. Something like this won't hurt him if it's meant for meditating and divining with, so I pass it to him, holding it by the very end of the handle so our fingers can't accidentally touch.

He grins at me again as he takes it, his big hands maneuvering it delicately onto his lap.

"Did you at least tell them they should mind their own business?" I ask Regan.

"Well, yeah, but you know they're not gonna listen to me. If it helps, they all think it was a hospital fuckup. Everyone that talked to me thinks it's crazy and amazing, but they feel for you, Christian. There's even a 'glad you're not dead' card going around fifth period art."

"Aw, cool," says Christian, noncommittal.

I worry my lip. His reluctance to hear any of this makes sense; I wouldn't know what to say if I were in his position. He's got a lot of people who care about him at school who haven't been able to text him. He's going to be swarmed by people who want him to rehash what he went through over and over. I've been anxious about it, and I won't have it half as bad as he will.

"You coming to school tomorrow?" I ask, nodding at him.

He lifts a shoulder, concentrating on his drawing. "I don't know. Are you?"

"Yeah," I say. Regan cheers. "My mom let me take today off but that's it."

"Pos . . . maybe."

I lean over to watch as he finishes his small sketch of the owl mirror. It looks good—more detailed than the bowls and candles he drew on the rest of the page sometime before today. He sets his notebook between him and Regan on the stones and places the mirror on his lap, looking down at the black glass. All I can see in the reflection is the gold glint of the round metal frames of his glasses in the dying sunlight.

Regan stands up, dusting the crumbling concrete pebbles off her thighs. Even in the evening chill, she's wearing shorts. Her hair is starting to frizz around her hairline in the autumn humidity.

"Can we get McDonald's now, or do you wanna show us the watch here?"

"The watch is the watch. And I'm not sure I trust you guys after the sickle thing."

"Come *on*," Regan whines.

"You can look at it," I say, pulling it out of the side pocket. "Don't touch, just look. Titi told me it's supposed to restore reanimated bodies the further back in time you set it."

Christian looks at it with a strange expression, somewhat subdued now. I watch the perfect lines of his pretty boy face, waiting for his reaction, but ultimately he turns his attention back to his notebook.

Does he remember it, I wonder? Did it remind him of the morgue?

"Anyway . . ." I say slowly. "We still have stuff to talk about. You know, like the three thousand links you sent me?"

"Can't we talk about it at McDonald's?"

I stare at her for a long moment.

"Regan, someone could hear us."

She rolls her eyes as she stoops down to pick up her backpack, rifling in the front pocket until she produces a pack of gum. "Who's gonna hear us? The meth-heads who hang out there sometimes? They'll think we're a bunch of weirdos. I mean, look at you, Jax."

I look down at myself when she gestures at me. I'm wearing a hoodie, jeans, and boots. What's so weird about that? I raise an eyebrow at her, waiting for an explanation.

"You always look like you're heading to a funeral, and you literally always are!" She bounds over to the hearse, patting it affectionately as if proving her point. "If anyone could sit at a McDonald's and talk about bringing people back to life, it's you."

"Christian, can you back me up here, dude?" I groan, turning to look at him.

He's still sitting on the stone foundation, his attention drawn away from his journal onto the mirror. His glasses sit at the very end of his nose, his thick dark lashes unblinking. It takes him a second to realize we're waiting for him to respond, but when he does, he looks up at us over the rims of his glasses.

"Isn't there something kind of strange about this mirror?"

Why did I let him touch anything? I hold my hand out for it. "I don't know. But you're undead and the mirror calls spirits, so—"

"It's not that," Christian says, handing it back to me. "I can't explain it. It feels like it's staring back."

I wrap it back up in a hurry, trying not to think about that. From what my mom's told me, the Gibsons didn't actually die out here in the ruins of their burned-down house, but we're close enough to the cemetery that I'm not trying to tempt fate. I don't want spirits staring at me or my friends until we know how to talk to them. Christian's got his notes—that's where we'll start.

The shadows deepen around us, darkening the orange leaves. "Fine. Fine, let's do McDonald's. If too many people come in, we can always get out and find somewhere quieter."

Christian looks at the hearse, running a hand through his hair. He gets up, careful to step only over the flagstones littering the ground in order to keep his sneakers the same sparkling white as always.

"Regan," he smiles at her nervously, "would it be okay if I ride shotgun?"

I gather up my bag and pass Christian's notebook to him. He shoots me a grateful smile.

"Yeah!" Regan reaches up, ruffling her hand hard over Christian's mop of curls. "I know, kinda mean of Jax to break out the hearse, huh?"

"No, it's not mean," Christian says quickly. He looks at me. "You're not mean. I don't think you're mean; you're giving us a ride to McDonald's."

I try to smile at him, barely managing a grimace. Regan's right. I shouldn't have come in the hearse. The last time Christian was in it he was dead—really dead. If I was him, I would feel weird about getting in too.

"You're not gonna be in the back of one of these again for a long time, okay?" I lie, hoping I don't sound as guilty as I feel, or that Christian is at least desperate enough for hope to pretend I don't sound like a liar. "Get in the front."

His eyes light up when I say that, and he hurries over to the passenger side seat. My stomach twists, both with anxiety and affection for him and his faith in me. Regan raises her eyebrows at me, patting my arm on her way to sit in the back. I feel it—their renewed resolve to do whatever it takes to keep Christian alive. They're counting on me to pull this all together.

That's the moment I realize I can't tell them how little time we might have. I really do have to figure out how to do this on my own.

TEN

The McDonald's is empty. I shouldn't be surprised. We live in a small town, and it's a Monday night. Still, we find a table as far from the counter as possible, half-hidden by the soft drink machine. This is the first time I've seen Christian eat since the accident, and I'm privately relieved he doesn't seem to be hankering for extra rare beef or something else zombielike. He eats a normal Quarter Pounder with his fries dipped in chocolate milkshake like a maniac.

A *human* maniac, at least.

Regan's the one with an insatiable appetite for meat. She sits next to me despite my trying to explain, again, that I need to be careful about touching people until I know what I'm doing. All I can hear, while Christian tries to explain his weird notes on scrying, is Regan chewing on her first Quarter Pounder right in my ear.

"Hold on, Christian," I say, holding up a hand before turning to look at Regan. "Look, I love you, but please close your mouth."

"My mouth *is* closed!" she complains through a mouthful of beef. "It's a big burger!"

I bite back a laugh in spite of myself, rolling my eyes as I turn back to Christian.

"Sorry, keep going."

Christian turns his notebook around so I can see it. I don't know why he bothers; I don't understand it. The most concrete part of his notes are the scrying tools doodled along the margins. The rest of the page looks something like a flowchart; a shield, eyeballs, words like "VEIL" and "INTERVALS" written in bold letters and underlined, all connected by arrows. "Well, basically, when you open up that kind of portal, anything can come through, I think."

"You think," I echo, resting my chin on my hand and eating a nugget.

"It's not like I've tried it that many times," he shrugs. "And you're the one with the powers."

"But you've tried it?" asks Regan, leaning forward with her elbows on the table. "Did anything talk to you?"

Christian smiles bashfully, shaking his head. "Nah, I kinda spaced out. Nothing like what it felt like looking into Jaxon's mirror."

I shrink against the booth as Regan leans closer, looking at the scribbles spread across Christian's page and pressing her finger against the drawing of the owl mirror.

"Does that mean anyone could do it with the right tools?"

"Maybe," Christian says, turning his notebook back around and drawing a long, curved arrow from the mirror to the shield. "I think, more importantly, you need to protect yourself when using a crazy strong artifact like that."

"Protect like how?" I ask, furrowing my brows. "Like salt or something?"

Christian scratches the side of his head with his pen, frowning down at his notebook. "Maybe? I don't really know. My grandma always said to pray first. I'd ask your aunt."

I nod. Titi was pretty unconcerned when she gave me the mirror, so she might not have anything to say to that. Although she did say she never got the hang of scrying. She might not know much of anything about it.

I wonder, with a sinking feeling in my chest, what my dad knew about this kind of thing. And whether my mom would know any of what he did.

"Okay." I squeeze my eyes shut, rubbing the heel of my palm against my forehead. "I'll figure it out."

However much it might suck to start asking Mami about Dad *now*, it'll be worth it if I can learn anything helpful. Christian's in high spirits, which is all the more reason to find answers as soon as possible. I watch him eat his fries as he looks through his notebook, eyes scanning back and forth behind his glasses.

"Let's talk research," says Regan, waving her phone at us. "There's all sorts of crazy shit online."

"I'm pretty sure one of the links you sent me was a Dungeons and Dragons thing."

She waves a hand impatiently, unlocking her phone. "There's actual relevant stuff too, like related-to-divination stuff!"

I smile at her. I know she's been researching her heart out. "Let's hear it."

"Gimme a sec."

In the breadth of time Regan takes to look through her bookmarks, my chest goes cold like ice water flooding up from the pit of my stomach. Automatically, my eyes flit over to Christian. He's frozen in place, eyes glued to the notebook in front of him but unseeing. Regan starts to say something, but neither Christian nor I hear her. Slowly, Christian's eyes lift up to meet mine.

He waits a beat, wordless, then turns his gaze toward the window fraction by fraction. I follow his line of sight, but the window is dark; only our reflections—Christian's horrified round eyes and Regan reading off her phone.

Christian waits for a pause from Regan before he whispers, "There's something out there."

Regan stops, glancing from his face to mine. "Huh?"

"I don't see anything," I whisper. "What's out there, Christian?"

Christian worries his thumb over the button of his pen, squinting through the window. I look through it again and now I see what he's seeing. Past the small stretch of green in front of the window, past the cars parked in the dark lot, a figure ambles jerkily, backlit by the yellow light of the McDonald's marquee.

"Some drunk guy," dismisses Regan.

Christian shakes his head tersely. "Something watching."

He's right. I can't explain it, but I can *feel* it. Something off about the way he moves. A chill in my chest, an unnatural vibration in the air.

"Watching us?" Regan leans away from the window, looking between both of us urgently. "Are you serious? How can you tell?"

I nod affirmatively, meeting eyes with Christian. His face is pale, cold sweat beading at his temples. I'm sure I look the same.

"I can feel it," he says, dropping his voice. "Watch."

We do, the silence at our table thick and suffocating. The figure outside staggers in our direction; even in the dark, I can tell his clothes are shabby and ill-fitting. He has a pronounced limp, like his thigh was haphazardly attached to their hip. He stops a few yards away, standing so still, it's as if time has stopped.

Regan emits a high, uneasy whimper, stuffing her fries and what's left of her burger back in the paper bag. I lean my face closer to the window, squinting out at them, cold sweat running down my spine.

He's dirty—dusted all over with dark, fresh soil. It's packed into his hair, smeared all over his skin, hanging in the folds of his clothes, and spilling from the black, empty sockets of his eyes.

My head swims, my heart pounds in my chest. I tear my eyes from the window, looking down at my hands. My nail beds are turning blue like they do every time a panic attack is about to grip me. I don't have time for this.

"We need to go," I urge, my voice leaving my throat thin and reedy.

Christian reels when he sees properly. He goes paler still, lips colorless, as he scrambles out of his side of the booth.

"We need to do something!" he whispers. "He's . . . he's . . . Jaxon, is he . . . ?"

"Yes," I hiss sharply, glaring at him as I jerk my head pointedly at the bored staff hanging by the counters. "We need to go. What else can we even do?"

I look at Regan to urge her to move so we can get up, but she's frozen in her seat, staring at the body. Her eyes are wide and glassy, one hand gripping the paper bag so hard her knuckles are white and the other shaking.

"Regan, we gotta go. Move," I insist.

Her eyes snap over to mine, nostrils wide with fear, jaw clenched tightly. She swallows and takes a shuddering breath.

"I don't want to go out there," she whispers. "Jaxon, did you do this? Tell him—tell him to sleep!"

"I don't know!" I groan. It's the truth. If I'm the one that woke him up, I don't know how I did it. But he's here, drawn to me. And I don't know the first thing about controlling my powers. "We're gonna be okay, Regan. But we gotta go now."

She gets up, her long legs shaking like a newborn fawn's, and Christian moves to help her walk. My entire body feels like it's made of cold, poorly made Jell-O, but I hold myself rigid as I walk out behind them.

"Go," I tell them as we get out into the cool night air. "Get in the hearse, lock the doors."

"You get in here, too," snaps Christian.

I shake my head, trying my hardest to keep my breathing steady even as the edges of my vision start feeling fuzzy and dark. This is my responsibility; I can do this.

"I'll be right back."

I don't know what I'm doing. I'll be the first to admit that. Maybe I should have Titi's sickle with me, but I don't like the idea of me in my hoodie walking up to a white man—even a dead one—with a weapon where anyone could see. It's dark enough that he really does pass for a drunk guy in dirty clothes if you don't look too closely.

The sickle . . . I was wrong. Unlike when I cut my hand on it back at the Gibson house, Christian and I didn't exchange anything this time. But whatever I did must have called this body somehow. We were a stone's throw from the graves at the edge of the cemetery. How could I be so dumb?

When I round the corner to the front window, the man—the

zombie—hasn't moved. He only swivels his head to look at me with his empty, earth-filled eyes. I can see him better without the glare of the window; he's been dead for at least a couple years by the look of him. His frame is skeletal, skin paper thin, the aging orange glow peeking out from under the crumbling remnants of corpse makeup, his actual tone long gone, skin shriveled with decay.

I walk toward him, hands out peaceably, as he watches me. The dim light of the marquee catches the silver thread of the corpse's tie; I recognize it in a flash of memory. I helped Mami knot that tie around Mr. Walker's neck. He was an astronomy teacher at the local community college; the tie was striped with the moon in all its phases.

"M-Mr. Walker?" I stammer, throat dry.

Mr. Walker's body shifts in my direction, limping heavily on his right leg. His right leg had been torn clean off at the hip joint in the car accident that killed him. Mami stitched it back on for the funeral. His bones click and grind against each other, his stilted movements turning increasingly frantic, skeletal hands extended toward me. His mandible moves, dirt falling from his weathered teeth. Is he trying to *speak*?

Is Mr. Walker actually *in there*?

I need to do something. It might go haywire without any tools, but I can't let him walk around out here, existing like *this*.

"Mr. Walker," I try again, stumbling backward to stay out of reach. I swallow past my heart where it's stuck in my throat, doing my best to sound firm. "I think you should—should go lie down again. You shouldn't be out here."

A sound finally escapes Mr. Walker. He has no voice left, just a shallow rattle like the bones in his throat clacking together. A beat later, he goes rigid, then crumbles. Like stone worn away by time and weather, only all at once. Pieces of his body, his face, crack, splinter, break off, falling to the ground only to explode into a pile of dust and rubble. I jump back, watching in stunned silence as he withers away to gray dust and bone fragments at my feet.

It takes less than a minute. When he's disintegrated into nothing but dust and scraps of fabric, I stagger my way back to the hearse, cold sweat prickling my temples. That's not what I expected to happen. Not a bigger problem, but I definitely don't feel in control.

All I can think of is Christian, freezing, cracking, breaking, and blowing away in the wind.

The drive back home sucks. Driving with Jell-O legs isn't fun, Regan is dead silent the whole way while Christian stares straight ahead. I get out of the car to hug Regan when I drop her at home, no touching rule be damned. Regan needs a hug, and I'm her best friend.

Christian looks more tired once Regan is gone. He slumps back against the passenger seat, staring down at his hands. The drive between Regan's house and his is short, but the silence feels long.

"Hey," I say, glancing at him sidelong as I drive, "I know that was . . . a lot. I'm sorry."

"Jaxon," he says, not looking up. "Can you feel what I'm feeling?"

"Huh?"

He turns his head, looking out the window at the houses passing by. "Like at the McDonald's. You looked at me before I said anything. Can you feel what I'm feeling?"

I take a hand off the wheel, rubbing the center of my chest.

When I think back to the first time Christian woke up, visiting him in the hospital . . . almost every time I've seen him since he woke up, it hits me that I've felt something that didn't feel mine.

"Sometimes," I admit. "I think I heard you in my head one time, too."

Christian's head swivels at that, staring at me with wide eyes. "Like my thoughts?"

"Kind of? Just that you didn't want to fall asleep. It was while you were at the hospital."

He sits up straighter, head almost brushing the roof of the van. "Can—can you feel what I'm feeling now?"

"No, man. I can tell you're freaked out, but I can't *feel* it. I've only really noticed it when you've felt something big like fear. When you woke up. When you noticed that . . . that zombie, I guess."

"Oh."

I don't tell him that his relief washes over me like a cool wave rolling over soft sand. I sigh, some of the tension escaping me. There's more he wants to say—I can tell by the way he goes back to staring at his palms, flexing his fingers—but I'm already pulling up to his house, so he's lost his chance.

He hesitates on getting out of the car, waiting a few breaths before looking at me.

"Jaxon," he starts again.

"Yeah?"

"I really don't think it hurts me when you touch me." He holds his hands up, looking at his palms at eye level. "I feel alive."

He looks kind of crazy when he says that, eyes round behind his dumb circle glasses. Even with crazy face on, he's stupid levels of good-looking. I hate it. I bite my cheek to physically keep myself from smiling at how ridiculous he is.

He's so annoying. I want to shove him out of my car.

"Well, let's keep it that way," I say. "Night, Christian."

"I'll be at school tomorrow, alright?"

"Okay." I hit the unlock button even though the door is unlocked already. "Good night."

He half smiles at me as he opens the door, climbing out. "Night, Jaxon."

ELEVEN

When the morning comes, I still haven't told my mom or Titi Clío about what happened last night. I know I should, but I don't know how. They didn't see me come home shaking and freaked out, so I haven't had to. Titi's still asleep when I head out for school; she was in bed before I got home last night. Mami's applying oil to her tiny curls in her bedroom when I pass by, dressed in a circle skirt made of heavy black fabric and a white, high-necked blouse.

"I'll give you a ride," she says, looking at me in the mirror. "Give me ten more minutes."

It's only about a twenty-minute walk to school, but I'm glad to accept a ride. I come into the room, plopping down over the bed on my stomach.

"Forgot my food last night," Mami admonishes.

"I know, sorry. Me and Regan were in the woods for a while, so I kinda forgot."

She catches my eyes in the mirror's reflection, smiling gently even as she shakes her head. "It's alright. Your titi's food wasn't the worst."

"Smelled pretty good."

"Smelled okay," she corrects. "You ate, though, right?"

"Yup." And, miraculously, didn't toss it all back up after seeing Mr. Walker. I press my face against the blankets, squeezing my eyes shut as I remember the blank, dirt-filled eye sockets.

After a moment, Mami's cool hand lays over my head. "I know it's a lot, mi amor. But you can't miss school again."

"No, I know," I say, muffled against the sheets. "It's cool."

"If you get overwhelmed, you can come home early. Stay through lunch, though, okay?"

That's generous. Mami isn't a huge fan of missing school in general, so she really must be worried. I turn to look at her as she strokes my cheek.

"Okay, Mami."

She only fusses for a little longer before it's time for us to head out. The ride is short and quiet. I consider telling her about Mr. Walker the whole time, but I don't. She's already worried; I don't want her to think I'm out of control on top of everything else.

Jacob's Barrow Regional High School is in the throes of Spirit Week, which I had completely forgotten about with all my anxiety about facing questions about Christian at school. Black and yellow posters and banners line the hallways along with flyers detailing the specifics of each day of the week. Today is Twin Day, which is clear from the moment I walk in. Every other person is dressed identically, or close to identically, with their best friend.

Spirit Week happens every year the week before Halloween. It's stupid every year. The only part I actually participate in is the pep rally on Friday because it's mandatory.

Unfortunately, when I spot Regan at her locker, she's taken away my ability to abstain from Twin Day. She's in her Misfits hoodie and a pair of black jeans, silver rings on every finger. Her boots are red, but other than that, it's uncomfortably close to what I've got on. Even the white print of Pinhead's face across my chest matches the size of the Misfits skull on hers.

I lean against the locker closest to hers, crossing my arms. "What are you wearing?"

Regan laughs when she sees me, holding up her hands and wiggling her fingers. Her rings are actually lengths of wire coiled around her fingers.

"Your fault for always dressing the same," she teases, grinning. "Happy Twin Day!"

I groan, thumping my head back against the locker. "I hate you so much."

Her grin turns impish, looking at me through her lashes. "Not as much as you're gonna hate me in a minute."

I know what she's talking about before I see it, but I don't believe it until Christian comes bounding down the hall in our direction. Sure enough, he's in a black hoodie with white words on the front. It reads, literally, "LOGO" across his chest. His pants are cooler than any I own, black, frayed, with silver-gray thread in the distressed patches, and his sneakers are black and silver too. It's nothing I would ever wear, so he just looks like himself in my color palette. I could strangle both of them. Regan for encouraging this and Christian for annoying me by constantly making me *like* him so much. He looks cute, I'm charmed, and it makes me want to bang my head against the wall.

"Regan, *why*?" I groan.

Christian's at our side in seconds. My stomach sinks as I notice his friends trailing behind him: twins Rhys and Rhiannon, Rhiannon's boyfriend Jae, and her best friend Ava. Ava and Rhiannon are the same brand of tall, intimidating pretty girl with alarmingly straight, white teeth. Ava has a sheet of white-blonde hair and skin the color of milk with eyelashes like snowflakes around slate gray eyes. Jae keeps his dark hair in a skin fade that's long at the top, falling fashionably over brown eyes and arched eyebrows. I only ever see him wearing his black and yellow crew team jacket; today is no exception, Twin Day or not.

Ava and Jae have equally intimidating, matching expressions of benevolent patience on their faces as Christian says hello to us. The twins, however, are worse. They're fraternal, but Rhys and Rhiannon have the same glowing, chestnut brown complexion and gleaming black hair. Rhys's hair falls to his shoulders while Rhiannon's is cut in a sharp, clean pixie well above her ears. They're both notoriously beautiful.

None of these people like me. I don't like them. In all the time we've shared school halls together, we've traded maybe five words between us. And that's a generous assumption.

"What's up, twins? Te quedó perrón, Regan, you're a genius!" calls out Christian, practically bouncing with excitement.

I don't understand how he and Regan got themselves together enough to pull this. I barely got myself together enough to change out of my sweatpants.

"Technically, we're triplets," I correct, eyeing his friends. "What's up . . . Christian?"

Christian looks at Rhys, who flashes a genuine smile at him, then looks at me.

"You know Rhys and them, right?" he says, grinning. "They wanna hear about what happened, so I told them to come say hi. You know like half the story better than I do, so . . ."

It's like Christian didn't actually hear a word I said the night we talked by the river. I don't *want* to know these kids, and why would I want to get hounded about what happened by anyone, least of all them? My shoulders tense, chest tightening with combined anger and anxiety. "Really."

Regan sucks in a breath next to me, opening her mouth to try to answer before I can say anything rude. She flounders for a moment before she finds her words. "Yeah, hey guys. It's like two minutes till the bell, and it's kind of a long story, so maybe at lunch or something?"

"We have the same lunch block, right?" Rhys says to me. This is the first time he's talked to me directly since we were on the same field day team in middle school. "Me and Ava will be there."

I don't know what to say to that. Christian thinks I want to sit around making up a bunch of lies about the single most traumatic night of my life to these people?

"Yeah!" Regan cuts in. "We do!"

Rhiannon's hazel eyes narrow, lips twisting in annoyance. "That's not fair. Jae and I want to hear, too."

"We have AP US History," says Jae, shrugging. "O'Brien won't care if we skip the first lunch block and make up the work during second."

I glare at Regan while Jae and Rhiannon argue about whether or not they can skip their class. Regan knows better than anyone that I want nothing to do with them, so I don't know why she's doing this to me. Spending time with Christian must be making the spinelessness rub off on her.

"Well, I'm not sure if I'm gonna be at lunch," I say, pulling away from the group. "I might go home early. Christian knows the story. I'm the least interesting part anyway."

"Aw, come on," whines Christian, following me for a few paces. "It'll be fun. We can all sit together and hang out!"

"To be honest," I snap, turning to narrow my eyes at him, "hanging out with you and your friends sounds as fun as a frontal lobotomy. I know *you* like being their pet dog, but I'm good."

Christian's expression shutters, reeling from the lash out. I don't know what he expected from me. These are the people who are too good to give me the time of day but not too good to go around feeding stupid rumors about my dad overdosing. I *told* him that, and then he still brings them to me when they apparently want me to dance for them.

"Hey, man," Rhys says from behind Christian, smiling as he puts on his best defusing tone. "It's all good. Chris wants us all to be cool since you kinda saved his life."

"We're not uncool," I object, throwing my hands up in confusion. "We're not anything. There's nothing here because we have nothing to do with each other. I'm good keeping it that way. So, thanks but no thanks to the pity invite, *Chris*."

Christian gives me a look of wide-eyed bewilderment, shaking his head. "That's not it at all, Jaxon!"

"Whatever it is, I don't want it," I call over my shoulder as I start walking away again. "I'm going to homeroom."

Regan shuts her locker in a hurry to chase after me, hugging her biology book to her chest as she catches up. I don't know how to parse out the concern on her face, but it makes me mad all over again.

"Dude," she says, eyes wide and round. "Are you okay? That was dramatic."

"*Dramatic*?" I echo, laughing. "After all the shit those kids talked? About my *dad*? Are you joking?"

"Jaxon, maybe if they get to know you, they might—"

"Nah," I interject, holding up a hand. "I don't want nothing to do with people who need to know me to stop themselves from talking *shit* about my *dead father*. I'm good."

Regan worries her lip, and I know—I can *tell*—she and Christian have been plotting this behind my back. Regan's always been the social one out of the two of us; she blends right in with the Davies twins and their posse. I'm the only thing that stops her from hanging out with them.

"You can hang out with those assholes if you want, Regan. I don't really wanna talk to you right now."

"Jax," she says, her tone a mix of disappointment and concern, but she stops following me.

I'm not going to bother trying to make it through the whole day. Today's already not worth it.

I sit alone at lunch, by choice, and text my mom that I wanna go home. I haven't had any run-ins since this morning, but I'm rattled and I can't shake it off. I gotta get out of here.

We're still allowed to take our lunch out to the hill by the practice fields until it snows, so I take my tray out without pausing to look for anyone and sit under the bleachers set up for this afternoon's scrimmage. It's cold today, so the gravy on my Salisbury steak stiffens by the time I sit down. At least it's quiet out here. The chatter of the kids on top of the hill is distant; there's nothing but woods behind the fields.

It feels good to sit in the quiet. I know I should feel worse about going off on Regan earlier, but I know she gets it, or she will eventually, even if she's pissed at me right now. Regan can't ever stay mad long. I *can*, but Regan and I never spend more than a day mad at each other. Anyway, she has tons of friends. There's plenty of people for her to sit with when I'm not around. I don't want to feel guilty or think about fixing Christian in this half hour. I need my brain to shut up a while. If I can get out of here early, all the better.

Leaning back against the steel beams supporting the bleachers, I spear the peas on my lunch tray individually, eating them one by one. Mami should be around to come get me soon; this is around her normal lunch hour. Even if she works through lunch, Titi Clío is around. The more I think about it, the more I feel the aura of a panic attack coming on. There's a hot, sick feeling starting to chew on my insides that I can't identify. It isn't quite nausea; it's more like I swallowed a chunk of hot copper and the fumes are climbing up the back of my throat. It started in second block. If it's a panic attack coming on, I gotta try to sleep it off or something before I make peace with Christian.

I shake my hands. They're numb at the tips of my fingers but, when I glance down at them, there's no trace of the blue tinge that usually signals a panic attack. Leaning back against the cold metal support beam closest to me, I look up between the gaps in the bleachers at the crisp blue autumn sky. A small flock of birds, loosely arranged like speckles of ink floating across a blue canvas, flies overhead. The birds are too small and too far for me to tell what they are, but even at a distance one of them is clearly out of sync with the others. It bobs and weaves out of the loose formation until, finally, it plummets.

As if it had been aiming straight for me, it bounces on the

bleacher right over my head with a sharp, metallic thud, like a hail-stone. The bird whizzes between the gaps, then lands on my tray, spattering thick gravy across the grass.

It's a house sparrow.

I stare at it, gray and brown feathers bathed in gravy now, prone on my tray. Could *I* have done that? It looked sick even in the sky, so I don't *think* so.

But how would I even know?

My hands tremble as I cradle the bird in my palms, lifting it out of the mess. I bring it close to my face; it lays perfectly still, eyes shut. I've never seen a sparrow's eyelids before; they're translucent, the black of its eyes showing through the thin white skin. It's still warm in my hands, fat and round, wet with gravy.

I wipe it carefully with one of the napkins from my tray, clean-ing up its feathers as best as I can. The gravy comes off easily enough, less sticky for being in the cold. When I finish wiping it down, I place the bird in my lap, trying to swallow back the hot, coppery, sick feeling threatening to overwhelm me.

I think back to the night I saw Christian, body cold, broken, still half in rigor. I remember being unable to accept the idea of him as someone dead and gone—waiting for him to open his eyes, or for me to wake up from a weird dream.

It's not the same now, but something similar. The unexpected-ness, the shock, the illogic of it.

The first thing my aunt thought to explain to me about nec-romancy was how using tools is important to the process; they facilitate it or fine-tune it. The night Christian came back, though, I didn't use anything until his eyes were already open. I don't know how I brought him back.

I spoke to him. I touched him. Was that all it took?

I scoop the bird up in my palm. It's worth trying.

"It wasn't your time," I say. My voice shaking as much as my hands. "Come back. Come back now."

My head swims, spots flashing before my eyes as blood spurts from my nose and splashes across the Pinhead decal on my hoodie. Flecks of it spatter onto the bird's feathers. I inhale sharply in surprise, coughing and choking on the iron taste of my blood, then bring my wrist up to hold against my nose.

Every time. Some variation of this happens every time. I remember Titi slicing her palm with the sickle to reanimate the fox, how my own spilled blood accidentally brought back Mr. Walker.

Blood must mean something too.

The sparrow's eyes fling open like Christian's did. My heart flies up into my mouth, beating faster than a hummingbird's wings, but I keep the sparrow in my hand. It doesn't make a sound or try to move away. Its body twitches, emitting a gentle vibration of life against my palm where it had been deathly still and silent before.

"I can call you back," I whisper, running my thumb across the sparrow's delicate wing feathers. "Shouldn't I be able to make you stay?"

My phone rings as a heartbeat starts pounding against the sparrow's chest feathers. The screen reads *Regan*.

I transfer the sparrow onto my lap, answering the call.

"I'm outside," I say.

"Can you come to the cafeteria?" Her voice is tight, words running into each other as she rushes to get them out. "Please? Right now?"

I'm up on my feet so fast I almost hit my head on a low beam. Below me, the grass has gone brittle and brown where I was sitting.

Just like Titi with the fox and the tree. The life transferred into the bird when I asked it to, moving through its body as its body twitches and registers its renewed life. There were no plants around when I brought Christian back, though. I was the only other living thing in the morgue.

My stomach churns as understanding dawns on me. The life I gave him came from me.

"Uh—what is it? Christian?"

"Just come here!"

The sparrow's wings twitch to life, then it screeches. It leaps up from where it had rolled off my lap, hopping across the ground in panicked confusion.

My head swims again.

"I'm coming!"

I sprint up the hill, leaving my lunch, my bag, and the terrified sparrow behind me. The kids at the top of the hill crackle with frenetic energy. They're shouting at each other, and I nearly trip over someone on my way to the double doors leading into the cafeteria.

I spot Regan with a small group of people—one of them is Ava—and two others I vaguely recognize from the handful of times I've hung out with her at the skatepark. All of them are looking down at something on the ground in front of them.

My chest constricts painfully, fearing the worst. I take stiff, faltering steps toward them, praying it's not what I think. Christian can't be dead, right? The teachers would be here. After the accident, everyone was talking about what happened at the funeral home. Someone would have at least called the nurse by now.

There's no way Christian died after I called him a fucking *dog*.

"Jaxon!" calls Regan when she notices me. She hops up on the table, reaching down for my hand. I take it, climbing up and over with her.

It's Christian, like I expected—but he's very much not dead. He's on the ground shaking in Rhys's arms, eyes blown wide, the veins in his whites bright red, pupils like pinpricks. He's twisted his fingers around Rhys's flannel, knuckles white, nail beds blue, lips pale, chest heaving fast as he gasps for air. Rhys looks pale too, half sprawled on the ground like he fell there with Christian.

I rush over, edging past Rhys, then squat beside him and Christian. My hands are still shaking but I try to present as level-headed as I can manage. "He's having a panic attack."

Whatever else is going on, I know *that* is true. I've had enough panic attacks to recognize one in action. I almost reach out for him before I remember my aunt's warning. Things are unpredictable enough right now without my tempting fate.

"Christian, look at me."

His eyes find mine immediately with that weird, unseeing obedience he showed me on the morgue table a few nights ago. He stares into my eyes, a soft sound leaving him with every hard exhale. His ribs must be hurting him; he's still wheezing.

"You're okay. I know it feels like you're dying, but you're right here with me. We're gonna get you to the nurse, okay?"

Rhys presses his hand against Christian's forehead and the side of his face.

"He's ice cold," he whimpers.

My stomach roils nervously. I shake my head.

"That's normal; his heartbeat's just going haywire. Can you try to breathe slow and easy for him?"

Rhys nods, taking deep, steady breaths as he presses Christian's head to his chest. Christian's knuckles turn whiter, eyes glassy as he stares at me.

"I can't breathe," he wheezes.

"Breathe with Rhys," I tell him. "Your body won't let you die. Let it take over."

"Yes, it will!"

"Christian," I say, as firmly and calmly as I can, "It won't. I promise you, it won't. Feel how Rhys breathes and breathe with him."

He listens to me, slowing his chest as he tries to match his deep, staggering breaths to Rhys's rhythm.

"Okay," I say, backing up with the other kids. "Can someone get the nurse?"

It's not far, at least. The nurse's office is at the end of the hallway adjacent to the cafeteria. I look at Regan for confirmation and she nods, sprinting off to get the nurse. I stay down at Christian's level; he doesn't show any signs of wanting to get up any time soon.

In the short stretch of time between Regan leaving and returning with the nurse, a wave of alarmed voices ripples through the cafeteria, crescendoing as the shrieks and gasps of surprise roll toward our end. I sit up on my knees to look around, but just as I do, it hits me.

There's an odor. Noxious and putrid like a pile of roadkill left to rot under the sun. The staff and students are in a state of pandemonium, tripping over themselves to throw their food into the dumpsters.

Everyone's food is rotten. All of it, not just the school lunches. The kids who whiz by me carry sandwiches with tumorous lumps of fuzzy mold sprouting from them, trays with Salisbury steaks webbed with yellow fungus and black with rot, fruits and vegetables turned wrinkled and discolored. I stand up, watching with wide eyes as students gag and hold their food as far as possible from their faces or abandon their food altogether as they run out of the cafeteria.

The smell is revolting. It coats the back of my throat so even holding my breath I can smell and taste the rot.

Did this *just* happen?

Regan and I exchange looks. She pulls the neck of her hoodie up over her nose and mouth, looking from me to Christian like she's waiting for something to happen to him. I don't know what. I imagine him ballooning with bloat, discolored with livor mortis. It turns my stomach more than the stench of everyone's rotten lunches.

"Jaxon!"

Titi Clío calls me—she's running up behind the nurse, who's staring in shock at the pandemonium, hands gripping the handlebars of the wheelchair she brought for Christian. Titi accidentally shoulder-checks her as she jogs up to me, a visitor badge clipped to her cardigan, tugging me into a bone-cracking hug.

"Me diste una clase de susto," she says, all in one rush of breath, then pulls back to look at me. "Your mom tells me you need to come home and you don't come when they call you over the PA and then I saw the nurse and I just . . ."

She trails off, grimacing at the mass rot around her. Then it clicks.

"Titi Clío, did *you* . . . ?"

"I told you!" She protests, squeezing my arms bracingly before turning me around and guiding me toward the exit. "It's not an easy thing to control!"

I look back over my shoulder, finding Christian's eyes following me. But Rhys and Regan are with him, helping him up into the wheelchair. Regan nods at me, using one hand to keep her hoodie over her face, giving me a little wave.

I wave back, then do a double take at Rhys. There's a streak of white in his long black hair, right at the front. There's no way I missed that before. It was me, wasn't it? His body was making basically full contact with Christian's while I was trying to keep him from freaking out.

I didn't mean to, but I must have gotten Rhys caught in the crossfire. The exchange between me and Christian must have leeched and marked him, like the grass and the tree.

My stomach turns anxiously as I tear my eyes away from him. White hair . . . he aged in just the flash of a second. He doesn't even know yet. I *have* to be more careful. No matter how big or small, Rhys didn't ask to give some of his life for Christian, and I don't know if I can give it back to him.

Titi Clío steers me out of the cafeteria, twitchy like she thinks someone might somehow put together that the sheer force of her presence launched every edible thing through all the stages of decay at once.

"*Did* something happen?" she asks, a slightly hysterical pitch to her voice.

Multiple things, I guess. The sparrow. Christian's panic attack. The food rotting. Rhys's streak. I wouldn't even know where to start. I swallow, but my throat is dry and sour from the smell. Even if I want to tell her, maybe right now isn't the moment.

"No . . . not really."

TWELVE

"We should talk."

Titi Clío and I have been quiet since we got home, up in my room while we wait for Mami to finish up with the body. I'm not sure what she wants to talk about now; nobody was hurt, at least, so even if it spooked me, the whole lunchroom rotting like that was more unnerving than anything.

"What about?"

"Last night." She tosses me a meaningful glance, then reaches down to the hemp bag hanging across her body. She pulls out a sickle, her own. A rough-hewn, dark wooden handle and a blade that looks like it's taken a beating over the past decades. "How could you not call me as soon as you saw what you saw last night?"

My head spins when she says that. Last night already feels so long ago after everything that happened at school. But what she's saying doesn't make any sense. I frown, replaying her words in my mind. I must have heard wrong.

"What I saw? How do you know I *saw* anything?"

Titi comes in, shutting the bedroom door behind her. In an instant, Grimalkin's at the door, scratching and meowing in protest at the audacity of a closed door in her house. Titi ignores her, giving me a smile that's halfway between guilty grimace and impish grin.

She spins the handle of the sickle between her thumb and forefinger. "Because I was watching. This is the boonies, remember? There's no shortage of dead animals to tail you with."

"*What*?" The word bursts out of my mouth louder than I intended. But really—*what*? Why would she do that? "You assumed I was lying, or . . . ?"

"I didn't *assume*. I wanted to see what you were up to," she said, raising a hand in disagreement.

"Well, no, because if you wanted to see what I was up to, that means you didn't believe me."

She sighs, looking at me like I'm being an unreasonable kid. "Jaxon, cariño, you *did* lie, first of all. I'm trying to understand *why*. Someone could have seen all of that. And it obviously scared you even though you've been around dead bodies all your life."

"Not bodies like *that*." Mami's brought home some gruesome bodies for work. She's dealt with dismemberment, discoloration, and bloating, but she's never had to set up a service for a body that was desiccated and covered in graveyard dirt.

I don't know what to say to her. She's had, presumably, a whole lifetime to get used to watching people and animals reanimated, shambling uncomfortably in their worn, inhospitable bodies. I didn't *mean* to disappoint her. Was I really supposed to know the right thing to do after something like that?

There's no time for her to put me on lockdown over my abilities being haywire. But the idea of having been seen by someone else *is* sobering.

"I'm sorry," I say finally. "I guess I didn't want you to think you need to hold my hand constantly or anything."

"Jaxon, it's not like that. This is dangerous stuff; I'm not trying to 'hold your hand.' I want you to feel like you can trust me in a crisis."

"I don't *not* trust you . . ."

It's complicated because of Christian. Without his life hanging in the balance, all of this might even feel cool or interesting. Instead, I'm learning to manage my abilities in a trial by fire.

Titi sits beside me on the bed, smiling and placing a hand on my shoulder. Even through my hoodie, I can feel a current of energy coming from her palm. It's pronounced, but not uncomfortable. I remember feeling a gentle little vibration from the sparrow when it came back to life in my hand, too.

"Titi, are you doing that on purpose?"

"¿Qué, mi vida?"

"Eso," I touch her hand gently. "I don't know how to explain it; it's like a really low-level current between your hand and my shoulder."

Almost electrical, though not painful at all. Steady, and impossible to miss now that I'm focused on it.

Titi smiles wider, squeezing my shoulder. "You're starting to notice it, huh? That's me, but I'm not doing anything. I'm alive, and you can feel it."

I wrinkle my brow, considering her fingers. Nothing *looks* out of the ordinary, it's purely a physical feeling. "So *I'm* not doing anything, right? If I can feel that, it doesn't mean I'm hurting your aliveness? Life force?"

"No, honey," says Titi fondly as she raises her hand to cup my face briefly. "You're not hurting me. It's a good thing you can feel it—you should keep trying to notice it. It's all around, everywhere, you know? Not just person to person."

That does seem like a pretty fucking useful thing to notice. But I can't sense anything at all when Titi isn't touching me. "Do you think I accidentally transferred some of mine to Christian or something? When I, uh, alived him?"

"From what you and Tessa have told me, that sounds about right. It'll get easier to manage yourself as you get better at noticing the life force in people and things around you. It'll help you develop more control over your abilities, too, so you aren't giving your life away."

"How? I just . . . wait to get better?"

"Well, no, like I said, keep feeling it. Keep noticing. Sit outside surrounded by living things and clear your mind, try to find it."

I almost laugh. This is the second time someone's told me I need to shut my brain up to make things work. "*Clear my mind? I don't know how to do that.*"

Really, I don't. My mind is almost constantly going at about a thousand miles per hour, spinning the worst-case scenarios for any given situation. I'm supposed to sit quietly by myself thinking of nothing?

Titi Clío smiles as she gives me a helpless shrug. "It takes practice. When you hone the ability to sense life around you, you can really start using your abilities. On purpose."

"For what?"

She widens her eyes, grinning like she's bursting to tell me all the possibilities. "Your dad used to help your mom make bodies look their best for the funerals. No life, just freshening up the body. He used to fix broken bird wings and one-eyed cats—all sorts of stuff. Your abuela could talk to spirits, and she helped people answer all kinds of questions. There's *so* much."

Hearing about my dad makes me grimace without meaning to. I think Mami does great making bodies look good without him around to cheat the process. Most of the memories I have of spending time with him, though, are of walking through the woods and stopping whenever we ran into dead animals to pay respects. He was the first person to teach me what an owl pellet was, and that porcupine quills are hollow, and how to tell eagle feathers from hawk feathers from owl feathers. He never talked much but when he did, it was about animals.

I think of the sparrow dropping dead on me today.

"What about the thing with the cilantro? And what happened today at lunch when you came to get me? I might also kill things? Or . . . ?"

"It's not killing," she reassures me gently. "And we don't really know if that's something that's going to pass onto you yet. That's why it's dangerous not to come to me when problems happen. You can't do this on your own safely, mijo."

I bite my tongue. How much does she know about last night? Does she know about Christian grabbing my hand even after I told him not to?

"I'm sorry," I murmur, looking down at my lap. "I shouldn't have lied about what I was doing."

Her eyes soften as she leans over, kissing the top of my head and shaking my shoulder gently.

"It's okay," she says. "I'm not mad at you. But if undead are following you, Jaxon, you have to tell me. Imagine if he'd followed you around all night!"

The thing is, he didn't. I get her point, but I, for better or worse, kind of handled it. There *is* something that's bothering me, though. I remember Mr. Walker's funeral; I remember his family had chosen a pine casket out of cost necessity, and I can imagine it's degraded a lot by now. But even if the wood is little more than mulch . . . *how* did he get out?

"Titi, how did his body function enough to dig his way out of his grave? He was brittle, barely held together by the embalming. At the point of decomp he was at, any ligaments in his body would be gone or hanging on by a string, *maybe*."

"He wasn't quite *alive*, you know?" Her brow wrinkles a little as she tries to parse out how to explain. "He wasn't really obeying the laws of physics in that moment. That boy Christian came back to life with his chest caved in, right?"

"Right . . ."

"The life force that enters them is greater than the limits of their bodies—to an extent. He probably couldn't run a marathon, but he could drag himself to you when he felt your pull."

I'm not sure I get it. I squint a little as I try to make sense of that.

"So what? His joints stitched together by necromantic magic?"

Titi Clío smiles wryly, shrugging a shoulder. "Is it easier to wrap your head around it if we call it a different kind of force? Like gravity or energy but not?"

"Maybe . . ." I say uncertainly. "Is that why he crumbled apart when I asked him to go away? Nothing holding him together anymore?"

"See? You're starting to get it." She gets up, smoothing her hands over the front of her chiffon skirt as she moves toward the door. "Come on. There's ice cream in the freezer downstairs."

I get up, furrowing my brow. "Titi, you're vegan."

She gives me a guilty grimace, shrugging. "We need comfort food."

"But Titi Clío," I roll out of bed, following her as she opens the door. Grimalkin rushes in, yowling indignantly. "I'm still confused on what actually *happened*."

"Did you recognize the body, Jaxon?"

"Yeah, Mr. Walker. He got his leg caught in the door when the car took off. It almost ripped him in half."

Titi's mouth makes a small *o* before she winces sympathetically. "Oh, Jesus Christ. Well—when you were talking to him, did you say his name?"

I nod and she takes my hands, grinning as she squeezes them tightly.

"Pues . . . cuando hiciste eso, you ushered that man's soul back into his body."

Most of the things that have happened have been terrifying, and I had no control over them. Every time I close my eyes, I keep seeing images from the last twelve hours on a constant loop. Mr. Walker's earth-packed eye sockets, the sparrow dead in my hands, the rotting food, Rhys having a visible change right in front of me, the look of abject terror on Christian's face.

But Mr. Walker—the *real* person, his consciousness—being dragged back into his uninhabitable body against his will? Did he understand what was happening? Could he feel or think anything with nothing but residual brain matter and withered nerve endings?

God. I hope not.

If I tell Titi everything, she'll think I'm a hazard. I *am* a hazard.

"Oh," I say softly, following her down to the second-floor landing.

She leads me into the kitchen, pulling bowls out of the cabinets, then circling over to the fridge.

My head pounds. An image of Christian flashes into my mind, waking up screaming in the dark, twisted in pain, crawling, desperate. I think of Mr. Walker, dried up and skeletal. I made him wake back up in *that* body?

I cross the kitchen stiffly, dropping down onto one of the chairs at the table.

"So putting Mr. Walker's soul back in that body, did that hurt him? Or . . . I don't know."

"Well, he was in a pretty advanced state of decay, like you said." Titi sets the tub of ice cream down on the counter, pausing to look at me sympathetically. "It was probably more confusing than painful, and it didn't last very long. He's at rest again now, cariño. It was one moment, and you didn't mean to."

That's not much comfort. It's a horrible thing to have put someone through, even for a second.

"But when Christian came back . . ."

"That's different," she says, holding up the scoop as she looks over at me. "You know those circumstances are completely separate."

I swallow, tracing the blunt edge of my nail against a groove in the wood of the kitchen table as Titi comes over, sets a bowl of ice cream down in front of me, and sits across from me with her own bowl. I watch her take less than half a spoonful, trying it daintily as if it might be poisoned.

"Yeah, that's true. I guess I'm just wondering, I would have had to turn the watch way, *way* back to restore Mr. Walker's body into decent shape, right?"

"Right . . ." says Titi Clío, narrowing her eyes like she's not sure she likes where this is going.

"Okay. So if I'd wanted to fully resurrect him, would it take a bigger sacrifice than it would for Christian? Or is it a soul for a soul across the board? Because when you reanimated that fox, you didn't have to kill a fox to do it."

"Honey, that's reanimation," Titi Clío looks at me, brows coming together seriously. "Not resurrection. To resurrect Mr. Walker and Christian both would take *time,* literally. You need to give Death the years those souls owe it."

I sit up straighter, interest piqued. "So it's *not* a soul for a soul."

Titi's cheeks turn red as she shakes her head, holding a hand up to stop my line of questioning. "Ya basta, Jaxon. Don't even start!"

I stare into my bowl as I bite my tongue. Time for time is a different thing than *a life for a life*. Time and life are connected, obviously, but if there's a loophole to be found, it's there.

Weirdly, I kind of wish Christian was here. He would know the right questions to ask my aunt to get a straight answer out of her.

"But like . . ." I lift my eyes up to her, squinting slightly. "Mr. Walker, theoretically, would need a way smaller sacrifice than Christian, then?"

Titi's lips press into a thin line, her impatience with the subject of Christian boiling over.

"Que ya basta, te dije." She points a stern finger at me. "Te advierto, Jaxon. Leave that boy alone."

"Titi, if we can fix this, don't you think we *should*?"

"No!" she snaps, voice sharpening with finality, her shoulders squaring. "Do you *want* to end up like—"

She falters, holding her hands up before taking a deep breath through her nose as she shakes her head.

"Just . . . no, Jaxon."

There was something there, where she cut herself off. What is she stopping herself from saying?

"Like what?" I press, leaning forward on my elbows. "Like who? Like . . . my father?"

"Stop pushing. The conversation is over."

I back off because I want to revisit this, which will be easier if I don't piss her off now. My heart beats fast even though I'm doing nothing but sitting here. Was I right? If she was talking about my dad, that would be more than I've ever learned about how he died. I shove a spoonful of ice cream in my mouth to prove my willingness to stop talking about it.

The act of eating gives me a visceral flashback to the kids at my school spitting rotting hunks of food onto the cafeteria floor. I imagine the ice cream souring and curdling, and it takes every ounce of self-control in my body to stop myself from gagging when I try to swallow.

I push myself through it as Titi changes the subject to my birthday on Saturday—Halloween.

With all this shit happening, I keep forgetting.

THIRTEEN

Mami gets a call from the school about the incident, but the admin plays it down so much all she does is ask me if my lunch was okay. They blame the mass rotting on the air conditioners being shut off last week and the unseasonable weather we've been having. I think about telling her the truth, but I don't.

It's getting easier and easier to not tell her things.

"Take a shower tonight," she says when I tell her I want to go to bed early. "Don't think I didn't notice you skipped yesterday. Don't be nasty."

"*Mami*," I groan, rolling my eyes before I can stop myself.

"Ah, I don't wanna hear it." She leans up to kiss my face, then drops down on the couch, toeing her shoes off. "There's going to be a wake tomorrow, and I don't want people thinking my son can't bathe himself."

"No one's gonna be looking at me," I mutter under my breath. However, I do as she says, leaving the sitting room for the bathroom.

I spend a long time under the hot spray of the shower. It rains down directly over the crown of my head and rolls over my face, so I keep my eyes closed. The heat feels good; the steam in the bathroom is so thick it makes me a little faint, but it's relaxing. I lean with my hands against the tile wall in front of me, letting the hot water loosen my shoulders.

I don't remember the last time I felt this tired. It's like my spine turned into a tightly coiled spring, constantly scrunched down by the weight of my head. I want to sleep, but I don't have time, and when I *do* sleep, I have nightmares. They're always nightmares about Christian—either him dead and crumpled in his smashed-up car or him screaming at me from the concrete floor of the morgue.

This is the closest to rested I've felt in days. Shrouded in steam, worries drowned out by the sound of the water hitting the porcelain. I stay until the water starts running cold and my fingers prune.

I wrap a towel around my waist, calling good night to my mom and aunt. Both of them call back to me as I head up to my room, holding the towel secure with one hand.

"Grim?" I call, craning my neck to look around as I click my tongue to call her over.

She doesn't come. Grimalkin does everything on her own time, as cats do. I head into my room, flipping the lights on, only to hear a meow.

"Hey girl, you in—" I cut off.

Grimalkin is sitting on my bed—curled up in Christian's lap. Christian holds a hand out and brings a finger up to his lips, but I shout before I can stop myself, clutching my towel tighter.

"*Jesus*!"

"Jaxon!" My mom yells from downstairs. "Are you okay?"

I gape at Christian, turning hot from my ears down to my chest. For a moment, I'm dumbstruck. Christian smiles up at me, half-apologetic and half-amused, and it takes everything in me not to curse him out for smirking at me from my *bed* while I'm sitting here barely managing to keep my heart in my chest. I don't understand how he got in here—why did he have to break into my house while I'm practically *naked*? This is the worst.

"Uh, I, uh," I stammer, trying to make my brain work fast enough to process all this. "Sorry! I'm fine; I stubbed my toe!"

I shut the door behind me, holding my hand up to keep Christian quiet as I cross over to pick up my phone and start a random playlist on my speaker. I pivot, looking down at him sitting on my bed like he belongs there, trying to decide how to start.

"Jax," he begins.

"*No*," I cut him off. "Shut up. What do you think you're doing? How'd you get *in* here?"

"Back door. I used the spare key and went up the spooky stairs."

"The spare key?" I blink at him in disbelief.

He shrugs, albeit guiltily. "It's not like I could call ahead. I'm sorry! You guys keep the spare in the same place as back in middle school!"

He keeps his eyes glued to my face pointedly, making my cheeks burn even hotter. I'm not built like Christian or Rhys or any of those guys on the crew team. Even tall and wiry like he is, it's clear that Christian's growing into broad, flat muscles.

I'm not. My torso is a shapeless thing. Worse still, I'm definitely blushing.

"Okay, weirdo," I say, taking a deep breath. "Can you look the other way or something? I need to put pants on, I can't handle this with my balls out."

Christian at least is also blushing. His cheeks go from brown to peachy pink as he turns his face up and away.

"Yeah, of course, dude!"

I move to the farthest corner of the room possible, changing into a pair of cotton pajama pants and a Mothra t-shirt. When I turn back around, Christian's still staring up at the far end of the ceiling as Grimalkin rubs her face against his hands.

"Traitor," I mutter to her, coming over. I sit down at the head of my bed with my legs crossed under me. Christian looks at me, fixing me with a blinding grin. "What are you doing here, Christian?"

"I had to come talk to you. I tried to throw rocks at your window, but you weren't in your room."

I narrow my eyes, tipping my head at him. "Why didn't you *knock*?"

He laughs nervously, rubbing one of his eyes under his glasses. "I'm still kinda embarrassed that I was, like, naked in your mom's lap when I woke up, you know?"

I pinch the bridge of my nose, sighing deeply. "Okay. Well, just so you know, this is psycho behavior. But you're here, so what do you want?"

Christian winces, looking down at Grimalkin who's curled up with her eyes closed. He scratches between her ears for a moment, then finally looks up at me from over the rim of his glasses.

"Sorry for being a psycho. I wanted to come and I guess say sorry? For being a dumbass today."

That's not what I expected. The fiasco in the cafeteria seems like a more pressing issue, but I nod at him, unsure what to say.

"Well," I start, "you're always a dumbass, so . . ."

"Yeah. I know I really hurt your feelings today. And after you told me how mad you got at me for being a coward about the stuff with your dad, I promised myself I was gonna do better. And then I didn't."

I look down at Grimalkin to avoid looking at him. I'm not sure what he wants me to say to that, but he waits patiently while I consider it. His fingers start to scritch faster against Grimalkin's fluffy fur. I can hear her purr from where I'm sitting.

"Okay," I say ultimately. "I'm sorry I said you're those kids' dog. That was mean."

Christian shakes his head, "No, it's okay. I know you were mad. It's really not like that, though."

I lift my gaze to meet his. When Christian needed help, Rhys was on it immediately. I can at least concede I may have judged him too harshly. Maybe.

"Yeah, I know. Rhys was really scared for you today."

Christian widens his eyes behind his glasses at me. "Did you *see* his hair?"

"Yeah. It wasn't like that before, right?"

"No mames, Jaxon, you know it wasn't," he says, scooting back gently to keep from startling Grimalkin. "He freaked out when he saw it. Last I talked to him, he wants to dye it, but he's scared to ruin his natural hair color."

I squint at him. "He's not more worried about how the fuck that happened in the first place?"

"Well, yeah! But Homecoming's on Friday, you know?"

I roll my eyes. Spirit Week is the worst even when doing the bare minimum spirit activities. I can't imagine what it's like for kids in student council or on sports teams who have to care about showing spirit and doing things at the rally. We're juniors this year—it's the first year our class is allowed at Homecoming—so everyone's turned up their spirit by a few decibels. Personally, I'd rather eat nails.

Though, judging from the look on Christian's face, he'll be there with bells on.

"People's food rotted as they ate it today, his hair turned white, and he's worried about Homecoming?"

Christian's smile falters as he swallows, looking down at his hands and picking at a hangnail. "It's nice to think about normal things when everything else is going crazy."

I rub the space between my eyes. "Can't relate."

"You don't really do anything normal," he teases, smiling.

"You didn't either. Before."

Christian's smile falls, a silence stretching between us. He frowns, adjusting his glasses by the edge of the frame.

"I was gonna say I'm still me," he says, looking up at me through his long, dark lashes. "But I guess I don't even know if that's true after what happened today."

I tip my head. "What do you mean?"

"That stuff today." He winces, wringing his fingers one by one and blinking at me like a guilty kid. "I think it was me. I think it was my fault. I don't even know how it happened. My brain feels all weird since you brought me back."

"What stuff? The food?"

He nods at me. "The food. Rhys's hair."

I shake my head, feeling my scowl soften sympathetically. Christian's probably never had a panic attack before, but I have them all the time. They make me feel like a freak too when they happen in public. In all fairness, considering what happened to Rhys, I think his panic attack got triggered by almost *dying*, and

I feel a little bad twisting the truth, but I don't want Christian to feel like he's a threat to others on top of everything else he's got going on.

I don't want him to be afraid of me either.

"It was just a panic attack. My tía, she's pretty sure the food was her by accident. I don't know if she noticed, but I think Rhys's hair was her too."

"Wait . . . really? By accident?"

"She says her powers are hard to control and when she came to pick me up today, she freaked out a little 'cause they called me over the PA but I was outside, so I didn't hear it. She thought . . ."

Christian nods along, expression clearing with understanding. "Makes sense there'd be an emotional piece to the puzzle, yeah . . ." He trails off for a moment, scratching under Grim's chin until she gets so into it, her eyes close and her whiskers push forward. His eyes meet mine over the rim of his glasses, a little smirk tilting the corner of his mouth. "So that means you were emotional when you did me, ¿verdad?"

I roll my eyes, huffing as my cheeks go hot. "Shut up. Don't even start."

Christian's smirk widens into a grin that doesn't disappear until Grimalkin jumps off his lap. He whines, fixing his glasses with one hand as he pats his lap invitingly with the other. "Grim, no! Come back!"

"Listen," I interject, "Something happened to me at lunch, too, while that was happening to you."

That draws his focus back sharply. He worries his lip as he looks at me, a crease forming between his eyebrows. "What happened?"

"I was sitting in the practice fields, under the bleachers, and a sparrow fell out of the sky on me, dead."

Christian widens his eyes, bringing his hand up to his mouth.

"I picked it up and told it to come back," I continue, suppressing a shiver at the memory of it. "And it did."

"It did?" gasps Christian, leaning toward me, eyes widening even more.

"Yeah. Screeching and confused."

"And then?"

I look at his hands, thinking of his pale knuckles and his blue nail beds. Do I tell him about the ring of dead grass around me when the bird came back to life? He's clever enough to ask if that has any connection to the way he came back. That means I either lie to him again or tell him the only living thing he could have gotten life from was me.

Better not mention it.

"Then Regan called me and told me to come to the cafeteria. And then I found you."

Christian looks alarmed at that, reeling backward and raising his eyebrows. He whispers like he's afraid he'll be too loud if he speaks to me normally. "What about the sparrow?"

"I don't know," I admit, wrapping my arms around myself, gripping my elbows. "When I went back for my stuff it was gone."

"Dude!"

"What?"

Christian shakes his head, gripping his hair with one hand in dismay.

"Dude, you set a zombie sparrow on the world!"

I roll my eyes, even though the thought does rattle me. Christian has a way of making everything sound stupid *and* a little cute.

He's right, I guess, but who knows how long the sparrow will last?

"I set zombie *you* on the world, too."

"Touché," he says, laughing nervously. He stares at my covers, tracing his fingers along the stitches on my comforter. We sit for a while in silence, the discomfort prickling the air between us like thorns.

"What triggered your panic attack?" I ask at length.

Christian doesn't look at me, bringing a hand up to rub his sternum. "I don't know. I felt dizzy and tired. Like my heart was slowing down. I freaked out; it happened so fast, you know? I kept thinking, 'Am I dying? Please don't let me die.'"

My skin crawls, a cold sweat breaking out over my spine. There's no way to know how much time Rhys's life force bought us.

"I'm sorry that happened," I offer. "And I'm sorry I wasn't there."

"You *were* there. You showed up."

He looks at me with bald-faced trust, eyes round and earnest, lips curving up in a hesitant smile despite what we're talking about. My chest aches sharply for a moment as it hits me. I *miss* him. I miss the days when he used to sneak into my house because I asked him to, when we stayed up watching my dad's horror movie collection on the ancient tube TV in the attic and Christian would "borrow" copies of my dad's books that he'd never give back.

"Christian," I say, forehead crinkling as I swallow past the anxious lump in my throat, "I'm scared I'm gonna fuck this up. Pissed at you or not, I really want you to be okay."

"I know, Jaxon."

I press my face into my hands, pressing hard against my eyes until I see stars. I can't stop thinking. I can't afford to sleep for an entire day, no matter how much I want to. Talking to my mom will only make things worse. I curl my shoulders forward, shaking my head.

"I'm really trying."

"I know," he says. "Me too."

He places a hand on my shoulder. I jerk away, glaring at him. "I told you—I could lose control, especially when I'm freaking out!"

He sighs through his nose, considering me for a moment, then opens his arms. "Dude, just come in for a hug. We both need it."

"Are you a moron? It could kill you. *I* could kill you."

He shakes his head. "No, man, I don't think you could."

I hesitate because I don't know how to answer that. I narrow my eyes at Christian. Does he hear himself? He takes my silence as a go-ahead, wrapping his arms around my middle, squeezing hard.

For a second, I try to pull away, but I'm already tangled up in it, and nothing's happened yet. In fact, he feels warm, his heart's beating against my chest. The relief that gives me pulls the air out of my lungs. Can he feel the way *my* heart is racing? We haven't been this close since we were in middle school.

I place my hands against his shoulders gingerly, still nervous something will go wrong. Squeezing his shoulders gently, I get a flutter of a current from him. It's faint, nowhere near as strong as my tía's. It's steady, at least as far as I can tell.

"See?" he comforts, squeezing me tighter before letting go and pulling back with a dumbass smirk on his face, glasses askew from hugging. "Nothing happened."

"I really can't stand you," I mutter, a smile pulling at my face against my will. I roll my eyes, but I do feel better. He's solid, living, breathing flesh and blood. He's nothing like Mr. Walker, trapped in that stitched-up body beaten up by time.

Christian fixes his glasses, staring at me with a doofy smile that makes butterflies erupt in my stomach, eyes wide like he expected me to hit him or something. He breaks into a grin, and I feel his relief as intensely as my own.

"Look, I was . . . I was thinking maybe we could sneak out to the woods, and I could help you out with the mirror. I mean, I'm not an expert on channeling helpful spirits, but we could try it together, at least."

I want to sleep so badly, but there's no time. Christian can't sleep well until this is resolved, and neither can I. If that means staying up to search for spirits that can give us more information on necromancy, then that's what we'll do.

"Yeah, alright. But we have to wait until my mom and aunt are asleep. I don't want them catching us."

"Okay," says Christian, reaching down to pull off his black socks, then scooting over to the wall side of the bed. "So we wait."

I look at him quizzically as he settles in, rucking up my comforter so he can burrow into it. I sigh, getting up to turn off the light and cracking the door open slightly so Grimalkin can come and go as she pleases. I grab my ear buds from the nightstand before climbing in beside Christian.

"Here." I offer him a bud, leaving the case on the nightstand. "If you hear anyone coming, hide."

He nods, pulling his glasses off his face and trading them for the bud. I place them on the nightstand, picking up my phone.

"What do you wanna listen to?"

"Can we listen to Spanish music?"

"Like what?" I scoot closer to him to bring the phone closer to his face, knowing he's pretty blind without his glasses. "Reggaeton or like that banda stuff your dad's always listening to?"

The phone screen lights up his smile as he takes it out of my hand, holding it about an inch from his face.

"Don't knock banda, it's cool. What about Zoé?"

"Man. Who are you? My titi?"

"Cállate, güey. They're cool."

So, we listen to Zoé while Christian does his best not to sing along. His shoulder touches mine, which I try not to freak out over. It's nice—it's familiar, lying side by side, trying to stay quiet. Just like in the past, my stomach is in knots. Every twitch of my muscles feels like a seismic, obvious sign that he makes me nervous. I'm hyperaware of how easy it would be to hold his hand. But, at least, there's a more pressing issue to focus on: I'm not going to hurt him. I want him *here* with me. And I can focus on the current from him here in the dark, when I manage to stop thinking about the fact that we're *in my bed*.

It's steady. It doesn't waver. His vibration is weak, but not so weak that I lose track of it. I wish I could compare it to my own, but how would I go about finding that?

The floorboards creak as my mom comes upstairs. Christian ducks under the covers, pressing closer. His breath is warm against the back of my t-shirt. It makes me shudder.

"Night, baby," says my mom as she passes by my door.

I don't call back. If she knows I'm awake, there's a decent chance she'll come in since I didn't see much of her today.

Shortly after that, my aunt passes by. Her footsteps are lighter than my mom's, but she doesn't know our floors well enough to avoid the loudest boards. One near my door groans particularly loud, and she hisses a swear, hurrying the rest of the way, her door snapping shut soundly behind her.

"Now?" whispers Christian, peeking up from the covers.

I turn on my side and shake my head, pressing my finger against my lips.

"Titi turns on a sound machine before she goes to sleep. Wait for that. Mami's a deep sleeper, but Titi will wake up."

He nods, turning down the volume on my phone even though it's already quiet. We stay a while longer waiting while Titi Clío does whatever it is she does before bed. Christian stays sunk down low in the covers playing some dumb game on my phone.

When the sound machine comes on, Christian sits upright automatically, but I hold a hand up to slow him down, reaching over to grab his glasses. I trade them back for my phone, sitting up slowly. Turning the light on as he puts them back on, we climb out of bed carefully, testing our weight on the floorboards.

Christian does seem to remember the loudest floorboards in my room, at least. He tugs his socks back on, steps into his sneakers, and pads over to the door, peeking through the slit into the hall before pushing it open carefully. He looks back, gesturing for me to follow.

I guess he *is* the one who sneaked in in the first place. It's kind of weird, thinking about it that way.

I follow him, grabbing the mirror from my backpack and cradling it against my chest. We tiptoe our way to the servant stairs entrance at the back of the hall, pulling the door open with bated breath, knowing it creaks.

The door gives a small, low whine as we crack it open enough to slip through but doesn't sound any different than the noises the rest of the house makes when it settles at night. Christian sneaks through ahead of me, while I pull the door shut behind us before Grim can chase us down. The staircase is pitch black so I turn on my phone's flashlight before Christian can miss a step and eat shit all the way down to the next landing. The wood on these stairs is old and hard. They almost feel petrified, so they're quieter than the floorboards, emitting only the occasional soft groan when we press our weight down on them.

I don't stop holding my breath until we make it out on the bottom floor in the butler's pantry.

"Wait a sec," I whisper, pointing to one of the lower cabinets with my lips. "There's extra candles in there. Grab some."

Christian's big white grin flashes at me. "Spooky séance."

I sigh, admittedly tinged with a *little* affection. "Also, a light source other than my phone."

Christian stoops down to search through the cupboard, producing a pair of tall, thick pillar candles and a long-reach butane lighter. He gives me a thumbs up as I get the door.

Grimalkin's orange eyes flash at me from where she sits, a yard away from the door. I fight back the urge to go over and pet her for being so smart; she always turns up exactly where I am in the house.

"Can't bring you, girl," I whisper as I head to the back door.

Christian falls into step with me out in the yard; I can almost feel him ready to burst out using his outdoor voice. It must be hard for him, staying quiet for that long. He opens his mouth to say something, but I shush him before he gets the chance, pointing my thumb back at the house.

He sucks his lips in, mouth turning into a thin line as if his lips are sealed.

I wonder, again, how much he's actually compelled to listen to me. Sometimes it seems compulsive, sometimes he doesn't at all, and sometimes, like now, it could be a coincidence.

When we're deep into the woods behind my house, Christian breaks his silence all at once like water breaking from a dam.

"That was insane! I've missed your house. It's so scary!"

In the trees directly above us, an owl screeches in surprise before silently pushing off into the air. The canopy of leaves is still too thick to see it, even with October coming to a close soon.

"Was that a barn owl!?" says Christian, not really asking. He looks at me with big round eyes, grinning and nodding at the mirror in my hand. "So cool, dude!"

"Yeah," I confirm, looking down at the heart-shaped barn owl face on my mirror. "I always hear barn owls around here, though."

"I still think it's cool."

"Yeah, I bet."

He carries on, spirit undampened, looking up as he walks in case the owl perches somewhere nearby. With how carelessly he steps on crunchy leaves and dry twigs, I don't think any animals are going to want to be anywhere near us.

"I can't believe you broke into my house," I say. "Not just because it's a weirdo thing to do, but also because you're this fucking loud."

"Pinche verga, Jaxon, I'm sorry!" He whines, smiling at me, not looking sorry in the slightest. "I told you, if I had a phone, I would have asked."

"That really isn't good reasoning, but sure."

He shifts the candles and the lighter into one arm as he fixes his glasses, looking ahead. "I couldn't wait till tomorrow."

"Why not?"

I watch the back of his head, tension radiating from the nape of his neck and the curve of his ears.

He shrugs. "Just in case."

I let the weight of that sink into my chest, the silence settling around us like thick dust. I'm not angry at him for breaking in, even if it is objectively a weird thing to do. Both of us are struggling to act rationally, to even keep it together. If I were in his position, I wouldn't be doing half as well.

"We gotta figure out the phone thing," I say, for lack of anything better.

"Oh, Jae says he's gonna hook me up with his old Galaxy. I'm trading him my Melos tomorrow."

"Your what?"

"Shoes, Jax."

The sneakers he has on now are different from the ones he had on at school today. Gray knit fabric and a black Nike swoop on the side.

"I don't even wanna know how many more shoes you've gotten since middle school."

He laughs. "Yeah, you really don't."

We come to the clearing Titi and I practiced in yesterday. This felt like a good place to her, so it should be good enough for our purposes. Christian scouts a flat spot to set down the candles, squatting down to light them. I turn off my flashlight, then stick it in my back pocket, carrying the mirror over to sit opposite Christian.

"So, what do we do?" I ask.

"Maybe set it down between us here? So we can look in together?"

I hold it to my chest, looking at him doubtfully. "Is that a good idea?"

"¡A huevo que sí! Why not?"

"I don't know." I look down, looking at my reflection in the black glass. It's almost impossible to see anything but the glimmer of my eyes. "What if something happens to you? Like it . . . like it sucks in your soul or some shit, I don't know!"

Christian grins, leaning back on his hand. "You been watching too many horror movies, young man."

"We are literally living a horror movie, Christian."

He laughs even though it's true. Or maybe *because* it's true. Either way, he stays firm by it, patting the ground between us.

"Anything that could happen to me could happen to you, too. You keep thinking I'm more vulnerable 'cause I died, but we're fucking with *magic*, man."

I open my mouth, trying to think of a rebuttal, but nothing comes out. I'm supposed to have control over what happens to me—I think, anyway. I'm the necromancer who doesn't know what he's doing. Christian's right.

"That doesn't really make me feel better."

"Look," he says, taking the mirror from my hands, "it's just scrying. It might not even work, we're giving it a shot. If it gets too scary then I don't know, lo dejamos a la verga and we can run to 7-Eleven to get hot chocolate instead."

"That's . . . okay. I guess that's *a* plan."

He laughs again, setting the mirror down. "Let's *try*, Jax."

I can't tell if he really feels confident or if he's hysterical, but we're both desperate for answers. I nod, looking down at the mirror between us, watching the orange light of the candle flames flickering at the edges. The glass is remarkable, smooth and black like a vortex behind a window.

"So what should I do?"

"Look at it," he insists, settling with his legs crossed, pushing his glasses up when they slide down the bridge of his nose. "You don't have to be focused on a point or anything, look and wait to see something."

"In the glass?"

"In your brain. The glass helps you focus."

I try not to get distracted by the intricate details of the ivory frame, watching the orange flashes of candlelight in the glass. I remember Christian telling me quieting the mind is part of this, and Titi also stressed that it was important for other reasons, so I try, but when we're both quiet like this, my brain feels louder than ever.

I think of my mom and aunt waking up to find me gone. I imagine Christian dropping dead out here in the woods with me, leaving me looking like some kind of demon warlock who killed him with my mirror and candles. If I can't stop *worrying*, how am I gonna know when the mirror is showing my brain anything?

"Shouldn't we, like say something?" I wonder out loud after a while.

"Like what?"

"I don't know. Didn't you say you felt like the mirror was staring back at you last time you looked at it?"

Christian nods, glancing up at me over his glasses. "I do."

That makes my stomach turn.

"So shouldn't we call someone? Whoever's watching?"

Christian tilts his head, a line forming between his eyebrows as he considers it. If even Christian hesitates at the proposal, I don't feel confident that it's a great idea, but sitting here trying to shut my brain up and staring blankly isn't working.

"Who do you think it is?" he asks.

In all honesty, I don't know. It's my grandmother's mirror, so it could be her. My grandfather made it, so it could be him.

I know who I want it to be, even if he's someone I'm nervous to talk to.

"It might be my father."

That makes Christian freeze. I watch his thoughts scramble desperately behind his eyes as he stares at me. It's annoying. My father's a sore spot between us—but I wouldn't have brought him up if I didn't feel it was necessary. He shouldn't walk on eggshells at a time like this.

He clears his throat. "Okay. So call him like how?"

"Like . . ." It strikes me that I've done this three times, apparently, only once on purpose. And never without a body. "I don't know. Dad, you there? I need to talk to you, so can you say something if you are?"

Nothing happens right away, but the only time that it was instant was with Mr. Walker, who was already on his feet. I wait, gazing down at the mirror and listening to the crickets, rustling leaves, and occasional flapping wings. I try not to focus on them too much; I try to keep my brain empty.

However, I do notice when the sounds start to fall away. First, the rustles become less until there are none. Then the flapping. Then the distant hoots and screeches of night birds. Last to go are the crickets.

The silence presses against my ears like they're stuffed with cotton. Is this what it is to have an empty head?

I pull my eyes away from the mirror, thoroughly creeped out. The sound doesn't come back. I open my mouth to ask Christian if the sounds have all disappeared for him too, but the sight of him makes me reel backward.

His eyes shine fully white and every visible inch of his skin looks like cracked ceramic. He looks like someone dropped him and shattered him into a thousand pieces and set him back together with lightning itself, the cracks shining viciously white blue and purple platinum.

"Christian!" I shout, the words floating out of me muffled like I'm screaming under water.

I scramble up on my knees, hands hovering uncertainly over him. I don't know what's happening. I don't know if I can do anything to help, or if trying to do something will make this worse. He looks alive. His chest rises and falls with breath, and every few seconds, he blinks.

Looking alive isn't good enough, though.

"Christian," I try again, the muffled sound almost unintelligible. "Look at me! Can you hear me?"

I can't tell. I can't even tell where he's looking—his eyes are two balls of light.

In the silence, the *whumf* of owl wings feels as loud as thunder. I look up at the sound to see a barn owl descending on the clearing, talons extending to land, wings spread behind him as he comes down. He lands on Christian's shoulder, talons gripping him securely as he folds his wings, staring in my direction. Christian doesn't react, still glowing and tranced out.

The owl ruffles his feathers, turning his head to the side at an uncomfortable-looking angle.

Christian opens his mouth to speak, but it's not his voice that comes out.

"He can't hear you," says my father, speaking through Christian. "Not now."

FOURTEEN

I stare at Christian, barely recognizable under the illuminated cracks across his face and his blank white stare. For a long moment, I'm speechless. Both Christian and the owl stare at me, waiting without prompting me.

It's not just the voice that gives my father away—it's the cadence, the dryness of tone, the rigid set of Christian's shoulders. That alone is disturbing; I've never seen a person become so unlike themselves so suddenly.

"Dad?" I ask finally. This time my voice sounds distant yet clear, like the last reflection of an echo.

"Yes, Jaxon?" asks my father, lightly, like this is a normal conversation.

I don't know what to say—or what to ask first. My heart is racing, pounding hard against my ribs, my throat feels tight. There are so many things I want to ask, and I know my first question should be about Christian, but the first question out of my mouth is:

"Dad . . . what *happened* to you?"

He considers me—or, I think he does; it's hard to tell where Christian's eyes are looking—taking a moment before deciding on an answer.

"I ran out of time."

I should have expected cryptic answers. However, that's the same phrasing Titi uses when she talks about Christian. I frown, narrowing my eyes at him.

"Were you undead?"

"Not exactly," he says. The owl turns its head to clean its feathers. "It's better that you don't know."

I bite my tongue, resisting the urge to push back on that. If I start arguing with him now, I'll waste time. I don't know how long this will last.

"Dad, I brought Christian back after he died. I brought him back, and I don't know what to do now because Titi says he's gonna drop dead if I don't find a way to pay Death the years he owes."

"That's how it works," he says plainly. "Death always gets its due, one way or another."

"Okay—fine." I'm beyond that at this point. Yes, alright, Death isn't going to look the other way. There are a million other questions beyond that. "So how do I do it? Do I have to trade human life?"

"How do you *do it*?" he admonishes, voice going hard with authority. "You're asking me how to sacrifice yourself for a friend? Did you forget you're speaking to your father?"

I wince. It's not that I *forgot*. It's that Christian is so prominent in my mind, it's hard to think straight about anything other than saving his life. It's hard to think straight about anything regarding Christian at all, actually.

I guess that's not fair. This *is* my dad, and I get why he'd have reservations about being open with me about this right now. But if he was like me, he must understand on some level, right?

How am I supposed to let it be?

"I'm sorry," I say earnestly. "This is *my* mess, Dad. It's my responsibility. Don't you think I should at least know what my options are?"

"I don't care if it *is* your responsibility—you're *my* son. It's my job to protect you."

I should have anticipated this. There's no impartial source of information for me to go to, not even in the spiritual world.

"Please," I insist. "This is *Christian* we're talking about, Dad. You *know* him, he used to come to our house all the time. He has parents too. You *knew* his dad, and Mami always says his parents were so nice to you both when she was pregnant with me. Can't you at least help me make an informed decision here?"

Dad goes quiet. I can't tell from his expression what he's thinking, but I press on, hoping that he's starting to see my perspective at least a little bit.

"You're saying *I* have to do it? I have to trade *my* life, or my remaining years, for his?"

"Jaxon," he says wearily. "Of course, you would have to make the *trade*. You're the necromancer. Is it really more palatable if I tell you it doesn't have to be *your* life that you trade? You feel ready, at sixteen, to deprive anyone else of their remaining years for Christian's sake?"

I press the heels of my hands against my eyes, but I don't feel any of the pressure. In fact, I don't feel anything at all. My body looks normal as far as I can see, but pressing my hands together and rubbing my palms against my jeans feels more like the memory of a sensation than actual feeling.

Glancing back, my physical body is sitting behind me, looking down at the mirror with eyes glazed over. It makes my head spin.

"Wait . . . this is . . . it's all in my head?"

"Not *all*," says my dad.

I squeeze my eyes shut—or I try, at least—but I can't stop seeing. It's like my eyelids are transparent.

"I don't *know* that I'm ready," I start again, trying to stay focused. "Maybe I'm not. But let *me* decide. When do I need to decide by? How would I even start?"

"Jaxon. These aren't simple questions with simple answers."

I glare in spite of myself. Obviously, it would be great if it *was* simple. I wouldn't be here if I hadn't figured out by now that it isn't. I can't lose my head about it; I need to get answers. I need *help*.

"I *know* that," I assure him. "But I don't know anything outside of a handful of things Titi has told me. If you can offer me any help at all, it would mean everything to me."

Dad hesitates for a long time. Christian's expression doesn't change, while the owl's stare burns through me. If he refuses me, we've hit a wall. We can't exactly go kill someone in Christian's place in the hope that it'll save him.

"Sometimes we have to face the natural consequences of our mistakes," he says stiffly. "Taking responsibility often means that, too."

That's not what I'm trying to hear. He's looking for reasons to refuse that don't amount to "I'm your dad and I say no." That's hollow. It's not a real reason to do nothing. Learning a life lesson by letting a kid my age die traumatically twice even though I might be able to do something? It's bullshit.

"You died knowing a lot more about who I am than I do," I say, trying not to sound angry or petulant. "If there's really nothing I can do, then there's nothing I can do. But I don't have you here with me to help figure that out. If you won't even help me now, did you seriously not even leave behind something to help me figure out more about who *you* were? Just a watch? I need to at least *know* I can't help before I give up."

My dad sits in reluctant silence for a long moment, the owl's eyes boring into mine. At length, he speaks through Christian again. "Go to the filing cabinet in your mother's morgue with the tax papers in the accordion file. Lift the file and take the notebook underneath. It was mine. It might help you understand."

My jaw almost drops. I didn't expect him to cave. I wonder what he'd look like right now if he was really here. Angry? Frightened? Maybe dry and stone-faced like always. I wish I'd had more time to get a sense of what he was like in a situation like this. I never gave him trouble when he was home; I didn't want him to have any reasons to leave home again.

"Does Mami know it's in there?"

"She didn't," he says, his tone softening slightly, "when I was alive."

Something in me shrivels at the thought of helping my dad keep a secret from my mom even after he's dead. When Christian's alright, I'm going to show her. I'll tell her everything if I come out of this alright too.

"If I call you again . . ." I start, not sure I want to ask. He wasn't around before. Why start now?

"I'll try to come," he offers. I try not to let the disappointment show in my face. "It's not always easy. Much easier with a body."

"Is Christian gonna be okay after being your host, or . . . ?"

The owl turns to look at Christian, observing him as the white light emanates from the cracks in his skin. The owl extends his wings, preparing for flight.

"I'm not sure," admits my dad. "Every time has been different."

I wonder how many times he's been called this way. Before I can ask, the owl releases Christian's shoulder and takes flight. I watch it go but I only see a glimpse of it soaring up into the canopy, the stars so bright they shine through the leaves like they're made of gossamer.

In the next second, something yanks me from behind my belly button, bringing me crashing back into my body. I gasp, coughing like I'm emerging from being underwater too long, as I catch myself with my hands against the earth.

All the sounds of the forest come rushing back at once, making my ears pound. I clamp my hands over them, squeezing my eyes shut, and everything from the pressure of my hands against my head to the darkness of my eyelids feels comfortingly real. I groan as my body starts making peace with being solid again.

When I open my eyes, Christian is slumped over on the ground with his head dangerously close to a candle. He's pale, the skin under his eyes dark, and his nose is bleeding profusely, blood dripping across his face.

"Christian!" I scramble to snuff out the candle before crawling on my knees to get beside him, shaking his shoulder. "What the fuck!"

He's unconscious, head lolling slightly when I move him. I need to be careful what I say and do when I'm freaked out, but it's hard to think straight. His skin feels cold when I grip his jaw in one hand, his blood smearing onto my fingers as I lean down to listen for his breathing, watching his chest.

His lungs wheeze softly, chest rising and falling. It's a tiny movement. I close my eyes, trying to suss out if I can feel the life inside him, and it's weaker than before. I need to put both my hands on him to make it out: a faint, flickering buzz under his skin like a lightbulb with a filament close to burning out.

A little bit. Just to keep him going. Focus.

"Christian," I say, trying to keep my voice steady. "Not yet, okay? Not yet. Wake up."

Christian's eyes snap open. He coughs and chokes on some of the blood from his nosebleed as he reaches up to fist his hands in my shirt. I help him sit up, thumping my hand against his back.

"Ah, pinche vida despreciable," he groans, pressing his wrist against his nose and looking down at himself, dirt and blood decorating the collar of his sweater. "Aw, dude, what *was* that?"

I stare at him, unnerved by his underreaction. A couple drops of blood fall from my nose, nowhere near the amount that's gushed out of Christian's face. But he's not *acting* any worse for the wear. That's good. This is good.

"You're an insane person. Are you okay?!"

"Ah . . ." Christian blinks hard like he's dizzy, looking down at his shaking hands as he licks the blood off his upper lip. "Not really. I blacked the fuck out."

"My—my dad. He talked *through* you!"

Christian looks at me, eyes going round in shock. After a beat, a grin spreads across his bloody face before he laughs in disbelief, looking at the mirror, then back at me.

"*What*!" He laughs again, pushing a hand back through his hair. "It worked? It worked! Oh—"

He winces like he's remembered something, hastily softening some of the intensity in his expression into something like concern.

"Are you okay, Jax?"

I laugh shakily at the ridiculousness of him and his train of thought. It's nice of him to worry about me in the throes of his occult nerdery while his life is literally hanging by a thread. Weird and shouldn't be his highest priority, but nice. I reach out for him to help him stand, feeling for the vibration of him again as surreptitiously as I can.

Better. Not much stronger, but it's grown constant and steady.

"I definitely wouldn't say I'm okay. It was scary as fuck, and it was extra bad because my dad's voice was coming out of *you*."

"I'm sorry," he says, genuinely like any part of it is his fault. "Did it help?"

Not nearly as much as I hoped it would. We're at least not walking away empty-handed and Christian's still hanging on. We have to keep pushing forward.

"I think so. I hope so. I gotta find something at home."

"Let's go, then!" Christian's eyes sparkle with promise, trying to take a few steps but staggering, knees still weak. I put my arm around him, letting him put most of his weight against me.

"You can't even walk, man. I'm not bringing you to my house, you'll be knocking shit over left and right."

"I can walk!" he lies. "Give me a minute!"

I watch him as he struggles to recover his strength, knees buckling. He keeps close to me as he steadies himself. Even when he manages to gain his bearings, he looks pale and exhausted and all the worse for being covered in blood. It can't be good for him to push his body to its limits in his condition.

"I'm gonna get you home, okay? You need to rest. You shouldn't push yourself too hard."

"Jaxon!"

I continue before he can say more. "I don't want you getting *hurt*, Christian. I need you to be okay."

He looks at me when I say that and, even though I know he wants to keep the mischief going, a small smile graces his face. He bumps against me, playful and affectionate rather than clumsy. I roll my eyes as I push him gently, watching the cogs turning in his head as he hesitates, thinking of something to say that'll keep me from dragging him back home.

"I can't go back like this," he insists, gesturing at his bloody face. "And I feel like I ran a hundred miles in the middle of a fucking blizzard. Let's go to 7-Eleven!"

"Christian . . ." I squint, though I already know I'm going to give in.

"Please? Come on. Then I'll go home, promise. I'll buy us that hot cocoa!"

It's a bad idea. Sneaking back into the house is gonna be nerve-racking enough without dragging this out longer, plus I'm afraid of running him ragged while I only have a flimsy understanding of the amount of life left in him, especially now that we've got something of a lead. But he really does look bad. If we can get him cleaned up and maybe even something to eat . . .

"Fine," I say, sighing as Christian cheers. "But this is it. For real."

"¡Simón! Definitely."

I jab my elbow into his ribs gently. "Can't you just say 'yes'? Weirdo."

The cashier at 7-Eleven barely bats an eye at me and Christian walking in dirty, bloody, and carrying candles and a mirror. I recognize her—she was one of the seniors that graduated when I was a freshman—but she doesn't recognize either of us. She sits behind the counter, chair leaned back on two legs, spitting sunflower shells into an empty Coke bottle as she looks at her phone. When we walk in, she glances up, squints, then turns back to her phone.

"I'll look for first aid stuff," I say, starting to head toward the back aisles. "You look for cocoa, I guess."

"I think they still have hot dogs!"

I bite back the many thoughts I have on eating 7-Eleven hot dogs that have been sitting in the warmer for God knows how long and carry on. Christian should eat, even if it's a lukewarm tube of mystery meat. I'm not positive what eating will do for him, but Mami always makes me eat when I've been sick or anxious, and it usually helps.

The first aid section of 7-Eleven is tiny, which isn't surprising. I find an overpriced box of gauze and a bottle of isopropyl alcohol, which is good enough for our purposes. I look for something to help him regain a little more of his strength—magnesium, maybe?—but there's nothing like that. Food will have to be enough. We're not far from his house anyway.

I come up to the front, where Christian waits at the counter, chatting up the cashier as he pays for the food and cocoa. Even though he looks like he's lost a fight and she couldn't be less interested in us when we walked in, he's managed to charm her enough that she's laughing at whatever dumb joke he's telling her now, pale freckly cheeks pink with mirth. I place the stuff on the counter, and Christian gestures at them.

"This, too," he says, grinning. "Jaxon, remember Becca? She went to school with us!"

"Uh," I squint at her. "Kind of?"

"Well, anyway," he continues, "lemme know when the next bonfire is! We'll pull up!"

"Yeah, you got it," says Becca, finishing ringing him up. "That'll be $11.68."

Christian pulls his wallet out of his back pocket, handing her a twenty, then sticking the change he gets back in the jar for St. Jude's hospital.

"Thank you!" she says, grinning as we gather our things before heading out to the parking lot.

"I don't get how you get people to like you so much," I say as we walk toward the big willow tree at the far end of the lot. "I mean, we were little dorks when she was in high school with us. There's no way she remembers us."

"We're still little dorks," he counters, grinning. "But I'm cute now."

I roll my eyes, sitting on the bench behind the willow branches. "You look the same, just taller." I can't look him in the face when I say it. It's unfair how he looks good even when he's pale and covered in blood and dirt.

"Yeah." The way he eases himself into the bench beside me rather than flopping himself down is a sure sign he doesn't feel nearly as well as he's acting. "Tall is cute!"

"Well fuck me, I guess." I turn to him, opening up the box of gauze and pausing to pour a little alcohol over my fingers before I take a piece. "Christian, tell me for real how you're feeling. I need to know if you're holding up, okay?"

Christian shakes his head, then pushes his glasses back up on his head, sitting and leaning his face in for me to clean up. I start dabbing at the blood caked on his face. It comes off easily, still fresh and tacky.

"I feel tired. Like really tired."

That makes my stomach churn sourly. That could mean any-thing. We've never done this before; it could be a normal response to using the scrying mirror. Or his life could be sputtering out of him right in front of me even after it seemed to steady in the woods.

"Can you hold on really quick?" I ask him. "I mean, can you sit there quietly?"

Christian blinks at me. "Sure . . . ? Why?"

"This is gonna sound weird, but I need to feel you for a second."

I place my hands against his cheeks and close my eyes, trying to push all thoughts of feeling embarrassed to do something like this out of my head. It *is* embarrassing to be cradling a hot guy's face right now, even if it is Christian. But I have to try harder to get the hang of sensing where he's at.

Taking a deep, slow breath through my nostrils, I try to empty my mind of everything except the energy signature of his life force.

It's there. About the same as it was last time I felt it. He's alright. It's holding steady. I let go of him, keeping my eyes closed as I reach blindly for one of the willow branches. Christian guides my wrist after I miss a couple of times, staying silent and letting go of me as soon as my hand touches one of the reeds. I ignore the way the light touch of his fingers makes my heart race.

It takes a couple seconds to acclimate. Once I find it, the current of the tree is so strong in comparison my eyes snap open in surprise. Christian's is *barely* a fraction of the strength.

Trees are long-lived, obviously. But a willow? Maybe fifty years with some luck? Christian's got next to nothing left.

"Jaxon . . . ?" Christian reaches for my hand again. As soon as his fingers touch my wrist, a jolt of static shock makes us both jump. My heart almost stops. For a split second, I'm sure I've killed Christian, but he just shakes his fingers, cringing.

"¡*Ay*, pinche madre!" he yelps.

"Are you okay?!" I take his face in both hands again, shaking. "Hold on, hold on—"

Christian reaches for *my* face, pulling his sleeve over his wrist and plugging it against my nose. "Jax, you're *bleeding*, dude."

"Shut up, shut up," I say, squeezing my eyes shut and focusing on him. After a few frantic seconds, I let out a breath when I find it. Still going, still steady—a little stronger? Maybe I zapped a little life into him again without meaning to. Even without the sickle . . . maybe it moved from me to him?

When I open my eyes again, Christian's still dabbing away the blood from my nose.

"Lot of blood tonight," he comments casually, though his face is visibly flushed even under the traces of blood still smeared on him. "Necromancy is messy business, I guess . . ."

I let go of his cheeks, suddenly self-conscious now that I've regained some amount of my wits about me.

"You're okay," I tell him, pretending I wasn't intimately

touching his face for an extended amount of time. "I can feel it. You're still doing okay."

"You can feel it . . ." he echoes, smiling slightly. "You can tell by touching me?"

I nod. "I'm still figuring it out. But I can tell."

Christian searches my face, though I'm sure he can't make out the full details of it without his glasses on in the dark.

"I trust you, ¿sabes?" He smiles a little brighter at me, enough affection in his eyes to make me look away in a bout of shyness. "I believe we're gonna figure this out."

"I really hope so," I mutter, watching his hands to avoid looking at his eyes. The fresh stain of blood on his cuff prompts me to check my nose, but my blood has already dried stiffly against my skin. "All this gauze we bought and you went and used your sleeve."

I chance a look up at Christian's face. He wrinkles his brow, confused, before he registers that I'm talking about the nosebleed a moment later.

"¿Qué? Oh . . ." He laughs at himself, shrugging. "Se me olvidó. I guess let's finish cleaning each other up now."

"Okay."

We sit for a while, eating in bashful silence after we've managed to clean off as much of the blood on us as possible, blushing and laughing awkwardly all the while. It's funny, getting up so close to Christian's face, getting an extended look at all the components that make him such a pretty boy up close. It's embarrassing, too, knowing he's looking just as close. I wish I knew what he thinks about my face, if he thinks it looks as nice up close as I think his does.

Then again, maybe it's better not to know.

It strikes me how weird it is that I came out here with him of my own volition, without Regan having pushed me into it. It's only been a couple days since Christian's accident, but after tonight it feels like that was eons ago.

Even this morning feels like ages ago. I was so angry with him earlier, and now we're here. I've never had a hard time staying angry before. Everything feels so unreal now that my biggest worry is Christian dying.

"Do you think . . ." I clear my throat, trying to think of how best to phrase this. "Should we talk to Rhys tomorrow? See if we can find out if he saw anything during the whole cafeteria thing?"

Christian pushes his glasses up his nose by the bridge, smiling hopefully. "Yeah! That's a good idea! You wanna sit together at lunch?"

I can't look at him because this is embarrassing to say, especially after I insulted Rhys and them today. "If Rhys wants to. And Ava. If they're pissed at me, then—"

"They're not!" Christian says quickly. "They're really not. They know they weren't cool to you before. I talked to them; I promise, they'll be nice. Rhys and Ava are really chill!"

"Then, yeah, alright."

He beams so bright it takes everything in me not to roll my eyes in secondhand embarrassment. I want to ask him if my approval only means so much to him because I'm the one that resurrected him, but I don't want to embarrass him. And I really don't want the answer to be yes.

"How are you feeling?" I ask him.

"I feel good," he says, smiling a little softer at me.

It'll hold. It's scary to leave him until morning, but I think he'll hold. Even in the shadow of the willow tree, I can tell the color is back in his face.

"Then I should get you back home."

That dims his megawatt smile a fraction. He nods, gathering all our trash in the plastic bag. "Okay. Let's go."

FİFTEEN

Christian leaves me at his doorstep with a reminder that tomorrow is '80s Day at school. I don't know what he's expecting from me, but if Twin Day was embarrassing to participate in accidentally, '80s Day on purpose will kill me.

I walk back home, wondering how Christian has room in his head for that kind of bullshit, and the walk is refreshing until I get close to my house. Where the air had been seasonally chill and filled with the soft rustling of leaves and nocturnal animals all along the way, the entire atmosphere around my house is as frozen over as a February blizzard.

My mom's sitting in one of the high-backed wooden rocking chairs on the porch, her hands on the armrests. I know she's seen me because I'm the only person walking on the street at this hour, but she doesn't move. Frost coats my insides, starting at the pit of my stomach before blooming out to the rest of me. I'm already caught so I keep walking until I'm climbing up the porch steps.

Mami watches me approach with narrowed eyes like chips of ice, her lips pressed tightly together, nostrils blown wide like she's holding back a scream. She probably is.

When she speaks, her voice is dangerously quiet. "What the *hell* do you think you're doing, running around outside at this hour?"

I look down at my feet, knowing I don't have much wiggle room to make stuff up while I'm holding a black mirror and candles. Whatever details I wanna omit, I can't leave out these crucial ones.

"I'm sorry, Mami."

"*I'm sorry, Mami*," she echoes, standing up and pulling her robe tighter around herself. "Jaxon, you be as mad as you want that I hid this stuff from you! But you don't get to act out like this, you hear me? Do you know what it's like to look for you in the middle of the night and find you *gone*?"

"I'm not acting out; I swear, I'm not."

"Get inside!" she demands.

I follow her into the main parlor downstairs as she turns on some of the low lights, pointing me toward one of the couches. I sit on it, setting the candles and the mirror beside me gently. Mami sits in the imperious-looking vintage armchair across from me, looking like an angry queen in her robe and satin bonnet.

"This *is* acting out, Jaxon. Hiding things, running off in the middle of the night without asking anyone. Tienes suerte que no te doy un cocotazo con ese espejo. What's gotten *into* you?"

I stare at my hands for a long time, examining the pale crescents at the ends of my nail beds. My mom's voice is thin with panic, even though she's trying to sound hard, but she's right. I *am* lucky she doesn't whack me upside the head with my mirror. It hurts, having to think about how much to say to my mom or what to leave out. Feeling anxious about talking to my mom makes me nauseous, so I lean forward, resting my elbows over my knees and dropping my head in my hands.

"Talk to me, baby," she says, her tone still strangled with worry.

I shake my head. Whatever I could consider telling my mom, I can't tell Titi Clío. Mami respects her authority on magic stuff and Titi's going to stay firmly on the no-helping-Christian side of this. Plus, ever since the situation with Mr. Walker, I can't get the thought that she might be awake, listening from somewhere, out of my head.

It takes me a long time to answer her verbally, but Mami waits like she always does.

"Can we go for a drive?" I ask. "A short one?"

Mami raises her eyebrows, searching my eyes with worry plain on her face. She looks at the grandfather clock in the corner, the big hand starting to creep toward the two already.

"Mi amor . . ." she murmurs, uncertainly.

"Please?" I insist, swallowing thickly. "Just you and me?"

She considers me for a long moment, thin brows drawn together, eyes brimming with concern. She stands up, sighing as she reties the sash on her robe.

"A really short one, Jaxon. You have to be up in the morning."

"*Thank you*," I say in a rush of love for her. She gets me. "That's fine. Short is fine."

I wrap her up in a tight hug. She folds her arms around me immediately, one hand reaching up to press my head against her shoulder.

She kisses the side of my head, letting out a long, shaky sigh. Her eyes are bright, fingers trembling against my arms. Guilt settles like a hot brick in my chest.

"Don't think this means you aren't grounded," she reminds me.

Whatever upset I feel about that is drowned out by how glad

I am that this moment, at least, feels normal. I nod before pulling back to look at her.

"Can I drive?"

"At two in the morning?" She gives a firm shake of her head. "*No*. It's past curfew and *you* really don't need more trouble tonight."

It's not illegal if she's with me, but I don't protest. This is the most surefire way of getting her alone with no possibility of interruptions—and even if I can't say all the things I wanna tell her right now, I miss being alone with my mom.

We take Mami's car. It's the little blue sedan my dad bought her after he got a big advance on one of his books almost ten years ago. The barn owl feather attached to the rearview mirror sends an electric chill up my spine; I reach up, running my finger along the ends of the barbs.

Mami drives in silence for a minute or two. I lean my head against the window, trying to sort through my thoughts as I watch the headlights illuminate the fog in front of us. She keeps both hands on the steering wheel, manicured nails biting into the leather steering wheel cover, but she looks composed otherwise.

"Um . . ." I start, glancing up at the feather between us. "I was . . . I was talking to Dad tonight."

Mami turns to me, meeting my eyes. She opens her mouth, takes a deep breath in, then nods, turning her eyes back on the road.

"With that mirror?"

"Yeah."

It's silent for a long moment. Her hands flex against the wheel.

"Did it work?"

I look ahead, watching the way the fog curls along the mossy borders of the road. "Yeah, it did."

Mami blinks a few times, staring straight ahead. She takes another deep breath and worries her bottom lip, considering her reply. "What did he tell you?"

I know she believes me because she has every reason to; this kind of magic stuff is more real to her than it is to me, given how long she's known about it. But it's hard not to feel like I need to prove myself, especially with all the lying I *have* been doing recently.

"He kinda went off on me a little. Because I was asking about the kind of sacrifice we'd need to bring Christian all the way back to life."

Mami doesn't respond right away, though her head swivels to look at me in alarm. She takes a while to think it over. Her lips thin as she thinks, corners of her eyes wrinkling, brow furrowed.

"Well . . . es tu papá. You can't expect him to endorse an idea that starts with you sacrificing *anything*."

"I know. In the end, I think he wanted to help me at least understand everything better, even if it means I might do something he doesn't want me to do."

"Jaxon," she says, shaking her head. "You need to catch me up here. A sacrifice of *yourself*? For Christian? Is that what we're talking about?"

"I'm not sure about anything. I'm still trying to figure it all out."

Mami's posture is rigid as she keeps shaking her head like she doesn't want to hear anything I'm saying.

"There's no planet—there's no *universe*—where I would allow you to do something like that."

"I understand," I say gently. I do—she's my mom, just like my dad is my dad. They're supposed to put me before everything, but that's what makes it harder for them to understand *my* position. "I'm not sure it has to be as cut-and-dried as 'I die so Christian lives'. What if there's another way? Shouldn't I at least try to find that out?"

"Do you *actually* think there's another way?" she asks, looking at me sidelong.

"I don't know," I admit. "But *what if* there is? I don't think it's impossible. This stuff—necromancy—it's too big to keep stumbling around in the dark like I've been. Titi doesn't want me digging about how to help Christian either. I don't know if she told you that I had something else happen."

"Baby," she says, taking a hand off the wheel to squeeze my knee reassuringly, though her tone takes on a slight authoritative edge, "forget what she might have told me or might not have told me. Talk to me."

There's something comforting about being in this position. Everything feels like it's spiraling out of control, but my mom always speaks with finality and intention. She makes my wheels stop spinning out.

I spill about Mr. Walker and how he turned to dust, the weird link between me and Christian, the way I'm starting to sense people's life force to the point where I can tell if they've got a long time ahead of them or not. Mami pulls over on the side of the road, squeezing the back of my neck as she leans close to search my face.

"Jaxon, I had no idea." She sighs, pressing the heels of her hands against her eyes. "Baby, I'm sorry."

"It's not your fault," I say, wrapping my arms around myself to grip my elbows. "I want to do something right. Or at least feel like I know what I'm doing. I want to *choose* what I do, not let things go haywire around me."

Mami looks at me when I say that, eyebrows knitting closer together, dark eyes heavy with anxiety. She shakes her head, reaching over to place a hand over mine.

"Jadiel tried to help, you said?"

"Yeah, I think." It wasn't exactly *direct*, but he wasn't exactly *willing* either. "I had to wear him down. If he'd talked to me about all this when he was alive, maybe none of this would have happened. It doesn't make any sense to me that he left me in the dark like this."

Mami grimaces in empathy for Dad, pressing her hand against her chest. "Your dad was always afraid of his abilities. Sometimes he worried there was something dark, I guess, or *evil* about them. Clío always had an easier time embracing it. When I got pregnant with you, he wanted desperately for you to be a normal kid. He was so scared of passing that stuff onto you, but we wanted to have you so badly. Eventually your dad made his peace with his abilities, though he still hoped you wouldn't have them. He was scared for you."

"I guess," I mutter, shrugging as I cast my eyes down to my knees. "It feels like he put so much distance between us because of that. I've been missing him since *before* he died. I never got a real chance to get to know him, and now it's like there's this whole part of *myself* I can't figure out, either."

"He really loved you, Jaxon," she says gently. "He kept some distance because he was paranoid he'd rub off on you, but I never saw him happier than the day you were born. You know he's the one that handed you to me?"

I sigh, pressing my forehead against the cool glass of the passenger side window. "I know, Mami."

"You were born feet first with your cord wrapped around your neck, and the doctors thought you wouldn't make it."

I've heard this story about a thousand times. I squeeze my eyes shut, letting her tell it because she feels like it proves my dad and I had a bond.

"You were all purple, and the doctors were worried because you didn't cry. Jadiel went right over and picked you up, and you smiled. You didn't open your eyes, you just smiled. They said you were born asleep."

I have a hard time imagining my dad looking anything but stone-faced or curious. I remember the sound of his laugh better than the sight of it. I remember his smile only because Mami and Dad's wedding photo is up in the second-floor sitting room; all the other photos of him around the house are neutral-faced if not plain sullen. When I picture my dad carrying me over to my mom on what she claims was the happiest day of his life, all I see is my father's arched brows raised in curiosity as he looks down at a purple-faced infant covered in blood and gunk.

I scrub a hand across my face, slumping forward. No matter how I try to change the picture in my head, it hurts too much to imagine my dad looking excited to see me. I wish we could have spent more time together. I wish I could go back in time and tell him to get over it, I was never going to turn out a normal kid.

"Yo sé, Mami."

She reaches over, brushing her thumb over my eyebrows, smoothing them down neater.

"When you finally opened your eyes, your father burst into

tears, you know that? The doctors said it was only about twenty minutes after you were born, but it felt like hours."

That's even harder to picture. Mami presses her palm against my cheek and sighs, wiping the corners of her eyes delicately with the tip of her finger.

"Tell me what *you* want to do."

I press my face against her palm, wishing I could think straight. I need space from everything and everyone. I want to press pause on the world and go sit in the woods for a few days.

"I want to find out *if* there's anything I can do for Christian. Before it's too late."

"Alright." She sighs, brushing her hand over the back of my head, then returning to the wheel, pulling back onto the road. "And Clío . . . ?"

"She's completely against the idea. Won't hear two ways about it."

Mami nods, shrugging slightly like she can't blame her. "It's scary for us to hear you talk about this. We love you."

I can't really argue with that. All of this is crazy. "I know. I get it."

"I'll talk to her," says my mom. "Maybe she can give us a couple days alone while you sort things out. Then she can meet you, me, and Regan up in Salem for your birthday?"

"On Halloween? The Pike is gonna be a parking lot, Mami."

"We can figure it out."

I try to bite my tongue, but I can't stop myself.

"Christian might be dead again by then," I moan, pressing my head against the glass again. "I don't think I'm gonna be in a party mood if that happens."

Mami falls silent for almost a full minute, eyebrows knitted together in worry as she stares out at the road. She squeezes the wheel so hard the leather squeaks against her palms softly, then she clears her throat before she speaks.

"He might not," she says softly.

"Well, we'd still be waiting for it."

She looks at me sidelong for a moment, sighing. "You know, I understand what you're trying to say. I know it feels like your responsibility to make things right. And I know it hurts letting nature run its course. But sometimes that *is* the right thing to do."

I watch the ground as it rolls by in the car window, clouds of steam rising up like wraiths intermittently from the heat of the car passing by.

"Do you really think letting him die without even trying to find a solution is the right thing to do?"

She weighs my question for a while, then, "I'm always going to pick the answer that keeps you out of danger, Jaxon."

I turn to look at her. "That's not really a yes."

She looks at me meaningfully. "It is a yes, for me."

I sit up, rounding my shoulders as I rub a hand over my face and hair. It wouldn't be fair to get frustrated with her. Between Mami and anyone else in the world, I wouldn't even think before choosing her.

But if I'm choosing between my safety and making Christian die twice, that's not really a choice.

"I'm going to try."

It's a relief to say it out loud, even though my throat tightens painfully and the skin around my eyes goes hot, tears stinging at the corners. My chest feels lighter, like my ribs had been made of lead before and now they're blood and bone again.

She slows on the road, blinking hard.

"I know, Jaxon." She sighs, resigned.

I know she's not happy, but it feels like acceptance. I press my hands against my eyes to stop the tears of relief from running. I swallow hard, trying to breathe normally. I'm shaking, lungs stammering for air. It's nothing like a panic attack; what I feel more than anything is release.

"Mami," I mumble, my voice thick and tight with tears, "I really want your help."

"We're almost home," she says, pulling brown napkins out of the glove compartment and piling them on my lap. "Okay? We'll get you to bed and talk it over tomorrow."

I wipe my eyes and nose with the napkins, wadding them tightly in my fists as the tears keep coming. Of all the people to have to see me like this, I'm grateful it's my mom, but I can feel her low-level panic in the way she grips my forearm as she drives.

"I'm okay, I'm just—"

"Of course you are," she says, reassuring both of us at once. "Of course you're okay."

At home, Mami makes me sit down to eat a slice of pound cake with a glass of milk because she firmly believes in solving all problems with food. She sits beside me at the kitchen table, watching the minutes tick away on the digital clock on the stove. Under the low lights, Mami's face looks gray with exhaustion. I can't imagine I look any better.

"Can I sleep in your room?" I ask when the digits on the stove read 2:30 a.m.

She pulls her arm around my shoulders, leaning in to kiss the top of my head. "Always, baby."

It's nice, having the comfort of someone alive and breathing in the same room as me when I'm alone in the dark with my thoughts. That's part of why I want to stay in my mom's room, comforted by the chemical smell of her work clothes in the hamper combined with the various scented lotions and body sprays she applies every day.

The other part is because I know my mom well enough to know she'll hop in the shower before going back to bed. It's part of her bedtime routine, and the drive we took disturbed the night too much for her to go straight back to sleep. If I take the time to look for the key to the cabinet my father told me about now, it won't be suspicious when she comes back to find me there.

While she's in the bathroom, I search her room. She took another shower earlier, so I know I only have fifteen, twenty minutes tops before she's back. Mami keeps her room pretty tidy and organized. There are a few spots I can think of where she would have extra, non-everyday-use keys.

I start with the miscellaneous drawer—formerly my father's sock and underwear drawer. As I look carefully through the various small boxes separating like knickknacks from different ones— lighters, earrings with lost matches, HDMI cords, Sharpies—I swallow back my guilt. I know I'm doing one more thing behind her back, but I can't afford to lose any piece that might help me with Christian.

The junk drawer is a bust, so I move over to the bedside table, first checking under the small potted ivy plant, then under the lamp, and finally opening the small drawer. The book my mom's reading is in there—some nonfiction thing about death across cultures—along with a box of lotion, tissues, and a ring with keys of various sizes. The smallest of them looks like it would unlock a little kid's diary; the biggest is barely smaller than a standard house key.

It seems like a good bet. While I don't have enough time to run down to the morgue to try them now, I have enough time to stash them before my mom gets back. I zip over to my room, flipping the lights on. Grim's curled up on my bed, blinking up at me in annoyance for waking her.

"Sorry," I whisper. I stick the keys in one of my backpack's side pockets.

While I'm here, I take a minute to make sure everything else is where I left it. The pocket watch is in the opposite side pocket and the mirror is still in the bigger compartment, wrapped in its scarf. The sickle doesn't fit with my books, so I leave it stashed under my mattress for now.

Grim rubs herself against my legs. I scoop her up, scratching under her chin as she purrs loudly against me.

"All set for tomorrow, girl," I tell her, burying my face against her fur for a moment.

"Sweetheart?" Mami says from my doorway, startling me into dropping Grim. "Sorry. Are you gonna sleep here after all?"

"No! Uh . . ." I shrug. "I don't know. The kids at school said it's '80s Day tomorrow. I hate that kinda shit but . . ."

She smiles, the expression almost nostalgic on her face. "Why don't you wear your *Evil Dead* hoodie? That counts."

That is, easily, the most '80s appropriate thing in my closet. It's one of the few brightly colored pieces of clothing I own. I don't actually plan on following tomorrow's theme, I just wanted to say something other than *I was shoving a key I stole from your room into my backpack*. But thinking about it now . . .

Then I remember.

"Uh . . . Christian wore that out of here. I haven't seen it since."

"Death by Stereo then," says my mom, heading to her room.

The hoodie is hanging from a hook in my closet. Mami gave it to me a few Christmases ago. It's a black zip-up with white, electric looking letters across the back reading "Death by Stereo" under a screaming skull that looks like it's being electrocuted by the letters.

I feel stupid thinking about '80s Day, even as a cover for what I'm up to. But I smile a little. It *is* kind of a cool hoodie.

I take it off the hook, draping it over my backpack for tomorrow. It's not like I'm going to do anything else. Regan and Christian are the only ones who'll get it anyway.

SIXTEEN

Walking into school in the morning is embarrassing. It's not so much embarrassing for *me*—it's second-hand embarrassing. Each year has a different decade to emulate: Freshmen get the '60s, sophomores the '70s, juniors the '80s, and seniors the '90s. It's the senior student body council that decides the Spirit Week themes, so it's no coincidence the seniors got off easy for today. The Davies twins pass by me in their '90s looks: Rhys wears a flannel and jeans, hair tied back at the nape of his neck, black and silver strands of hair loose around his face. Rhiannon wears a burgundy skort with a white crop top and one of those fake plastic tattoo chokers.

Rhys smiles at me. Rhiannon makes eye contact. I don't know how to react to them, so I settle for raising a hand in greeting and move along.

Sophomores are easy to spot by all the giant sunglasses and tie-dye they broke out, and most of the freshmen were too self-conscious to do more than a tie or a Peter Pan collar for the '60s. The juniors, though . . .

Regan and Christian stand at the lockers looking . . . well, kind of dumb. Regan's got sections of her ponytail crimped, tied closer to the top of her head than usual with a scrunchie the color of one of those vaporwave Dixie cups. She's wearing a clear pink plastic jacket over a rainbow striped ringer t-shirt and a denim skirt with electric blue bike shorts underneath. Two pink plastic hearts the size of tealight candles dangle from her ears. It's insane-looking, but I always think Regan looks pretty.

Beside her, Christian's in my red *Evil Dead* hoodie with the sleeves rolled up. A blue shirt collar peeks up from the top, his shirt tails showing underneath. He's in acid-washed jeans that I'm pretty sure he acid-washed himself and a pair of blinding white sneakers. He braided his hair into two neat cornrows that meet in a curly puff at the back of his head. It doesn't look '80s, but it looks nice. There's no sense denying at this point that I always find him nice to look at.

To myself, anyway. I might still deny it if anyone asks.

"This is more embarrassing than yesterday," I groan as I approach them.

Close up, Christian's got visible shadows under his eyes. I frown at him, the usual worries churning in my stomach. Christian grins, greeting me like usual.

We *were* up late last night, I remind myself. It could be that. I'll check on him as soon as I get a second.

"Oh my God!" Regan grabs my shoulders and wrestles my backpack off, spinning me around to face her. "Look what he wore!"

This is the reaction I was hoping for. Christian gasps in delight, stepping back into my line of vision to point at his ear. He has a fang dangling off one of his earrings.

"Death by Stereo! Same thought!"

I can't stop the smile pulling at the corners of my mouth, but I roll my eyes, with more feeling.

"Yeah, same thought."

Regan, Christian, and I discovered *The Lost Boys* in summer of sixth grade. The dark-haired vampire that dies by stereo was a sexual awakening for all three of us, I'm pretty sure.

"I like your sweater." I nod at him and place my arm around Regan's shoulder, pulling her into my side for a brief squeeze. "And you look like a nutcase, Regan."

"I think I look cute," she says, squeezing her arms around my middle.

"Yeah, you do."

Christian looks down at himself, pressing his hands against the *Evil Dead* decal of the hand bursting out of the earth.

"I can give this back," he says, smiling apologetically. "I probably should have by now . . ."

I shake my head. The idea of taking anything from him feels shitty. Besides, whatever happens, I won't be able to look at that hoodie without thinking of him.

"It looks better on you," I blurt without thinking, blushing immediately because what the fuck? Did I really say that? "I . . . I mean . . . I don't wear bright things like that a lot, so."

Christian's cheeks light up peachy pink, ears bright red. He rubs at his cheek like it'll make the rush of heat back down, looking at the ground, smiling.

"Uh . . . thanks, dude!"

Regan taps her fingers against my ribs and presses her lips together, dimples forming in her cheeks as she tries not to laugh.

"Um," she starts, clearing her throat, "he changed his hair, too. Really cute, right?"

I shove her away from me gently, but when Christian turns redder and takes his glasses off to polish them with the sleeve of my sweater, I know I don't have any other recourse. I guess I *won't* deny it if anyone asks after all.

"Yeah, it looks good. You look really good, Christian. Jacob's Barrow's resident heartthrob for sure." It's hard to resist embarrassing him when he's already flustered, even if I'm embarrassing *myself,* too.

Anyway, it's not like he doesn't know he's cute.

Christian's still blushing, furiously wiping at the lenses of his glasses like the force of his blush fogged them up. The brightness of his smile lights up his face more than the pinkness of his cheeks. When he's wiped his glasses to satisfaction, he sets them back on his face, adjusting his collar as he beams at me.

"Thanks," he says, as genuine as ever. "I think you look good, too. You always look . . . uh. You always look great. I gotta go find Jae, so I'll see you at lunch? Yeah, see you at lunch!"

With that, he hefts his backpack onto his shoulders, hurrying off down the hall. Regan waits until he's around the corner before she bursts out laughing, punching my shoulder a few times.

"What was that?!" She laughs again, eyes wide. "What are you gonna do if he asks you to Homecoming?"

"You're getting so carried away right now," I say, turning to my locker and spinning in the combination. "He's being Christian. He's, like, weird. And dumb. But sweet or whatever."

"So you think he's sweet, huh? I'm getting a vibe from him, I don't know. I think he's sweet on *you.*"

"Regan." I shake my head, maneuvering around the mirror to pull my first block books out of my backpack, then shoving my bag into the locker. "Be quiet. Anyway, you're the only person I'd drag my ass to Homecoming for."

It's not worth mentioning that I'm going to have to be wherever Christian is regardless. If something happens to him . . .

I don't know if trying to wake him up again would work, but it's worth a shot. Whatever buys us time is worth a shot.

Regan's head is a million miles away, though. She looks at me with impish eyes, her lips curved into a devilish half smile. "Actually, about that."

"Homecoming?"

She grins, "Someone asked me! But I can't tell my parents, so will you please be my pretend date?"

Regan's parents are notoriously strict about boys. Even as little kids, we weren't allowed to have sleepovers together. Her parents only budged on that rule when I came out in middle school. Even if they're backward about boys, they've never had a problem supporting me being gay. As such, I've been the best alibi option since Regan started having an interest in dating.

"Do I have to do anything?"

"Pick me up from my house. We can even go back to your place, and Rhys will pick me up from there."

That sounds like a small enough commitment that I can keep focused on the Christian thing in case anything goes—

My brain grinds to a stop. I replay what Regan said in my head, squinting at her like I must be missing something. No way. No way she'd wait this long to tell me a guy asked her out.

"Don't get mad!" she squeals before I even open my mouth.

"*Rhys*?" I ask, eyes going wide. "Rhys Davies?!"

Regan's cheeks darken, whipping her head around like Rhys is going to jump from behind a corner and surprise us. She reaches up to twist a lock of hair from her ponytail around her finger, shrugging.

"He asked me yesterday . . . I don't know!"

"And you're telling me *now*?"

She shrugs helplessly. "Well, yesterday was nuts! And you were mad at me before everything went crazy!"

I take her point. There were more important things happening yesterday. In fact, the cafeteria is shut down today because they haven't been able to air out the smell of rot, so health inspector people are coming in to check out the kitchens.

"Okay . . . still. I didn't know you guys were close?"

"We're not! We have Humanities together, so we talk in class. I didn't know it was like that!"

"Do you like him?" I ask, grinning in spite of everything.

Regan's practically glowing, shrugging even as she can't stop smiling and blushing. "I haven't really thought about it."

"Right . . . sure. So is it like a date, or . . . ?"

"I don't know!"

With how flushed and excited Regan looks, it better be a date. All the more reason to talk to him with Christian today, I guess. The first bell rings for homeroom, so I spin the lock on my locker, heading to the stairs with Regan. We're in different classrooms, but she's on the way.

"I can't believe you're giving me so much crap about Christian *giving you a vibe* when you've got this going on."

She laughs. "I'll give you all the crap I want. You think Christian didn't tell me you guys had a little midnight meeting without me?"

"Yeah, well. It wasn't very romantic." I shudder, thinking of the way Christian's skin seemed to split at the seams, glowing like he'd swallowed a lightning storm.

"You better fill me in," she says, wagging a finger at me as she hovers by the door of her homeroom.

I roll my eyes, waving at her as I pass. "You know I will."

At my homeroom door, my phone buzzes in my pocket. I pull it out as I head over to my seat and an unsaved local number flashes up on the screen.

GUESS WHO GOT A NEW PHONE!!!!!!

I smile, depositing my books on top of the desk at the far corner of the room closest to the window before sitting down. This is good. This will make it easier to worry less about Christian; he can reach me when he needs me. I save his number, then text him back while the other kids file in.

Delete this number.

He sends back several crying emojis and a skull. I lean my elbow against my desk, leaning my face against my hand as I text back with the other.

Hi xtn. See you at lunch.

Practice fields? he asks.

Nowhere else to go.

The stink from the cafeteria carries all the way down to the practice fields. It's not strong, but it's persistent as hell. Me and Regan are the first ones under the bleachers. I forgot school lunch would be a problem today, so Regan's sharing her arroz con habichuelas with me. It's special sharing food with her; since my dad and abuela passed away, Regan's family is basically the only Puerto Rican family I get to see on a daily basis.

"Don't look now," I say, spotting Ava in a Barbie-pink sweater and banana yellow leg warmers, her white-blonde hair reflecting the autumn sunlight as she walks beside Christian and Rhys down the hill to the practice fields, "But I see your little *boyfriend*."

Regan scrunches her nose at me distastefully before smoothing her hands over her hair and fluffing her ponytail fastidiously. She glances over her shoulder as they approach.

"Yeah? Well, I see yours, too."

"Stop fussing," I tell her, ignoring the comment. "You're beautiful. Relax."

She smiles, leaning back on her hands.

Christian and the others duck under the bleachers, setting down their lunch bags before taking their seats next to us. Rhys sits next to Regan, greeting both of us with a flash of his notorious grin, and Ava sits between him and Christian, which leaves Christian next to me.

"Sup, guys?" he greets us. He looks down at the Tupperware between me and Regan, raising his eyebrows. "Oh, Jax, do you not have lunch? You can have some of mine."

"Me, too!" offers Rhys, unbidden.

They both start unzipping their lunch boxes, and I stammer, watching Christian unwrap his torta as Rhys unpacks several Pyrex containers. Ava looks at both of them, then pulls her wheat bread Fluffernutter sandwich out of her bag, holding it out to me.

"Uh . . ." I shake my head, laughing nervously. "That's okay, Ava, that's all yours. You guys don't have to feed me, it's all good."

Christian presses half his torta into my hand anyway. It's packed with onion, avocado, and chorizo. Even cold, it smells so good it drowns out the sick rot rolling down the hill.

Christian's already tearing into his half. Regan gives me the most annoying little smirk she can muster.

"Okay, well . . . thanks, man."

"Anyone can have some of mine," says Rhys, pushing his Pyrex containers into the center of our circle. They display an array of grilled chicken with vegetables, pasta salad, trail mix, hummus with baby carrots, hard boiled eggs, and apple slices. When all of us stare, he smiles self-consciously. "My mom goes overboard. So, seriously."

"You don't have to twist *my* arm," says Regan, going in for a baby carrot.

Rhys and Christian laugh. I look down at the half of the torta Christian gave me, struck by how weird this is. Last Friday, I never would have imagined myself having lunch with Rhys Davies and Ava Knightly. Christian, maybe. He always went out of his way to say hi to me, even before all this. I was the one always blowing him off.

What's weirder is how different today would feel if Christian had stayed dead. They probably would have canceled the pep rally on Friday to do a memorial service or something. Instead, I'm probably going to have to actually pay attention to the pep rally for the first time to keep an eye on Christian.

It's only been a few days, but everything is so different. It's hard to eat thinking how quickly this could all change again.

Christian's hand comes up, wrapping around my upper arm gently. He looks at me over the rims of his glasses.

"You okay?" he asks.

"Sorry, yeah." I bite into the torta. Even with the queasiness from anxiety, it tastes amazing. The warm flavor of the chorizo and the cool smoothness of avocado, it's been way too long since I ate at Christian's house. Some of the unease in my stomach ebbs away.

Christian rubs my arm soothingly, looking over at Rhys, mouth still half-full of bread as he speaks.

"Dude, Rhys, how you feeling? I still can't believe your hair!"

I almost choke on my mouthful, but Regan thumps on my back until I hold a hand up for her to stop. Christian's bringing this up *now*? In front of Ava?

Rhys's brown skin flushes pink from the top of his ears to the dip in his collarbone showing over the collar of his shirt. He reaches up, tucking the silver strands of his hair behind his ear. "Man, I know! Mom says it's impossible for something like that to happen from one day to the other. She thinks I *dyed* it."

Ava tilts her head, chewing on her sandwich thoughtfully. "It doesn't look dyed, though," she says, pointing at him which makes him blush harder. "Like, it's not one chunk. You've got a bunch of random silver hairs around it."

Rhys laughs self-consciously, running a hand over his hair and pushing all the loose strands back.

"I know, yeah. I'm freaked out. Right before Homecoming, too." He shoots a furtive glance in Regan's direction.

"I think it looks nice," she offers, right on cue. "It's not like you look old or anything."

"Yeah, you're still hot dude, but like . . ." Christian sits forward on his knees, pushing his glasses higher up on his nose. "What was it you were saying yesterday? About what you felt like when it happened?"

The embarrassed smile that started forming on Rhys's face falls. He bristles visibly, staring hard at Christian like there's more he wants to say. Judging by the tight expression in his eyes, I wonder if Christian sprung this conversation on him the way he tends to. "I don't even know when it happened. But yeah, I felt weird yesterday."

Ava hums sympathetically. "Did you eat any of the rotten food?"

"Who knows?" wonders Regan, grinning like it's cool rather than scary and disgusting. "It rotted right in front of us. Maybe it rotted in our *stomachs*."

My stomach gurgles in complaint as I shoot Regan a dark look. She shouldn't be adding fuel to the fire of everyone's curiosity about that and I also really didn't need to hear it.

"I think we all felt sick yesterday," I offer, glancing over at Rhys. "But you felt something other than sick? Are you okay?"

Rhys looks at Christian again, something unspoken passing between them, Rhys's eyes round and uncertain and Christian's narrowed in thought. He swallows a mouthful of food before clearing his throat, giving Rhys the slightest of nods.

"I'm gonna go grab some napkins, I'm getting shit all over myself. Ava, wanna come with?"

Ava blinks, not at all convinced by Christian's ruse. She looks at Rhys, then at me, then up at Christian, trying to understand. Then, she shrugs, taking Christian's hand and standing up.

"We'll be right back," he calls, jogging up the field with Ava at his tail.

I want to call out to him. Why is he *leaving*?

Rhys sits, watching them retreat over his shoulder as he picks nervously at his fingernails. Regan gives him an encouraging smile, though the set of her eyebrows tells me she's as confused as I am.

"Okay, uh . . ." He sighs as he pushes his hand through his hair, accidentally pulling more stands loose from the front. "I'm trying not to sound like a crazy person, so bear with me. Chris says you guys'll get it, so . . ."

Regan and I exchange glances. Christian already got answers out of him; why not spare him the awkwardness by telling us himself?

"You're good," says Regan, leaning forward with her elbows on her knees. "We're not gonna judge, promise."

"Um . . . This is gonna sound weird." He rubs the center of his forehead, frowning down at his lunch for a long moment. "You know how I was, like, holding Chris when he had his panic attack?"

Regan and I nod.

"Okay, well . . ." Rhys clears his throat, meeting our eyes. "I think I blacked out or something . . . ? I guess only for a second, but it felt a lot longer."

I squint at him, furrowing my brow. That's definitely unusual. "Like how?"

"Like for that second or whatever, everything went black and quiet. Like I fell into water. Then I heard a big loud cracking sound—like thunder, almost, in my head. And then I was back. Everything looked normal. The only thing was . . ."

"The food," Regan finishes for him, looking at me with round eyes.

"Right." He nods, the fine dark and silver strands of his hair falling forward to frame his handsome face. "I don't know what it means. That was the only weird feeling I got before I saw my reflection again."

"That's . . ." I flounder on how to respond. I don't want him to feel like he imagined it, but I can't just tell him he's confirming my suspicions here. "It doesn't sound crazy."

He brightens up a little when Regan nods in agreement. He has kind of a funny smile, canines noticeably pointy and outer incisors smaller than his front teeth and canines.

"With everything that's happened to Chris, I don't even know what to think." He folds his arms over his chest, tipping his head. "I mean, dude wakes up in a morgue after the doctors say he died from his chest getting caved in? And now weird shit starts happening?"

He shudders, illustrating his feelings on the matter. I find myself stuck on what he just said, but Regan speaks my thoughts before I can put them together in a tactful way.

"Whoa," she says, laughing nervously. "How much did he tell you about all that?"

Rhys looks at her quizzically, raising his thick black brows.

"I don't know, everything? I'm his best friend."

That rankles something in me, so much so that I have to bite my tongue before responding. The back of my neck is hot as I take a breath, focusing on keeping a neutral face.

I shouldn't feel defensive. Christian and I haven't been best friends in a long time. We're not dating. I have no reason to be jealous or weird about it. Christian's best friends with normie sports guys now, which is fine. There are more important things to worry about.

I shake my head, clearing it. "When did he get the chance to tell you anything?"

"I walked him home. Rhiannon and me were gonna give him a ride, but he said no and I was worried about him, so . . ."

"Right."

Rhys's eyebrows scrunch together, green eyes flitting between us fretfully.

"He told me you guys already know about what the hospital said and all that. You do know, right?"

"*Yes*," I say, sounding defensive even to my own ears.

Regan places a pacifying hand on my knee, shooting me a meaningful look before smiling at Rhys.

"Yeah! It's fine; you're fine. We didn't know he told you anything."

"I haven't told anyone," He assures us, looking at me like he thinks that's the reason I'm giving him attitude. "I promised I wouldn't. Not even my sister."

"Okay." I sigh, rubbing my fingers against my temples. "Yeah, good."

I should check on him. Christian probably wants me to, right? But I only know one way to do it, and I'm still not great at it.

"Uh . . . Rhys, I don't know if Christian mentioned anything about *me* in all this . . . ?"

Rhys nods. "He said you're into witchy stuff or whatever so you know a lot."

I'm not sure how to feel about that. Reductive, I guess, for the sake of not spilling all my business to Rhys without my permission. I sigh.

"Right. Sure. Okay. Uh . . . this is gonna sound weird. Can I hold your hands for a minute?"

Rhys smiles brightly, extending his hands. "Dude, nothing sounds weird these days."

Regan scoots closer curiously, having missed everything from last night. "What're you gonna do?"

"I wanna check on him," I say, taking Rhys's hands. "I've been learning this trick. Be quiet for a bit? I need to focus."

"This is magic?" Rhys asks eagerly.

"Shh." I take a breath and close my eyes, trying to empty my mind as I focus on finding the energy under his skin.

It only takes a moment. The life within Rhys is the strongest I've felt yet—much more than a gentle current. Touching his hands fills me with it, seemingly boundless and exuberant, every hair on my body standing on end from the static of him. He's fine. More than fine. I can't have taken anything substantial from him.

"Hold on," I mutter. "Don't say anything. Don't move."

There has to be a way to measure it. Obviously, Rhys is a teenage boy with many more years ahead of him than anyone or anything I've done this to before now. I need a better metric to judge how Christian is doing than "worse than a tree." I already know he's got way less time ahead of him than Rhys, but there has to be a way to get a clearer sense than that.

Rhys and Regan are obliging about being quiet. I try not to think about how weird I probably seem, sitting here with my eyes closed holding hands with a guy I barely know. I need to stay focused here.

A seventeen-year-old with an average lifespan has, what, sixty or seventy years ahead of him? This has to be something like that, right? There's a definite sort of pulse to it, slow and overwhelming. It pounds along the column of my spine, filling my skull, ebbing and flowing in a deliberate pattern. Each pulse has its own sort of symphony of currents beneath it, difficult to pick out individually.

A deep, unwavering hum. Beneath that, a constant, steady flicker.

My father's pocket watch pops into my mind's eye. Three hands: hours, minutes, seconds.

Three currents.

"It's like a clock," I blurt, opening my eyes and staring down at Rhys's hands. "Years, months, days . . . ? Maybe?"

"What is?" Rhys asks, staring at me with wide-eyed curiosity.

"Uh . . ." I waffle uncertainly, releasing his hands and shuddering when the swell of his life drains out of me. "You're doing fine. Whatever happened in the cafeteria, it didn't do you any real harm, I think."

Rhys looks at Regan, baffled but apparently exhilarated by what must have looked like the world's most boring witchy thing.

"What did you do?! Were you reading my vibes or something? What *was* that?"

That's not an entirely incorrect way to put that, actually. I laugh nervously, shrugging.

"Uh, yeah, I guess? Kind of."

Regan grins, stars in her eyes at the new development. She holds her hands out, bouncing against the grass a little. "Do me!"

It's a little intimidating to do, actually. There's no exact science to it yet, and even if there was, I would really hate to find Regan had anything less than a typical lifespan ahead of her. But I take her hands and close my eyes again, focusing.

A relieved breath escapes me when her life force feels similar. The pulse of hers is slower and longer, like the waves of her energy crest higher than Rhys's. I wish I knew the significance. Is it slower longer-lived or shorter-lived? It has to be longer, right? Christian's last night was flickering fast and unsteady.

"You're fine too," I tell her, smiling gratefully. "Vibing amazing, like always."

Regan doesn't react right away, staring at me in alarm. I let go of her hands, suppressing a second shudder, and find Rhys looking at me with wide, shocked eyes, too.

"What?" I ask, touching under my nose. "Am I bleeding?"

But no, it's dry. However, Regan nods, pointing at my ear. I touch both, then pull my hands away to find both of them coated in fresh, dark blood.

My head spins. Even sitting down, my body sways slightly. What the fuck? As if nosebleeds weren't enough.

"You're not okay," says Regan. "We need to get you to the nurse."

"I'm fine," I insist. "I think it's stopping."

"No, dude . . ." says Rhys gently. "We gotta make sure that's not something serious. It *looks* serious."

Behind me, the sound of approaching footsteps jogging toward us tells me Christian and Ava are back. It only takes spotting the looks on Rhys and Regan's faces to tell him something's wrong.

"What's the matter?" He asks urgently, dropping down on his knees beside me. When he spots it, he gasps sharply. "¡Ay, verga, Jaxon! ¿Qué pasó?"

"I don't know. I just noticed."

"It literally came out of nowhere!" says Regan, still wide-eyed in disbelief.

Christian starts cleaning me up with the napkins he fetched, Ava passing him some when all the ones he'd had get saturated with blood. His hands shake as he does it, face pale, and even with the blood still warm on my face, I have the urge to do one more check.

I went overboard, I think. Too much, too fast.

"Are *you* okay?" I ask Christian, locking eyes with him.

"Duh, I'm not the one bleeding," he retorts. "Come on, I'll walk you to the nurse."

"I don't *need* the nurse." What's she going to do for me? There's no actual health issue here. She's going to shove gauze in my ears and tell me to go to the hospital.

"No seas terco, Jaxon." Christian looks into my eyes, raising his eyebrows meaningfully. "Vámonos."

I relent, though not without heaving a long, suffering sigh. I'm a little unsteady from the shock of having bled out of my *ears*. Regan steadies me as I try standing, handing me my backpack to prevent me having to lean down again.

"Just to be safe," she says, squeezing my arm affectionately.

I *feel* her when she touches me, not as powerfully as I did when I was trying. Each time she makes contact with me, my body registers her deep, steady thrum of energy.

"Sure," I say. "See you later."

Christian grabs his things as he bids goodbye to the others. I'm confused as to why he's saying *bye* when he'll probably run into them at least a couple more times before the end of the day. All becomes clear when we reach the top of the hill and Christian turns toward the path leading to the sidewalk rather than the building.

"I thought you were taking me to the nurse?" I ask.

"A la verga con eso," says Christian. "Let me walk you home, Jax. Unless you think you're actually hurt?"

It's possible, I guess. But there's no pain, and as far as I can tell my hearing is still the same.

"Nah. Think I went too hard trying to see if Rhys was alright."

"*Was* he?" Chrsitian asks quickly.

I ignore the little surge of jealousy his concern over Rhys gives me. They're best friends. I need to get a grip.

"Totally fine, far as I can tell."

Christian lets out a deep sigh of relief, then fixes me with a brilliant smile. "Thanks. I thought for sure I hurt him or stole life from him or something."

I watch my feet as we walk. Christian really *is* sweet. Unreal for him to have the capacity to worry about Rhys like that with all he's been through. And is *still* going through.

"You're a good person," I tell him.

He grins even brighter, shrugging. "So are you!"

I don't know how to respond to that. I'm trying, I guess. The school recedes into the background as we walk into town. Sneaking out during lunch is insanely easy, but I've never done it before.

"Maybe I should take a selfie so I can prove to my mom I was bleeding out the ears and had to go home. Do I still have any blood showing?" Mami already let me skip a day; I don't know how she'll feel about me cutting class of my own volition.

"A little," says Christian. "I'll vouch for you."

"*You* won't get in trouble for skipping?"

Christian laughs at that, waving a hand. "Nah. After the accident, I could legit murder someone, y no hay pedo. My mom would probably help me hide the body."

Conce would probably do that regardless. Christian's the baby of his family and the only son. Every time I went over to his house when we were younger, they treated him like a little prince. I don't point that out.

"Wanna cut through the cemetery?" he asks.

I look up at him witheringly. "I don't think that's a good idea. Do you?"

"Right," he says, turning to walk behind the pie shop at the corner of the street. "Bike path, then."

SEVENTEEN

It's quiet on the bike path in the middle of the day. Goldenrod and Queen Anne's lace line the edges of the pavement, along with the trees adorned in fiery-toned leaves. Christian looks like he's in good humor, smiling as he walks along, shoulder bumping into mine every few steps.

Each time he does, I feel the rapid flicker of his life counting down.

"Did Rhys tell you he's taking Regan to Homecoming?" I ask.

"Yeah!" Christian lights up. "Cool, right? Rhys is kind of goofy and weird like her. I think he'll show her a good time."

"Are *you* going?"

"To Homecoming?"

I nod, raising my eyebrows expectantly. What else would I mean? His best friend's going, my best friend's going, I figure he is. If so, I'll have to tail him there to keep eyes on.

He flounders for a moment before answering. "Uh . . . I don't know. I'm guessing you don't wanna go, right?"

"Doesn't matter." I shrug, stepping off the bike path when we get to my street. "I'll be wherever you are. I'm getting a better sense of how to tell where you're at, as far as . . ."

Christian slows his pace, expression dimming slightly. "As far as dying?"

"Yeah."

"Can you feel it from there?"

I shake my head, reaching for his hand. Christian meets me halfway there, brushing his index against the curve of my wrist-bone before linking his fingers with mine. I try not to choke, ignoring the way my ears burn.

"Uh . . . I have to touch you. I'm still not sure how to measure it completely. I was trying with Rhys and Regan and then my ears started spurting blood, so . . ."

"How am I today?" he asks. "Rough estimate."

A flicker, barely. If I had to guess, I'd say he's running on fumes. Bits of life I've zapped into him by accident extending his time by hours, or maybe a day or so.

"Close," I admit quietly. "Very, very close."

Christian tries not to let his face fall completely, but I know that's not any easier to hear than it is to say. I squeeze his hand before releasing it, pausing as the turret at the top of my house comes into view.

"Guess I'll see you later?" I ask.

Christian hesitates, looking at the turret for a moment, then back at me. "Is your family home?"

I shrug. "I don't know. My mom's probably out getting stuff for the wake tonight. My aunt might be."

"Oh, okay."

"Why?" I press, raising my eyebrows. "Did you wanna come over?"

He looks at me, faint lines between his eyebrows as he gives me a nervous smile. "Yeah? I miss you. You know?"

My chest clenches even as my stomach gets buffeted by butter-flies. I miss him too, which feels extra ridiculous when we're right next to each other. But I missed him before he died, I missed him *when* he died, and now he's dying and I'm anticipating missing him again.

So yeah. I know.

I open my mouth to tell him so, but a familiar car pulls out of my mom's driveway a few yards away, and I shoulder Christian into Mrs. Chee's overgrown bushes.

He yelps as we crash into them. He falls on his butt into the fallen leaves and goldenrods growing at the base of the bushes. I squat, peering through the stems at the road as my titi's mint green Outback drives past us.

"That's Titi Clío," I whisper, even though there's no way she can hear me. "I wonder where she's going."

"Out to lunch, maybe?" offers Christian, awkwardly trying to make his height and his long limbs fit within the bush.

"Maybe but there's no vegan joints around here."

I wait, paranoid that she'll change her mind and drive back around. When the hum of her engine is long past, leaving only the sound of the crows up on the power lines, I clamber out of the bushes. Christian catches my arm, disentangling himself from the clinging stems and leaves, straightening up as he brushes the twigs and pollen off his braids.

"So . . ." He catches my eye, smiling. "Your house?"

We shouldn't. Even if Titi's gone out and Mami's not home yet, either of them could come back at any minute. However, time is undoubtedly short, and I still haven't had Christian take a good look at the pocket watch sitting in my bag. There's also the key to the filing cabinet. With so much to sift through, it only really makes sense to split the work.

Christian smiles hopefully at me.

I roll my eyes fondly. "At least you asked this time."

He laughs, widening his eyes like he doesn't know what I mean as he follows me home.

"I didn't have a phone!"

"Yeah, yeah."

The only car in the driveway is the hearse. Christian and I walk up the front porch steps, as I reach into my backpack to pull the house keys out of the front pocket. Unlocking the double doors, Christian reaches up to hold it open for me, so I enter first.

"Lock it," I remind him. It won't buy us much time if someone comes home, but every second counts.

He snaps the lock into place, coming up to my side again, pressing his hand between my shoulders. "You wanna take your PRN, dude?"

I'm taken aback that Christian remembers I take a PRN anxiety med. It's been years since the last time he saw me take it, and it doesn't feel like that would be something particularly memorable about me. Christian doesn't even blink when I stare at him in surprise, so I guess it's not weird to him.

It's not a bad idea. My anxiety's been at a constant dull roar in the back of my head. I can't afford to have a panic attack until *after* I've taken care of Christian.

"Yeah, they're upstairs," I say, heading for the big stairs at the end of the foyer.

"I'll come with you!"

I'm starting to see why Christian and Rhys are friends. *Best* friends. They're both the same brand of helpful jock with sunny dispositions. I don't hate it as much as I thought I did, in either of them.

In the kitchen, Christian bounds over to check the cabinets for glasses so he can get me water to take my pill with. I get my bottle of Ativan out of the cabinet my mom keeps the important and daily meds in, shaking one out onto my palm.

Christian presents the glass of water to me with a flourish. I smile at him in spite of myself as I take it from him, washing down the pill. It'll kick in fast, with any luck.

"Hey," I say. "Can you pass me my backpack?"

Christian does and I hoist it up for a moment, pulling the pocket watch my father left me out of the side pocket.

"I want you to look at this." I hold it out to Christian, urging him to take it from me. "I didn't really show it to you before. But I trust you with it, alright?"

Christian's eyes go huge behind his glasses as he stares at the gleaming metal of the watch cover. He turns his big eyes to me uncertainly, holding out his hands.

"You're sure?"

My fingers hold onto it tighter instinctively. I don't *know* that it won't do anything if he doesn't turn the hands, but I really don't know anything.

"Yeah. Drop it if it makes you feel any kind of way, alright? Be really, *really* careful and don't play with the lever or the dial."

"I'm always careful," he says, taking it in both hands.

My brain flashes the image of Christian lying on my mom's prep table in response. A time when he wasn't so careful put him there. I blink hard to erase the image, keeping quiet as he turns the watch over in his hands, examining it reverently.

"So this is it, huh?" he says softly.

"Yeah."

"Looks really old . . ."

I shrug, watching the way his fingers skim across the smooth surface of the metal. "I think it belonged to my grandpa's grandpa or something."

"Wow." He sighs. He flips the watch cover open, looking over the faded inscriptions inside. They're not professional—it's clear that my father, and my great-grandfather, etched their names in themselves.

"Why isn't your name here . . . ?"

My ears go hot as I drop my gaze, shrugging. I don't know how to answer that without feeling kind of dumb and self-conscious about the whole thing. I try anyway.

"It never really felt *mine*. Didn't really feel like I'd 'earned' it, if that makes any sense?" I clear my throat, glancing up at him and finding him watching me with an inscrutable expression. "I wish I'd known what it meant to my dad, I guess. I kind of know now, I just wish he could have told me himself. Sometimes I'd look at it and it'd make me miss him more."

Christian closes the watch cover, running his thumb along the smooth, gold surface. "I wish I had been there for you, Jaxon. Fui un pinche cobarde. I regret being such a coward so much."

I don't know what to say to that. I don't have the energy, nor the desire, to be mad at him about that anymore. A silence falls between us then, thin and awkward. I return to my backpack for something to do in the quiet, searching through the front pocket to pull out the key to the filing cabinet downstairs.

Christian breaks the silence. "Your mom has a Dremel, right?"

"Uh, downstairs somewhere. Why?"

He smiles at me, snapping the watch shut carefully before sticking it in the pocket of his hoodie. My hoodie.

"Can we go get it?"

I squint at him, unsure what he's trying to go for, but nod slowly.

"I guess, if you can find it? I have to go down to the morgue anyway."

Christian visibly blanches at the mention of the morgue, and I reach out instinctively, bracing a hand against his upper arm.

"You don't have to come. The Dremel's in the butler's pantry somewhere."

He swallows, the relief washing some of the color back into his cheeks.

"Okay," he says.

We drop our backpacks off in my room, then head downstairs into the big show kitchen. Christian turns to search through the cabinets in the butler's pantry while I open the door to the basement and descend the stairs, flipping on the fluorescent lights.

There's a body on the table, which shouldn't surprise me, but I gasp and miss a step on the way down. I stand at the stairs, bracing myself on the banister, heart pounding as I stare at the body. It's lucky Christian was smart enough to remind me to take my PRN.

I don't recognize the person on the table, though he's about ready for the casket. With his makeup done, hands folded over his chest, salt-and-pepper hair neatly brushed into a conservative style, all that's missing are his suit pants. They're hanging up beside him on a rack, split into two panels because they no longer fit him. When she comes back, Mami will stitch them on him as best she can before putting him in the casket for the showing. The legs are the least important anyway.

I breathe out shakily, going down the rest of the way as I try to keep a cool head. I won't touch the body. I won't even look at the body again. I'll go to the file cabinet, look for Dad's notebook, and go.

I enter the office, going behind my mom's desk, where she has her papers in neat, perfect stacks and family photos in pristine silver-edged frames. There's me as a red-faced baby in her arms at the hospital as she smiles down at me tearfully, me as a toddler on my father's shoulders in an apple orchard, one of my elementary school pictures where my front teeth look cartoonishly big and awkward compared to the rest, and one of my dad pressing his ear to my mom's pregnant belly.

I pick up the picture of my parents together, looking at it closer. They are young in the picture; Mami was still wearing box braids back then, strands of electric blue and white braided in. She was in the process of getting her mortuary science degree and, instead of the pencil skirts and blouses she wears now, she wore fishnet gloves with vampiric looking blouses and strappy black skirts with black platform shoes. She's skinny in the photo, her belly a petite but prominent bump that peeks out under her blouse, with more facial piercings than I have by a mile. Dad is even weirder to look at; I remember him best in sweaters and jeans, crisp and ordinary. At twenty-two, he had half his head bleached blonde, and wore baggy pants with a big orange *Dragonball* shirt.

They look like kids. They look lamer than *me*. But they look happy. Mami's grinning, her pierced dimples catching the light in the photo. Dad's smiling serenely.

"Please," I whisper to my parents in the photo. "*Please* help me."

I set them down, taking a deep breath as I turn to the filing cabinet behind the desk. The key fits smoothly in the lock and turns. I almost laugh in relief, whispering a litany of *thank-yous* to my dad as if he might be right here with me. I pull each of the drawers open until I find the accordion file full of tax papers, tugging the whole thing out. Underneath, like my father said, there's a notebook.

It's ordinary-looking for the most part; it has brown leather binding with the shape of an owl's face embossed in the front and a strap of leather holding it closed. I pull it out, replacing the accordion file before I forget, then lock the cabinet again.

I resist the urge to open it now. I'm still down here with a body, and I don't want to run the risk of something happening that I don't understand. Instead, I hold the notebook in both hands against my chest and hurry out of the office, racing up the stairs to the kitchen.

The whirring screech of a Dremel tool against metal greets me. My teeth ache instinctively, the sound a little too close to a dentist's drill. I duck into the butler's pantry, but Christian stops almost as soon as I poke my head in. He grins at me, my watch open-faced in his palm.

"I really didn't think you'd have the nerve to do it," I tell him, raising my eyebrows.

"Why wouldn't I?" He challenges, still smiling as he holds the watch out to me. "It *is* yours, Jaxon. You *have* earned it."

I take it, face growing warm as I look at my name inscribed under my dad's. It doesn't bother me that he did that—not at all, actually. I couldn't get myself to do it. I didn't even really consider doing it.

It looks right.

I stare at it for a long moment. He tried his best to make the letters look consistent, but there's a distinct wobble in the X. I hate how much that makes my throat grow tight with affection for him. If anything happens to Christian now, I'll really never be able to look at this fucking watch again.

"It *is* okay, right, Jax?" he says nervously, tucking the tool back into its drawer. "You told me where the Dremel was, so I figured . . ."

I snap it shut, shoving it back into my pocket. Trying to hide how emotional I feel is a complete failure. I try anyway, doing my best to give him an annoyed expression.

"I hate you so much," I say, unconvincingly shaky.

Christian comes toward me, still grinning, hands shoved in his pockets. "You really, really don't."

I don't give him the satisfaction of a confirmation. Instead, I hold up my dad's notebook, which diverts his attention immediately. He raises his hand to run his fingers across the owl's face on the cover.

"Your dad loves owls, huh?" He smiles.

"Loved," I correct.

He looks at me, squinting doubtfully. "He doesn't really seem to have stopped."

That is an unsettling thought. I suppress a shudder, pulling the book in closer to me again.

"Let's do this upstairs," I say.

"Cool," agrees Christian, heading for the pantry again.

There's no reason to take the back stairs; I think Christian just likes that we have "secret" stairs in our house, even more so for how dark and creepy they are. I follow him up; he automatically goes to the third-floor landing, where the bedrooms are.

In my room, I leave the door cracked open for Grimalkin and sit next to Christian on my bed. He toes his sneakers off, sitting with his legs crossed under him, radiating excitement but clearly doing his best to remain level and cool.

I set the book down between us and stare at it. It's harder than I thought it would be to open the cover. Even on my meds, anxiety presses tight on my skull at the idea of opening it only to find nothing helpful inside.

Christian seems to read my mind. He reaches over and puts his hand over mine, tipping his head down to make me meet his eyes.

"Jax, whatever we find or don't find, we'll keep figuring it out. Okay?"

I swallow, acutely aware of his hand on mine as if the nerve endings are sharper and keener there than the ones in the rest of my body. Beneath the rush of my own nerves, I count the flickers of his life force buzzing under his skin. "Okay."

His fingers close around mine, warm light brown against the cool dark brown of my skin. It's weird; I feel weird. My stomach feels like it's been crumpled up into a ball, heart aching from beating so fast and hard. I curl my fingers around his, too.

"I'm so fucking scared for you," I say, so quietly Christian has to lean in.

Christian's fingers squeeze mine, looking at me with his best brave face though I know he's scared too. His dark eyes search mine while he tries to think of what to say. I shift my hand under his until our palms are pressed flush together, the crests of his cheeks blushing pink. His fingers slip between mine, locking in place as his eyes find mine again.

"I'm *not* going anywhere," he swears.

I can't say anything in response. My heart is wedged in my throat so firmly it's hard to breathe. I explore the curves and divots of his knuckles with the pad of my thumb and exhale slowly, trying not to betray how hard my breath is shaking in my lungs. His skin is smooth, soft and warm, but my chest tightens remembering the first time I held his hand a few days ago when it was stiff and cold.

"Uh," I stammer, voice thin, "Christian, we should . . . let's look. Now."

"Yeah! You're right."

He doesn't let go of my hand. Instead, he adjusts his glasses with the free one, scoots closer to me so our hands can rest comfortably between us, our knees touching as he reaches for the cover of my dad's notebook.

"Do you want me to do it?" he asks.

I swallow nervously, trying to take my focus off the point of connection between us.

"Yeah. Please."

Christian opens the cover without further question. It falls open easily, like it's been used so many times the binding is weak. The front page is brittle, yellowed paper with nothing on it but *JAD-IEL SANTIAGO* written in block letters and the guy from *Cowboy Bebop* doodled in the corner.

Christian's eyes light up in surprise and amusement. Honestly, it eases loose some of the knots in my chest. If Dad drew anime guys on his fucking grimoire or whatever, maybe personal, powerful things don't have to be sacred.

"He was definitely kind of a weeb," I say, reaching over to turn the page, feeling emboldened after seeing that. He probably did it when he was a teenager, but he never saw any reason to tear it out. It makes the notebook feel a little friendlier to me.

The next page is full of writing in tiny, cramped letters, almost margin to margin. I squint at the words, then realize he used this page as a kind of index, listing everything in as specific detail as possible. The words *observations*, *artifacts, families, rings* and more, all with several sub bullet points listed under them.

Christian's fingers squeeze mine again, then he releases me so I can take the book in two hands. I lift it up closer to me, flipping through the pages. Every last one of them is thoroughly covered in black ink letters and occasional diagrams.

"I wish my notebook looked this good," admires Christian, leaning in to look with his shoulder pressed against mine.

I run my fingers along the index. It doesn't list any page numbers or hints as to where any of these things are; it only promises that there is more about these things within. There'll be something in here. There has to be.

"Let's start looking, I guess?"

I turn the page, scanning my eyes over the shaky, jagged letters written by an adolescent hand.

Christian nods, propping his chin on my shoulder so he can read along with me.

EIGHTEEN

Dad's notebook is denser than it looks. Every page is full of methodical categorizations of things like spirits by type and death, preliminary sketches of a family tree he wanted to draw but it doesn't say where, and general rambling thoughts. It doesn't surprise me to learn he loved my abuela's mirror, nor that he had high aspirations of being a medium and a diviner like her.

On any other occasion, I'd be interested. I never heard my father speak as much as he has to say in his notebook; it's like getting to know him for the first time. But it's frustrating, scanning all of his thoughts for anything relevant under the anxiety that my mom or aunt will come home, plus the added pressure of needing answers *now*. I try a few times to flip to random pages, hoping to happen upon what I'm looking for, but no such luck.

By the time twenty minutes have passed, I'm lying back in my bed, holding the notebook above me in my outstretched arms. Christian lies beside me, not quite touching but close enough that I feel the heat of his body. I snap the book shut when my eyes can't take reading more of my father's cramped handwriting, and squeeze my eyelids closed for a long moment.

"Want me to keep looking?" offers Christian.

"Give me a minute."

"Okay."

I place the book down beside me, staring up at my ceiling. Christian's watching me, waiting for me to say something, so I turn to meet his gaze.

"I just want *one* part of this to be easy," I tell him.

He smiles wryly at me. "Keep dreaming."

"I wish I was."

Christian lowers his eyes, long black lashes brushing over the smooth, thin skin under his eyes, as his index finger slips its way under my palm.

"I don't."

The itchy pull of sleep tugs at my eyelids; the meds are making me tired. I uncurl my fingers to welcome his between them again, and he seals our palms tight together. The faint, steady flicker of his life force beats familiarly against my skin.

"Hey," I say, voice softening involuntarily. "Why do you keep doing that?"

He turns his eyes back to mine again, round and earnest. "Ya sabes, Jaxon. Come on."

I'm warm from head to toe. My heart races all at once, making my head spin. I shake my head, still locked on his face. "I want to know what *you*'re thinking about it."

His face goes pink from his hairline down to his neck, while he clicks his tongue impatiently at me. "Kinda fucked up to mess with me right now."

I don't answer that. It's hard to fight the heaviness pulling on my eyelids. I shouldn't have laid down, it isn't helping, but I don't want to move now.

"Jaxon," he says, tugging gently on my hand to bring my attention back to him.

Now is not the time to be half-asleep, and it's especially not the time to be holding hands with Christian instead of reading, but I turn to him anyway. His cheeks are redder now, lips pressed tightly together like he's trying to stop himself from talking until he has the right sentence in his head.

My phone buzzes in my pocket. My first thought is to ignore it. The buzz is long and extended, starting again a beat after it cuts off.

"Someone's calling," I say, reaching for my phone.

Christian exhales like a tire deflating as he lets go of my hand, looking relieved and disappointed at the same time. He leans on his elbows, watching me as I pull out my phone, the name *TITI CLÍO* lighting up the screen.

I look at Christian, pressing a finger to my lips as I answer.

"Titi?"

"Nene." Her voice rushes out of her, breathy like she's been running. "Where are you? Why can't they find you at school?"

My insides turn cold for a second—caught. But I relax a little; Titi isn't the type to get upset, and she definitely isn't the type to rat me out to Mami.

"I'm cutting class," I admit. Christian widens his eyes at me like I'm a crazy person. "Sorry. I felt like I was gonna have a panic attack, so I went home. Did they call you? Were you going to pick me up?"

"Where are you? You're already back home?"

"Yeah, I got back a few minutes ago," I lie.

"I'm coming to get you."

"Why?" I raise my eyebrows, shooting a glance at Christian, who's still watching me, listening.

"Mijo . . ." Titi cuts off, the line going silent for a beat before she continues. "Jaxon, sweetie, es tu mami."

My head goes blank when she says that. Of everything she could have been calling about, that was the last possibility in my mind. Christian sits up straighter, eyes going wide behind his glasses as he leans in to listen in better.

"Mami?" My voice sounds hollow and distant. "What about her?"

"The hospital called. She was in a car accident; she's in the ICU. I don't know anything else."

I stand up all at once, unsteady on wooden legs. Christian surges up after me, pressing a supportive hand against my lower back.

"I'm going. Don't come back for me. Make sure she's okay. I'm taking the hearse now."

"Are you sure?" she asks urgently. "Are you alright to drive?"

"Please go see her! I'll be there as soon as I can."

I hang up before she can say anything else, bones rattling in my skin and blood racing through my veins. I'm lightheaded but stable enough; I'm lucky I took my meds before Titi called me. Christian is in my space in a heartbeat, squeezing his hands around my upper arms like if he doesn't anchor me down, I'll float away.

"You have to get back to school," I tell him.

He looks at me, eyes firm. "You're not driving on your meds. And I'm not leaving you alone."

I don't have room in my head to argue. After a beat, I nod, chest tightening with gratitude. He squeezes my arms for good measure, then catches one of my hands, pulling me toward the door urgently.

"Come on."

At the hospital, Christian handles interacting with the lady at the desk. She directs us to the waiting room for the ICU, and Christian keeps his fingers clasped tight around mine as he leads us down the labyrinthine hospital hallways.

"My aunt," I say, pulling him back when we see the waiting room sign.

"Jaxon, me vale verga what she thinks, okay? She can deal with it." He doesn't bother pausing, pulling harder on my hand as he presses forward.

For what it's worth, Titi's reaction when she sees me is pure solace. She hurries over, barely glancing in Christian's direction before sweeping me up into a hug. I squeeze her with only one arm because Christian is still refusing to let go of me. Even as addled as I am, the contrast between her energy—distinct, flowing waves— and Christian's is staggering.

"Hi, honey," she says, stepping back to take my face in her hands as she looks me over with tearful, brown eyes. "They haven't told me much of anything. She's in surgery. I don't know for what."

The word *surgery* sends my stomach into revolt, and it's all I can do to keep my knees from buckling.

"You're next of kin," Christian cuts in. "They'll tell you what they know."

Titi turns her pale eyes onto Christian's face, then down to our joined hands. Her thoughts whir visibly, but I don't have the brain space to worry about that now. Even with my Ativan doing its best, I'm only a few shallow breaths away from a panic attack.

"Okay."

"I'll ask with you," Christian reassures me. His eyebrows knit together, determined to support me. His face relaxes when I nod, and Titi runs her fingers across the side of my face before backing up.

"Let me know what they say," she says, wringing her hands.

Christian walks me up to the desk in front of the ICU doors. The walk feels longer than natural—like the waiting room is a fish tank, and we're walking against the weight and pull of water. Christian does all the talking again, which I'm grateful for because my head feels like it's stuffed full of cotton.

"Your mom's in surgery for multiple leg fractures," says the nurse, clicking through the file on his computer. "That's all I have for you right now. It's going to be a few hours. I don't see any other significant notes on here."

"Is it a very complicated surgery?" asks Christian.

"It's complicated," agrees the nurse, "but the doctors know what they're doing. It usually goes fine. Your mom should be out of the ICU and in a recovery room shortly after surgery, then back home within a day or two, my guess."

Hearing the nurse say that with casual confidence loosens the clamp-like feeling in my chest that was holding my lungs closed. Christian rubs his thumb against my knuckles as I slump my weight against him.

"Cool, thank you!" Christian smiles brightly at the nurse.

"Thank you," I echo faintly.

Christian guides me back to sit in the seats closest to Titi. I can't relax completely while my mom's still behind those doors having her leg operated on, but the way Titi's face and shoulders relax when I recount what the nurse told me soothes me. She scrubs her hands over her face, sighing deeply.

"That's not so bad," she says, leaning back in her chair as she rubs the center of her chest. "Gloria a Dios, let's hope the surgery is short and easy."

"Yeah," I agree, leaning over and closing my eyes because I'm still sick to my stomach and my head keeps swimming. Christian's hand comes up over my back, rubbing big soothing circles over it. "Can you tell Regan, Christian? She's gonna want to know."

"Yeah, man. Anything you want me to do."

I press the heels of my hands against my eyes, racking my brain for anything else that would be helpful right now. I remember the whole reason my mom was out driving in the first place is because she had to get supplies for the wake happening tonight; I have to make sure that's taken care of. I pull my phone out of my pocket, handing it over to him.

"Can you also call my mom's assistant? She's the only Monica in my contacts. Tell her she's gotta run the wake tonight. Body's already prepped and half-dressed; he's just gotta get in the coffin."

"You got it," says Christian, squeezing my shoulder. "I'll run out to the hall, okay? Be right back."

Titi Clío and Christian meet eyes, sharp and wary like cats being introduced to each other for the first time. Christian doesn't see that I notice, but Titi does. She watches Christian head out to make the phone calls, waiting until he rounds the corner before she says anything.

"Jaxon, mi vida," she whispers, looking at me with wide eyes. "What do you think you're *doing*?"

"What about *you*?" I ask, shaking my head. "He's keeping me together right now; why are you looking at him like that?"

Her eyes dart toward the doorway Christian walked out of and she chews her lip, thinking before answering. "This is why you're so focused on saving him, isn't it?"

I don't want to answer that, even though it raises my defensive hackles even under the haze of my anxiety and medication. No, this isn't why. *This* hasn't even been a thing until, what? An hour ago?

"I'm focused on my *mom* right now, Titi."

Titi has the decency to look abashed, cheeks blushing soft pink. She blows out a deep sigh, bringing her fingers up to massage the space between her eyebrows.

"I'm sorry. I'm sorry, just . . ." She shoots another glance through the doorway, features tight with something I can't identify. "You're right. Let's be here for your mom now."

We sit down in adjacent chairs, Titi pulling me in so I can lie my head on her shoulder. She scratches her nails lightly along my scalp, settling some of my frayed nerves. I close my eyes, counting the seconds between the long, slow waves of her life force, until Christian comes back and tells me everything is all set.

When he settles down next to me, my aunt tenses slightly. She cups her hand against my head and takes a breath to relax again.

"Shouldn't you be getting back to school?" she asks Christian.

"This is more important," he says breezily. "I already told my mom. She says she's gonna make pozolito verde for Tessa, so she doesn't have to eat the hospital food tonight."

"That's really sweet," says Titi, going back to scratching lightly along the edge of my hairline.

I look at him sidelong from my aunt's shoulder as he looks down at his hands, where he's holding a phone in each one. I hold out my hand to him, startling him a little, before he places my phone in my palm. I pocket it, then hold my hand out to him again.

Christian's expression brightens as he lifts his eyes to meet mine. I can't manage a smile right now—not until I've processed what's happening to my mom and my stomach has settled enough that it doesn't feel like I'll throw up if I open my mouth. I extend my fingers toward him instead. He touches his fingers to mine, tracing the soft parts between the creases, before knitting our hands together. It feels slightly more intimate than I meant to be in front of my aunt so my heart flutters nervously, but I let our hands rest between us as we wait.

NINETEEN

Christian doesn't leave my side for anything other than to run to the cafeteria to grab water or food for me. Titi doesn't give me any more of a hard time for it. She sits in silence, chewing down her thumbnails and staring into the middle distance, lost in thought.

I can't help feeling guilty now for asking my mom to tell her to leave for a while. When she's well, and when we get a minute alone, I'll have to tell my mom how worried she was about her and that she should stay at least until my birthday.

When the doctor finally comes out, my legs almost give under me when he confirms that the surgery went well, no complications. Titi exhales like she hasn't taken a breath since she arrived at the hospital, and Christian grins at me, eyes bright with relief.

"Is she awake?" asks my aunt.

"Just waking up. She may still be a bit loopy from the anesthesia, but she's already asking to see her son."

That sounds like my mom.

I rub a hand over my face, some of the tension in my shoulders finally releasing me, as I make a beeline toward the door. "I'll go see her now," I say, and the nurse behind the counter presses the button to unlock the doors.

I hurry down the hall until I reach my mom's room with TESSA NOBLE SANTIAGO written in dry erase marker on the white board. Her blinds are closed, which makes my heart speed up, my blood turning cold for a split second.

When I duck into the room, there's a nurse helping her adjust her hospital johnny. One of her legs is in a cast from foot to thigh, elevated on a sling hooked up over her bed. Besides the broken leg, the only other thing is a bit of bruising darkening the side of her face.

"Mami?" I call. My voice sounds small even to my ears, and I feel smaller still standing helplessly in the middle of the room as the nurse tries to make my mom comfortable.

She registers my voice after a delay; the effort it takes for her eyes to find me tells me that she's definitely not all there yet. She reaches out when she sees me, smiling drowsily.

"There you are, baby," she says, beckoning me closer. Then, to the nurse, "This is my son. Isn't he so handsome?"

The nurse smiles kindly and agrees as I approach the bed, taking in all the machines she's attached to. Reading the tension on my face, the nurse places her hand on one of the monitors, smiling at me. "We're keeping an eye on her because she has a concussion, but she'll be on the way to a recovery room really soon. She'll have to be off that leg for a long time."

I take my mom's hands, squeezing her fingers delicately for fear she might have bruised them too. My throat squeezes tight, face hot. I sit at the edge of the mattress, trying to breathe in as I take a second to feel for her. For a moment, I'm positive I'll feel her fading like Christian, but the current of her life force comes in strong, filling me with enough relief to make my eyes water. Not soon. Definitely not now.

"We have a lot of stairs," I say. The downstairs is all accessible for clients, but upstairs and getting down to the morgue are going to be impossible for her.

"She won't be able to manage that for a while," says the nurse. "And she's going to need a lot of help in general for the next six months. There'll be more recovery time once the cast is off, too. Femoral fractures are a nasty business."

Behind me, my aunt speaks up. I didn't register her coming in until now.

"We can figure out the stairs," she says, standing at the foot of my mom's bed with her fingers curled around the footboard. "Don't worry, Tessa. Me and Jaxon will make sure you have everything you need."

"Oh no, no," my mom slurs, letting go of one of my hands to shake her finger at my aunt. "You gotta go, Clío. Jaxon needs some time alone."

My ears turn hot. I widen my eyes at her, squeezing her hand and mentally trying to will her to stop. Titi takes it in stride, though. She smiles placatingly at my mom, like she's a little kid telling a fanciful story.

"Like it or not, Mamita, you're gonna have to let other people take care of you for once."

"Mami," I murmur, brushing my fingers over her hair gently. "It's okay."

"Yeah," she agrees, though it's clear she only has partial understanding of what we're talking about.

Titi Clío watches us, biting her lip as she pulls her key out of her bag.

"Jax, I'm gonna go get some pajamas and some clean underwear for your mom, okay?"

"Okay, Titi," I say, grateful for her presence and clarity of mind. "I'll be here."

"And your little friend is outside the door. ¿Qué le digo?"

Mami raises her eyebrows at me, smiling slightly. I scrub my hand against my face, sighing. It's not like I can leave Christian out there after how much he's done for me today.

"Tell him he can come in. He knows my mom."

"Who knows me?" says my mom, widening her eyes. I sigh and run my hand over her arm, watching Titi leave. A few beats later, Christian peeks in through the door, then edges into the room, holding up a shy hand in greeting.

"Hey, Tessa," he says, coming in with his head ducked, shoulders stooped like he's afraid to be too big. "Glad you're doing okay."

Mami doesn't react to Christian right away, staring at him like she's still processing what she's seeing. I know part of her slow reaction time is the anesthetic wearing off, but I realize she hasn't seen Christian since the night she brought him to the hospital. This is the most normal and healthy she's seen him since he woke up screaming, shaking, and bleeding in her lap.

"Hi, Christian," she says softly.

He smiles as he sits in a chair at the edge of the room, giving me and my mom a wide berth. I appreciate it—both his presence and the space to be with my mom. I shoot him a grateful look, and his features soften for a moment before he gives me a little wave.

I'm glad my mom's not cognizant enough to read anything into how much I'm blushing, in spite of everything else going on.

"He really helped me a lot," I tell her. "He drove me here after I took my Ativan, and he's been sitting with me."

That makes a small smile spread across my mom's face. She squeezes her fingers around mine. "That's good, baby. I'm glad. I'm okay, see?"

I nod. Behind me, Christian lets out a slow, relieved breath.

Mami moves into a recovery room quickly, as promised. By then, it's nighttime. Christian stays, mostly a quiet, friendly presence, until Conce comes to drop off her green pozole. My mom's anesthesia has worn off by that time, so she welcomes the distraction from the pain, but once Conce starts getting ready to head back, she takes Christian with her.

We say goodbye quietly, with our arms at our sides, my face flushing furiously, eyes glued to his. He smiles guiltily like he feels like he shouldn't be, but he can't help it, lingering for a long moment while his mom waits at the edge of the door. Surrounded by our moms and my aunt, there isn't much we can say.

"Mi vida," says his mom, tapping her hand against the door frame gently. "We have to go home. Vas a ver a Jaxon mañana. Vámonos."

I wish I could think of a reason for him to stay. What if I *don't* see him tomorrow? What if he needs me tonight?

"Ya voy, Amá." He taps his fingers against his pocket and raises his eyebrows at me as he mouths *text me*.

Right, his mom doesn't know he has a burner phone. Struggling not to roll my eyes affectionately at him, I nod, patting my pocket to make sure my phone is there.

"If you get the chance," he adds, grinning as he walks backward toward the door. "Obviously, you got a lot going on. Let me know if you need anything, okay?"

"I will. You too, okay? Go home."

"Bye, Christian," says my mom, waving. "Bye again, Conce. Thank you so much for dinner!"

Conce's eyes crinkle with her smile as she waves again. Her smile looks like Christian's. I don't know if I've ever noticed that before. I watch Christian leave, trying not to feel embarrassed by my own longing in front of my mom and aunt.

Mami waits until we can't hear Conce and Christian's footsteps anymore before she addresses my aunt. "Cli, can you do me a little favor?"

Titi scoots forward to lean over my mom's bed, tucking her locs behind her ear.

"Whatever you need. What's up?"

"Can you go tell the nurse I'm feeling a lot of pain right now? And would you also grab me something sweet from the cafeteria? Please?"

Titi smiles, but the worry tugging at the corners of her eyes dims the brightness of it. She nods, placing a hand on my mom's shoulder.

"Claro que sí. I'll be right back, okay?"

When she runs off, Mami beckons me closer, patting the side of the hospital bed. I come over. Too broad to settle next to her comfortably, I fit myself on the edge of the mattress as best I can. Mami runs her thumb over my eyebrows, smoothing them down, then looks at me seriously.

"Jaxon, mi vida, you've gotta go back home."

My eyebrows shoot up. "Huh? Now? Why?"

"Tonight, you need to go back home. You wanna help that boy, right?"

"Yeah, but . . ." This is the most straightforward endorsement I've gotten from her; I don't know how to process. I sit up, balancing with one foot against the ground. "I can't leave you here like this."

She shakes her head. "I'm okay, Jaxon. There's nowhere better for me to be right now. After your aunt saw you here with Christian, I'm sure she's panicking. She's going to try to stop you; you can't let her get back to the house on her own. It's better if she stays here with me."

"Are you sure about this?"

"Yes, I'm sure. I love you, and I want you to be safe, and I'm giving you my trust, alright? Find a way to do what you need to do that doesn't take you away from me." She takes a deep breath, lowering her voice. "Your dad's got a trunk in the attic you should have a look at. There's a key in the morgue, okay? Check my desk. It's a skeleton key; there shouldn't be any other keys you can mistake it for."

I stare at her, speechless for a moment. Her eyes are bright, face determined, refusing to show any lingering doubt on her decision. It means more than I can say. I know it can't be easy to extend this kind of faith.

"Alright," I say, standing up and taking a shaky breath. It doesn't make sense to me to leave her alone; she's hurt. What if something happens? What if *she* needs me?

"Mami, are you really gonna be alright?"

She smiles at me softly. "I know how scary this must have been, baby. But it's just a leg. I'm gonna beg the doctors to let me go home by your birthday so we can at least have a movie marathon or something, okay?"

"Okay, then. I'll go home."

She reaches for a hug, so I lean down, only loosely looping my arms around her. I don't know what's bruised on her, and she's already in pain. She presses her lips against my cheek, keeping a firm hand against the back of my neck for a moment.

"Love you, Mami."

"Love you, baby. Text me when you get home."

Before I leave the hospital, I find Titi to let her know I'm leaving. She looks at me with round eyes, covering her mouth like she's desperate to say something.

I stop her before she can open a conversation with me.

"Titi, I gotta get home." I don't know how to be convincing about this. Everyone who knows me knows I'm an unrepentant mama's boy. "I have school in the morning, and Mami doesn't want me to miss another day this week."

She blinks at me, processing that for a moment. "Mijo, isn't it more important to be with your mom right now?"

"Yeah," I agree, nodding firmly. "But you know I can't really say no to her. Can you stay with her tonight?"

Titi and I stare at each other for a long moment. Her eyes flicker to the side, searching for a reason to force me to stay. I wait, wondering if she'll think of something or if she'll demand to know what I'm really going to do at home. In the end, she sighs and nods.

"Okay. I'll stay with her." Her voice is tight, eyes, avoiding mine. "Pero you shouldn't stay home alone. Why don't you go stay over Regan's or something?"

"It's too late for me to be dropping in on her," I lie.

Titi Clío doesn't look like she buys that, which is fair because it *is* bullshit. But she backs down. "Be careful getting home, then."

"Yeah, I will." Some of the tension in me dissipates, relieved that I don't have to argue her down or evade any accusations.

I excuse myself and hurry home, knowing I can't really relax until this is all over.

TWENTY

The wake is still going when I get home. I pull the hearse into the designated spot, curving around the house. Then I walk in through the back door. It's dark downstairs, all the lights on the lowest dimmer settings and thick pillar candles set up strategically to bring warmth to the dark corners. The glimmer of candlelight reflects off the polished hardwood as the bereaved speak in hushed murmurs about their lost loved one.

This is familiar to me, almost comforting. It would be more comforting if my mother were home, but it's nice that Monica is here. One day, when I take over this business, I hope my mom will still be living with me in the house. There's nothing like the quiet loneliness of an empty funeral home with a full casket in a dark salon. I almost want to ask Monica to stay over, if it wouldn't be weird.

As I ease open the door into the butler's pantry and head up the back stairs, I pull my phone out of my pocket to text my mom that I'm home. I pause on the second-floor landing, as I open up Christian's chat. The last thing he sent me is a dumb GIF of a sad-looking dog waving.

You're so annoying, I type.

The three dots that tell me he's typing pop up immediately. Then, a second later:

How's Tessa??

I step into the second-floor hall, trying to avoid the creaky boards. Wake attendees tend to get particularly freaked out by phantom noises.

She's okay, I guess. She sent me home so I can make sure my aunt doesn't interfere with me trying to help you.

Christian's dots appear and disappear a few times as he types.

Dude, didn't she go alone to your house to pick up stuff for your mom?

My chest goes cold. She *did* do that. In all the panic, I forgot. She could have gone through my stuff. If she found my dad's notebook, we could be right back at zero. I shove my phone into my pocket and hurry, tossing out my concerns over which boards I step on.

My stomach drops when I step into the room; someone was definitely here. The comforter's on the ground and my backpack's been upended. I reach into my hoodie pocket, closing my fingers around the cool, round exterior of my dad's pocket watch. Even as my blood rushes in my ears in panic, I'm grateful I had the foresight to keep it on me.

But I think I lost something more valuable.

I shake out the comforter, kick around the laundry scattered along the floor and check under the mattress. The mirror is gone from my backpack, the sickle is gone from under my bed, and my dad's grimoire is nowhere to be found. She took it all.

I cover my nose and mouth with my hands, trying to slow my breathing, staring at my aunt's door across the hall for me. What are the odds she put them somewhere in her room? They don't feel great. Is it worth looking?

My phone buzzes in my pocket for what feels like the millionth time. I finally pull it out, looking at Christian's name lighting up the screen.

"Christian, I'm freaking out," I blurt, bypassing any actual greeting.

"I know. I was texting you, listen—"

"My aunt ransacked my room at some point, and she fucking took everything back! And she took my dad's grimoire too. I don't even know how she let me leave the—"

"¡Aplácate!" Christian says. "I was trying to call you before you panicked! Your dad's notebook isn't gone, okay? It's with me. I took it before we ran out to see your mom."

My brain does cartwheels trying to understand what he's saying. A flash of anger makes my cheeks burn hot as I stand up, pressing the heel of my hand against my temple.

"You *what*? Why wouldn't you tell me that?!"

"I'm sorry! But you were busy with more important stuff— like your mom! I figured you weren't gonna want to leave her side, man, and—and I don't even *know* how much time I have left, so I thought—"

"How were you going to figure this out on your own?" I demand, belatedly remembering I shouldn't raise my voice while people are downstairs. "You were gonna do it *without* me? How?"

"Jaxon," says Christian, his voice aggravatingly calm. "I know there's a lot going on right now. Breathe, okay? I'm trying to pull my weight here, dude. I'm trying to *do shit* while I still can!"

I scrub a hand over my hair, sighing. It's not worth staying mad over; the grimoire is safe because of him. My relief that Titi Clío didn't get her hands on my dad's notebook outweighs my anger at Christian taking it. Even though we haven't gotten much out of it yet, it's the most personal thing I've ever gotten from my dad. The pocket watch is personal, but in a way, it was like a contingency gift. An "in case of accidental necromancy, use this" sort of deal.

My dad gave me the grimoire because I asked for help.

"You took my dad's notebook, you literally broke into my house—you can't do shit like that. What's your deal?"

"Okay, I know breaking in was kinda crazy. And I'm sorry! But obviously I wasn't gonna lie about the notebook to you, Jaxon! I didn't think you needed to be thinking about me while you were scared for your mom!"

"Christian . . ." I stumble for something to say. How can he be so stupid? "I left my mom at the hospital to figure out how to help *you*! I'm *always* thinking about you!"

The line falls silent on his end. I wait, trying not to read into his silence. I know how that sounds, but whatever way he hears it, it's true. I *am* always worrying about how to help him, and I *am* always thinking about him.

"Jax, I'll come over," he says finally. "Okay? Maybe we can find your stuff or something."

"Okay."

"I'll sneak out as soon as I can."

"A wake's happening, so come through the back. I know you know your way in."

Christian laughs nervously. "How many times am I gonna have to apologize for that?"

"Until I get sick of hearing it."

My aunt's room is useless. The box she presented the mirror and the sickle to me in is empty except for the scarf that had been wrapped around the sickle. Her duffel bag is completely unpacked, clothes hung up in the standing wardrobe we put in the corner of the guest room, all her toiletries and underwear neatly tucked into the drawers of the vintage vanity across from the bed. There's nowhere for her to hide the artifacts, but I check under everything before giving up.

They must be in her car. I definitely don't plan on being the Black kid breaking into a car in a hospital parking lot under constant video surveillance, though.

Christian's footsteps come up the backstairs. I meet him in the hallway, wiping the anxious sweat off my palms over my jeans in the half second before he emerges through the door.

"Hi," I say as he steps out into the hall. "Thanks. For—for bringing the notebook."

"Hi, Jaxon," he replies. He's wearing one of those drawstring backpacks that usually have a sports team logo or a school name on the back, but his has a glow-in-the-dark flying saucer. He swings it over his shoulder, pulling it open to show me both his overstuffed notebook and Dad's grimoire, side by side. "We're all good. So what specifically are we missing?"

"The sickle and the mirror. I've got the watch, you've got the notebook, so I think that's it."

"Okay!" Christian grins, encouraging. "We got this, we've at least got a couple of really important pieces."

It's hard to share his optimism, but it's nice to hear it. "I gotta get a key from downstairs. You should stay up here. It's in the morgue."

"I can come down to the first floor with you, at least."

I shake my head, holding my hands up. "There's a body in the showing room. The less time you have to spend around that kind of thing, the better."

Christian looks like he wants to argue, but the desire to stay away from dead things and symbols of death wins out. He nods, biting the corner of his lip.

"Okay, fine. Hurry back."

I head down. All the lights are off downstairs, so I use my phone to light my path. There's a barrage of messages from Regan about my mom's accident, but no time for that right now. She'll understand; I'm a bad texter at the best of times.

When I open the door to the morgue, my gut sinks when I'm met with a sudden scratchy, scrabbling sound thundering up the stairs. I almost trip over myself, until a beat later a familiar yowling announces Grim before she sprints past me in a gray blur. How long's she been down there?

"Jesus—Grim, you scared the shit out of me!"

Still shaky from the fright, I flip the morgue lights on before heading down. There is no body out on the table tonight. Everything is spotless and sparkling, and I'm grateful for my mom's assistant. She runs as tight a ship as my mom does, so when Mami's ready to get back to work, she'll be able to slip right back into her normal routine without missing a beat.

I duck into the back office, leaning down to pull out the skinny drawer. Inside is the skeleton key to my father's trunk, like Mami promised. I loop the key's string around my neck, then hurry back up.

"Got it?" asks Christian as soon as I'm on the third floor.

I hold up the skeleton key. Christian's eyes go wide behind his glasses, the corners of his mouth quirking up.

"Whoa . . . qué chido." He leans in to get a better look. "You have so much cool old shit in this house. What is that, cast iron?"

"Keep your pants on," I tell him, stepping around him to pull down the string for the attic stairs. "This key's for a trunk of my dad's stuff. I need you to use your weird-stuff nerd brain to figure out if there's anything useful in there. Or even, I don't know, stuff that makes you feel healthy or strong or whatever. Anything that might help."

Christian nods, fixing his expression to convince me he's taking this seriously. I know he must be. He looks more and more tired up close. I reach for him, closing my fingers around his hand and closing my eyes.

There's a distinct pattern to his flickering current now. Clusters of many in rapid succession—twenty or so, too fast to count reliably—with a rest in between. I let go of him, trying not to look worried.

"How am I, doc?" he asks, smiling nervously.

I hold back a sigh. "Still here, so . . ."

Christian nods, taking that for what it is. "Right. Yeah."

"Come on."

The attic is wide, mirroring the size of the third floor without rooms to separate it. The ceiling comes down lower than my head at the far corners, but at the center stands about a meter taller than Christian. I make my way to the center, navigating around the boxes of our Christmas decorations in the dark, and pull the cord that turns on the single lightbulb. It only helps illuminate the room a little, mostly lighting up the shimmering cobwebs laced along the exposed beams.

"This place is great," says Christian, glasses flashing in the dim light as he looks around.

"We're looking for a green trunk."

"Knowing your mom," says Christian, turning on his phone's flashlight as he heads toward the far end of the room, "it's gonna be with all the other green things."

I press my hand against my stomach for a second, feeling both affection for my mom's organizational habits and unease over her current state of being. I take the opposite end of the room, turning on my flashlight as well.

"I'm sure she'll be home soon," Christian offers after an extended silence. "She's a pretty badass mom, you know?"

He smiles hopefully at me from across the room. I smile back despite the sick feeling in my stomach.

"Yeah, she is."

We move boxes around until, as Christian predicted, we find a green trunk tucked in among our old blue and green suitcases. We haven't traveled anywhere that needed more than a carry on since my dad passed away; I forgot we had these. I push them aside, grabbing the end of the trunk and dragging it out to a clear space on the floor.

"Is it heavy?" asks Christian, bounding over boxes to come over to my side.

"Kinda, yeah."

I kneel in front of the trunk, leaning in enough to stick the key into the lock. It turns easily, and I lift the lid. Christian shines his light into the trunk, squatting down beside me. The inside smells musty and warm, like all the sweltering summers it's sat up here have concentrated into one scent. The lid is lined with a threadbare patterned silk, once white and pink, now faded with age. Yellowing paper is taped to the lid with waxy-looking Scotch tape, bearing a faded hand-drawn family tree: my dad and Clío are at the bottom. As the branches spread up, they go further and further back until I don't recognize the names, some of them nothing more than first names; the years attached become approximations.

"My dad was working on this in his journal," I say, touching the tip of my finger to the worn edge of the paper.

Christian sidles a little closer, shoulder touching mine. "Is this for real? This is way bigger than the ones he sketched in there." He traces over the names at the topmost branches. "'Saturnina, born circa 1550?' and 'Karaya, born circa 1520?' That's *real* far back . . ."

I shrug, honestly not sure. "The bottom is accurate, but my dad *did* love fiction, so who knows?"

The inside of the trunk is neatly packed with sentimental items. Close to the top, there is a thick yellow envelope labeled PICTURES. Under that is my father's laptop, covered in years of stickers. I pull both out of the trunk, finding an old, worn copy of the first paperback horror my dad ever published underneath.

Christian's hand comes up between my shoulders, anticipating a need to support me. I pick it up and flip it open, thumbing over the well-loved pages. On the cover page, he wrote:

To Tessa and Jaxon,
The loves of my life and my
biggest (only real) fans.
Jadiel

I run my thumb over the familiar, cramped handwriting before closing the book, setting it aside. I don't want to think about my dad when he was young right now. I need to know what he knew. As I dig, Christian picks up the paperback, flipping through it reverently and doing his best to geek out quietly over it.

Everything in the trunk is covered in a dusty film and soon my fingers are caked in it too. I pull out several clear, generic CD cases, the discs inside them reading things like "road trip mix," "best anime openings," and "PROM 2000." For a minute I'm sure that I'm on some kind of wild goose chase. So far, it's all been mundane-looking memorabilia.

We bring down the yellow envelope of pictures, deciding that's probably the most likely to have anything of note, and return to my bedroom to search through what we've got on my bed. Christian keeps poring over the journal as I open the envelope.

There's about a million pictures shoved in here. Old-school type photos like polaroids and blurry disposable camera ones, but also beautiful film prints, grainy old black-and-white, and digital camera prints.

"This is gonna take forever," I say, pulling out a small stack of Polaroids. Mostly my mom, maybe in high school, judging by the amount of black eyeliner and lipstick. "Let me know if you see anything."

Christian grins. "There's a lot of interesting shit here. Like some of your extended family had abilities, Jaxon! I don't know who, 'cause your dad's not dropping a lot of names. He's saying his mom keeps track of the ones she hears about."

"*Kept* track of," I remind him. "She's dead."

"So? Maybe we can talk with her!"

"With what mirror?"

Christian shakes his head. "That can't be the only way, dude. There's gotta be something else."

That's easy to say, but what am I supposed to do? All I've gotten from anyone are vague suggestions to look around for something helpful. I don't know how to tell what that is. I groan, looking hopelessly at the stack of Polaroids in my hand.

Even if there's something in these photos, I don't think it's gonna help me replace the mirror.

"It's late," Christian says, observing my frustration. "Maybe we can call it a night and start in on this stuff early tomorrow? I can skip school and come straight here. You're not going in tomorrow, right?"

There's no way I can *rest* with things the way they are now. There's no time. "I'd say I'll try to sleep, but . . ."

"Ya sé. I haven't been able to sleep either. I get freaked out. It feels like dying."

He doesn't look at me when he says that, instead looking down at my dad's grimoire without reading. He tucks a gum wrapper into the binding to mark the page he left off on before closing it, setting it down on the foot of my bed. When he finally meets my eyes again, his usual eager smile is back on his face, refusing to spend any longer in that moment of vulnerability. But I don't think I should let it go.

"Christian," I start slowly, not sure exactly what I want to say yet. "You know you don't have to put on a brave face all the time. You can tell me when you're scared, or . . ."

He laughs a little, humorlessly. "I'm scared *all* the time."

"So am I." I stretch my hand toward him hesitantly. "So you can tell me."

He takes my hand automatically.

"I really wanna make it," he whispers. "I wanna keep living."

I nod, closing my fingers around his and pulling him closer to my end of the bed.

"Me, too," I say, looking at his bony knuckles. A heavy knot forms in my stomach, sinking deep in me with guilt. "Christian, I'm really sorry for doing this to you. It's not fair."

Christian scoots closer until our knees touch, then pulls our hands into his lap, holding mine in both of his.

"Whatever happens, I'm glad I got a little longer. With my family and with you. I'm glad I got to make it better between us."

My face flares hot with embarrassment at the same time my chest sinks with despair. I squeeze his fingers tight, swallowing thickly.

"I don't think I'll be able to let you go," I say, acutely aware of the watch's weight in my pocket.

Christian smiles, leaning closer. Our knees bump. I can see each individual eyelash behind his glasses.

"I don't think I could stop coming back to you."

My heart stops when Christian's lips touch mine. The first thought that fills my head, loud and echoing, is that I've never done this before. I don't know what I'm doing. My heart kicks into high gear, rising up into my throat, thumping furiously, and I try not to let my breath shake as I move closer to him.

Christian's hands come up, cradling the edges of my jaw, moving his lips against mine with the kind of reckless certainty I've come to expect from him. This close, he smells like Old Spice and spearmint gum, and when he tilts his head to the side, the cool metal of his glasses presses against my cheek.

Lost in all the sensations of him, I try to push away the thoughts about being inexperienced for now. I reach up to place my fingers on the arms of his glasses, pulling back to leave enough of a gap between us to push his glasses up on top of his head.

Christian smiles at me, close enough that he doesn't have to squint, his cheeks and ears bright pink. He laughs nervously, leaning into me again, nose brushing against mine as he brings our lips back together.

"I never thought this would happen to me," he murmurs breathlessly, lips moving against mine as he speaks.

"What?" I sound embarrassingly breathy too, but I hope I sound as good to him as he does to me. "Kissing?"

He laughs, eyes bright as he shakes his head. "Kissing *you*, menso. I can't believe I had to die to get here."

I don't know how to react to that. The idea that Christian wants to kiss me is already new and hard to process enough. The fact that he's *been* wanting to is too much for me right now.

"Don't joke about that," I say instead, pressing my hand to the center of his chest. He's still wearing my hoodie. "Don't joke about dying until I've gotten you out of it."

"Who's joking?" He presses a hand against mine, keeping it tight against his heartbeat. "You don't know how long I've been literally dying for this."

I don't know what to say to that either. I push him back with the hand he's keeping trapped against him.

"I really can't stand you, you know that?"

Christian lets me push him, but he doesn't let go of me. He's all flustered confidence, and I don't understand how he can manage that when I can barely string words together.

"You're such a liar," he says, reeling me back into him.

If he has any problem with me not knowing what I'm doing, he doesn't say anything. Christian takes his time kissing me, hands roaming cautiously. By the time I've gotten the hang of it, my lips are soft and swollen, everywhere else his mouth has traveled on my face, neck, and ears is more sensitive.

"I want you to stay over," I tell him at one point when he's lying on top of me on the bed, tracing his fingers along the shell of my ear as he presses his lips under my jaw. "Just to sleep. Please? I don't wanna be far from you tonight."

He leans up on his elbow, looking down at me as he trails his fingers up into my hairline.

"I'm gonna be in so much trouble if I'm not in my bed when my mom wakes up and checks."

"You can say no," I tell him quickly. "That's fine. It'd be . . . nice."

"It'd be really nice," he agrees, leaning down to press his face against my cheek for a second. "So obviously, I'm not gonna say no. It's just not the smart thing to do."

I raise my eyebrows, smirking. "Good thing you've never been too bright."

Christian rolls his eyes, still smiling, still flushed. His weight is warm against me, my hands settling in the curve of his back. He looks at me through his thick, dark lashes, shaking his head.

"We gotta work on your pillow talk, Jaxon."

TWENTY-ONE

In the morning, the sound of rain lashing against the windows wakes me up. The thick gray clouds outside blot out enough of the early sun that it still looks like night in my room, but the green numbers on my alarm clock read 5:57 a.m. I shift, stretching to turn off the alarm before it rings in the next three minutes, but Christian's weight pins down my other arm. I don't know if I can reach it without waking him.

Christian's face is slack and peaceful in the dim purple glow of my sheep eye jar, his chest moving against mine with his slow, rhythmic breathing. Last night, I fell asleep listening for the sound of his breath, lulled by the rhythm of his life force beating weakly against me, making sure he wasn't really slipping into nothingness like we both feared he might. He slept with his fingers twisted in my shirt, face pressed into the space between my neck and my shoulder, and now he's heavy against me, one arm draped across my middle. If I wake him now, he might be too scared to sleep more. If I don't turn off the alarm, he's going to wake up anyway.

I bring one hand to his side, curling my fingers over his ribs carefully. He slept in his boxers, having no pajamas, and his bare skin is warm against my palm. I hold it there, keeping him close to me, pressing my face against his hair as I try to slide my other arm out from under him.

Inevitably, Christian stirs, making soft sounds of complaint in his sleep, burrowing closer against me.

"Shh." I run my hand down to the widest part of his ribs. "I'm right here."

Christian huffs a short, content sigh as he settles, eyelashes stopping their fluttering. I manage to pull my arm out into the space between us, propping myself up enough to turn the alarm off successfully. I settle back down as fast as I can, and Christian only stirs a little more before letting his exhaustion win, slipping back into deep sleep. Digging my phone out from under my pillow, I wind my arm around him again to hold it up behind him, scrolling through my notifications.

It's still too early to text my mom; she's recovering from surgery, so she's got to get all the sleep she can. Regan should be awake by now, though, assuming she's going to school again today.

Her text window is a wall of messages demanding to know if my mom's okay. I feel guilty for having ignored my phone last night. She must have at least gotten some answers from Christian because all her texts were sent within the span of twenty minutes, then abruptly stopped.

Christian probably told you, I type into the window, that my mom's okay. Her leg's fucked up, but she'll be fine.

Regan doesn't respond right away. I wait, Christian's face pressed against my chest as he sleeps. I don't know how we managed to nod off this way—especially me. If I had woken up today, alone, to find that last night had been a weird fever dream, that would have surprised me less. Then again, the past week has felt like a fever dream.

The rain picks up outside, pelting the windows harder. A gust of wind howls through the tree branches, creaking through the old wood of my house. Instinctively, I tug the comforter up higher, more securely around us.

Christian's phone lights up on the bedside table, blaring out the sound of an old-timey car horn. Both of us jump in surprise, Christian's head knocking into my chin and clacking my teeth together. He turns over, swearing under his breath, reaching out blindly as it keeps honking louder and louder.

"Sorry," he mumbles, voice thick and rough with sleep as he flaps his hand around for his phone. "Se me olvidó. Chingao, espérame."

He grabs it, swiping to disable it and accidentally dropping it on the floor when he tries to put it back a bit too close to the edge of the table. He groans, rubbing the sleep out of his eyes, then turns so he's face down on the pillow.

"Forgot to turn off my alarm," he says, muffled.

"It's okay. You can go back to sleep if you want."

Christian turns his head, so his cheek is against the pillow, facing me. His ears and the back of his neck go red, like he's just remembering I'm actually here. He blinks at me blearily through blurry eyes.

"Did I sleep normal?"

"Yeah," I whisper, nestling closer so he doesn't have to squint to see my face. "I could feel you all night. No change yet."

"Did I snore?"

I shake my head. He slept like a rock the entire night as far as

I know. My phone buzzes in my hand, but I don't look at it right away.

"You were fine."

"Thank God," he says, reaching out for me under the covers. His fingers find my free hand, curling around my wrist first, then slipping down until our hands lock together. "It was cool, falling asleep with you. I felt safe."

My heart hammers against my chest, and I lower my eyes, staring at the comforter rather than his face. I don't get how Christian just *does* what he wants like this. How does he keep from getting tangled up in his own thoughts or flinching away from the raw newness of whatever this is between us?

"I liked it, too," I murmur, softer than I mean to.

Christian's hand comes up to my jaw, tilting my head up gently. When I lift my gaze, his eyes are dark and hooded, searching my face.

"You have extra toothbrushes, right?"

I blink at him. "Uh . . . yeah, I think?"

"Cool. 'Cause I wanna kiss you pero mi boca huele a puro pedo." He grins, fanning his hand in front of his face as if warding the smell away.

If nothing else, that grounds me a little. I'm definitely not dreaming or hallucinating any of this. I roll my eyes.

"You should sleep a little while longer, Christian."

He shakes his head, sitting up to grab his glasses from the bedside table. "Waste of time."

He rolls out of bed, shivering exaggeratedly when his feet touch the floor. I sit up on my elbows, watching the muscles in his back shift as he reaches up to muss up his sleep-rumpled curls.

"You coming?" he asks over his shoulder.

"I gotta, I guess," I say, leaving my phone on my bed before pushing myself up. I slip past him, rubbing my eyes and rolling my shoulders as I lead us out of the room. As I pass my closet, I grab one of the hoodies hanging off the hooks on the back of the door, tossing it back to Christian. It's cold today, and the bathroom tiles are even worse than the wood floors.

"Thanks, man," chirps Christian, pulling it over his head. The Creature from the Black Lagoon stares at me from his chest. "How's it look?"

I turn ahead again, winding down the hall to the bathroom. What's a cool way to tell someone they look cute? I wish I could be like Christian and say every stupid thing that comes into my head.

"Looks good," I mumble, pushing the bathroom door open and pausing to let him in first while rubbing the back of my neck. "You look good. All the time."

Christian lights up, hesitating in the doorway for a second like he wants to grab my hands again before doubling back for the closet to search for the extra toothbrushes.

I leave him to it, and he sniffs them out by the time I've started brushing my teeth. He joins me in front of the sink and ornate bathroom mirror, bumping into me gently as we clean up. He's gross; he still lets the foam get all over his mouth like when we were kids. I try not to laugh at him in the mirror, elbowing him out of my way so I can spit and rinse.

"You're nasty," I tell him, taking the opportunity to splash my face with cold water. "Even if you're cute, you're nasty."

"Brushing teeth isn't nasty!" he complains, toothpaste foam spraying the mirror. "Shit, I'll get that!"

"You better. That shit's silver."

Christian goes wide-eyed and he scrambles, toothbrush hanging from his mouth as he pulls one of his sleeves over his hand and reaches out for the mirror.

"Ah!" I wrap my hand around his elbow, tugging him back. "*Not* with my Creature hoodie, dude."

Christian holds back a laugh, pulling his toothbrush out of his mouth as he leans over the sink to spit and rinse, too. He tosses his guest toothbrush into the cup holding mine and my mom's, like he belongs here, then takes hold of my arm, pulling me into him.

"I'll fix it, gimme a minute," he says, before leaning down to kiss me.

I reach for him in spite of myself, stomach fluttering uncontrollably, every inch of my face and chest turning hot. I take his face in my hands, kissing him back, our mouths cool and minty from having brushed.

"Don't let that stuff dry," I say against him.

"Gimme a *minute*," he insists, letting go of my arm and placing his hands under my ribs instead. "I'm feeling this right now."

I know this is a distraction from how fucked up things are, and I should be thinking of nothing but how to help Christian, only I can't help feeling happy right now. It's like I'm on a weird high. No matter how much I remind myself things are still shit right now, I can't stop the adrenaline rush or the way the corners of my mouth keep pulling into a smile.

Christian pulls back to look at me, scanning my face like he's committing it to memory. I still wish he'd drop his default happy-go-lucky thing sometimes, but I think I'm also starting to count on it. I wonder if his carefree affection is what's keeping me from sinking. Does my perpetual anxiety weigh him down?

"If I get to keep living, Jaxon, I wanna make you smile every day. Literally every day."

I shrink away from him, blushing so hard my head spins. "Ew, don't say shit like that."

"I'm serious!" He places his hands on my shoulders, shaking me gently like I don't already understand he's being serious. "I put that on everything. That's what I wanna do with the rest of my life."

"Okay." I shake my head, looking down at the floor because I can't look at his face right now. "Stop embarrassing me."

"You wanna smile, I can tell," he teases, tapping his fingers over my cheeks. "I can still see your dimples."

I glare up at him to rob him of the satisfaction, reaching up to push his face away from me toward the mirror.

"Clean up my mom's mirror before she gets discharged from the hospital."

Christian lets me push him away, holding his hands up like he's surrendering. "Okay, okay. Lemme get the Windex or whatever."

"Down in the kitchen. I'm gonna get dressed."

Christian sighs, dragging himself out of the bathroom with his shoulders sagging.

"*Fine*," he says.

I wait until he's rounded the corner before leaning back against the bathroom wall. I'm weirdly winded, but I blame it on being on an emotional high and an emotional low at the same time. I keep marveling at how much Christian's come to mean to me in such a short amount of time—in new and different ways.

A week ago, I lost someone I used to be friends with. Now, if I lose him, I'll be losing a lot more.

✦ ✦ ✦

Christian's mom has been blowing up his phone for most of the day. When he finally bites the bullet and talks to her, she's furious. He steps out into the hallway, but her tinny voice is clear as day. Christian's doing his annoying calm, rational voice while she yells at him, which I can't imagine helps her mood any.

I take the opportunity to call my mom too. When she picks up, she sounds well—lucid, at least.

"Are you okay," I ask, trying not to sound as frenzied as I feel lately. "Are you in pain?"

"Mijo, they have me on a morphine drip. I'm more than fine."

I chew my lip a moment, parsing through everything that's happened and trying to decide what's most urgent to tell my mom.

"Are you alone?"

A pause on her end. "For now, but not for long. ¿Qué pasa?"

"How does Titi seem? On edge?"

She laughs a little. "She's a mess. Jumps up to ask me what I need if I so much as cough."

I guess that was kind of a stupid question. Of course, she's on edge, that wouldn't seem suspicious to my mom given the circumstances.

"She said anything about me? Or tried to run home at any point?"

"No, not at all," says my mom, tone rising with curiosity. "Why? Did something happen?"

"Ma—Titi took my things . . . the mirror, the sickle. I still found Dad's watch and I found the trunk and everything, but . . ."

She's quiet for a moment, though there's no real surprise in her silence. We both know Titi doesn't want me doing anything that, from her perspective, I might regret.

"Ten fe, okay, Jaxon? Have faith in your dad. And yourself. There's no sense worrying about that stuff now. You've got to keep moving forward with what you've got."

"I know. I wish I had a better idea of what I'm looking for."

Mami tries to reassure me for a bit longer before abruptly changing the subject to being okay with calling me out of school, presumably because Titi walked back into the room. I tell her I love her and promise to call again soon to check on her before hanging up, still feeling adrift but glad to have her in my corner.

Christian comes back into my room a moment later, tucking his phone into my hoodie's pocket, then flopping down on the bed beside me.

"You're in trouble, huh?" I ask.

He pulls his arm around my shoulders, pressing us close together as he scoffs. "Please. I came back from the dead. She yelled at me for scaring her and said que si yo vuelvo a hacer una cosa así, she's gonna freak out or whatever."

I look at him dryly. His mom's a nice lady; it sucks that he's so flippant about scaring her like that. He really can't handle being anything *but* flippant about all of this. I can't help feeling partially responsible for asking him to stay with me in the first place.

"Dude, don't forget your whole family went through the trauma of seeing you dead. She's kinda right to freak out."

Christian's eyes dim a little. He nods, leaning his head against mine. "Yeah, I know, you're right. Were you on the phone too?"

"Yeah, I called my mom. She says my aunt's been jumpy, but

she didn't say anything or try to come back here. I told her Titi Clío took the things she gave me, and then my mom changed the subject like a second later."

"Changed the subject?"

I shrug, "I think my aunt must have walked in."

"I wish we could get your mom alone for like ten minutes even. I bet she'd have some insight on your dad's journal entries."

"Yeah, if we get a chance, I was thinking I'd ask my mom if she's got any ideas or, I don't know, if she knows how to find any of his contacts."

"That's a great idea!" Christian rolls over to lie on his back beside me, grinning at me.

"Yeah?" I ask, scrunching my brow uncertainly. "I don't wanna focus all our effort on that, though. It could be a dead end."

He reaches up, curling his hand around the back of my neck. "No pienses así. You're defeating yourself before you even try. We're gonna do everything we can, so don't worry."

He tries to pull me down, but I resist the weight of his hand, rolling my eyes. The whole morning has been him interrupting us to make out. My lips feel used up—which I didn't even know was possible.

"Aren't you tired of sucking face?"

He widens his eyes at me like I said something crazy.

"Not even close," he says, running his fingers up to the base of my skull. "I could go all day, Jaxon. No pee breaks."

I fake gag as I push the notebook aside, pulling his glasses off his face and setting them on the bed beside us.

"What stamina," I say.

"Endless reserves." He grins, waggling his eyebrows at me.

I scoff in mock disgust, but we kiss anyway. The first time my phone rings, I ignore it. My mom's ringtone is a submarine dive alarm, so I know it isn't her calling. When it rings again, though, I pull away from Christian despite his complaints, grabbing my phone from the bedside table.

My stomach drops when I read Titi Clío's name. My mom might have said something to her—or worse, something could be wrong with my mom.

"It's my aunt," I say. "Gimme a minute; it could be about my mom."

Christian nods, lying back with his hands behind his head, as I answer the call.

"Titi? Is everything okay?"

"Hi, Jaxon," she gasps, a bit breathless. "Yeah, honey, everything's fine. Your mom's doing good, I was with her all night. Listen, are you home? You're not going to school, right?"

Christian meets my eyes, shaking his head. No sense lying; I'm pretty sure she was in the room when my mom was talking about calling me out of school and, even if she wasn't, she could show up and find out I'm not there anyway.

"I'm—I stayed home. I was gonna stop by the hospital later."

"That's fine. I'm gonna head over, okay? I need to talk to you about some things."

I want to ask her outright about the artifacts, and by the grim expression on Christian's face, I can tell he's thinking the same thing. I wait too long trying to find the right way to ask, and she keeps going.

"I'll be there in a few, okay? See you soon. Dios te bendiga."

"Uh—"

The line goes dead. Christian and I look at each other, both trying to find words in the moment.

"She already knows we've been spending time together," I begin.

He shakes his head. "But she's not gonna say anything about the shit she stole in front of me; it's better if I hide."

I lean my face against my hand, grimacing. "You're way better at asking the right questions. Your brain is built for this stuff."

He shakes his head again, firmer this time. "Your brain works fine for this too, dude. And bueno, pos. Aquí estoy por si la cagas, ¿okey?"

Hopefully I won't need backup. Even if I did, Christian might be the person Titi Clío is least likely to drop her guard around right now. If anything, I wish Christian could write out a script for me—but there's no time for that.

"Do you wanna hide up here? She might pick up on your energy if you're too close."

Though it's weak. If it's hard to pick up even by feel, he should be easy to hide with just a bit of distance.

"Okay. I'll try to keep within earshot."

TWENTY-TWO ✦

Titi arrives through the double doors in the front looking like hell. The shadows under her eyes are deep purple, her locs wrapped up into a haphazard bun on top of her head, clothes wrinkled from sitting in one of the hospital chairs next to my mom all night. Her hands shake with that buzzing sleepless feeling I know well by now, and when she sees me in the foyer, she beelines for me, taking me by the elbows as she kisses my cheek like she hasn't seen me in ages.

"I'm so glad you're home," she says, shifting her big burlap bag on her shoulder. "I really need to talk to you. I didn't realize how out of control things were getting."

"Is that why you took my stuff?" I ask before I can stop myself.

"Yes. Things were getting out of hand before that, but yes, I have a reason. I promise."

I don't know what I expected. I thought she might deny it, so I guess I'm glad she isn't lying about it. It's almost weirder that she's saying it outright. I gesture at the parlor room, heading into it.

"Okay, then let's talk about it."

She follows me in, both her hands wrapped tight around the strap of her bag, sitting at the edge of one of the couch cushions.

I sit in the high-backed armchair across from the couch, placing my hands over the arm rests, trying to keep myself open for this conversation.

"I wanted to talk to you at the hospital, but you brought that boy, and—"

"Titi," I start, already bristling.

"No. Listen to me. I didn't realize you were so *close* and mi amor, I can't get behind what you're doing. I'm sure he's a nice kid, okay? I get that you like him, but hanging around him is draining you like a battery."

The blood rushes out of my face, knowing Christian is presumably listening in. She's right; I haven't been able to perceive my own life force like I've been able to do with other people's, but the link between us is almost definitely transactional. However, it's only happening in tiny bits, judging by how little his energy fluctuates. It's in a constant state of almost spent, as far as I can tell. Christian doesn't need to know the impact on me unless it gets dire.

"It isn't like that," I lie. "I don't feel any different."

She holds a finger up to me, eyes wide. "You don't *know* that. And *he* wouldn't know that, either. You're both taking risks without understanding them fully. You haven't seen what *can* happen to people in this situation, you don't know what *has* happened to people who've tried to sustain people who were supposed to be dead. I know you don't get it, but I'm trying to save you from yourself."

I blink at her, stammering, not sure how to begin answering that. In her exhausted state of jitteriness, each of her words comes out with as much urgency as the last, but I try to stay focused on one thing at a time.

"Slow down and give it to me straight. What do you actually know about what's going on with Christian? Because I'll be straight with you, too; all I wanna do is help him. From the minute I saw him on that table, Titi, all I've wanted to do is give him another chance."

Is she thinking that I'm wrapped up in this because I have a crush on him or whatever? It's not true. He didn't deserve to die for being a dumb teenager. Whether or not it was right for me to bring him back, even involuntarily, he's back now. He has the right to stay.

"You're a really kind soul, Jaxon. You're a good kid, I get why you want to help. And being in love for the first time—I know, alright? I understand how powerful that feels."

This is way beyond the point, but I wish I could bury myself under the floorboards listening to her say that while Christian is within hearing distance. *Jesus*, we've barely had our first kiss. Somehow I'm sure that wouldn't make my aunt feel any more amenable toward my cause.

She continues, ignoring my obvious embarrassment as I cover my face with both hands. "Your dad died this same way, but at least it meant something! *Really* meant something!"

Anger flares in my chest. I sit up straight against the chair, narrowing my eyes at her.

"Wait—*what?!* You know how he died?" I demand, voice dripping with accusation. I'm so sick of family secrets. And I'm even more sick of secrets about my dad. "Why haven't you told me? You come here to tell me all this stuff that I have a 'right' to know. Don't you think that should be like the first thing on the list? You should have told me that before you told me anything else!"

She shakes her head, biting her lip as she turns her eyes up to stop them from welling up.

"I promised him I'd never tell you, Jax! I know that feels unfair, and I'm sorry. He was my brother; he means more to me than I can describe."

I clench my jaw, fingers curling in until my nails bite into my palms. I guess, when I was little, no one had any problems making promises to lie to me for my dad. As if me being little meant I had less of a right to know things that pertained to me.

"Okay, well?" I ask tersely.

She takes a deep breath, sucking her lips over her teeth for a moment as she exhales through her nose.

"Jaxon, honey, you were stillborn. Your dad put the life back into you and gave everything he had into keeping you alive, and now, he's gone. I can't let something like that happen to you."

I stare at her, uncomprehending. The inside of my head feels hollow and cavernous, like my brain has shriveled down into the size of a raisin. My mouth goes dry. *Stillborn?*

"What?" My voice comes out reedy and thin. "That . . . that doesn't make any sense."

Even as I say it, I know it kind of does. How many times has my mom told me that I was born a 1 on the Apgar scale, with my cord around my neck and silent? That I didn't open my eyes until my dad pushed through the doctors and held me himself?

My blood runs cold and sluggish in my veins, the inside of my head roiling like seasick waves. I lean forward over my lap, wrapping my hands around the back of my neck, trying my best to breathe evenly.

"You're alive, sweetheart," assures my aunt, trying to smooth out the sharp anxiety in her voice to be soothing. "You're okay. I just don't want you to end up like your father. Don't tie yourself to this boy. Let him go before it's too late."

That jabs something in me. My chest tightens again, my heart like a hot coal inside my ribs, and I scrub my hands over my face.

"What are you even saying?" I sit up straighter, hands shaking so hard I have to clench my fists again to make them stop. "Christian's gonna sap the life out of me like I did to my dad?"

"No, no," she says quickly. "Jaxon, you don't understand— having a kid was always going to be a gamble, but your dad fell in love with Tessa, and from the moment she showed him the pregnancy test, it was like he was a changed person. He wanted you, and he wanted to take care of you. No matter how much it scared me when he decided to give his life for yours, or how angry I was with him—that he'd cut our time together short—this was what your father wanted. This was what he was willing to do for you. He stayed as long as he could, but—"

"But then he died," I finish for her, finger bones grinding painfully as I squeeze my fists tighter. "Because of me. And now you want *me*—"

"Jaxon, that is *not* what I said."

"—to let Christian die because it might kill me? Because it wouldn't *mean* anything if I died for him?"

"That's not what I'm saying, and you know it!" Titi Clío sounds shrill, slightly hysterical with stress. She's out of her seat in an instant, holding her hand up. "You're my nephew! You're all I have left of Jadiel, and I'll be damned if I let you give up your literal *life* for your first boyfriend!"

"This is an actual life-or-death situation, Titi! Whatever he means to me now, he's not . . . he's not just special to *me*. He's a human being with a family that loves him! I brought him back, and I'm going to find a way to make it work! I'm not going to say 'oops!' and let Christian suffer for my ignorance, alright?"

Titi reels, chewing her lip nervously as she shakes her head, watching me with wide eyes. "No! Not alright! You and Tessa are the only family I *have left*! I am not losing you like I lost Jadiel! And after what I just did to Tessa—" She cuts herself off, snapping her mouth shut and breathing shakily through her nose.

I stare back at her for a long, tense moment, my heart sinking to my stomach. What she *just* did to my mom?

She must know something more about my mom's accident. She must have done something. But she *can't* have. Titi Clío wouldn't ever hurt someone.

Right?

"What?" I ask, barely above a whisper.

The silence stretches. For a moment, I think she'll try to blow past without spitting it out, but eventually she pries her jaw open to admit it.

"I caused the accident," she confesses, blurted fast like a gunshot. "But I didn't—I didn't mean for it to be so *bad*, Jaxon, believe me! I would never *really* hurt her. I could feel you pulling away and I needed you two to need me a little longer, so—"

I'm breathing fast, lightheaded already. I *could* have gone the rest of my life without hearing this, any of this, and I would have been better off. That I cost my father everything; that I wasn't even supposed to be here, living this life, in the first place; that my aunt would gamble with my mother's safety—her *life*—to keep meddling with mine. It's too much to process all at once.

"You . . . did *what*?! How?"

"I didn't think it would—" she stammers, voice strangled, pressing her hands against her face. "I made the fox run out in her path, I wasn't even—I thought she'd swerve and hit the guardrail but—"

"You should go," I say. Though my voice shakes, I try to sound firm and final about it. "I need you to go. Please."

"I still have to talk to you," she insists, a tinge of desperation in her tone.

"I can't right now. I can't even think straight. Please, I need to be alone."

Titi Clío looks torn. On some level, she must understand that I can't carry on talking after she dropped several bombs on me. After finding out my mom was seriously hurt because of her.

In the end, she backs down reluctantly. Taking a deep breath, she reaches for my hand. I consider rejecting her for a moment, but I know what she's doing. Upon contact, the flow of her life emanates from her palm and, I suppose, she feels mine. It doesn't do anything to reassure the anxiety in her eyes, but she at least doesn't look *more* alarmed.

"Please go," I say again. "I can't talk to you right now. I can barely look at you."

The guilt twists Titi's face, but she doesn't argue or insist anymore. She lets go of my hand, leaving the way she came.

A second after her car door slams shut outside, Christian steps into the parlor, looking at me uncertainly.

"Jax . . . ? You alright?"

I stand from my chair, unsteady on my feet as my head swims. Wrapping my hand around his arm for balance, I pull him gently into my side. He shakes his arm out of my grasp, looking at me with all the color drained from his cheeks leaving him ashy brown, almost gray around the eyes.

He heard it all.

My throat tightens, teeth clenching as I try to think of something to say. What *can* I say?

I can't speak. I can't even breathe. This is what my dad knows. This is what did him in. This is why he wouldn't say anything straight.

But my aunt knows. And now Christian knows.

I feel faint. The room spins and pulses around me as I crumple toward the ground. I squeeze my eyes shut against the waves of sickness rising in my chest. Scrambling a little, I fail to stand until Christian helps me, hands under my armpits. Even as he hefts me up, it's like I'm sinking into cold water. It rises up on all sides of me until it blocks out even the rushing in my ears, then everything goes black.

For a while, I swim in and out of consciousness. I'm on the couch, and each time I open my eyes, Christian sits in front of me with his hands buried in his hair. One time, I think I see a barn owl sitting on the fireplace mantel, but he doesn't do anything. He stares blankly at me until I close my eyes again.

When I start feeling myself wake up for real, the thunder and lightning outside is raging, jolting me into awareness with each crack. I reach out for Christian when I'm awake enough, touching my fingers to the back of his knuckles.

"Christian."

He looks up at me, scooting closer to the couch until our faces are less than an inch apart.

"Hey, I wanted to make sure you were okay. I should probably get going soon."

My head feels overloaded with new information—all of it horrible. But Christian wanting to *leave* makes no sense.

"Go? Go where? We still have shit to do."

"¿No escuchaste lo que dijo tu tía, güey?" he says, worrying his lip for a moment. "I'm like some kind of life leech to you. I shouldn't even be here now."

I push myself up on my elbow which makes Christian back up, but I reach for him to keep him close to me.

"She said *maybe*. This is theoretical on her part, and she *could* be wrong! If my *mom's* willing to trust me to try to help you, why can't you?"

"Because your aunt knows more about this stuff than your mom does? Hello!" he cries, widening his eyes at me like I'm missing something obvious. "And your dad really did die, and no one knew why, right? That shit adds up!"

"After thirteen years of me being alive! Even if she's right, I'm pretty sure you don't have to run off *right now*! We have time!"

Christian's eyes search mine silently for a few seconds. "Tell me the truth. Do you *really* think she's wrong? Do you *really* feel fine?"

I take a deep breath. Christian shouldn't have to bear the burden of my death on top of his own. It feels wrong to be honest here, but I can't blatantly lie anymore with him looking me in the face and begging for the truth.

I pivot instead, feeling like shit all the while.

"What, exactly, is your plan? Leave me alone, *die*, and then you think I'll get to live happily ever after? After all the *shit* we've been through?"

He stares at me, silent. His mind races behind his eyes, but it's clear he's coming up short with anything to say that sounds good. I sit up, my entire body shaky and unstable, like I split apart at the joints and someone taped me back together.

"You heard what she said about me, right? When I was born?"

Christian nods once.

"You're the only person I know who even slightly understands what I'm going through right now. Let's find more answers, for both of us. Please."

Christian takes his glasses off, wiping them fastidiously with the sleeve of my hoodie. He's still pale. Even his nail beds are stark white against the brown of his skin. He swallows as he thinks it over, pressing his ashen lips together. It must be uncomfortably real for him now that there's another life at risk. He can't laugh in the face of danger if the danger's aiming at both of us.

The thing is, constantly reconfiguring how I understand death—and my father—makes me want to know everything.

"A little longer," he finally agrees. "It's not like I *want* to leave you alone, Jax. Especially not *now*; you gotta know that. But I'm not giving you the option to die for me. I wouldn't give that to anybody."

"Please," I say. "Let me try to help you. I can't do it without you."

Christian nods, looking up at me without seeing since his glasses are still in his hands. He takes a breath, leaning forward until his head rests in my lap. I fold over him, cradling my arms around his shoulders and pressing my cheek against the back of his head. His life force is still there, fluttering against me in short bursts of energy. It's still fighting for him. I can't give up either.

"You really think we have time?" he asks, voice small and muffled by my pants.

"I can *feel* it, Christian. You're still here. And I don't think my dad would've said anything if he didn't think there might be another way or if we didn't have any time."

Christian's shoulders release, his head sinking heavier into my lap.

"That's . . . that's true. But if there's another way, then why did he . . ."

That is the obvious flaw in my logic. If there *is* a way for me and Christian to keep living our own lives, then why didn't my dad do that instead of dying for me?

"I don't know. But I'm not ready to give up on this."

TWENTY-THREE

Christian is a nervous wreck. I can't blame him. I don't feel any better. His foot bounces against the wood floor as he pores over my dad's notebook again. Watching him heightens my anxiety, but I can't afford to take my meds right now. With my luck, I'll fall asleep. There's too much to do to take that risk.

I don't know how to comfort him in this moment, and I know he's thinking the same about me. Looking for rational solutions is how Christian helps.

I text Regan, Everything's spiraling out of control. I wish you were here.

Almost immediately, she answers. I'll be right there after school!! I'll ask Rhys to drop me off!!

Okay.

Christian and I decide to return to the envelope of photos, but it's been sitting sealed and untouched on the ground between us for a while. He's leaving it up to me when we decide to dig through them, but I'm paralyzed by the fear that they'll be useless to us.

I slide closer to the envelope, pressing my hands against the cool floor. With the way the storm winds batter the house, the rain a constant, comforting hum in the background, the whole house feels a little colder. If things were normal, this would have been a fun day to skip school with Christian; a couple days shy of my birthday and one day after being kissed for the first time.

Christian looks up as I pick up the envelope, turning it to fold back the ears on the thin metal clasp in the back. I turn the envelope face down, catching a stack of photos in my hand.

"These are old . . ." I recognize my dad in one of them. He's no older than twelve or thirteen. He has the same narrow eyes and sharp brows as me, scowling at the camera with his hands stuffed in the pockets of his oversized baggy pants. Beside him, Titi Clío grins at the camera in a silly wide-legged pose with one hand on her hip and the other out in a peace sign. She looks maybe eight, her hair split into four braids tied off at the ends with different colored hair bobbles, wearing what looks like a corduroy jumper over a turtleneck.

Christian leans in, raising his eyebrows. "Whoa. This looks like they're on *Fresh Prince*."

I pass the picture to him, and he holds it up closer to his face, fascinated. "Yeah, you're not wrong."

The next picture in the stack is them with my abuela, long before she passed. In the photograph, she doesn't have the silver-streaked hair I remember. Instead, her hair is fully black, blown out into big fluffy waves, her bangs making a tall arch before swooping over the side. She has my dad's sharp brows and narrow eyes, all the narrower for her black eyeliner, smiling at the camera with an arm around each of her kids. They're younger in this one, my aunt's face is round, her curls pulled into little puffs, the three of them wearing windbreakers in bright colors. My abuela's lips are painted brown and she's grinning, showing off the big white front teeth that she passed on to me and Dad.

I turn the picture over. It reads, *Cape Cod con los grillitos, 1992.*

"Hey, does that one have writing on the back?" I ask Christian.

He turns his photo over as well. "It says 'Jadiel y Clío, primer día de octavo y tercer grado, 1995.'"

I turn the stack of pictures over, spreading them out on the floor. All of them have neatly written descriptions on the back.

"Here, help me look at these. Tell me if you see any years or anything my dad might've mentioned in the notebook."

We split the pictures, Christian gathering some up closer to him and picking each one up to examine. I do the same, wondering at the names and faces I don't recognize, placing them closer to Christian. For his part, he's sucked into his own pile, laughing and gasping with excitement every time he sees my parents looking like the goth teens they once were.

One in particular draws a surprised cry out of him. When he turns it toward me, it's only a picture of me as a toddler. I'm sitting in a patch of dead grass, a black crocheted hat with cat ears on my head, bundled up in a thick black onesie, my stubby arms wrapped around an unhappy Grimalkin.

"I must be a year or two there," I say, reaching for it. "Looks like Halloween."

Though, knowing my parents, could be any day of the year.

Christian doesn't hand it over; I'm not sure he even heard me. His eyes are glued to the back of the photo, eyebrows reaching for his hairline.

I sit up on my knees, leaning closer. "What? What is it?"

"Look . . ." He turns the photo. In my dad's script, it reads

Welcome back, Grimalkin. 1990–2005, 2005–?

I snatch the photo from him, turning it to look at the image again. Grimalkin looks normal, just angry. The dead patch of grass around me, however . . . on closer inspection, it looks charred. Some brown, streaks of black and ashy gray.

Like the tree and the fox. Like the cilantro. Like the grass that died under me when I revived the sparrow. My insides go cold as Titi Clío's voice fills my head.

I'm also constantly trying not to suck the life out of things. Ojalá no hayas salido a mí.

"Can you check the journal?" I ask, throat suddenly rough and dry. "Look around Halloween 2005 if there's anything."

Christian scrambles to pick up the journal, shoving his glasses up the bridge of his nose and flipping frantically.

"Yeah, uh—here." He clears his throat, then reads. "'Jaxon's birthday was almost a disaster. Fixed things before Tessa found out, thank God. I guess Grim's going to be with us a while longer.'"

I pull the journal over, but that's all it says under that date. The next entry is months later, no relation to my birthday or Grimalkin.

"I need to talk to him," I say, slumping forward and dropping my head in my hands. "But I can't. Not without the mirror."

Christian squeezes the back of my neck, stooping down to bump his forehead gently against my cheek.

"Ten fe. Maybe we need to put more heads together."

I don't get why Christian keeps pulling Rhys into this, and I don't think Rhys gets it either. We link up with him and Regan at the old plastic playground by the Snack Pit, and he looks as confused as he is happy to be there while Christian tries to catch the both of them up on our findings. Hearing him recount it while watching the skepticism slowly wrinkling Regan's brow, I worry that maybe we're trying to shoehorn a solution here. Dad really didn't give us much to go on.

Even when he's being met with confusion and skepticism, Christian carries himself with utter confidence, all earnest eyes and determined smile. I try to shake off my own uncertainty. Christian has good sense for this stuff and, anyway, he's never been afraid to go back to the drawing board.

Rhys and Regan sit on the swings, both of them too tall to actually swing on them without kicking up a wood chip shower or snapping the old ropes. When Christian, straddling the top of the blue plastic tube slide coming off the play structure, finishes, she squints at him, scrunching her mouth to the side as she thinks.

"Couldn't your dad have *told* you if you accidentally brought back your dead cat when you were a baby?"

I shake my head. "I don't think so. He was super cryptic, like, I don't know if it's a ghost thing or what, but he didn't give me any actual answers outright."

Regan furrows her brows, spreading her hands. "How do we know he'll tell us anything *this* time?"

"Well, we don't," Christian admits, still smiling confidently. "But there's nothing else glaringly obvious for us to check out, you know?"

"It's worth a shot!" Rhys grins at Christian brightly, tucking his hair behind his ears. "The worst that happens is we don't learn anything new, right?"

Christian grins back at him, matching dumb jock smiles. I cross my arms, leaning against the slide as I glower down at the purple laces on my black combat boots. Stupid to keep getting jealous, but here I am anyway.

Regan sighs, pushing herself gently on the swing and digging the heels of her sneakers into the wood chips. "Alright, alright. I'm with you. Obviously. It just feels like we're going out on a limb."

I laugh, short and a little desperate. "So what? To be honest, I feel like I've been dangling off a limb this whole fucking time."

Regan softens her eyes sympathetically, nodding. "I guess that's fair."

It's quiet for a few seconds. Did I sounded sharper or more upset than I meant to? My face goes hot in the silence, and I go back to looking down at my feet, waiting for Christian to go on doing his thing. Instead, Rhys clears his throat, speaking up uncertainly.

"So the problem is we don't have a mirror? I'm pretty sure my grandma's got a couple antique mirrors. She lives like a half hour from here."

I shake my head, looking up at Rhys even though my face is still burning. "We're missing a special mirror. It's black. My grand-father made it."

"Does it really have to be that mirror, though?" asks Regan.

"I think it's important that it's black." Christian swings his leg over the slide, hopping down like he's climbing off a horse. Standing next to me, he sets one arm across my shoulders. "I'm not pretending like I'm some kind of pro here, but the whole point of scrying is like clearing the mind and letting images come and stuff, right?"

The rest of us trade glances, each as clueless as the other. I remember him saying that before, but my mind didn't feel empty at any point when we did it back then.

I squint. "I wouldn't say that's what happened to me . . ."

"Right, yeah, but you were focusing on trying to clear your mind, right? It was kinda easier with it being dark and the mirror being black and all, wasn't it?"

"It wasn't easy, period." Christian's starting to press his lips thinner as he loses patience, which almost makes me want to laugh. I try to make amends anyway. "I guess it would be kind of harder with a normal mirror?"

Christian sighs. "I could be totally off. But I feel like the dark reflective surface is important."

There's no reason to question how he feels, for any of us. I don't think any of this works for me exactly the way he imagines it, but he hasn't actually been far off the mark on much of anything.

Regan seems to come to the same conclusion, clapping her hands together, businesslike. "There's gotta be more black mirrors around here somewhere. What if we hit up that witchy shop out in Northampton?"

"You mean the one with all the rainbow dream catchers dangling off the ceiling?" I wrinkle my nose. "Hard pass."

"Well, I don't know!" huffs Regan, gripping the ropes on the swing as she kicks her heels against the wood chips. "It's not like we're gonna find any kooky stuff like that in Jacob's Barrow!"

"What about—" Rhys starts, then stops again when everyone's eyes fall on him. He smiles brightly. Even in the dwindling daylight I can see his cheeks have gone from sunny brown to pink. He clears his throat. "Uh. What about the river? Out back behind the Pit?"

I blink, not following. "What about it?"

Rhys looks more embarrassed but keeps smiling as he ducks

his head a little, tone half-apologetic like he's sure he's wasting everyone's time. It's frustrating that, even intimidated, he's still kind of charming.

"Well . . ." He gestures vaguely. "Water looks pretty black when it's dark? Or even a bowl of water in the dark? I guess that might be a little more reflective . . ."

Christian inhales sharply, straightening up as his face splits into a grin. He holds his hands out in Rhys's direction, laughing. "Rhys! Yes! That's a great idea!"

Rhys, Regan, and I all say, "It is?" at the same time, glancing at each other, then back at Christian.

"Yeah!" Christian smacks his hand over his forehead lightly. "I don't know how I didn't think of that. Water scrying is totally a thing! There's all sorts of shit about divination and oracles and prophecies and whatever involving water! Jaxon! We should go in the river! Tonight!"

I stare at him. I know it's been warm but it's still October. Even if we still have a few days where the heat sticks, the nights still tend to get cold.

"*In* the river?" I echo, making sure I'm understanding him right. "It's gonna be like forty fucking degrees out tonight! What about the bowl idea?"

Christian's enthusiasm is undampened. "I'm sure it won't be that cold; it was almost seventy degrees yesterday! I've read some things about people having visions and shit when they get wet. Let's try it!"

Rhys jumps in to help him, of course. "The river's not that cold yet! We're always getting wet during crew practice, it's no big deal."

I'm sick of this team-up already.

I scrub my hands over my face, wondering if I really believe in Christian enough to let him drag me into a river at night in fall. Thankfully, Regan cuts in, brow furrowed skeptically.

"I do feel like we should try the drier option first at least," she offers.

"Exactly," I chime in quickly. "Me too. I'm not trying to freeze my balls off for no reason without at least exploring my options first."

Christian hooks his arm around the back of my neck, bringing his broad hand up to pat over my head. I shove him off gently.

"Okay, okay." He grins at me, shaking my shoulder. "Fine. First, we try it dry, and if it doesn't work, we go in."

What are the odds that I'm actually going to get through the night without getting wet? Knowing Christian and his luck, I'd venture to say slim to none.

To Christian's credit, we do try multiple avenues for a while. He brings a variety of mirrors even though he doesn't seem to think they'll work. It's strange, because they do look quite black in the dark, but it's not the same. When I look into them, there's the flickering of the candles we brought and the faint glimmer of my dark eyes in the reflection. It doesn't feel quite right, and my mind stays as cluttered as ever looking into them.

We try the water in a bowl, which doesn't feel right at all. Even in the blackness of the cloudy night, I can see straight through the water into the bottom of the bowl. I try anyway, gazing into it with Christian sitting across from me like we did last time, but nothing changes. If anything, the night sounds around me are louder than ever. The occasional car driving past is thunderous, the bugs click and trill, and somewhere in the canopy of trees, a crow caws intermittently.

I lean back on my hands, sighing in defeat.

"This is stupid. Let's do it your way and get in the water."

Christian, at least, tries not to look like he's psyched to have been right. I know Rhys is probably doing the same from where he's sitting next to Regan, but the candles don't provide enough light for me to actually see his expression.

Christian squeezes my arm, then takes my hand to pull us both up. "I'm here with you. Let's do this like last time."

We leave our shoes and socks on the bank with Regan and Rhys. When my feet touch the cold edge of the stream, toes sinking slightly into the soft silt, I stoop over to roll the cuffs of my pants up over my calves.

"How deep do you think we have to go?"

He shrugs, bending over to do the same thing. "No clue. Let's feel it out."

As we wade out, the water is colder than Christian and Rhys promised. Despite the warm streaks we've had this October, the deeper in we go, the more it feels like wading into an ice bucket, the pebbles at the bottom frozen and sharp underfoot. We are far enough in that the river comes up over our knees, both of us stopping at the same time to glance at each other.

It's hard to see tonight. The sky is thick with clouds, no stars peeking through. Christian's face is shadowy, his glasses glimmering when he moves his head.

"Should you have worn those? What if we fall in?"

"At least I'll see it happening?" The white of his teeth gleam when he grins at me. "Come on. Let's give it a shot."

This part always feels stupid. The water is so black in the dark that I can't see any part of my legs under the surface. It's blackest where my shadow sits over it, so I keep my eyes there, taking a breath as I decide what to say.

"Dad?" I try not to cringe. At least my dad probably won't be offended by amateurish summoning attempts. "Can you hear me? Can you come back, please?"

I keep my eyes down on the black surface, waiting, trying to keep my thoughts from lingering too long in my head. I wait for the sounds around me to fall away and, slowly, they do. The quiet rush of the river falls away first, then the soft huffs of Christian's breath. The cars out on the road stop thundering past us, the bugs go silent. The last one to go quiet is the crow. He beats his wings in the silence, gives a farewell caw, then takes off.

Lifting my eyes from the water, Christian stands stock-still in front of me looking like he did last time. Cracks all over him glow a brilliant purple white, his eyes like sightless electric suns. Out on the bank, two sets of matching glowing white eyes stare at us.

I look at Christian, waiting for something to happen.

"Dad?" I try, the word burbling out of me like I'm underwater.

The silence persists. For a moment, dim panic blossoms in my chest. Did I fuck this up? What if I got us all stuck this way? There's a whisper of wings above me as a barn owl circles over us, stretching his wings back and extending his legs. He lands on me this time, but there's no sensation when the talons grip my shoulder.

He doesn't speak through Christian or through me. The owl's beak clicks, he shifts his wings slightly, and my father's voice echoes in my head.

"I'm here." His talons close around my shoulder tighter, even though I still don't feel anything.

"Dad, everything's going to shit," I blurt before I can stop myself. Even in this plane where I'm mostly not in my body, I can't help the panic bubbling up in me. "Titi took my things, she told me I was dead when I was born and you brought me back, and then I found that picture of me and Grimalkin where—"

I cut myself off. I'm going too fast, though my dad doesn't say anything or make any sign that he needs me to start over. I have to stay focused.

"Sorry," I continue. "I'm desperate, and I want to know . . . Grimalkin died a long time ago, didn't she? And I brought her back?"

The barn owl stretches out a wing, turning to clean his feathers. His beak clicks softly, the only clear sound in the silence blanketing us. At length, my father's voice fills my head.

"I fixed it. I wanted to keep you safe."

"Okay, but I did it initially, right? Grimalkin's apparently been alive for like thirty-five years, so what part did I play in it?"

Silence. Long and heavy with reluctance. Christian glows in front of me like a frozen lightning storm and I wait, praying that I don't lose focus and that my dad doesn't decide to drop this conversation without giving me anything to go on at all.

Eventually, my dad says, "You were a conduit. You saw her there and I guess you couldn't imagine anything was wrong with her. You were too little. So you put your arms around her, killed every plant in a six-foot radius, and she woke up."

"*How?*"

"I don't know," Dad admits, a little less distant, more like a voice speaking in my ear. "Resurrection is the hardest feat for any necromancer to accomplish; to do so without tools and as a child was unheard of until you. I tried to get you used to death so it wouldn't happen on accident when you grew up."

"Didn't work."

"No," he agrees. "It's part of who you were born to be, and I shouldn't have hidden it from you. But I felt protective of you. With the way life and death move through you, I could only imagine it would kill you."

I can't say it makes sense to me. But my dad's not the first parent to try protecting their kid by barring them from something completely. Regan's parents refuse to let her have a boyfriend, which turned out similarly successful.

"How come Grim's still alive? If I brought Christian back but he's dying?"

Dad hesitates. The owl's head turns so I can only see the blank back of his head. "Because your life was connected to Grimalkin's very literally. After everything it took to keep you alive, I wasn't going to let your life depend on the whims of an animal. I sacrificed a cat to make it a true resurrection."

"My life was connected to hers?" This is it; this is where all the big question marks lie. What does that mean in the long term? "In what way? What did you think was going to happen if you didn't resurrect her?"

"I've never encountered anyone like you, Jaxon." The owl turns to look at me again. "I could feel Grimalkin siphoning life from you even after she'd come back to life. Neither of you seemed to be doing it on purpose, but I felt it distinctly."

"The way that I did with your life?"

A silence follows that, the owl's dark eyes boring into mine.

Though he doesn't speak, there's a distinct thread of offense in the atmosphere.

"I *gave* you my life," he corrects sharply. "Every time I did so, I did it on purpose exactly as I wanted to. You had no control over it, just as you had no control over the amount of life you kept pouring into Grimalkin. Just as, I assume, you have no control over how you're keeping Christian alive now."

I wouldn't say I have *no* control over it. Maybe very little. It's not a good time to argue with my dad, though. He obviously doesn't like having his role in me still living and breathing taken away from him.

"Then how *did* you bring me back?"

"It was easy because of your nature. The same reason it was effortless for you to bring Grimalkin back. I asked you to live, and you latched onto my life. For you, sharing a life between two bodies comes naturally, even without tools. But it hurts you, it runs your time down faster. I tried to keep you steady by controlling the amount we shared. Year by year I gave you my time, but you kept having accidents . . . close calls. Death was coming for you, so I gave you all of my life."

It's a lot to take in at once, basically confirming what Titi said. He sacrificed himself for me. But he was able to do it in bits and pieces, he was able to watch me grow up. And I did grow up with more stitches and broken bones than any of my classmates up until recently. Mami's always said I'd grow out of it, but I guess she didn't know. She thought I was just a clumsy, accident-prone kid, like I thought.

"Why did it have to be your *whole* life? Couldn't it be enough to keep doing it little by little?"

"Perhaps the debt would have been different if it weren't for the fact that you died of natural causes," he says delicately. "And so did Grimalkin. When you resurrect someone that was never meant to live any more years, the sacrifice necessary is greater."

But Christian didn't die of natural causes. Without the accident, he could have gone on to live many more years—possibly. This is good news, isn't it? That makes his situation much different than mine.

"How do I do it? Slow, like you did?"

My father extends his wings. His parting tone is thin and desperate. "Please, Jaxon. I don't think you can. Death will follow until you find a way to pay the price—whatever it turns out to be."

"Stop," I demand. "Don't go! Just—wait a second."

His wings fold down, head swiveling to look at my face again. It shocks me so much that he listened that, for a second, I don't even have words.

"Wouldn't you have done it for Mami?"

"Of course," he says at once.

I stare at his black eyes, hoping he gets my meaning. "And how old were you when you fell in love with her?"

His beak clicks, but he doesn't answer right away. It doesn't matter. We both know: they were seventeen. They fell in love, had a baby, and got married real fast, and neither of them ever seemed remorseful about it.

"*No*, Jaxon," he says finally. "I can't control you. If you're looking for my blessing, I'd rather die again before giving it to you."

It isn't until he says it that I realize that kind of *is* what I'm asking for at this point. He's told me what happened to him, he's told me what he knows of how my powers function. I need him to explain *how* to do what he did, but he needs to approve of what I'm asking to give that to me. Putting it that way, it feels impossible to get. How do you ask your father, who died for you, to endorse you putting your life on the line?

"It's not fair. You hid this from me all this time, and you and—and everyone, Titi Clío and Mami—you all act like I don't know what I'm doing, I'm throwing my life away. Didn't you know Mami was worth it? I bet it didn't take you that long to feel that way about her. You were ready to give everything up for me the minute I was born. Why is this so different?"

"It just *is*."

"But *why*?"

"Because!" he snaps, tone heated, feathers fluffing up, then slowly deflating again. "You are *my son*. My *kid*. You were my reason to live and die for. I can't make you understand that. I don't know how."

Even in this weird, spiritual state, my chest aches mournfully. I wish I could bring my dad back. I wish he and I could have been together through this situation, figured it out together. He made a huge sacrifice for me, and he must feel like I'm spitting in the face of it. But Christian isn't just some guy I like. We've known each other since we were babies. We used to share secrets and dreams with each other as kids. He's not *just* anything—he's a huge part of my life.

"I know it's not exactly the same," I say gently. "Try to understand me. You had someone you would have died to protect, and you did. Christian is so important to me. I don't know how to put into words how much he means to me. He's someone *I'd* die to protect. And if I have to, then I will. But maybe I *won't* have to."

He's quiet for a long moment, then finally extends his wings again. His voice sounds as sorrowful as it does scolding. "Try to be more selfish. For me."

When his talons release me, I jerk back into my body, staggering and falling on my ass in the freezing river. Christian hauls me up by my arms as Rhys and Regan shout from the bank, splashing as they run in.

"He's okay!" Christian helps me upright, leading me out of the water as I choke on the mouthful I got when I fell. "Jax, what happened?"

I wring out my hoodie when I'm back on land, still coughing up river water. Rhys strips out of his sweater and Regan pats me dry with it, looking into my eyes. Christian's soaked too, still holding onto my hand, watching me with rapt attention.

There's a decent chance that all I need to do is donate enough of my life force to Christian to balance him out—that's not as bad as dropping dead right now. But even if I knew exactly how to do that, Christian will shoot it down. They all will. It's not a small sacrifice to make. It sounds scary and I suppose it is.

"He said . . . uh, he said I'm basically kind of a conduit."

"A conduit . . ." Christian echoes. "You can reroute energy. That makes sense."

"Yeah. Also, Dad says that the sacrifice necessary to bring you back isn't as big as for someone who died of natural causes."

For a moment, no one says anything, the word *sacrifice* heavy in the air. Rhys wrings his hands, eyeing Christian, and Regan turns to look at him too, a worried line forming between her eyebrows. Christian, like always, refuses to show any fear. He grins encouragingly, coming closer to brace my shoulders. His hands tremble when they touch me. "Well, that's good, right? We just have to figure out how big it needs to be."

My chest sinks with cold, heavy guilt. I should tell them. I *should* tell Christian. There *is* a solution here. He just won't like it.

I can't say it. Not here. I need to talk to him alone.

TWENTY-FOUR

Christian asks me to spend the night at his house and everyone's still awake when we get there late in the night. Conce, his mom, sits on the couch watching a late-night telenovela with Christian's older twin sisters, Rosa and Alondra, sitting on either side of her. I'm surprised to see them still home from college, but with circumstances being what they are, I guess it makes sense that their school is being a bit lenient about letting them have time with their family.

Conce and the twins sit up, twisting to look at us, raising their eyebrows in matching looks of surprise when they see me. From the kitchen, Christian's dad pokes his head out.

"Christian, ¿estaban nadando?" asks his mom, taking in his damp clothes, then mine. "¿Con este frío? ¡Ave María Purísima . . . !"

I answer before he can, speaking in my halting Spanish. "No, we weren't swimming. Estaba conmigo. I've been really nervous about my mom and we went for a walk and I slipped on a river rock. Christian helped me out, es mi culpa."

The twins swap glances behind her back, but Conce doesn't look entirely convinced either. Rather than looking at me, she eyes Christian, an eyebrow just slightly raised. Christian widens his eyes at her innocently and spreads his fingers.

"¡Así fue, Amá!"

Christian's dad rolls his eyes, ducking back into the kitchen, as Conce sighs, deciding to drop it. "Ay, pues. ¿Cenaron?"

My stomach growls. I don't even remember the last time I ate, now that she mentions it. She smiles like she's caught us and hops up.

"Pónganse las pijamas y les caliento alguito ya rapidito. Vayan."

Christian smiles and tugs on my arm, leading me down the hall to his room to get pajamas. The space is meticulously cared for, the open closet organized by color, the shoe rack on the far wall almost as tall as me and lined with what looks like a million varieties of sneakers. His bed is made, blue and red sheets crisp and bright, his glasses case propped open on his bedside table, a lens cloth folded inside.

I watch Christian bend over his bureau drawers, searching for pajamas. His drawers are as fastidiously organized as the rest of his room.

"I forget you're a neat freak," I say, dropping my bag in the corner so it doesn't feel out of place.

"Not a neat freak. It's easier to find everything this way."

"What's your mom do with all that time she saves not yelling at you to clean your room?"

Christian gives me a small smile over his shoulder, shrugging. "Watch novelas and yell at me to eat more."

My heart aches sharply in my chest, imagining this house without Christian in it. Conce with her son gone, no one to fuss over since his sisters are grown and rarely home. The image hurts. The thought of letting Christian go feels so innately wrong, it makes me sick to think of it down to my marrow.

I know Christian doesn't want anyone sacrificing themselves for him. That doesn't make it any easier to shut down the idea.

"You wanna shower first?" he asks.

I nod, eager for the quiet, embracing warmth of a steamy shower. It's homey here, exactly as I remember it. Despite the circumstances and how long it's been since I spent any time here, it's easy to feel at home. And it's hard not to feel a rush of affection for Christian's parents when I see they've still got their weird little paintings of old people sitting on toilets decorating the bathroom walls.

After we've showered and changed, Conce sits us down with heaping bowls of chorizo and potato mashed together, a stack of warm corn tortillas between us at the table. Christian whines that he wants less, arguing with his mom for a bit until she notices I'm already on my second serving.

Pride lights up her black eyes. She presses her lips together in a pleased smirk, coming over to stand behind me and squeezing my shoulders.

"Jaxon, you eat here any time. ¿Ves, mi vida? Por eso es que Jaxon se ve tan grande y fuerte."

I smile at him, cheeks full of food. It's been about a million years since someone unironically told me I look big and strong, but I haven't forgotten it's the highest of compliments in the Reyes house. Christian rolls his eyes.

"*Amá,*" he whines, "No manches, ¡yo también soy grande y fuerte!"

"Pero tan flaco," his mom laments, clicking her tongue. She goes back over to him, kissing the top of his head. "Go to bed early. Jaxon can sleep in, pero tú vas a ir a la escuela mañana."

Christian groans irritably, but he turns his face up so his mom can press a kiss against his cheek before going back to the living room with the girls. His dad comes up behind him, setting down glasses of Tampico next to our plates before cuffing Christian's head affectionately.

"Ándale, hijo. Come bien para complacer a tu amá."

"*Sí*, Apá. I'm eating, I'm eating," he says through a mouthful of potato and chorizo.

Later that night when we're lying in Christian's bed facing each other, fingers loosely linked in the small gap of mattress between us, I watch his face in the dark. His curtains are open, filtering in some of the orange light from the streetlamp on their corner. It's enough for me to see the glimmer of his eyes and the light bouncing off the smooth curve of his cheek. He's quiet, but it's charged, eyes a little distant like there's a question forming in his brain.

"Jaxon," he whispers after a long silence. "Can I ask you something stupid? You can say no."

"Sure," I say, heart speeding up as my mind races through possibilities.

"I know you've got a lot going on. I mean, we both do. And I trust you . . . and I think whatever we decide, that's gonna be the right thing. But I don't know how much 'normal' life I've got left, so if your mom doesn't need you tomorrow, do you think you'd wanna . . ."

He trails off, clearing his throat nervously. My entire face turns hot and I'm grateful for the darkness and that Christian's glasses are folded up in their case. Am I sweating?

He starts again, "Jaxon, you think you'd go to Homecoming with me? I know it's kinda dumb."

I don't know why this is so heart-racingly embarrassing to me.

After everything we've gone through in the last week, something like being asked to Homecoming shouldn't even be a blip on my radar. Even if Homecoming is stupid, Christian wanting to spend what could be his last normal teenage days or hours with me means a lot.

"Yeah," I say, barely more than a whisper. "That'd be cool. I just gotta ask my mom."

Christian lets out a breath in relief, close enough that the mint of his toothpaste and mouthwash fills my senses. He scoots closer to me, our fingers still tangled together.

"Cool, okay."

Although Christian's mom insists that I can stay at their house and sleep as long as I want, my mom calls me at the exact time my alarm usually goes off to encourage me to go to school so I don't fall behind.

"They're discharging me today, but Conce is picking me up, so don't worry." She pauses. "I was trying to get a hold of Clío, but I don't know where she's at."

I don't know what to say to that. My mom deserves to know what happened and who's responsible for her accident, but there's so much going on right now. Maybe she's better off keeping as much of her focus on recovering as she can. Given how our last conversation went, Titi Clío definitely might have bailed. I doubt she'll have left my stuff behind if so.

"Really?" I ask lamely.

"Mhm. Is she at the house?"

"Uh . . . I'm not sure," I say, blushing. "I'm not at home. I stayed over Christian's house."

"*Oh?*" says Mami, unable to hide the smile from her voice. "Are you okay? You're being *safe*, right?"

My skin burns hot from my hairline to my chest. Is she insane?

"Mami! We're not—I haven't exactly been thinking about that, alright?"

"You haven't been thinking about sex or you haven't been thinking about condoms? You know where they are at home, right? In the bathroom closet?"

I drag a hand over my face, stewing in embarrassment. If Christian overhears the words *sex* or *condom* from my mom, I'll join my dad in the afterlife and call it a day. He's only barely half-awake now, though, dragging himself out of bed. "Neither, Ma. Please don't be weird."

"I'm not, I'm not." She clears her throat, taking a more serious tone. "How is he doing?"

"Still hanging in there."

"Have you found out anything helpful?"

Nothing she'll like. It could be worse. However, most of what I know will scare her even more than it would scare Christian. They'll both have to stay in the dark for a bit until I figure something out.

"I'm not sure yet."

She sighs sympathetically. "Well, let me know anything that comes up. And let me know if your aunt calls or texts or anything, alright?"

"Okay, Mami. I love you. Bendición."

"I love you, baby. Dios te bendiga."

When I hang up with my mom, Christian is stumbling around

the room with his glasses on, squinting in the overhead light. He looks at me, bleary eyed and smiling.

"It's Spirit Day today," he says, grabbing something from one of his drawers, then tossing it at me. "You can wear that for the pep rally."

"The pep rally?" I echo in mild disbelief. "Christian, we've got problems. Like, my aunt-may-have-bailed-before-I-could-get-my-shit-back problems. We're at square zero."

The smile falls from Christian's face, eyes still puffy with sleep but wide and anxious. "Not square zero, we have the watch. And she can't've gone far, right? Doesn't she live out in Boston? We can get to her if we need to."

"Lawrence," I correct weakly, digging my fingers into the jacket Christian tossed me. "And then what? We break in?"

"I mean, if there's no other option. It can't be any scarier than dying, right?"

I groan. He doesn't get it, and why would he? I haven't told him anything. The morning's barely started and I'm already exhausted.

I unfold the jacket in my hands. It's a black zip-up hoodie with a yellow pair of crossed oars and the word CREW over the left part of the chest. I turn it over; the back has the words JBRHS ROW-ING in big yellow block letters over another, bigger pair of crossed oars. Above the oars are the letters XTN.

I stare at Christian.

"Are we in *High School Musical*?"

Christian's face changes, brightened by the accusation of corn-iness. "Aw, come on, Jaxon! Please?"

Christian doesn't wear his hoodies as big as I like to, and even if he did, the act of showing up to the pep rally in school colors is embarrassing enough without it being Christian's hoodie with *his* name on the back. I rub my hand over the top of my head, trying to decide how much dignity I'm willing to give up for this guy.

He watches me with round, hopeful eyes. It's corny, but I can't say no to that face. I drag a sigh out of my lungs and try it on. It's tighter than I like my sweaters to be, but it fits.

"I'll get you back for this," I tell him.

He grins, pushing his glasses up to look at me better. He comes over, hauling me up off the bed by the hands to turn me around.

"Dude, look at your shoulders! You should join crew."

"You are seriously pushing me right now."

He drapes himself over my shoulders, stooped to press the side of his face against mine with his arms wrapped around my chest.

"Alright, alright. I'm kidding but don't take it off. It looks good. I like it."

It's an easy way to lift his spirits, so I leave it on even though I'm already withering on the inside knowing I'm going to be sitting on the bleachers looking like an idiot today. If his mom thinks it's weird when we head into the kitchen, she doesn't say anything about it. We're both wearing school colors, though, so that might satisfy any suspicions that arise in her.

We eat a quick breakfast of scrambled eggs and warm tortillas while Conce packs us lunches, sending me off with a torta twice the size of Christian's. She kisses both our cheeks at the door and waves us off, promising me she'll make sure my mom eats when she gets home today.

"Man," says Christian as we head down the street, looking back over his shoulder. "I think she missed having you around."

✦ ✦ ✦

It's embarrassing how much of the school shows up in black and yellow. Some of the sports kids even painted their faces or wear Jacob's Barrow Regional Golden Eagle spirit hoodies or sweatpants. Even Regan shows up in a black sweatshirt with yellow sleeves. She runs to us when she sees us and wraps her arms around me, squeezing me so hard my bones creak.

"We only have like half a day today," she says to me, shaking me by the upper arms. "Then we can sit on the bleachers for a couple hours and go *home* and end this hell week."

Rhys greets Christian emphatically. I raise my eyebrows at Regan.

"Then back to school for Homecoming, huh?"

Her cheeks darken, smiling as she blushes. "Maybe. If we're feeling up to it."

I don't know what's wrong with me, but I have to bite my lip to stop myself from smiling. Regan raises her eyebrows, eyes flitting between mine quickly like she knows she's missing something.

"Well, let me know if you end up coming too," I say.

A smile dawns across her face, eyes lighting up as she squints at me like she's not entirely sure she's catching my meaning right. She looks down at my hoodie, the stupid crossed oars over my heart, then takes my arm, turning me around.

"Jaxon!"

This is so stupid and embarrassing, but I'm grinning even as the heat spreads from my face down to my chest. Regan runs her fingers over the "XTN" across my shoulders.

"*Wow*," she says, seizing my shoulders again to turn me back around. "No, he didn't. Did he ask you?"

I raise my hands, spreading my fingers helplessly. "Yeah, I guess. Dumb, huh?"

Even through her smile, there's a torn look in her eyes. I get it; that's how I should feel too. There's a lot on the line, and it's resting in my hands. If Regan and I switched places, I would feel nervous about her getting excited about a stupid dance too.

"It was nice," I mumble quietly, acutely aware of Christian only a couple yards away. "To be asked."

"Of course it was!" she says, reaching out to squeeze my hands. "I'm . . . I knew he wanted to. Didn't I tell you? You should be excited. You should be happy. I'm sorry if I don't look—"

"No," I say, squeezing her hands in return. "It's cool. Don't be sorry. Let's try to have a normal day today, okay? We can talk about all the bad stuff tonight."

Her eyes darken a little more with worry, but she swallows back whatever she wants to say nodding.

"You're right. Let's get through this."

"For real," Christian chimes in, coming up behind me like he did this morning, folding his arms around my chest and propping his chin on my shoulder. "Seven more hours."

Regan rolls her eyes at him, leaning into Rhys as he comes up beside her. "I know *you're* happy. Listen, don't go around embarrassing Jaxon or I'll drop-kick you."

Christian laughs. Regan laughs with him but shakes her head and continues.

"Seriously. Like, in the nuts."

Christian's laugh turns a little nervous. Rhys takes Regan's hand in his, pulling her gently. "Let me walk you to homeroom," he says, smiling his easy, sharp-toothed smile at us and lifting a hand. "See you at the rally, guys."

We wave at them, watching them go. Christian tilts his head forward so he can catch my eyes with his head propped against my shoulder.

"Can I walk you, too?" he asks.

I press my lips together, pretending to think it over. "I guess. Not like this, though."

He laughs as he releases me, slinging an arm around my shoulders instead and herding me into his side as we turn to head down the hallway.

TWENTY-FIVE

When it comes time for the rally, thick clumps of white clouds drift across the sky leaving barely any gaps of blue. I'm grateful for the cloud cover because, while in the past years Regan and I sat under the bleachers away from the autumn sun, this year we sit *on* the bleachers directly behind the crew team.

As part of the School Sports Team Relay Race, Christian, the Davies twins, and Jae all wear matching jerseys—yellow and black with CREW printed on their backs in big bold letters above the eagle head logo. We sit on the next riser up, Christian leaning back on his seat to rest against my knees as I lean forward enough to drape my arms over his shoulders.

"This feels so fucking *mainstream*," I whisper as the principal and the vice principal jog down to the edge of the football field together, wearing matching Golden Eagle sweaters.

Christian laughs, leaning his head back to look at me.

"*We* aren't mainstream," he says, winking and shooting me a devilish grin.

I roll my eyes and push his head upright, so he won't catch me biting back a smile as my cheeks heat up. I can't stand his cute, stupid face, and I can't believe he's got me sitting here feeling like

Taylor Swift at this dumbass rally.

The crowd cheers as the showcase begins. It's the football team that cares most about the pep rally since this whole week is a desperate attempt to make us show up for the Homecoming game, but the admin always takes the opportunity to present all its athletes while trying to convince us that being on a sports team is cool and fun rather than expensive and painful. The captains all give more or less identical speeches; we're gonna take state this year, we want new blood on the team, et cetera. When it comes time for the crew team to say their piece, they all file down, and, surprising no one, Rhiannon Davies announces herself as team captain this year. Whoops and hollers chorus around us from Rhiannon's friends, fans, and teammates in the bleachers. Ava and her fellow cheerleaders shake their pom-poms.

Regan claps, giving a little whoop, and I automatically clap with her. However surreal, this is our scene today.

Other than watching the crew team say their bit about wanting new blood on the team and Ava getting thrown around in the air by her fellow cheerleaders, the rally is as boring as every other year. The clouds keep gathering, and some of the teachers squint up at the sky, searching for rain. They probably want this to be over as much as I do.

When it comes time for the relay race, Christian stands up in front of me on the bleachers, shrugging off his jacket as he takes a minute to stretch his limbs.

He grins at me. "Wish me luck?"

"What's the point?" I jab my thumb toward the track and cross-country kids, already down on the track that rings around the football field. "Track always wins."

"That's the spirit," Rhiannon says, tilting half a smile in my direction before following Jae down the steps.

I stare after her for a moment, surprised. She's acknowledged me before in class, but I didn't realize getting close to Christian would put me on joking terms with the cool crowd.

I smile sheepishly at Christian. "I mean, good luck, I guess."

He bites back a grin. "Wow, thank you."

"Christian!" Regan snaps her fingers up at him. "Your team is down there. Stop making heart eyes at your boyfriend and go!"

The word *boyfriend* echoes in my head. I'm kind of Christian's boyfriend, and people know. Not even just Regan—Christian's friends, too. Judging by the huge grin on his face and his bright red ears, Christian also likes hearing someone say it out loud.

We could probably sit here smiling at each other like idiots for an hour.

"Seriously. You're holding your team up, boyfriend."

"*Fine.*" He gives an exaggerated sigh, taking the steps down two at a time. He trips over the last four, barely catching himself as he falls on one knee and grasps at the bleacher. I jump to my feet, but he's standing again in the next second, laughing it off and looking back to give me a thumbs up before hopping down onto the grass.

Regan touches my hand when I don't sit back down, the hair at the back of my neck standing on end. That didn't feel right and, looking at Regan's expression, I know it didn't feel right to her either. "He's okay. We're here," she says. "When . . . if anything happens, we'll be ready."

"I know . . ." I can't shake the sinking feeling in my stomach. My eyes follow Christian as he takes his position at the last leg of the race. His life force has felt about the same—flickering in bursts—all throughout today each time I've touched him. But I should have checked closer. I should have pulled him aside and tried to tune in to him. "I think we should be closer." I stand, heading down the bleacher stairs.

Regan follows me without question. We hustle over to the sidelines closest to the finish line, standing by the fence separating the field from the woods. Regan snuggles into my side, and I put my arm around her, glad to have the comfort of her weight and familiar scent of heat protectant on her hair.

"I love you," she says, looping her arms around my waist. "I'm glad you're here."

"At the pep rally?"

She rolls her eyes, clicking her tongue impatiently. "You know what I mean, Jax. But, you know what? Yeah, here at the pep rally, too. If I was the only one dating a jock, you would've bitten my head off."

"'Dating' is a strong word," I protest.

"Is it?" she says, looking back down at the field. Her eyes look dark, a little distant. I know this is about more than sweaters and pep rallies and stupid things like dating. Like Christian, she tries to hide when something's bothering her, and she's pretty good at it. But it must wear on her, too, to feel helpless while we try to figure out how to save our friend's life.

I squeeze my arm around her. "He'll be okay. I'll do whatever it takes, you know?"

Regan's face grays a little, like I've confirmed something unfortunate. She presses her cheek against my shoulder, still not looking at me. "That's what I'm afraid of."

I don't know what to say to that. For a second, I think about admitting what my dad told me to her. Christian and I are sharing one life right now, and it's running down fast. I'm not sure how fast and I'm not sure how often I might be doing it unintentionally, but that's the reality. Would she keep my secret? Or would she tell Christian and give him the opportunity to "spare" me? Every time I slow down enough to think about how all the effort we've put in could amount to nothing, it feels like the air around me turns into a gaping, vicious void. But even with the dread threatening to swallow me, I don't think I can stop trying.

I can't tell her.

"He's worth it," I say, watching him flail his arm in a big animated wave toward us from the track. "He deserves it."

Regan looks up at the sky as a fine mist of drizzle starts to fall over us. She crosses her arms over her head, groaning. "It wasn't supposed to rain today."

I shrug off Christian's hoodie, draping it over her head. "It's almost over anyway."

The race starts, the cheerleaders dancing and chanting from the sidelines, shaking their pom-poms at the crowd to inspire us to cheer for whatever sport team we want since they all belong to our school. Ava looks extra pale under the gray clouds in her black and yellow uniform. Her silver ponytail hangs heavy, already partially saturated from the drizzle, but she's bright-eyed and smiling more than I've ever seen her, chanting, "V-I-C-T-O-R-Y! That's the Eagle's battle cry! Victory! Victory! Victory!"

Christian doesn't give off any visible signs that he's not okay while he cheers on his teammates as they run, but I can't stop alternating between scanning the horizon and looking at him, waiting for something bad to happen. Nothing would shock me at this point. The longer it takes for something to happen, though, the sicker I feel.

Rhys gets the baton, running his quarter of the race as Christian readies himself, getting into position to take the baton from him. At this point, the track kids have more than pulled ahead—they're about to cream all the other teams. The faster they do the better because the rain is picking up, soaking through my shirt, and the crowd up on the bleachers shifts impatiently.

Christian gets the baton, feet flying, pounding against whatever that weird shit they make tracks out of is called. My breath catches in my throat, eyes glued to him as he moves around the bend. Other than Christian, jocks have never been my type. But the way his muscles move as he runs, thighs flexing under his running shorts, brown skin shining from the rain, it's beautiful. His body's powerful, strong, and so *alive*.

I stare so hard that when the flash of lightning comes, it blinds me in slow motion. A brilliant, jagged streak of pure electricity strikes the wet track inches from Christian's foot. The current is strong enough to launch him a foot into the air and send him skidding on the ground. Then he's still.

Regan's hands come up over her mouth, muffling whatever she's screeching. More screams come from the crowd; Christian isn't the only one knocked off his feet by the lightning. The water conducted the electricity in a wide radius, the smell of ozone and burning potent.

Rhys staggers toward Christian. Most of the other runners, despite the proximity of the strike, are getting back up.

I can't let him get too close to him. He might need me to *do* something if he's dying, and if Rhys is too close, all I can think of is his hair and the sparrow and the picture of me and Grim with a blast radius of dead grass around us.

"Rhys! Don't!" I don't think my voice carries over the clap of thunder that comes.

Before I can try again, Regan cups her hands around her mouth, bellowing so loud and booming it makes me stagger. "Rhys, STOP!"

Rhys freezes, definitely hearing that, looking up at us wide-eyed just feet from where Christian's crumpled on the ground, completely prone.

I have to help him. But I don't know how. Fuck. *Fuck.* What can I do? I look around helplessly, the boughs of the young maple trees that reach over the fence above us with their wet, heavy yellow leaves make me wish, desperately, I had that stupid fucking sickle to grab some of their energy.

No, I can do this. I've transferred my own life force accidentally plenty of times without any tools. I can do *this* on purpose.

I reach up, wrapping my hands around one of the boughs, mentally begging it to give me something. Anything. A little life, just for right now.

"*Please*, let me . . ."

As if answering me, the yellow maple leaves around us shake as they shrivel and turn brown, some snapping off, drifting down in the rain like wet feathers while others dissolve to nothing, reduced to dust and swept away by the water. The bark under my palms splinters as it turns brittle, flakes of it falling over my head. Beneath me, the grass at my feet goes dead and yellow.

There's no time to think about what I've done. The bough rots through, nearly cracking off right over my head, so I release it, taking off down the track.

My hands are thrumming, warm and pulsing with what I hope is life rather than adrenaline from my panic-induced tree-sapping. As soon as I'm close enough to Christian I drop onto my knees on the wet track next to him, holding my hands out in front of me with my fingers splayed wide as if I've dipped them in something viscous. Christian's out. His clothes are singed, knees scraped and bleeding. I don't know if he's still alive; his whole body is limp.

"You're okay," I assure him, though I don't know what the hell I'm doing. I put my hands on him, dragging him onto my lap and circling my fingers around his bare arms. "Keep breathing—you're fine, I've got you. It's not time yet."

I'm hoping the energy just goes into him, because I have no idea what I'm supposed to do. For a second, I can't tell if anything happens. My hands are still pulsing, Christian unresponsive in my lap. Rhys and Regan close in to shield Christian from view, Rhys leaning against Regan heavily, wearing a pained expression.

I rub my hands over his cold, clammy arms, as if the friction might help zap the life back into him faster. He's pale—like, *30 Days of Night* pale—lips turning blue from lack of oxygen. It strikes me that, for all the times I've seen dead and undead people, I've never seen someone *dying*.

There's no way I'm letting it end like this.

The buzzing of energy in my hands blasts out of them all at once. My body jolts, ears ringing and popping like I got in a car and turned on the ignition only to find the last person driving left the stereo turned up to max. For a second, I can't hear anything but the ringing, a hot, crackling pain bursting from either side of my head and spreading across my brain until it flares behind my eyes.

I clench my jaw, holding back a scream. Jesus, maybe I'm the one dying.

My vision flashes white and the ringing subsides. The pain goes down from unbearable to annoyance, lingering around my temples.

On my lap, Christian breathes in sharply, and I sag with relief, even when he starts hacking and coughing. Color floods back into his face, healthy brown, and when his eyes open, I swear they have a dull film over them for a second before they clear. Bright-eyed as he gasps for breath, his frantic gaze meets mine.

My hands are numb and clumsy, but I manage to bring them up to hold his face, wiping his cheeks with my thumbs—tears or raindrops, I can't tell. The flicker of his life force flutters against my palms again, renewed. "See? You're fine. I got you."

He sits up, still half in my lap, which he's way too big for, but I'm not about to move him off. He throws his arms around me, burying his face in my neck. We're cold and wet, the rain pelting us harder than before. He trembles against me—or maybe I'm the one trembling—so I squeeze my arms around him, nose pressed against his cheek.

When I look up, we're surrounded by more people than just Regan and Rhys, all their eyes on us. I freeze, even though it's stupid to be embarrassed by something like this right now.

"We have an ambulance on the way," says one of the teachers. "Don't move, they'll be here in a minute to take care of you."

Christian shakes his head against me and says, softly, a little choked up, "I'm fine." He clears his throat, pulling away from me, though not far enough to let go of me completely.

When he blanches, I fear something has gone wrong. He brings his hands up to my ears, wiping urgently. When he pulls them away, there's blood on his palms. More than a smudge of red; it's dark and wet.

Shit. Not again. Stomach dropping, I touch my ears expecting to feel a river of warm blood, but whatever gushed from my ears is already starting to grow stiff and sticky where Christian wiped it away.

Everyone closest to us must've seen it happen. I glance around once more. Jae's eyes are wide and Rhiannon reaches in our direction like she wants to haul us up to drag us to the nearest teacher.

"It's okay!" I pull my fingers away and hold them up, only slightly smudged with blood. "See, it's stopping!"

In all honesty, apart from the splitting headache, I really don't feel any worse for the wear. The ringing's even stopped already. That's not to say I'm not worried, but this isn't the place to freak out about it.

The paramedics show up, but Christian flat out refuses to go with them. He allows them to check him over, patiently waiting for them to assess him as largely unharmed. Though Rhys encourages him to go to the hospital just in case, I think Christian's had enough of being a medical marvel.

In the end, no one was watching Christian as close as I was. All anyone saw was a blinding flash of lightning and several runners knocked down. Rhiannon, fretting over her twin, suggests hopefully that it looked worse than it was and all of us vehemently agree with her. With no one having anything but superficial injuries the sentiment spreads and everyone starts saying we lucked out by missing the lightning strike by a hair.

Rhys offers us a ride back after he's been bandaged up, trying and failing not to look as rattled as he feels.

By the time we're on the road, Christian's fully committed to playing his usual self despite the grim expressions on everyone's faces. Rhys does him the courtesy of smiling back from the rearview when Christian cracks a joke, but Regan sits stiffly facing forward in the front seat and I have a hard time unraveling any meaning out of whatever he's chosen to babble about. Something lame and geeky, knowing him. The only thought really registering in my brain is how close to the end we are.

How Christian must have been running on fumes.

How Death decided to come and collect.

How I haven't figured out how to save Christian yet.

How I have no idea what any of this is doing to my life or my body.

Rhys leaves us at Christian's house. I want to make sure he lies his ass down, first of all, and it's not a far walk home for me from here anyway. Now that we're alone, Christian drops some of his cheeriness—his expression droops a little with exhaustion, his eyes turn dark and melancholy. But he doesn't stop smiling.

"Christian . . ." I take his hand, rubbing my thumb over his knuckles. "I think Homecoming is a bad idea at this point."

"Jaxon—"

"No, hear me out. Let's stay in at my place tonight. You can bring a movie, or we can watch one of mine. You know I haven't seen *Eyes Without a Face* since I watched it in middle school with you?"

Christian starts shaking his head before I can finish. "No way. Jaxon, no way—I never got to go to a dance with a boy I liked when

I was alive, okay, I'm not giving that up when I'm obviously—when time is . . . I mean, do we even say 'running out' at this point? Time's up."

"*No*. No, I haven't given up." I squeeze his hand. "And you're not allowed to either."

I refuse to give up. I didn't know I could purposely drain life out of things without the sickle until I did it. I'm a conduit, right? This is what conduits *do*. If nothing else, I can keep energizing Christian like this a little longer, can't I? We can outrun Death until I can figure out the price for Christian's life. Until we figure out a more permanent solution.

For now, I gotta keep him alive. "I think it'll be dangerous to be in a crowded room after what happened to you today." I can't help the waver in my voice as I say, "You were almost *gone*. It could happen again. Or something worse could happen."

Christian lets go of my hand to rub his eyes under the frames of his glasses. When he pulls them away, his expression threatens to split my heart in two. It's a mix of pleading and desperate that I want to immediately soothe however I can.

"Let's go only for a little bit. Please, Jaxon? I'm not giving up, I promise. I'm just . . ." he swallows, lowering his voice, "Tengo miedo, okay? I just want to go out with my boyfriend and feel normal for a little bit. Please."

At the best of times, it's hard to deny him anything. I really can't fault him for being afraid, or for wanting to do something that feels fun and normal, something he's always wanted to do. I don't have a great argument against it because, thanks to me, Christian really is mostly unharmed.

"Okay." I scrub my hand over my head, looking up at him

uncertainly. "Alright. Fine. But we split immediately if anything feels off, alright?"

Christian lights up, genuinely, and my stomach flutters as a grin spreads across his face before he leans down with his hands on my shoulders to kiss me square on the mouth.

"Oh!" He draws back, face turning pink. "Verga, I hope my mom's not home! Okay. Alright, ¡qué perro! Thank you, Jaxon, seriously. I'll come get you at seven, alright?"

I'm agreeing to this against my better judgment. But making Christian smile like that does something to me. Makes me dumber, I guess.

"Yeah, okay."

TWENTY-SIX

Christian arrives at seven, and as soon as he's through the door he throws his arms around me in a spine-cracking hug, pushing my mask up so he can rain kisses on my face like we've been separated for five years rather than five hours. I laugh in spite of all this being in front of my *mom*, which is more than a little embarrassing since I'd tried to play off the Homecoming thing tonight as no big deal. Christian's smile and high spirits are infectious; I can't even bother trying to feel shame when she shakes her head with a big smirk on her face, snapping candid photos of us with her phone.

"Mami!" I laugh as I call her out, still wrapped up in the whirlwind of Christian's positive energy. "At least warn me!"

Christian slings his arm around my shoulders and pulls his harlequin mask down over his face, grinning for her camera. I do the same with mine, a black mask with silver ram horns sprouting from the top that Mami dug out for me when I asked about Homecoming, and she takes a couple pictures of us. Her eyes sparkle as she does, a huge grin dimpling her cheeks, close but not quite rivaling Christian's sunny excitement.

"Can I see?" Christian bounds over to her, stooping down by her wheelchair before moving his mask up again to adjust his glasses. Mami swipes through the photos for him and he bounces on his heels before coming back to me, taking both my hands. "¡Se ven bien chidos! Jaxon, you look so good!"

I'm not wearing anything special other than the mask. The same black suit I wear anytime I have to be part of a funeral service and black sneakers because fuck if I'm wearing church shoes to a school dance. But Christian's eyes comb over me repeatedly like he can't get enough of looking and my stomach twists pleasantly under the attention.

"Alright guys," Regan says, setting her hands on her hips as she looks at us impatiently. "Get a room, huh? Tessa, did you know about all this?"

Mami laughs. "I'd be lying if I said it's a surprise."

Regan takes Rhys's hand, tugging him closer to my mom. She poses next to him as she adjusts her mask on her face, nodding at my mom's camera expectantly.

"My parents aren't ready to hear I've discovered boys, so I need you to do the excited mom thing for me too."

"You don't have to ask me to do the excited mom thing for you, mija." Mami snaps photos of them, rolling her wheelchair back to frame them better in the shot.

They're cute, Regan in her ginger cat mask and matching sunset orange dress and Rhys . . . well, Rhys went full normie with his Zorro mask and black suit, but he's a cute guy anyway and he looks good with his hair tied back. Christian's definitely shown him up, though, in his red trousers, black shirt, white suspenders, and gold bow tie and sneakers.

I turn to tell him that, but his eyes are already on my face, making me stumble over my words. How long has he been staring at me?

"Rhys looks good," I blurt. "But I like you better."

Christian laughs. "Oh man, gracias a Dios. I was worried."

I shake my head, face burning. "I mean your outfit. Obviously, I also like you better, but I was thinking how—how nice you look."

Christian's eyes soften, even though he's still chuckling at me. Part of me wishes Homecoming was already over. I want to be home with Christian watching a scary movie with his head in my lap while we keep thinking on how to keep him here for good. But another part of me is glad I caved on this Homecoming thing. He's happy, and if I fuck things up, which I won't—I *can't*—I'm glad we'll have this night.

"I gotta look nice if I'm going out with you." Christian winks.

I smile. "So corny."

"Oh, Tessa!" Regan claps her hands together like she's just remembered something. Pushing her mask back off her face, she lifts her arm to sniff her armpit. "Yeah—I forgot deodorant, can you hook me up?"

Mami laughs and nods, pointing upstairs. "Medicine cabinet in the bathroom." She looks at Rhys, still laughing. "See, take notes. Now you know you've gotta keep a travel-sized deodorant on you for your lady."

Rhys grins, not at all put off. "Yeah! That's a good idea."

Cute. *Maybe* he's worthy of Regan.

Christian tugs my arm, nodding toward the door. "Let's head out to the car, we should get going."

"Okay!" Rhys jabs his thumb vaguely in the direction Regan went. "We'll be right there."

"You, okay?" I ask as we head out the door, crossing the lawn to Rhys's car in the driveway.

"I feel fine," Christian says as he opens the back door, letting me go in first. "Like, really good, actually. Are *you* okay?"

I nod.

Once we're seated, he turns to me. "What . . . what exactly did you do?"

"I don't know *exactly*. I grabbed the nearest living thing that wasn't Regan and leeched it or something. Like the sickle does, except with my bare hands. I think the energy went through me so hard my body freaked out a little. It's happened before. On accident more or less."

Christian doesn't say anything for a moment, resting his elbows over his knees and pulling his mask off. He's wearing his glasses under it which makes me smile a little, but his expression is dark with worry. He rubs a hand over his chin and sighs, glancing over as Rhys and Regan get in the car.

"Okay. Ten cuidado, Jaxon. Please?"

"You, too."

We both silently agree to drop it once the car rumbles to life. Despite all the smiles and clowning around while my mom made us pose for photos, the air in the car is thick and suffocating. I open a window like it'll help, waving at my mom on the porch as we pull out of the driveway.

Just an hour. If we can make it through an hour of Homecoming without anything dangerous happening, I'll feel a lot better about tonight.

Making the gym look spooky for Homecoming isn't really that hard. The building is old as fuck and whatever purpose it served before they dropped a school around it involved having a massive vaulted ceiling with sloping support beams and arched windows with glass too old and scratched up to see anything out of. It looks like a gothic crypt someone gutted and fixed up with a shiny hardwood basketball court, four brand new hoops, and bleachers. The Homecoming committee did their best to mask the court with cobwebs and fake gnarled trees around the sidelines, string lights tangled up in their branches. Honestly, even with the corny fog machines and all the green and purple gels over the lights, it's pretty effective.

"¡Qué perro!" Christian laughs as he takes it all in, taking my hand to drag me over to the photo station they set up off to the side. A million photos at home are apparently not enough.

One of the yearbook kids gets her camera ready as we come over to pose in front of a papier-mâché wrought iron arch with a sign hanging off it reading CEMETERY in a gothic font. Behind the gate are a handful of wooden painted tombstones reading RIP.

"*Perro* is one word for it," I mutter.

Regan and Rhys come over to pose with us, and she digs her elbow into my side. "This is right up your alley, Jax, come on."

I take offense at that, but only a little.

The Homecoming committee did, at least, clearly bust their asses trying to Halloween the place up.

Christian's hand stays glued to mine as we walk away from the setup. I tug him toward the dance floor. This might be embarrassing *and* anxiety-making for me, but tonight means a lot to Christian. So I'm gonna check off everything he wants to do, and I'm not giving myself any time to feel dumb doing it.

"One dance, okay?" I say. "I won't even fight you on it, but let's get it out of the way before I get a chance to overthink it."

"Wait, wait, no!" Christian digs his heels in, gripping my hand tighter so my tugging is completely ineffectual. "You're my *boyfriend*, this is Homecoming! I'm not wasting our one dance on a fast song! A slow dance. We do one slow dance and then we can bounce, no questions asked."

I groan, rolling my eyes up at the cavernous vaulted ceiling and the huge, round fluorescent lamps hanging above us. Every inch I give, I know Christian's gonna try to take a mile. When I look at him again, he's lifting his mask for me so I can see the cute sad face he's making.

Why am I this weak?

"If you keep doing that, we're not dancing at all. Put your mask back on."

"Jaxon, *please*."

I don't actually know much about how they organize school dance playlists or if they organize them at all, but the dance itself is only a couple hours. Some slow tune will come up before long, then we can get out. The irony of the haunted cemetery theme of this masquerade isn't lost on me. I'm not trying to tempt fate.

"Ok, fine."

Christian tackle hugs me and I'm high enough on the gesture that, in keeping with the growing pattern of me doing things because Christian likes them, I end up dancing more than one dance.

It's not as embarrassing as it could be, though my version of dancing is basically nodding along with the music while shifting my weight to the beat. Anyone else would look dumb strutting around, flailing his arms like Christian's doing, but because it's him and even that harlequin mask can't hide his huge grin, he looks awesome. Better still, he looks like he's having the time of his life.

I'm glad I caved about coming.

Everyone kind of melds together to dance in a group to the faster songs, which makes it less awkward than I expected. It's not so bad. Christian's having fun, he looks well, and Rhys and Regan, as much as they both seem to want to hover as close to us as possible, also seem to have forgotten most of their worries, getting wrapped up in the music and the atmosphere.

All the same, I don't think I can keep up the dance stamina as long as my friends can. I reach for Christian's arm, leaning up to speak into his ear over the pounding music.

"Christian, I'm gonna tap out for a little, okay? Grab a soda or something."

"Oh, I'll come with you!"

"No, it's okay! Keep dancing, you look like you're having fun."

He grins, shaking his head. "Not as fun if you're not with me. Ándale."

I almost trip over my own feet at his sweet words. He needs to stop doing that.

The dance floor is packed. It seems like the whole school turned out, which I guess I understand since there's not much else to do on a Friday night in our town. Christian, being tall, cranes his neck, apparently looking for the clearest path out to the edge where the drink table is.

"The crowd thins out this way. Ven." He puts his hand on the small of my back, pushing me gently in the direction he's decided on.

I'm glad we're choosing now to pause for a bit because the song playing is obnoxious with its repetitive bassline and a weird, tinny instrument I can't place. My ears have felt fine since I got home, but the sound is grating anyway and the strobe light is going for this dance, which is even more annoying.

Finally, the crowd thins. We hurry to duck out past one of the tall speakers mounted up on a stand at the corner. I stick my fingers in my ears, cringing at the way the music seems to pound in my chest, teeth, and brain from this close.

"*God*," I yell over the music. "That's so fucking—"

The speaker in front of us crackles, showers sparks from behind, then makes a popping sound so loud it rattles my skull. In the next moment it topples over like a tree coming down. Christian and I jump apart with barely enough time and luck to avoid being caught as it slams down on the hardwood floor.

Multiple people scream in surprise and a moment later the other speakers stop playing as the tech department runs to try to fix everything. I stand frozen, staring down at the ten-foot speaker that almost landed on Christian's head.

I take his face in my hands, closing my eyes as I try to focus on the current of life in him despite my pounding heart and the buzzing, startled dance floor. Not an hour ago, he'd been flickering in a constant pattern but already it's whittled down to bursts punctuated by short rests. It's draining faster than before. It's been faster each time.

Every part of me turns ice cold. I dimly register it when someone comes on over the mic tells us they're going to check things out before resuming the music and dancing. I can't read Christian's expression behind his mask, but he's looking at me like he's ready to argue what I'm going to say next.

"We should go," I say. "Let's go now."

Christian steps over the speaker, grabbing both my hands. "But I'm fine. Nothing happened, Jaxon!"

"Are you kidding?" I shake my head at him, looking from his face down to the speaker. "You are *not* fine. This isn't nothing. This is Death. We need to *go*."

"Faulty wiring happens," he counters immediately, squeezing my hands before pulling them up to kiss my knuckles repeatedly. "This isn't anything. Death'll do better than trying to squish me under a speaker."

"Christian," I snap. "You're being stupid, we *can't* risk you!"

"Sorry! Just please not yet. I'll ask the tech kids to put a slow one on once they're set back up, how's that? We'll do our dance y nos vamos a la verga."

I can't tell what's going on with him. If he's genuinely positive that this isn't Death coming for him or if he's just so desperate to knock this off his bucket list before it catches up to him. Either way it feels like a bad idea, and I want to scream at him that it isn't worth it—that I'm *not* going to let anything happen, no matter what that means for me. But now isn't the time for that conversation, which I *know* won't go well when it comes.

"If the next song isn't a slow song, we are leaving, get me?"

He grins, tugging me into his chest and squeezing me. "Gimme two seconds!"

He bounds away as I stagger shakily to the drink table. I'll never understand how Christian keeps it together. My heart is pounding a mile a minute and there's a sick knot in my stomach that won't be going anywhere anytime soon. My hands tremble as I reach for one of the plastic cups of soda.

Regan and Rhys appear beside me in a second.

"You, okay?" Regan side hugs me. "What the hell happened?"

I shake my head.

"That thing almost got him this time," Rhys says.

"Yeah," I agree faintly. "Almost." How long can we keep tempting fate?

I tell them again that I'm fine and to go enjoy the dance. Regan gives me a glare that says I better be alive when she sees me next or there will be hell to pay, before leaving with Rhys. I stand to the side of the refreshment table, trying to breathe.

The students and chaperones around sound like they've successfully brushed off the incident. Chatter and laughter bounce off the walls of the gym as students fool around, waiting for the music to come back on. I push my mask up, feeling suffocated by it, by the crowd, and by the dim, colored lights.

I loosen my tie with my free hand, draining the Sprite out of my cup in two big gulps. Just as I am about to call it quits and find Christian so we can leave, the music starts up again.

Sure enough, it's a slow song.

Okay. It's fine. This is good.

One three-minute dance, then we can go home.

I scan the dance floor for Christian among the crowd, but my eyes catch two pinpricks of light, back beside the folded-up bleachers pushed against the wall. I do a double-take and they're still there; two greenish dots staring out from the shadows of the gym, like a cat sitting in the darkness.

Or a fox.

I thought Titi Clío had split, but could she have sent the fox to watch me again? Can she control it from Lawrence? Did she decide to hang around?

I reach into my pocket for my phone, and there's nothing from my mom. When I look up from again, the eyes are gone. My head swims, stomach churning uncomfortably. I *did* see that, didn't I?

"There you are!" Christian surfaces from the throng, making a beeline for me and taking my wrists to drag me back out onto the dance floor. He stops, no doubt catching the spooked expression on my face, and pushes his mask up. "What's wrong?"

I look around, trying to spot the greenish dots around the perimeter of the gym. I don't see them anywhere, like they disappeared into the ether. "I'll tell you after. Let's go dance, huh?"

If my aunt is watching, she's not going to make a fox run out into the dance floor in front of everyone. At least, I don't think so.

Christian smiles, leading me to the least crowded part of the floor, then pulls me close and we finally dance a slow song. With all the ups and downs so far tonight, I'm glad to take a breath and focus on Christian like this. Despite my distaste for things like Spirit Week and Homecoming, I can't deny there's something about being cheek to cheek with him, our arms wrapped around each other, swaying to a ballad that makes my heart feel soft and achy.

Part of the aching is the fear of separation. But there's also something about Christian that makes my stomach clench and my heart swell up in a nice way. I pull back a little to look at him, glad his mask is still pushed up so I can see his whole face, dark eyes locked onto mine. He raises his eyebrows, smiling a little like he always does, visibly nervous like he's waiting for me to deliver bad news.

"It's not awful," I say. "Homecoming. It's not that bad with you."

His face splits into a beautiful grin. "Oh? You think?"

"Yeah. I guess." Every other couple on the floor is swaying along to the music at least as awkwardly as we are, so there's no reason to feel self-conscious about that. "Killer speakers notwith-standing, it's alright."

Christian scoffs playfully. "No mames, that speaker barely tried. If I'm gonna get taken out at Homecoming, I want full-on *Carrie*."

I glare at him. "Can you not? We're still *here*, idiot. Don't ruin the moment. I was literally just thinking about how much I like you."

By his megawatt grin, the last part is all he heard. He spins us around once, waggling his brows at me. "Yeah? Well don't be shy, let me hear it. How much *do* you like me?"

"You know how much," I grumble.

"I don't. I'm not a mind reader."

I roll my eyes, not even bothering to fight the heat surging in my cheeks like it always does when Christian acts goofy to get me flustered. And he's become a master at it. Damn. This song has got to be ending any minute now, right?

"I'm waiting," he singsongs.

I press my lips together to keep from smiling, my nostrils flaring slightly with the effort. If he thinks I'm going to whisper sweet nothings to him while we slow dance at our school, he's dumber than I realized.

"I know you wanna smile, Jaxon," he teases. "I can tell by your dimples."

I pull my mask down, heart pounding, ears burning. I can't stand him when he gets like this. "You *know*, Christian. You know I'd literally die for you."

We stop dancing and stare at each other, letting the weight of my statement hang in the air between us. He's not goofing around anymore, and I am dead serious. Christian believes me. Already shaking his head, he opens his mouth to argue.

"Christian, I—"

A flash of white blinds me. For a second, I think they've set off the strobe light at the end of a ballad for some reason, which seems like a weird choice. When it keeps happening sporadically, it's clear that it's not a dance effect. The flashes illuminating the entire gym are coming from the fluorescent lamps hanging up high from the rafters. Everyone gasps or groans in irritation as they squint up at the ceiling.

The slow song playing starts to fade to its end, but it sounds strange as it does. Off-key, burbling and slightly muffled, as if the speakers were bobbing in a pool of water. The ending notes stretch longer and warp. Although the song is clearly ending, the volume warbles, growing louder. The floor shakes under the strain of the volume and I bring my hands up over my ears, looking up at Christian in alarm. The lights flash more insistently, Christian's eyes widening as he looks around, tightening his arms around me.

"We gotta get out of here," I yell, but my voice falls flat against the push of sound all around us. My teeth ache like I've been grinding them against aluminum. The lights above us screech and whine audibly even over the speakers, sparks showering down from each lamp as they strobe violently—the colored lights for the dance follow suit.

People start to run out of the gym, and Christian herds me into his side, trying to do the same. There's a crackling burst overhead as hard, jagged pieces of fiberglass rain over us. The backboard on the basketball hoop closest to us shattered from the sound.

Panic rises in my chest, closing my throat, pulsing in my

overtaxed ears. The flashes are blinding, the sparks coming from every direction—including the fog machine, which now emits actual black smoke.

This was a mistake.

My body goes cold, my hands numb, stomach tight and painfully hollow. The all-consuming fear makes my legs weak, stumbling as we get jostled around by the people running past us. I fist my hands in Christian's shirt, praying this place doesn't explode before I can drag him out. More glass showers directly over us, this time from above, along with a brilliant spray of white sparks. With a metallic groan, one of the lamps comes crashing down from the rafter—a rush of heat, a hunk of metal, and shards of glass speeding down toward us like a meteor.

I yank Christian to the side and it misses his head by a hair, but he's still too close. It hits his shoulder, sending him down onto the floor and me along with him. Around us, the warbling speakers explode with ear-splitting screeches, muffling the screams of everyone around us as they rush faster to the door.

Christian's shirt is still trapped in my painfully clenched fingers, my whole body trembling so much I can barely get up on my knees. In the flashes of light, Christian's eyes are closed, his left arm and shoulder pinned to the ground by the blisteringly hot lamp.

I bring my shaking hands to his face. "Christian? Come on, we have to go." I pat his cheeks urgently, trying to get him to open his eyes.

But then I see it.

A dark, steadily growing pool of blood behind his head.

TWENTY-SEVEN

"No, no, no . . ." My voice is hardly more than a wheeze, all the air knocked out of me by the sight of Christian. By the blood. Frantically, I press my fingers to his face and neck, feeling for any flicker of life from him, but every inch of my skin is numb. I can't stop trembling. My nail beds are white, tinged with blue. Cold sweat prickles my temples.

Not now, please. I can't have a panic attack now. Not while Christian needs me and the gym is falling to pieces around us.

I take a shaking breath, faster and sharper than I mean to, holding it for a second before blowing it out as slowly as I can manage. I have to get it together. Pressing my hand flat against Christian's chest, it rises under my palm. Just a slight shift, but unmistakably a shallow breath. I lean down with my ear close to his nose and mouth, but I can't hear or feel anything in the chaos of thundering feet and exploding electronics around us.

"Wake up," I beg. "I need you."

If it were me under that lamp, knocked out and bleeding on the ground, Christian would have figured something out already. Why did I let this happen? Homecoming? How could I give in to something like this? I already struggle in crowds and parties. It's not like I don't know my brain leaks out of my ears when I need to focus most.

I yelp in surprise when someone grabs my shoulders from behind. Regan's fingers dig into me as her eyes, turning pale with shock, land on Christian. She sways on her feet, but her hands hold steady to me as she forces her eyes to meet mine.

"We have to get out of here," she shouts over the din of panic around us. "Jaxon—we can't stay here!"

"I'm not going anywhere without Christian." I'm shaking from head to toe, my brain is pudding, but I can't go now. Christian's trapped.

"If a fire starts—" Regan begins arguing, but I cut her off.

"I'm not leaving him!" My voice tears through my throat, leaving it raw in its wake. My breathing is so hard and erratic that my head swims. Even on hands and knees, I can't stop wobbling.

Regan makes a strangled noise in her throat, torn between wanting to drag me out of the fray and the knowledge that this is *it* for Christian. Leaving him now, like this, is losing him all over again.

"Okay," she says, dropping to her knees next to me. "What are we doing? What do we do? We gotta move fast."

Only a few steps behind her, Rhys manages to push past the throng of evacuating bodies to catch sight of us. He goes stock still at the sight of Christian. Staggering toward us, his hair is disheveled from his formerly sleek ponytail, white bangs sticking to his face from the sweat of panic and the actual heat of all the smoke and spark showers in the gym.

"Don't touch him!" I lean over Christian again, shaking my head urgently. "He's dying, don't touch him!"

If he hears me, he doesn't react. He squats down, shrugging off his jacket and wrapping it around the hot, metal lamp pinning Christian's shoulder and arm. Hefting it up with a grunt, he drops it a foot away where it crashes against the wood floor, splintering it. Now freed, Christian's arm and shoulder are dark with blood, blistered lacerations on his visible skin.

"Let me help," Rhys pleads, meeting my eyes.

I stare at him, unsure what to say. Christian has shown so much stalwart belief in me throughout all this; Rhys doesn't seem to doubt for a second that I can do something.

"Okay. Just . . . just let me think . . ."

My eyes sting, the skin around them prickling as tears blur my vision. What *can* I do? The only living things around me are people I care about. It's enough that I accidentally took some of Rhys's life; I can't just ask them if I can take some of their life for my boyfriend.

I crawl up a little higher by Christian, lifting his shoulders off the ground and lying his head on my lap instead. His warm blood soaks through my trousers as I brush his curls away from his face, blinking hard to keep my tears from falling. It doesn't really work.

"I'm so sorry." I cup his cheeks, running my thumbs gently over the dark fans of his eyelashes. "This is my fault. Please can't you *take* it from me? Everything you need, take it from me."

It's not fair to call him back for another fucked up half-life. Christian didn't ask for this mess, and the only real solution I have is the one my father took. The least I can do is give him life, time, whatever it is that I have in me.

Regan drops down on her knees beside me, gripping my

shoulder as she pushes her face into my field of view, refusing to let me look away.

"Jaxon, *don't* say that," she whispers urgently. "It might—*he* might . . ."

"He deserves better than this, Reg."

"So do you!"

Rhys's hand gently circles around Christian's injured arm. His eyes are red-rimmed and tearful, his cheeks wet.

"Let me *help*," he says again. "Please. He's my best friend."

With his other hand, Rhys touches my knuckles on one of the hands I have around Christian's face. I gape at him, realizing he knows exactly what he's asking for here. A transfer of life, to give some of his own for the sake of someone he loves.

And why not? I would do it for Regan too. And, judging by her face, she would do it for me.

She stares at us, brow wrinkled with anxiety, lips pressed together as she breathes quickly, thoughts churning behind her dark eyes. She follows Rhys's example, taking Christian's other arm and touching my other hand.

"Can we?" she asks. "The three of us. If it's three of us, then maybe . . ."

Maybe we all make it out of here alive; maybe this is the answer.

Not one whole life, but part of three to make a whole.

It might work. I *have* to make it work.

I give Rhys and Regan both one last look, making sure to meet their eyes. Neither of them wavers. Nodding, I take a deep breath, shifting all my focus onto Christian.

"Take it from *us*," I beg. "Everything you need, Christian, take it from us."

My palms start pulsing, growing warm against Christian's cheeks. I press them firmer against his skin as I close my eyes, trying to breathe evenly. Visualizing life energy streaming through our hands into Christian, reviving him. Replacing what's seeped out of him. The familiar rushing fills my ears. My eardrums ache from the building roar of sound, but I breathe through it as pain flares at my temples, hot and crackling like electricity.

Can the others feel it? I wish I'd warned them.

My mouth forms the word "please," but I can't hear anything. All at once, my vision goes painfully white. I cry out as my ears pop and ring, intense heat flushing my face. Hot tears run down my cheeks, coppery blood streams into my mouth as it drips from my nose. I gasp for air, coughing and choking as I breathe the blood in.

What if I die? What if we all die?

As that thought appears, the rushing in my ears grinds to a stop. The distant sounds of chaos around me fall silent, snuffed out in quick succession. The world is silent and my stomach lurches, a strangled sound coming out of me faint and muffled like I'm underwater.

Titi Clío's voice cuts through the stillness and the silence.

"What are you *doing*?!"

When I open my eyes, she's the only thing still in motion, though her eyes shine white. Everything and everyone else in the gym is frozen. Sparks float in mid-air, students static with panicked faces mid-run. All of them have brilliant, pulsing stars where their eyes should be.

Christian's eyes are closed, but like before, his skin is webbed with lightning-like trails of blue-white light. There are even more than last time, some large and bright enough to shine right through his clothing.

Titi Clío showing up here, after everything that happened, shocks me so much I can't even react for a moment. I just stare at her, the skin at the back of my neck prickling in panic. If she gets in the way, it's over.

"Please don't stop me, Titi," I beg.

"*Stop* you?" She's slack-jawed in disbelief as she shakes her head. "I can't! You've already—you're already *doing* it!"

To my surprise, instead of grabbing me to drag me away, she wraps one hand around my arm and places the other on Christian.

"Be careful," she says, voice shaking, growing muffled like everything else. "Feel it, Jaxon. You'll feel it. You'll *see* it, when it's done."

I don't have time to react to her diving in, my head spinning with combined gratitude and disbelief that she's helping me. I do as she says, trying to concentrate on the feeling—the way life pulses through me, out of me, the current of it so strong I'm sure I'd explode if it wasn't filtering out of my hands just as quickly. This kind of thing comes naturally to me—since I was little, according to my dad—I just have to control it. Do it with intention. Christian's body accepts it eagerly as brilliant white cracks begin to litter my fingers, spreading up to my knuckles. Faint cracks form around Regan's eyes, Rhys developing some over his brow up to his hairline, Titi along her hands as well.

It's working. What we're doing, for better or worse, is having an effect. But Christian shouldn't look like this. Until now, he's been the only person I've ever seen with light shining through him like he's been badly glued together. It's not enough that his energy is vibrant and living; it has to stay inside.

"Come on, Christian," I say, the words distant to my own ears. The pulsing of my life matches his. My whole body—or my being, whatever I am right now—aches as I beg him, "Don't leave me."

I don't know whether the words make the difference, but the cracks of light on my hands stretch wider and crawl up toward my wrists faster. Titi Clío's, Regan's, and Rhys's spread and grow while Christian's shrink. Like watching a video of a vase cracking in reverse, all the shards of him knit themselves back together seamlessly, starting from the large glowing patch under his shirt and spreading in a smooth wave all along his extremities.

I pull my hands back, meaning to look at the shining carnage done to them. The moment I do, the world crashes back into focus. I'm drenched, freezing, and shaking. We all are; the sprinkler system in the gym went off at some point and is still raining down on us.

Christian is still unresponsive on my lap, his chest rising and falling with the rhythm of his breathing. Rhys and Regan stare at me expectantly, both looking like they crawled out of a pool with watery blood smeared all over their faces. Rhys's hair is whiter than before, his eyebrows and everything from the top of his head forward snowy white. Regan's eyes are cloudy, like a white film's been painted over them. They double-take at Titi Clío down on the ground with us, when she most definitely hadn't been before.

She'd been watching. She knew to come.

Glancing down at my hands, I realize we've all been marked in some way. They're gaunt, the skin sagging and loose, knuckles thick and bones spider-like.

I swallow past a big knot that's starting to form in my throat. No words come when I try to speak, so I nod as my shoulders crumple from the relief.

It worked. I'm sure.

"We gotta get out of here," says Regan, reaching for me.

"I'll take him," offers Rhys, voice ragged. He scoops Christian up in his arms, hefting him up easily, though Christian's long legs dangle close to the ground.

Regan and I wrap an arm around each other, helping each other up to follow after Rhys. Titi Clío comes to my other side, face pale, helping to steady me.

"Careful," she says faintly, voice trembling. "Come on."

With the sprinklers quelling the smoke and short-circuiting the rogue electronics, getting out of the gym is eerily easy. Titi vaguely mutters that it's a miracle we don't get electrocuted navigating past the dead speakers, and I hold my breath, hoping she hasn't jinxed us. All that just to get done in by a busted power cord in a puddle?

Miracle or not, we make it. Outside, the bus loop in front of the school is a clash of blaring sirens and flashing red and white lights as ambulances and fire trucks come rushing in to help. Rhys practically shoves Christian into the arms of an EMT but, with the three of us cold, drenched, and still smeared with trace amounts of blood the sprinklers didn't get to wash off, we all get pulled away to get checked individually.

Titi hovers by me, wrapping me in a shock blanket after the paramedics finish cleaning me up, looking me over. They scratch their heads at all the blood on me with no related physical trauma, but they write me off as unharmed pretty quick to keep moving through all the kids coming out of the gym.

Titi lets out a breath slowly, taking my hand in hers. A wrinkle appears between her eyebrows as she studies it.

She sees it, of course. My hands look more like the hands of a sixty-year-old than a sixteen-year-old. My stomach turns; that'll definitely take some getting used to. But I make no apologies. The price could have been higher, and I still would have gladly paid it. Her hands paid similarly, spindly and covered in liver spots.

"Titi . . ." Her eyes find mine, squeezing my fingers briefly before letting me go. "Why? Why'd you do that?"

She laughs, eyes glittering with tears in the flashing emergency lights. Shaking her head, she spreads her hands helplessly like she has no answer for me.

"You're my nephew," she said. "I love you so much. I know you and your mom might not ever forgive me for what I did, but I didn't want you to give up even a second more of your time than you needed to."

I shake my head, still trying to wrap my mind around what this means for her. She went over the line with my mom for sure, but she's my aunt. She's older than me. How much did she give up?

"Are you going to be okay?" I ask. "Can you tell how much time you have left?"

Titi Clío laughs again, wiping her tears before putting her hands around my face. The current of her doesn't feel *so* different. The same long, slow pulse, maybe a tiny bit faster.

"I'm thirty, cariño, not ninety. I'll be okay."

I lean into her, weak with relief once more. She wraps her arms around me tightly, pressing kisses against my head. Tears spill out of me, a couple at first, then a torrent as my shoulders start shaking with sobs.

"We're okay," Titi whispers against my hair, rubbing my back. "We're all going to be okay."

She drives us home once she's stopped shaking enough to get behind the wheel, both of us sitting in shocked silence in the dark. Has my mom heard what happened at school? She hasn't blown up my phone yet, so I can't imagine she has. Maybe she went to sleep early.

The house is dark when Titi pulls into the driveway. We both stay seated after she kills the engine, the air thick with unspoken words; both of us too shaken to break the silence. After a couple of false starts, Titi finally takes a stab at it.

"Jaxon, I'm really sorry. For everything. Especially your mom." She takes a deep breath, like she's steeling herself. "And that I didn't tell you about me, and your dad, and *you* sooner. I should have. Jadiel was wrong to try and keep it from you. I should have known better."

I don't know how to respond to that. All I can think about is how sorry I feel for roping her into giving up years of her life, however many or few. For that alone, I want to forgive her. But I don't think I can do that until my mom's heard everything and decided if *she* can forgive what happened.

"You were desperate to protect me," I say, sighing shakily. "And you were close to my dad. I get it."

"No, it's not just that. I . . ." Titi Clío leans forward until her head touches the top of her steering wheel, hands gripping either side. "Jadiel was an amazing brother, you know? He was the best. We weren't like siblings you hear about, always fighting and whatever.

We didn't always see eye to eye, obviously, but he would have done anything for me and I would do anything for him."

I reach across hesitantly, resting a hand between Titi's shoulders and rubbing gently to the rhythm of her life force. "I know."

"No, listen. When I talked to you before, I made you feel like— like it's *your* fault that we lost him. And it's not. That's not true." She sits up straight again, swallowing thickly before looking me in the eyes. "It's *my* fault."

I sit in the silence that follows for a moment, taking it in. That doesn't seem right, though. My dad said nothing like that when he talked to me, though I guess he wouldn't necessarily want to throw his sister under the bus. Still, that would be a big omission to make.

"Titi, I don't think that's true."

"It is," she insists. "You know, even *now* sometimes I do things I don't mean to, like in your cafeteria the other day? I've gotten a lot better, though. It used to be way worse. And your dad, Jadiel was *amazing*. He could always bail me out of a bad situation."

She reaches for my hand. They feel foreign, linked together with loose skin and arthritic knuckles.

"He should have been able to spend so much more time with you, you know? But the year he died, I had a pretty bad episode at my job." She laughs dryly, her eyes glimmering with tears in the dark. "I was working in a lawyer's office as a receptionist. Just me and the lawyer. I pulled the life out of him—by mistake, it . . . it just *happened*—and it looked—it looked *really* bad. I called Jadiel because I needed him to die on his own, with enough time for me to resign and be nowhere near any of that when it happened, but I couldn't bring him back to life. I could only reanimate him."

I take her hand in both of mine, leaning closer to her to try and search her eyes. There are a lot of gaps in that story that feel deliberate, like it's painful to recount the story in full. There's something missing.

"Something must have happened for you to lose control . . ."

Titi Clío smiles wryly, wiping her eyes with her free hand. "He was . . . not a good man."

"Okay . . ." I say, stroking my thumb over her knuckles. I don't need to make her say anything she doesn't want to; that tells me enough. Whatever happened, he wasn't sitting minding his business when Titi had her episode. He'd triggered the episode somehow.

"If your dad hadn't had to help me with that," she says, sniffing back tears. "You would have had more time. It's not *your* fault. It's mine."

My immediate thought is that's ridiculous. It's not her fault. It isn't really *anyone's* fault. Titi Clío was in a bad situation, so my dad protected her. If there's one thing I've learned about my dad through all this it's, even dead, he can't stop trying to protect the people he loves. He'd never regret helping his sister, like he never regretted giving his life for me.

"Titi . . . he chose." I smile at her resolutely, though my hands shake a little around hers. "You would have chosen the same, right? And you wouldn't have wanted him to spend every day after that blaming himself."

She shakes her head, pulling my hands up to kiss my knuckles.

"Ay, mi amor. It's not that simple."

"I think it is," I say quickly. "It *is* that simple. I don't blame you. He doesn't blame either of us. You're the only one holding yourself responsible. He did what he did because he loved us. Neither of us *made* him do anything. He wanted to."

Titi Clío leans across the center console to wrap her arms around me, pressing her face against the top of my head. Her tears soak into my hair as I embrace her.

"Well, I could say the same to you, you know. All this with Christian—you kept beating yourself up for failing. How could you have done any different when you didn't know anything?"

I didn't expect her to turn it on me that way, but it's not like I don't know that on some level. It's just hard not to feel guilty.

I'm kind of like my aunt, in that way.

She's right. I didn't *choose* to bring Christian back the way I did. What I did choose was to try and save him . . . and I *don't* regret that. I don't ever want him to think I regret it.

"Yeah," I say, pressing my face against her shoulder. "I'm sorry. I'm really sorry for pulling you into it, Titi."

She pulls back, taking my face in her hands and smiling at me tearfully.

"Ay, nene, no empieces. I chose too."

TWENTY-EIGHT

I leave for the hospital before Mami wakes up. Visiting hours haven't started yet, so I park the van to wait a while, listening to music and staring at my phone hoping Christian'll text me that he's well.

By the time 8:00 a.m. rolls around, the only messages I get are from my mom asking where I am and Rhys and Regan confirming they're still alive. Getting out of the car, I shove my hands in the front pocket of my hoodie and head in to find Christian.

It's chilly today, but it's a classic Halloween morning. The sky stretches bright blue and cloudless over the red brick hospital building, the trees half-bare from the rain reaching out of the ground like claws, only a smattering of red, orange, and yellow leaves still clinging onto the branches.

Inside, I follow the directions the nurse at the front desk gave me. Christian's room is easy to pick out; he already has so many people crowded in there that some of his younger cousins spill out into the hallway, sitting with their backs against the wall as they play on their Switches. I wave awkwardly at them, then lean into the doorway, peering past the group of people.

Christian's eyes are closed, though the wrinkle in his brow and the frown on his face tell me he might be either trying to keep sleeping or pretending to sleep. Around him, his parents, a priest, a couple aunts, and his sisters sit in chairs or on the foot of his bed, talking animatedly over Styrofoam coffee cups. After a moment, his mom notices me, a huge grin spreading on her face, tired eyes lighting up.

"¡Jaxon! ¡Ven, mijo!"

Everyone turns to look at me at once, including Christian, whose eyes open as he reaches for his glasses at the sound of my name. I shove my hands deeper into my hoodie, sidling in awkwardly as everyone talks at me at once, patting my shoulders and marveling.

"¿Este es el de la funeraria?"

"¡Mira, Christian, quién llegó!"

"Este baboso, ¿ah? Apenas le salvaste la vida y mira como casi se mata otra vez."

"¿Hablas español, mijo?"

I grimace. I don't speak nearly enough Spanish to keep up with everyone here. "Un poquito . . ."

Christian's mom takes me by the elbow to lead me over to Christian's bedside. "Pero entiende bien." She sounds proud. I can't help smiling, despite the anxiety gnawing at me in front of all these strangers.

On the hospital bed, Christian looks surprisingly well even with his head still wrapped in bandages and his arm wrapped tight against his body. His skin is bright brown, eyes fairly alert considering the hour and the concussion. When he smiles at me, pink tinges his ears and cheeks.

"Hey, birthday boy," he says quietly, as if he might prevent his relatives from hearing despite them hanging on his every word. "What a night, huh?"

"You're telling me. How're you feeling?"

Christian shifts in his mattress, cringing slightly as he tries to sit up. One of his sisters comes over, pushing the button to make the bed sit up higher.

"Broke some things, buncha staples on my head, but otherwise, perfect."

My heart pounds against my throat. I bite down on my lip and ball my hands into fists inside my pocket, bouncing on my heels a little. I don't know how to respond to him right now. We're surrounded by his family, but I want to throw my arms around him and cry in relief. I smile, the expression wobbly on my face. Christian seems to read my mind.

"Can I get a minute alone with Jax, Amá? Please?"

"Claro, mi cielo," says his mom without hesitation. She herds his relatives—*and* the priest—with impressive speed, shuffling them out the door. Closing it shut behind her, Christian and I are alone with nothing but the beeping of his monitors.

I sit next to him on the edge of his mattress, eyes warm and prickling until tears blur my vision. Sighing shakily, I wipe at my face with the cuffs of my sleeves pulled over my hands. It's quiet for a long moment. Christian smiles awkwardly, pushing his glasses up the bridge of his nose, preparing to break the silence.

"I really paid for that *Carrie* comment, huh?" He jokes.

I laugh, for a second, before I cry and press my hidden hands against my face so he can't see. It's not like he's never seen me cry before, but it doesn't get any less embarrassing to do it in front of him.

Christian stammers, panicked. "Sorry! Sorry, I shouldn't have joked about that! Pinche imbécil, valgo verga."

"No—no, it's fine, it was just . . ." I shake my head, waving vaguely. Scary? Horrible? Exactly what I was afraid of? Any of the above, I guess. "Christian, tell me honestly—do you really feel okay?"

Several expressions pass through Christian's eyes at once, all of them gentle. The back of my neck gets hot; I wish I could get a grip.

"Jax, I feel better than okay. Seriously." He reaches for me, concern wrinkling his brow. His hand curls around my arm, tugging gently. "What about *you*? When I woke, I thought you might be . . . I don't know. What happened? Are *you* going to be okay? You're not dying, are you? Tell me you didn't do something too desperate, please."

I wish I had answers based on anything other than feelings. I wipe my eyes again, sniffing wetly, then push my hands out of the sleeves to hold his in both of mine.

"Not anytime soon, I think," I offer, watching his eyes grow behind his circular glasses as he takes in the sight of my hands. "But we all die eventually."

Whatever Christian's thinking, his face doesn't betray anything. His brown eyes scan over my hands, while no other part of his expression moves. I squirm, increasingly self-conscious under his scrutiny. They aren't subtle. They're startling to look at, spidery and strange, thick knuckles and thin, loose skin webbed with visible veins.

Eventually, he pulls my hands up, pressing his lips lightly against my knuckles, then rests his cheek against them. A sharp ache blooms in my chest as I squeeze his hands, leaning down to press my nose against his hair. He smells like blood and antiseptic, but I can't pull away.

"I'll keep you safe," he promises softly.

I don't know how he'll do that. But I know better than to doubt him. "Alright."

He tips his head up carefully so our faces are pressed against each other's, the rims of his round glasses cool against my cheek. His lips find mine and I let go of his hand to hold his face between my palms instead, kissing him slow like we have all the time in the world.

"I love you," I whisper, though I can barely hear it over the pounding of my heart.

Christian holds my wrists as he kisses all around my face, lips, cheeks, eyebrows, ending with my eyelids.

"I kinda figured," he says, smiling against my face. "I love you too."

I leave Christian to spend time with his family not long after, though I wish I could spend all day and all night making sure he's really here. He's not going anywhere.

As I'm not quite ready to leave, I head over to the tall, sloping hill behind the hospital that serves as a notorious sledding spot in the winter. In the fall it makes a good place to sit on sunny days to admire the swaths of fiery colors the trees put on display. It's peaceful up here, and Christian isn't far even if I can't see him.

I spend a while there, watching the occasional flock of birds migrating south overhead, the seat of my pants increasingly damp from sitting on the wet grass. My phone goes off a few times, but I ignore it. With everything that's happened in the past week, my brain needs a little quiet before I can go back to reality.

By the time I feel ready to go, the afternoon sun is hot and bright in the sky, though it doesn't do much to keep me warm against the bite of the October breeze. I take the long way home, taking a detour down by the potato fields before finally making it back.

There are multiple cars in my driveway. My aunt's, Rhys's car, Regan's dad's car, and Christian's mom's car. As I climb out of the van, Regan runs out onto the porch, waving at me.

"We've been calling you for hours!" She widens her eyes, pressing her fingers against the skin under them, like she's trying to open them as much as possible. "God, it's like looking through a foggy window—Jaxon, get your butt over here, birthday boy!"

I jog over to the porch and pull her into my arms, squeezing her tightly before leaning back to look at her face properly. The cloudy film over her dark eyes makes it hard to make out her pupils. Guilt wrenches at my stomach as I squeeze her shoulders. It's my fault—how can I ever be sorry enough?

"Shut up," she says before I can start apologizing. "I don't wanna hear it. This is nothing compared to all the things I'd do for you. You should know that."

"How are your parents taking it . . . ?"

"Papi's been trying to get our health insurance to give him a straight answer about cataract surgery and if they'll cover it for a seventeen-year-old. Tessa and Clío are in there telling him and Conce what happened."

My eyebrows shoot up. That's a far cry from where they were at a week ago.

"They—what!? Like the *truth*?"

"The truth," Regan affirms, widening her eyes in a sort of panicked grimace. "Shit's been so crazy, I don't think they have any choice but to believe it."

"Oh God," I groan. "Carlos and Conce are gonna forbid you and Christian from ever speaking to me again."

Regan laughs, like she'd dare them to try. "Not a chance!"

I pull her in again, squeezing her even tighter. She squeezes back, kissing my cheek before making a wet fart sound against my face.

"Regan!" I push her away, gently, laughing as I scrub my cheek dry. "You're disgusting."

She grins, pulling me into the house.

To my surprise, it's not just Christian, Regan, and Rhys who came. Rhiannon's here too, examining the funeral services binder in the high-backed armchair of the main parlor. Rhys sits beside her on the ground, his two-tone hair tied back, raising his white eyebrows at something Christian's saying.

Everyone's eyes fall on me, but mine are glued to Christian. I didn't think he'd be discharged already, but here he is, in neon orange sneakers and a black hoodie with a big, white Ghostface mask printed on it.

"Why weren't you answering your phone!" He demands, though his face splits into a grin. "Your mom was worried!"

That's probably true. But probably not the whole truth. "Just my mom, huh?"

He clicks his tongue dismissively, lumbering to his feet and trying to stay balanced with one arm out of commission. When I'm close enough, he tugs me into a one-armed hug.

"We wanted to celebrate your birthday," he says, nodding at

Regan, Rhys, and Rhiannon in turn. "And Rhiannon's never seen, like, any scary movies so we forced her to come."

Rhiannon rolls her eyes before squinting at Christian disdainfully, then looks at me. "No one forced me. My brother never keeps anything from me, and suddenly he's sneaking around and risking his life with *you*. I figure that means it's time we get to know each other. Right?"

Definitely not something I ever would have expected to hear from Rhiannon Davies. I guess the cat's out of the bag with her too, though I'm not sure if it was Rhys or my family that told her. I glance at him, and he grins guiltily.

That answers that, then.

"Right," I agree. "And you're in good hands for a horror movie night, you know?"

"That's what I'm afraid of."

Titi Clío clears her throat, sidling over to me and squeezing an arm around my shoulders.

"For what it's worth . . ." She says slowly, exchanging glances with Mami and nodding as she holds up her own spindly hands. "I think . . . we can do something about what's happened to us. Or, rather, *you* can, Jaxon. With your father's watch."

"Oh . . ." Right, my dad used his abilities to help my mom with cosmetic things in the funeral parlor. That's more than plausible. "You're so right, Titi . . ."

Rhys and Regan perk up, hopeful smiles conflicting with confused eyes. They trade looks, then Regan squints at me uncertainly—or maybe because of the cataracts, I don't know.

"I thought the whole sacrifice thing was an issue . . ."

Rhys looks down by my feet as Grimalkin stalks up to greet

me, bumping her face against my shin and wrapping her bottle brush tail around my ankle. "I guess if it's just a small thing, a small sacrifice?"

Grim and I react to that almost simultaneously: she turns her big, orange eyes onto Rhys, staring at him like she'd dare him to try. I shake my head vehemently, crossing my arms in an X gesture. "Dude, you must not have pets. *No,* we're not sacrificing Grim. It's not a resurrection, it's . . . well, cosmetic, I guess."

Christian grins brightly, endorsing the idea. "Let's give it a shot!"

Out of all our family members, I think Conce is the one having the hardest time coming to grips with what, I guess to her, walks, talks, and quacks like brujería. She whispers to my aunt, my mom and Regan's dad, repeatedly, that this *must* be a gift from God. Her tone is as hysterical as it is attempting to be reassuring.

And, as I cut my hand open to dab blood over my friends' faces like some kind of twisted Ash Wednesday, I guess I get why she needs to talk herself down.

This part is Christian's idea. He pointed out that bleeding has been a common denominator in every ritual type thing I've done and put out the theory that drawing blood on purpose might make it easier. So, I paint a stripe over Rhys's forehead, dab over Regan's eyelids, and draw X's over the back of Titi Clío's hands before pulling out my pocket watch, flipping it open.

"You ready?" I ask Regan, taking her hand.

She shrugs, smiling nervously. "Nope! But let's do it."

"Don't be scared. I've at least done this a couple times."

Literally only twice, but I don't tell her that. And this is my first time with an audience. I glance around at everyone's faces; Mami looking on with a concerned grimace, Carlos squinting like he's still not sure what to think of all this, Conce repeatedly crossing herself as she mutters prayers and self-reassurances. Rhiannon is on the edge of her seat but composed as ever.

Christian meets my gaze, giving me a small, reassuring nod before I can start to doubt myself.

You got this, he mouths.

Right. I start turning the hands back. And though pain bursts behind my eyes, I don't bleed this time.

By the end of it, Regan's eyes are clear, Rhys's hair is back to black, and mine and Titi's hands return to normal; even my self-inflicted wound closes up. Carlos hugs Regan incessantly, elated with relief, Rhiannon is all smiles—which is *rare*—and she and Christian laugh as Rhys fusses over his hair. Conce watches at me with a wrinkled brow, tapping her fingers over her lips.

I look at her helplessly, offering a cautiously hopeful smile.

"This was how . . ." I say, gesturing at my chest then glancing over at Christian. "Cuando desperté a Christian . . ."

She sighs through her nose and nods, dark eyes glittering with tears as she places a shaky hand on my shoulder.

"Me lo imaginé," she says, then pulls me into a hug. "Pero al fin, no me importa. No sé cómo darte las gracias, pero *gracias*, mijo. Desde el fondo de mi corazón, te lo agradezco."

Her willingness to accept it makes my throat tighten up. Necromancy is a lot to swallow even for someone who's not religious. I wrap my arms around her, looking at Christian over her shoulder. He looks back at me, grinning fondly. My stomach flips.

"You don't have to thank me," I tell her quietly. "He means a lot to me."

She pulls back, patting my cheek as she looks at me knowingly. "Ya sé." With that, she releases me, turning to my mom, squeezing her hand briefly. "Vamos, Tessa. Tienes un comal, ¿verdad? Te voy a enseñar cómo se hacen unos tacos de mi pueblo."

"Um, sí . . ." My mom follows Conce into our kitchen, tugging Titi Clío to come along as well. "Pero—Clío doesn't eat meat."

"*¡¿Cómo?!*"

I'm glad Titi Clío is still here with us. I don't know if Mami quite knows how she feels about what happened with the car accident, but hearing about Titi helping me with Christian took a significant amount of the edge off her anger. If nothing else, Mami seems determined to try moving past it.

Christian bounds over to me as they disappear into the kitchen, pulling me with an arm around my shoulders. He leans in to press his lips against the side of my face.

"Told her about us," he admits.

I laugh, stomach twisting happily as warmth climbs up into my cheeks. "Yeah? Did she faint from shock?"

He snorts. "Nah. I think she could tell I liked you anyway."

"*No way*! You're so subtle."

"Vete a la chingada." He laughs. "C'mon. I wanna watch a seriously gay slasher."

"*Nightmare on Elm Street II*?"

Christian shakes his head, grinning. "Gayer."

I smile, some of the tension that's been knotted up in my chest for days now loosening up. It's fun having a horror movie virgin around for this kind of thing. And it's nice having Christian right beside me, surrounded by our friends. Regan pulls down the projector we usually use for memorial slideshows and videos so we can kick things off with Christian's favorite extremely gay slasher: *Hello Mary Lou: Prom Night II*.

"Does it matter that I haven't seen the first one?" asks Rhiannon. Christian laughs. "Not at all."

He and I sit on the blue-patterned rug with our backs against the couch. He wraps his uninjured arm around me as I rest my head on his shoulder, starting the movie. This was one of the first slashers we watched together. We were maybe nine, way too young. I remember how his eyes had been huge behind his glasses and his mouth hung open in delight and fascination for most of the movie.

Christian catches me looking at him, but I don't look away. He leans down, pressing his lips to mine briefly. "Pay attention to the movie," he chides playfully.

I nod, though it's hard to take my eyes off him under the flickering light of the movie on the big screen. He's warm and happy against me, and when he laughs and gasps, we're so close I almost feel his breath in my chest.

For now, that's enough.

ACKNOWLEDGMENTS

There are so many people who were instrumental to the process of bringing this little idea of mine into being in the form of a book, but I will try my best to thank you all.

First, thank you to my parents for always supporting me, for being insistent that I speak Spanish, and for always keeping me closely anchored to my culture. There were times that I fought you guys on that, so I'm incredibly grateful that you held fast to it. Thank you to my siblings, too, for always cheering me on.

Thank you to my beloved spouse, Christian. We fell in love throughout the time I was writing this book and for that, it will always be incredibly special to me. Thank you for everything you do for me and for being my biggest fan, bar none.

Caitlin, Hannah, and Bryce, without the three of you I probably would have lost hope in finishing the book much less querying and then going through submissions and beyond. You are my ride-or-dies, I literally could not do this without you.

Faridah Àbíké-Íyímídé, speaking of ride-or-dies, you have been an incredible friend and mentor to me for years now. Thank you for holding my hand throughout this process. You've checked in on me, you've been honest with me, and you've always boosted my confidence. You inspire me and you make me want to be the best writer I can be.

Thank you also to all my writing friends, especially H.E. Edgmon and Jonny Garza Villa. They were both instrumental to me getting my query together, picking agents to query in the first place, and letting me know what to look out for—both green and red flags. You're both incredible writers and amazing friends.

I would be completely lost without my agent, Saritza Hernandez. You are an incredible agent and advocate, Sary. I'm sure you know you are great at what you do but I just want to reinforce that: you are AMAZING. Thank you for your passion and dedication, thank you for asking the questions I'm too afraid to ask, and thank you so much for looking out for me and my work. I feel honestly blessed that you are in my corner.

Carolina Ortiz, thank you so much for loving my book and taking it on. When I was still doing pitch contests on Twitter, you were the first editor to ever like my pitch for this book, and your name was stuck in my head since then. It felt like fate when you offered, and after seeing your hard work and dedication I am absolutely positive that it was fate.

Thank you so much to my entire team at HarperCollins for all your work. You all have made my book the best it possibly could be along with a cover I couldn't have even dreamed of. (It is really INCREDIBLE, an extra thank-you to Hillary D. Wilson.) I did not imagine that I would feel so at peace with my book going out into the world, but I genuinely believe it is ready to fly thanks to you.

Last but not least, thank you to you, dear reader. You have taken time out of your life to open this book and see what's inside and that means so much more than words can say.